LOW BIRTH, HIGH ADVENTURE

"It is your turn now, Thorian," I said, as we crouched hiding in the dark. "What is your tale?"

There was a pause, then a sigh which seemed to last for several minutes—the product of an unusual lung capacity. "Alas, Omar! It is nothing. The tale of Thorian will compare with yours as the mud of the paddy field below the glory of the lotus. Not only has my brief existence been totally bereft of incident, but I lack your felicity of phrase and facility of pharynx. You come from far and exotic lands, overflowing with wonders. You have viewed deeds of heroes and the wrath of gods. Beside your peacock splendor, I am the maggot in the filth of the chicken run."

"That is indeed an inspiring opening!" I declared, much impressed. "Pray proceed."

By Dave Duncan
Published by Ballantine Books:

A ROSE-RED CITY

The Seventh Sword
THE RELUCTANT SWORDSMAN
THE COMING OF WISDOM
THE DESTINY OF THE SWORD

WEST OF JANUARY

SHADOW

STRINGS

HERO!

A Man of His Word
MAGIC CASEMENT
FAERY LANDS FORLORN
PERILOUS SEAS
EMPEROR AND CLOWN

THE REAVER ROAD

A Handful of Men
THE CUTTING EDGE*
UPLAND OUTLAWS*
THE STRICKEN FIELD*
THE LIVING GOD*

*Forthcoming

THE
REAVER
ROAD

Dave Duncan

A Del Rey Book
BALLANTINE BOOKS • NEW YORK

A Del Rey Book
Published by Ballantine Books

Library of Congress Catalog Card Number: 92-90144

ISBN 0-345-37481-9

Manufactured in the United States of America

First Edition: August 1992

Fondly dedicated to
KEVIN MICHAEL PRESS
in the hope that he
will grow up to enjoy
books and even perhaps
(some time next century)
this one.

Prologue

❋

You do me wrong, milords! I am no beggar. In my time I have been many things, from lowly tinker to royal tyrant—once, even, I was a god!—but I would never stoop to begging. I am by avocation a trader of tales, and this humble garb is my normal wear.

I travel this desolate trail from choice, honored sirs. Distant places have a fascination for me. In my time I have visited almost every town or city this side of the Rainbow. Name it and I can speak of it.

No, my only purpose in accosting you was to suggest we might exchange stories upon the way, to shorten the road and ease the burden of sunlight. Tales of love and war? Tales of glory and failure? Tales of wonders? No, I do not mind waiting while you eat . . .

Well, that is most generous of you, milords. I admit your stew pot smells enticing. Certainly I can speak and chew at the same time . . .

Being a god? It was a most unpleasant experience, and not one I should ever care to repeat.

But I do not mind telling you of it, although it is a lengthy tale, which may well stretch even to the next meal stop, or beyond. It happened long ago, when first I dreamed of Zanadon, fairest city of the plains . . .

1

1: The Reaver Road

As it had been prophesied, I came down from the hills and walked over the sunbaked plain. Very soon I noticed fresh horse droppings on the baked red ruts of the road, the first I had seen for many weeks. I saw also that the way was empty of the stragglers who had kept me company all that time. Sensing the danger, they had taken cover.

I walked on, feeling odd in my sudden loneliness, but knowing that a careful scan of the hedges and hayfields would reveal the missing wayfarers cowering in the foliage. Soon one man, bolder than the rest, rose and called a warning. I acknowledged with a wave and continued on my way, whistling as before, confident of my destiny.

The sky was very huge and blue, and the heat wearisome. I wondered if the faint shadows to the north could be the famed Kulthiar Range, or merely some trick of the haze. The east was still streaked by the smokes of yesterday. Every morning the smokes were closer.

To be out of the endless olive groves was a relief, for I was not yet desperate enough to eat untreated olives, but I missed the shade. The plains' fertile fields and orchards that I had been hoping might offer some nourishment had been picked clean by the army of locusts preceding me. A whole day and a night had gone by since I licked the crumbs from my provender bag.

I never pester the gods with complaints. They are well aware that a minimum sustenance is necessary if I am to perform my duties. Gauntness has a certain appeal. Possibly I had created a miscalculation by sharing the last of my victuals with little Bulla. If so, I did not regret the act,

2

for her breasts were as rosebuds and her tiny hands restless as summer butterflies.

Since the night Dom Wilth burned, I had met no one coming from the west. I had traveled faster than most, for there had been few able-bodied men upon that road of sorrows. Children and cripples and old women yoked to carts had been my companions. Penniless, homeless, and dressed in rags, they had yet been kindly and uncomplaining in their misfortune. Despair clears away pettiness. Many had been alarmed at first by my outlandish garb and appearance—it is part of my trade to be visibly a stranger—but once I had assured the refugees that I was not a Vorkan, they had been content enough to talk, while I lingered awhile at their slower pace.

Thus I would gather a tale or two. Soon, though, aware of the urgency of my mission, I would bid my companions good fortune, and they would call down blessings from the gods upon my back as I strode ahead to the next group.

Now I walked alone through a deserted land, hearing only my own whistling and the rumbling of my belly.

I arrived without warning at the wide glare of a river and a ford, and they seemed familiar to me. Although the river was too large to be any other than the great Jolipi, I saw no boats at all. Admittedly the water was low at that time of mellow summer, a tress of silver braids winding among shoals of golden sand.

Charred ruins showed where a ferryman's house had stood, but weeds sprouted within the blackened timbers, and there could have been no ferry there for many years. A legacy of a garden remained in the form of six green willows and a tulip tree flaming scarlet. I had no recollection at all of house or ford, but I recognized the tulip tree.

Sprawled on the black carpets of shadow in the grove, a squad of soldiers was taking rest while keeping careful watch on their chomping ponies and also on a group of near-naked men crouching in the sunlit water. These bathers were splashing listlessly and making none of the cheerful noises that such activities normally provoke.

As I approached, soldiers turned their heads. I knew how hot they must be in their bronze hats and metaled corselets, their greaves and vambraces, for I have worn such absurdities in my time, although never willingly. I knew also that their unfortunate mounts would never rise above a trot when so burdened. These stalwart warriors might be competent at intimidating peasants, but the Vorkans would ride gavottes around them.

Their leader was easily identified by a crested helm and a bronze cuirass. Even sprawled on the grass, he was a man of authority, thick chested and narrow eyed. He leaned on one elbow, and his calm was a symbol of power in itself. His beard of black ringlets hung almost to his waist, lush even by the standards of the Spice Lands. Indeed, he had a magnificent head, which might well have graced a marble bust, or a golden coin. It would have looked splendid on a pike, too.

I headed in his direction. Some of the nearer soldiers sat up, reaching hands to sword hilts and regarding me with distrust. My hair and skin are lighter than is common in the Spice Lands, and my eyes are gray. I wore my beard close-trimmed in those days. Even without my foreign garb, I would have been visibly a stranger to these warriors, and warriors' violent instincts always rise to the surface at the sight of strangers.

I smiled back guilelessly at them and was allowed to pass unchallenged. Arriving at the leader, I dropped my staff, swung my bindle from my shoulder, and then sank down cross-legged.

"May your life amuse the gods, Captain," I said cheerfully.

He raised one bushy black eyebrow. "That is not a greeting I have encountered before."

I pointed out that it was a worthy one, and asked if he would prefer the hazards of boring them.

"Indeed, when you express the matter like that, then I see the wisdom in it. I hope you also will provide amusement."

I smiled to set his mind at ease. "Such is always my aim, for I am a trader of tales, and amusement is my business. Sir, my name is Omar."

The captain's large hand stroked his apron of beard.

"And I am Publian Fotius, captain in the army of Zanadon."

"Ah! Then you may be able to assist me. Is not the city of which you speak that same Zanadon of renown and glory, the Zanadon whose fighting men are so furnished with valor and hardihood that it is known throughout all the Spice Lands as *Unvanquished* Zanadon?"

The soldier studied me with care and then nodded solemnly. "Such indeed is the case, thanks be to the Holy Maiana and Immortal Balor."

"Thanks indeed. I am indeed honored to meet one of its outstanding citizens. But my geography is hazy, noble Captain. I have been following the Reaver Road toward Shirdle and Thang these past many days. Dare I believe that this rolling flood I see before me is the celebrated Jolipi River of ancient story, and that therefore I am within a day or less of Unvanquished Zanadon itself?"

"You are overly modest, Trader of Tales Omar," the captain said in his sonorous voice, "for you have stated the situation exactly. But an hour's stroll up the river will bring you within sight of the granite walls and many shining towers of Zanadon the Unvanquished."

I ran a thumb thoughtfully over my own trim beard. "In these times of troubles, when the flagitious hordes of Vorkans ravage the land, defiling the very plausibility of the gods with pillage and slaughter—when mighty cities such as Forbin and Polrain and Dom Wilth have gone down to destruction—then surely Zanadon the Never Vanquished must stand forth as a sure refuge against the marauders."

"We shall resist them with all vigor and, if Holy Maiana wills it, grind them beneath our heels."

"Spoken like a brave soldier, a noble citizen, and a faithful servant of the Holy, er, Maiana," I said with enthusiasm. "But . . . you will pardon my presumption if I seek to pose a further question, or even two, perhaps?"

The captain turned his noble head to study the men in the river. "I must needs be on my way shortly, but pray continue, for I am rarely regaled by conversation so learned and inspiring."

"Your kindness illuminates your greatness, Captain.

This, then, is the matter that now troubles me. Many are the refugees I have observed upon the road, fleeing the fury of the Vorkan horde. Many mark out my way ahead and many I have overtaken. Great though Unvanquished Zanadon may be—however renowned her mercy and hospitality—there surely must be limits to the number of unfortunates she can succor in her bosom?''

"Alas! You speak of a matter that sorrows us greatly."

I sighed. "Then were I to make this trifling journey up the river that you mentioned, might it not be that I should be turned away, and my petition denied?"

Publian Fotius sat up. As if that was a signal, the troop began struggling to their feet with sounds of clanking bronze and creaking leather. I noted that some needed help to rise, they were so loaded.

"Be of good cheer, Trader Omar. I ween that the gods have guided you to the very man who can assist you in your ambition to enter into the sanctuary of Mighty Zanadon, the Unvanquished."

"Then may the gods be praised for their mercy!"

He regarded me with sudden chill. "And may I inquire what business you have within the city?"

"I have been ordered to proceed there," I explained.

"Ordered by whom?"

"By the gods, Captain. I am not certain which gods, or god, although I suspect that the mighty Krazath, or Balor as you term him, is at the heart of the matter. You understand, therefore, my joy at having encountered one who can win me admittance? It is a curious tale, with which I shall be happy to enlighten you. It begins some two years ago, when I was first sent a dream, which—"

"The matter is not quite certain." The captain braced his hairy knuckles on the grass, drew up his boots, and sprang easily erect. His bulk darkened the glade.

I clambered to my feet, also, feeling like a willow by an oak. "I beg of you, honored sir, to inform me what impediment may lie in my chosen path, and how I may seek to circumvent it."

Publian looked me up and down. He waved a wordless signal to his men. Some hurried to attend the ponies, others went over to the water and began summoning the bathers, addressing them in crude and peremptory terms. The captain continued to consider me, stroking his flowing beard.

"Your wisest course in my estimation, Trader, would be to remove your clothing immediately—all of it."

I frowned in mild surprise. "Sir? I have received such instructions from common vagabonds and cutthroats in my time, and I confess that similar sentiments have been conveyed to me on other occasions by members of the opposite sex, usually more by way of insinuation. But I am at a loss to understand how such an immodest act now could benefit my chances of favorable consideration by the civic authorities of Unvanquished Zanadon."

"Then consider the corporal here," said Publian Fotius with an expansive gesture. "His name is Gramian Fotius, the son of my youngest brother. Is he not a fine, strapping lad and a credit to the army we both have the honor to serve?"

"Indeed," I said, looking up at the giant so indicated, "if I may make allowances for his comparative youth, I can truthfully say that I have never observed a warrior to match him in either quantity nor the awe-inspiring quality of his demeanor."

"Then you will understand the wisdom of my advice when I explain that, should you delay further in implementing the course of action I recommended, Corporal Fotius will rip off your right ear with his bare hands."

I admitted that this insight clarified the advisability of compliance, and proceeded to strip off my hat, shirt, breeches, and sandals without further delay.

"Search his bedroll," Publian said. "Turn around, prisoner. No brands? Nor do I see even marks of the lash. You have been as yet deprived of the salutary experience of being flogged?"

"I fear so, sir. My audiences do not invariably greet my narratives with enthusiasm, but I have yet to provoke negative response as drastic as you describe." I completed my turn, and waited, enduring the captain's continuing inspection with untroubled good humor. No one who has spent as many years as I did among the Bushmen of Gath-oil will ever be troubled by nudity.

"And no weapon scars! You were never a soldier?"

I admitted that I had been, once or twice, but assured him that Mighty Krazath had always smiled upon me and turned his terrible frown upon my opponents.

"Praise to the god," Publian said, "although he is un-familiar to me by that name. I fear I must conclude that you are a spy, stranger. What gold?"

The soldier who had been ripping my bindle to shreds now rose and sheathed his sword. "None, sir."

"Try his clothes. Trader, I do not see your knife. How does any man survive without a knife?"

"With a fuller belly, for the first few hours."

"The tales you trade have so depreciated that you must deal your very knife away?"

"Alas," I admitted, "my tales have not depreciated, but the value of food has risen to levels hitherto unprophesied. It was a good knife, with a handle of carved bone in the form of warring demons."

The captain nodded reassuringly. "I suspect you are better off without it, then."

I watched with sadness as my breeches were shredded—the fine breeches that dark-eyed Illina had made for me, fashioned from soft brown camel leather and stitched with scarlet thread. They had covered my knees comfortably and left my shanks bare for the heat of the day. My sandals had been the price of a night's entertainment at the Seven Gods, in Wailman, and they, too, were now disassembled. And so, finally, was my shirt—a garment of strong linen, and still good, a gift from a caravan leader down near the coast, for shirts are unknown in the Spice Lands. The road dust of a continent obscured its pastel dye, dark sweat had mapped oceans upon it, but I was sorry to see it so ruthlessly treated. My hat I had made myself, of yellow straw, and I did not mind that being returned to its component parts.

But no gold was thus revealed, and Publian smiled for the first time, glinting teeth as shiny amber as cats' eyes amid the midnight of his beard.

"You are fortunate indeed in your poverty, Traveler, for I cannot envision a spy without either gold or weapon. You are also either fortunate or clear-thinking in approaching me to relieve your prospect of imminent starvation. As you so acutely postulated, Never-vanquished Zanadon has regretfully closed its gates to the rabble that the Vorkans drive before them. Were they to be admitted, they would undoubtedly congest the streets, pollute the air, and disturb the nights with strident ululation. One small exception only is permitted."

"I pray you to disclose it," I said.

The captain waved a paw at the clinking line of unfortunates now emerging from the water.

"My men and I were dispatched in search of able-bodied volunteers of good character to aid our citizens in their arduous labor of raising the walls. And, while you hardly measure up to Corporal Fotius as a paradigm of manhood—nor would you ever be chosen to pose for a statue of Immortal Balor in the temple—I descry that you are healthy, acceptably thewed, and may be worthy of the daily gruel with which our civic leaders will reward your willing service."

Paying no heed to the smirking soldiers closing in around me, I stooped and selected the largest remaining fragment of my linen shirt. I knotted it expertly around my loins. It was less than adequate, but I would still be one of the better-dressed members of the company.

"I am at your service, Captain."

"That much was evident from the first," Publian said.

2: The End of a Tether

※

I have been part of a slave gang often enough. Having just been washed in the river, this one was considerably more pleasant than most in my experience, and I marched willingly over to the end of the line, cooperating as the bronze collar was locked around my neck. I noted a few surprising points, though.

The pickings had been poor. There were thirteen men in the coffle, and only one of them looked capable of surviving very long in the stone quarry that was our most probable destination. That one was as stalwart as the hulking Corporal Fotius—more imposing, even, as more of him was visible. A ragged poorly healed scar angled down from his collarbone to his hip, and an arrow wound in his calf made him limp. Furthermore, his back bore an assortment of red and purple welts.

This titan had been placed at the rear of the line, and burdened with the unused length of chain. When I was locked in behind him, he shot a furious glare at me under brows as imposing as battlements, baring teeth in his sodden jungle of beard. His black hair hung in wet tangles to his shoulders.

Correct procedure would have been to put this most dangerous specimen near the middle, and to load the leftover chain on a pony, so that the gang would be tethered at both ends. Captain Publian Fotius was being curiously inefficient.

However—as I once remarked to Vlad the Opprobrious, or possibly his grandfather—the only thing that ever surprises me is the expected. I did not, therefore, seek to advise the captain on the finer points of his trade, and I shouldered the weighty, corroded burden without complaint, although I could see from abrasions on my predecessor's shoulders that it was going to be onerous. When the escort mounted up and the coffle lurched off along the towpath, I quietly redistributed the load so that a few stray loops hung down my back, for the two young lads equipped with whips looked unpleasantly enthusiastic.

Of late my feet had grown accustomed to sandals, and the chain grew excruciatingly hot in the fierce sun, but I ambled along cheerfully at the requisite pace, whistling softly through my teeth. My main concern was that Unvanquished Zanadon might feed its slaves in the mornings and not the evenings. Had I been a praying man, I might have mentioned that worry to the gods. The most interesting activity in my field of view was the tortuous paths the sweat beads found down the battered back of the hairy giant in front of me.

The chain clinked, the ponies' hooves thumped, and my belly rumbled. As we departed the Reaver Road, though, we began to see more settled country, secured by the might of the city—we passed several troops of armored men. The fields here had not yet been looted, nor the hamlets burned. Peasants bent to their toil without looking up as we trudged by.

Captain Fotius had stated literal truth when he said that an hour's walk would bring us within sight of Zanadon. Truly its granite walls and beetling towers are an inspiring sight, and I was stirred by seeing at last what I had viewed so often in my dreams. Regrettably, the great city stands at the top of a solitary and imposing mesa. It is visible a long way out across the plain.

Soon we began to see traders and mounted caravans and women carrying bundles on their heads. Among these, inhabitants of the city itself could be recognized by their grander attire.

The climate of the Spice Lands is benign, and only in the hills is clothing ever needed for warmth. Even the winter rains are usually warm enough to ignore. In the villages men tie a cloth around their loins and leave it at that. In the cities that most basic of garments has been expanded into an ornate swath, whose detail comes close to being a cult, rigidly regulated. The lawmakers fuss endlessly over the colors, the patterns, the fineness of the cloth, and the number of times it has been wound around. The height of the lower hem is even more critical. Slaves and the very lowly must leave both knees in view, but increasing status is indicated by covering first one knee, then two, and so on, until the wealthy and important drape both legs to the ankle.

To the initiated, a swath reveals the wearer's rank or trade, his fortune and family and patron god, and how many children he has sired—they work those loincloths harder than the king of Klulith's ox! Moreover, the swath must be held by a single pin, located just below the navel—this is obligatory. The ornamentation permitted on the pin is a study in itself.

The cities' sumptuary laws usually allow cloaks to some groups—the rich, the royal, and the religious—but most men rarely wear anything above the waist except pot-shaped hats and square black beards. In some cities a man may not marry until his beard reaches down to his nipples, which is why in Urgalon pretty girls are known as "neck-benders."

Women seem to wear anything they please.

As evening fell, we drew near to the base of the ramp, and the soldiers halted to rest their mounts and eat a brief snack. They allowed us to lie down in a cool, reedy ditch after the ponies had been watered. Strict penalties were announced for anyone who spoke, and one of the whip-bearers patrolled up and down the line to compel obedience.

I arranged my face close to the back of my neighbor's head, and waited until the guard was at the far end of the line.

"Omar," I said without moving my lips.

"Thorian," came the whisper.

I remarked that we were going to be worked to death or slain when the siege began, to conserve food.

The nod was barely perceptible, but quick. I was encouraged to surmise that this Thorian had more than bone inside his thatch, not counting the lice. I closed my eyes until the guard had come and gone, and then asked if he could break the chain without my help.

He shrugged. He must think he had a chance, though, or he would not have been so annoyed at losing the hindmost place.

"If you need me, stoop," I said, "so I can reach over you."

Another nod.

"I'll tell you when the time is right. And let me lead when we run, for I can take us to safe haven."

The guard returned and departed.

"I may need your help carrying this load," I admitted reluctantly. A companion who could snap one chain could probably snap two and depart alone.

"Quarry?" he muttered. "They won't take us into the city tonight."

"Yes they will. I am certain."

Cracks and screams from farther up the line ended our attempts at conversation. That was just as well, I thought. Thorian might next inquire how well I knew Zanadon.

3: The Great Gate

As we began to ascend the ramp, the soldiers dismounted and proceeded on foot, leading their ponies. The incline is so long and the ascent so high that the army has standing orders for all returning patrols to proceed on foot, lest they overstrain tired mounts. Most officers have more sense than to antagonize their men for the sake of a footling regulation, but Captain Publian Fotius was an exception.

The burly Gramian Fotius appeared near the rear of the line, and he was not in a jovial mood. A vexed expression marred the customary tranquility of his countenance. He was leading his pony with one hand, and in the other he bore a whip of plaited oxhide.

He paced along for a while beside Thorian, eyeing him as a strong man may seek to take the measure of another, for they were of comparable stature. The slave, despite the other's social and strategic advantage, matched him scowl for scowl.

The soldier opened the conversation.

"Want some more *pain*, Slave?" he inquired jocularly. "Want me to do your back again?"

"No."

"Didn't hear that. Speak up."

"Please don't flog me anymore," Thorian growled.

Fotius grunted in disappointment and thought for a while.

"You got a wound," he remarked at last, pointing at the half-healed scar that transected the other's torso. "Where did you get that wound, Slave?"

"Fighting Vorkan scum."

Fotius then pointed out that in future Slave Thorian would be required to fight nothing more than blocks of stone, and that those were undoubtedly more suited to his abilities and prowess.

The other indicated that he was entirely satisfied to leave the Vorkan problem in the hands of the capable Corporal Fotius, and had every confidence that the blood-drenched reavers of Dom Wilth, razers of Forbin, and rapists of Polrain would suspend their advance, cease their ravaging, and flee in terror immediately upon learning the identity of their new opponent. In cultured and measured discourse, Thorian further implied that, wound or no wound, he would be happy to take on the corporal at any contest or form of competition known to man or god, and would thereupon employ his person to clean dog droppings from the gutter. And furthermore, he was at a loss to know why the corporal was perspiring so copiously at the moment, on this trifling hill.

I concluded that he was a man of spirit.

Fotius might reasonably have pointed out the unfairness of Thorian's final observation, in that he was struggling with a skittish pony in a crowd and was personally encased in almost half his own weight of bronze-upholstered bullhide, while the slave wore only a metal collar and a small rag. He did not do so, but who among us has not at some time overlooked a possible witty rejoinder and only thought of it much later, when the debate was over and the opportunity missed?

The earlier challenge having escaped his notice altogether, due to the careful phrasing employed, the corporal decided to drop back and taunt me instead. I could sympathize with his frustration—there could be little satisfaction in flogging a chained captive, and in any case the press of the crowd would inhibit the limber arm motion needed for satisfactory results.

In most realms I have known, it is decreed that travelers when passing must veer to one side of the way, the choice being specified. On the great ramp of Unvanquished Zanadon, the law explicitly requires those approaching to walk in the middle and those descending to stay on the outside.

I do not know the reason for this, but I do know that the result is to add greatly to the confusion of traffic when the ramp is, as it then was, crowded to overflowing. The parapets are low and in places the drop from the sides is considerable.

Gramian Fotius eyed me with a puzzled expression. I was the madman who had walked up to his Uncle Publian and just asked to be made a slave. I had not been ridden down and clubbed like the others. He could tell I was crazy just from my smile.

"Teller of tales, huh?" he said.

"*Trader* of tales. I tell you one, you tell me one. Fair trade."

Bronze jangled as the corporal shrugged. "You start."

A descending camel train caused a momentary delay. Fotius's pony reacted in the way ponies always do to camels. The corporal eventually settled the matter by striking the beast with his fist, half stunning it. Then he was ready to listen, and I could begin.

"Ever since I came to the Spice Lands—"

"You weren't born here?"

"No," I said. "I was born on the Isle of Evermist, in the far north. My father was a carver of ivory and my mother a professional wrestler. You want to hear a tale of Evermist or of the Spice Lands?"

"Spice Lands, of course."

It did not matter to me. "Well, then. Often since I came to the Spice Lands, I have been told tales of the mischievous god Nusk."

"Never heard of him."

"He is the god of doorways and beginnings."

"Oh, Nask, you mean."

"Perchance he is known here as Nask. He is said also to be the god of adolescence, frequently associated with virgins. Many tales depict him in that wise, as a comely youth of spirit. It is told among the Wailmanians, for example, how Sky, the Father of Gods, discovered Nusk among the rushes of the Nathipi River, philandering with a group of mortal maidens. Being most exceedingly wroth at his wilful son's behavior, Sky ordered him to complete a great work for each of the maidens he had thus dishonored so that mortals would evermore be reminded of his shame.''

"What was he doing with the maidens?"

I sighed. "The details were not specified, but I fancy much what you yourself do, Corporal, when a group of the lovely creatures besets you in a secluded place. The works that Nusk was thus constrained to attempt were to be monuments so mighty that no mortal could have achieved them.''

"How many maidens?" he demanded, showing genuine interest.

"Your perception has penetrated to the nub of the heart of the center of the mystery! By establishing how many works the god completed, we may know how many maidens he had used so shamefully. The estimates vary, depending on the teller of the tale. In all regions west of the Nathipi, though, it is agreed that this great granite ramp of Zanadon, rising so straight and direct from the plain to the giddy height we have now achieved, level with the clifftop, must be considered first among all the wonders of the god. You will not argue with that?''

Gramian Fotius considered the question, crunching up his forehead under the brow of his helmet. Before he could reply, the parade stumbled to a halt, jammed in the press before the gates of the city. Grunting angrily, he went shouldering forward to see what the delay was, dragging his pony behind him.

Thus I never did hear his conclusions.

Relieved of the obligation to entertain the corporal, I thankfully slid my burden of bronze chain to the ground. Flexing my aching shoulders and rubbing my scrapes, I appraised the marvels before me.

Truly, all the legends of the world do not do justice to the great gateway of Unvanquished Zanadon.

The gates themselves are mighty and many layered, each twice as thick as a man is tall, wrought of thick oaks from the forest of Ghill, and bound in bronze. Teams of plodding oxen turn the windlasses that move them, but so long is the ramp leading up from the plain and so high the watchtowers above them that no marauder has ever managed to charge the portal fast enough to prevent their closing.

The gates themselves are therefore generally assessed as the second of the wonders of Nusk.

And the granite walls that enclose the city are assuredly a third. They stretch off out of view on either hand, topping the sheer cliffs of the mount. I have seen more city walls than other men, I suppose, but never any to match those of Zanadon. Why the elders should seek to raise them farther was an enigma to puzzle a god.

But then I decided, as most visitors do, that the two figures flanking the arch are greater marvels still. My dreams had never shown me those. Carved in high relief from the warm brown stone of the walls, they shine like living flesh. Their eyes are inset in ivory and jet, so cunningly fashioned by ancient craft that no viewer can evade their fearsome gaze. They watch each traveler arriving, from the time he first sets foot on the apron of the ramp, far out on the plain, until he passes between them. No mortal may enter Zanadon unnoticed by its gods.

On the left stands Holy Maiana and on the right Immortal Balor—eternal lovers, parents, and preservers of Zanadon, twin children of Father Sky and Mother Earth.

Maiana is crowned by her crescent, inset in silver, and the horns alone are four times the height of a man. Her nipples are inlaid with a man's weight of precious rubies; the hair of her head is set in diamonds and that of her groin in sapphires. Immortal Balor is even larger. His sword and armor are of solid gold, his beard of darkest hematite.

My enchantment was broken as a passing mule attempted to nip my knee. I stepped back hurriedly, almost tripping over the heap of chain at my feet and jarring the tether that bound my neck to Thorian's. The big man choked and grunted angrily.

I apologized, and aimed a kick at the hindquarters of the departing mule. The mule retaliated, narrowly missing two yellow-cloaked priests and a laden porter, and they were all swept away down the ramp by the press of the crowd.

The guards had vanished in the throng, so it was safe to talk.

"It seems to me," I remarked, "that the Vorkans have small need to vanquish Zanadon itself. Even if they cannot penetrate the gates, they can loot those two figures. They will thereby gain more riches than may be culled from a total pillage of all other cities in the Spice Lands."

Thorian chuckled into his matted beard. His eyes gleamed black under the sweaty tangle of his hair. "Then you have not heard the story of Susian, O Trader of Tales?"

I admitted that I knew of him as Great King of Thereby, and something of the wonders of cruelty and conquest he achieved, but I recalled no narrative relating him to Unvanquished Zanadon.

"Then hear it now," said the giant, "for it was where you stand that Susian met the fate he so eminently deserved. Having conquered all the nations between the Kulthiar Range and the sea, and all peoples from Forbin to the Edge of the Sown, Susian of Thereby came in his might to challenge Zanadon, and his hordes darkened the plain."

"Hordes always darken plains," I observed.

"Darker than usual," said Thorian. "The gates were slammed in his beard, of course. He marched three times around the city, promising mercy if it surrendered, and the priests hurled cats at him from the walls."

"Why cats?"

"That is not recorded. Apparently it was an insult."

"Doubtless." I apologized for my interruption.

"Then Susian, thinking as you do, that to strip the riches from the guardian god and goddess would amply repay his efforts, began construction of a scaffold. Two scaffolds, I estimate, one on either hand."

"A noble ambition," I admitted. "The cliffs fall sheer a hundred spans beneath the holy feet."

"Exactly. And the citizens spitefully dropped rocks upon him, wrecking serious hurt upon his workers and damage to their morale. And thus was he foiled."

"Your conclusion lacks a certain artistic finality. Did the mighty Susian merely march off in a huff, then?"

Thorian pushed back his bush of hair with fingers like the handles of trowels. "Far from it. He contrived a ram of enormous length, purposing to bring the whole might of his army against those very gates you observe. And such was the multitude of his legions that he filled the entire ramp with armored men, from the fevered paddies of the plain even to where we stand below the towers."

"Ah! The image bears intimations of impending disaster."

"Verily. Before the gates could be forced, they were flung open, and the army of Zanadon swept out with Immortal Balor himself at their head."

"Great was the slaughter?"

"Great was the slaughter."

"They ran like vermin?"

"Not so. Susian himself was smitten by Balor in person, of course."

"Of course. But some must have escaped. The ramp is narrow when we consider the magnitude of the forces involved."

"They all perished! The van was struck down by Balor and his cohorts in conventional fashion, I admit, but so great was the torrent of blood that flowed down the ramp that the rearguard drowned in it and was swept away into the Jolipi! Not a man survived to bear the story home to Thereby."

"It has scope," I admitted. "It conjures an epic vision. I am grateful to you for this, Thorian."

"You are most welcome. But now I observe that we are free of the attentions of our guards, and I feel ready to hazard the strength of my arm against these insolent bonds. There is a link here that seems inferior to its fellows."

"Let your manifest virility be curbed by patience," I said. "There is no sanctuary there." I gestured to the ramp, running down forever, straight and steep, crowded with refugees and camels and mule trains. "Two fugitives may evade pursuit in this tumult, I grant you, but we need refuge. The Vorkans are coming, and we must enter the city.''

"We shall have no better opportunity," the big man said, scowling suspiciously at me.

"Yes we shall!" I insisted. "Did I not assure you that they would bring us to the gate, and not to some distant quarry? Trust me. More important—trust the gods! Tonight we shall sleep in freedom within Unvanquished Zanadon, I promise."

Thorian stared hard at me and then shrugged his great shoulders. "You have much faith in the power of prayer!"

"I never pray," I snapped. "It is the worst of errors. Now hush, for I think our captors return."

I had no reason to say so; I wished only to contemplate my surroundings, for this was an experience worth savoring. One leaf of the gates stood closed, and the remainder of the passage was packed with a screaming, struggling multitude:

Soldiers in bronze armor, shining bloodred in the sunset, raised empty hands to show they came as suppliants, clamoring of their prowess and the battles they had fought . . .

Bulky merchants in their many-colored swaths, howling that their permits were still valid and fumbling for bribes as they were evicted from the city . . .

Smug, black-bearded citizens showing their passes calmly and being bowed in through the throng . . .

Pack beasts, and wagons, and slaves bearing carrying chairs . . .

An ambassador and his entourage in cloth of gold, spluttering purple outrage at the indignity being heaped upon his monarch—and being turned away regardless . . .

Noble ladies in silks and gems, seeking to sell their bodies on any terms to anyone who could win them residency . . .

Rich men sobbing as they offered their all . . .

The Vorkans were coming.

I sighed, hungry for all the tales I saw there and would never hear, and for the irony, also. Because, when the evening chaos was settled, then fourteen near-naked men would be admitted before the gate was closed—admitted merely for a spell, of course, until they completed their labor or it killed them. That was the intent. I have a weakness for irony.

Far below the plain was shadowed now, and the lights of fires showed a litter of campsites as far as the eye could see. There were the richer refugees, leaders with many followers—petty kings who had abandoned their cities, defeated generals with the remains of their armies, displaced tribes of the uplands, all come to offer allegiance to Unvanquished Zanadon and pay the price of entry with the blood and muscle of their young men. Eventually the young men would choose to enter as slaves—for a spell— and the leaders would starve outside. The Vorkans would loot their bones. Or the Zanadonians might. It would depend on timing, I decided.

Oh, the tales to be gathered on that plain! The threads of ten thousand lives . . . love and death, rape and sacrifice, hate and friendship. Could I but stretch one evening to a mortal life span, I could not gather all those stories, and I must shun them all, for the sake of what awaited me within the walls of Zanadon the Never Vanquished.

As the sun dipped into the plain, a whip cracked, and we were driven forward through the gates, into the city.

4: Escape

✳

The vista disclosed to the traveler as he first enters ancient Zanadon has been praised since the dawn of tourism and lauded by poets unnumbered. I was thus unfortunate in that I could see nothing except Thorian's wide back.

I do not complain, though, because I regard complaint as a paramount sin. I was steadfastly disregarding my weariness and the weakness of hunger, and doing my best to ignore my burden of chain. In truth, I was very glad to escape from the minatory scrutiny of the sentinel gods, whose obvious suspicion was worrisome.

But I did want to see the view.

Progress was slow and frequently blocked altogether. At those times I could stand on tiptoe and peer over the big man's shoulder at the fabled splendor of the jeweled city. I saw it through a forest of pot-shaped hats, but I saw it.

"It is impressive," he muttered. "I deplore untoward ostentation as a rule, but there is a point at which sheer excess can raise vulgarity itself to the stature of an art."

"They say no true count of the shining towers has ever been made, and the domes are without number," I countered.

"But they have only one temple. I call that paltry."

"Narrow-minded, perhaps."

"I am at a loss for further comparisons."

I informed him that the poet Fimloo had praised the king of Urgalon's new palace by deeming it *"Fit to be a slum in Zanadon,"* and the king had rewarded his flattery with gold.

Thorian twisted his head around in his metal collar and regarded me skeptically out of the corner of his eye. "Monarchs rarely appreciate such subtlety of metaphor!"

"Melted gold," I admitted. "He washed out Fimloo's mouth with it. But all witnesses agree that this street is without peer."

The Great Way, to which I referred, is paved in whitest marble and wide enough to march an army fifty men abreast. It is flanked by mansions and palaces, ornamented with statues and fountains, and shaded by enough great trees to furnish a small jungle. Seen from the perspective of the gate, it narrows like an arrowhead, whose point rests at the entry pillars of the temple on the highest point of the mount, far away and high above.

The ziggurat itself is no mean edifice, and it is capped by the House of the Goddess, although all that could be detected of it at that distance was the gleam of its golden dome. Yet the pyramid is quite overshadowed by the two statues that flank it, Maiana and Balor. In design they match the figures guarding the portal, but are free-standing and greater in size. Eagles fly around their heads like gnats, and they overlook everything.

Thus I found myself again under the foreboding gaze of the twin deities. They could obviously see me peering at them over Thorian's shoulder, and I found their frowns worrisome.

"Truly," I murmured, "no city is better guarded by its gods than Zanadon the Unvanquished."

"That sounds like a prayer," said Thorian.

"It was intended as a statement of principle."

Conversation was interrupted when our bridles yanked us forward again. The area of the Great Way just inside the gate was crammed to bursting with citizens and soldiers. Slaves brandished flaming torches before their masters. Odors of people and livestock and evening meals warred in the air. Wagons of provisions rolling in jostled empty wagons hurrying out, ponies and mules and camels pushed through the tumult, and everyone seemed to be cracking whips and shouting oaths and orders all at once. The weeping rich who had bought their way in were being methodically stripped to the garb of paupers, so they could be evicted the following dawn, as the law required. The fair women were being led off to whatever vile servitude they had accepted.

The coffle halted again. Again I rose on tiptoe to admire the view. Maiana and Balor still stood at the top of their city, shining red in the sunset as if enraged by this unseemly pandemonium. They were still staring right at me.

For some time Captain Fotius and his men struggled to clear a way through the crowds. They were tired and eager to complete their task and return to their homes. They bullied and shoved and shouted themselves hoarse in the din, but so great was the press that they made little progress, while the sky overhead darkened to slate and the smoky torches flamed ever brighter.

Had I not been watching for the opportunity I expected, it would have killed me. A binding failed on a wagon, and great barrels of wine went rumbling off. The horses of the following wagon shied and reared.

"Now!" I yelled, and threw myself against Thorian's back, grabbing with both hands for the chain between us. Thorian seized his own tether with intent to snap it, but he had no chance then. The runaway team plowed through the crowd and into the chain gang.

The other twelve slaves died instantly, of broken necks. Many of the guards and bystanders were less fortunate. I was yanked forward inside my load of chains and then whipped bodily into a party of jugglers and acrobats being deported as undesirables. I thought my bronze wrappings had crushed me, but they granted me some protection as I was dragged through the carnage.

When I came to a stop, I was under the wagon, with my nose touching one of the rear wheels, so close had it come to rolling over my head. I surmised from the incredible amount of noise I could hear that I was still alive, and I forced my fists to relax their death grip on the tether. By twisting my head, I could see Thorian's familiar back, although at an unusual angle. It rippled, strained, and then said, ''Ha!''

Having thus freed himself from the corpse ahead of him,

Thorian rolled over. His hair and beard were spattered with blood. "You are profligate with your powers, Sorcerer!" he said angrily.

I made incoherent noises through a bruised larynx and a broken neck.

"Can your magic sever this tether?" Thorian demanded.

I shook my head. I licked my lips and tasted blood, although probably not my own.

Thorian wrapped the chain around his fists. The muscles of his arms bulged like melons, and veins swelled in his forehead. I joined in, and we heaved together. The chain stretched but did not come apart. We relaxed with simultaneous gasps.

"Pity," the big man said. "As I postulated, there was a defective link in the other. Nevertheless, I am minded now to view the sights of the city, including all points of historic and artistic interest, and I propose to drag you along in the hope of furthering your education."

I made no demur.

We wriggled out from under the wagon and then struggled to our feet. Onlookers were attempting to aid the wounded, while shouting descriptions of their own narrow escapes over the screams. Flaming torches waved in the gloom. Amid the confusion, we two slaves were barely noticed.

"Heavy!" I croaked, indicating the chain still looped about my neck. Despite Thorian's wounded leg, he could probably manage the additional burden better than I.

"Permit me this indignity," the giant said, and scooped me up bodily. "Look damaged, if you can."

"That I can manage," I groaned.

Shouting for a medic, Thorian bulled through the crowd, using me as a battering ram. As we reached the outskirts, however, we came face to face with the towering mass of Corporal Gramian Fotius.

Clearly, although the names might escape him, the faces were familiar. He said, "Hey!" and then, "Huh?" and went down before Thorian's charge in a crash of metal. Thorian stepped on his face and kept on running. Shouts went up behind us. Pedestrians stepped hurriedly out of the way, and we disappeared into the darkness of an alley.

Limping harder as he tried to make speed, Thorian rounded a corner, into an even narrower alley, flanked by high walls and roofed by the last glow of twilight. It was familiar. I said, "Stop here!"

Thorian stopped and set me down, panting loudly. "More magic now?"

"No magic." I hauled off my burden of chain. "There are spikes atop this gate."

"A regrettable display of inhospitability," the giant said, accepting the chain. He arranged the loops as best he could in the dark, swung them to and fro a few times, and then hurled. The snake seemed to hiss as it unwound upward, and so great was the violence of the throw that my collar almost yanked my head off. Then the string crumpled and fell back to earth, rumbling against the far side of the gate.

"Awrk!" I said, having to rise on my toes to breathe.

Thorian tugged on the dangling end. "It would appear to have caught on one of the spikes," he said resignedly. "No magic?"

"You should have retained some slack," I gasped.

"I shall keep that procedure in mind for next time." The big man cupped his hands for my foot and hoisted me as high as he could—which was not very high, because our necks could not be located much more than a cubit apart. I leaned a knee on his shoulder until I managed to locate one of the metal collars. I put a foot in that for support.

Thorian spurned such aids. Using the chain as a rope, he went up it hand over hand, bracing his feet against the planks. I preferred to utilize the empty collars as ladder rungs. The procedure was awkward and noisy, for the tether joining us restricted our freedom. The chain rattled on the gate, the gate clamored against its hinges, I was repeatedly banged against it, and Thorian swore a string of resonant oaths. Soon half the city must come running to investigate. I tried very hard not to think what would happen to my neck if I fell, especially if the big man came down on top of me.

We were both half choked when we came level with the top and peered over. The space below was obviously a kitchen yard for some great mansion, enclosed by storage sheds and the side of the house itself. An alarming amount of light was streaming from the windows, but as yet no one had come to investigate the racket.

My companion had noted the silence. "No dogs, even?"

"Mayhap we have stumbled upon a holy hospice for the chronically deaf," I suggested.

Thorian began hauling himself up to a precarious perch between the closely spaced spikes. Had he slipped and toppled over, of course, I should have been shredded on the spikes as he dragged me after him. I tried not to think about that, either.

When he was safely over, hanging on to the top, I followed, and I also succeeded in passing the spikes without impaling myself. Anyone coming along the alley was going to have a clear view of these two foolhardy burglars performing acrobatics, backlit by the bright windows of the mansion. The occupants should be able to hear us, or see us, just by glancing out a window.

The only really surprising thing is the expected.

Side by side, we clung on the far side, while Thorian struggled to free the chain, for the lucky link had been well jammed onto its anchoring spike. Just as I concluded that my arms must come loose first—and Thorian was hanging on with one hand only—he solved the problem by ripping the spike from the wood. "On three," he said. "One. Two. Three."

With two thuds and a jangle, we were down. For a moment we just sat there, sweating and panting, side by side.

Angry shouts and a patter of sandals went past in the alley.

"Your mastery of timing is the mark of a true professional," Thorian said. "You must have done this hundreds of times."

"The true artist never repeats himself," I replied modestly. "The followers of the Ineffable Hasmarn eschew the eating of fowl. Have you religious objections to consuming the flesh of birds?''

''Your interest in my beliefs has been provoked by that large goose cooling on the windowsill?''

I said I believed he could reach it.

''I am sure you are mistaken, but let us investigate.''

We rose to our feet simultaneously. I gathered up the excess chain. Like Siamese twins, we walked together across the yard. Thorian could not reach the goose, but I cupped hands for him to step on—to show that I was capable of the feat, even if only briefly. With that advantage, he grabbed the prize. He jumped down.

''Ouch! This brute is hot!''

''I detest people who complain all the time. Let us see what these elegant amphorae contain.''

The gate we had come over was large enough to admit wagons, and a platform alongside the house was obviously intended for unloading them. Several large clay ewers were standing on it. I sniffed at the seals.

''Not olive oil, to be sure.''

''That is encouraging.''

''Wine, I think. Have you any religious obj—''

''None whatsoever. Now produce a safe place to drink it, Sorcerer.''

I glanced around. There would be somewhere safe to hide, of course. The white-painted storage sheds were generously barred and padlocked. They probably contained not only household supplies but the stock in trade of a family business. The doors had obviously been designed not only to resist burglars, but also to reveal any attempt at tampering.

Another door led into the house itself, and the windows were attainable, if my friend could remove the gratings. Even as I considered the prospect, I heard laughing voices within. People were coming. I knew there would be *somewhere* . . . I took a harder look at the loading dock.

''Consider these steps,'' I said. ''They are well made, you agree? Good fieldstone, smoothly finished but unmortared. If you were to leave off your disgusting gnawing for a moment, I believe you could lift one edge of this topmost tread?''

Thorian dropped the bird and gripped the slab. Again his muscles bulged, and the great stone slowly tilted upward. I slipped the wine jug into the gap as a prop. I dropped the loose chain inside and clambered in feet first. The space was not high enough to stand erect and was restricted to the area of the steps—it did not extend under the dock itself. No matter that it seemed to be paved with broken glass, nothing had bitten me or stung me. Thorian followed with the goose, then braced his shoulders against the lid so I could remove the amphora.

With a gentle grating noise the slab settled back into position, and we sat down together in the dark.

For some time thereafter, the only sounds were those of chewing and swallowing.

5: The Tale of Omar

"**I** do not believe there is anything left on this carcass," I remarked. "Do you wish to try another gnaw?"

"Certainly! I do not give up so easily. More wine?"

"I think not. It is a worthy vintage, but I might become drowsy."

There was a sound of bones crunching. "You promised me," Thorian said with his mouth full, "that we should sleep as free men in Zanadon. At the risk of seeming ungrateful, I concede that I had hoped for more expansive quarters."

"These are temporary. I chose them on the grounds of privacy and quiet. The ventilation is barely acceptable, I agree."

"And my left knee is in my right ear. Furthermore, the long-dead artisans who constructed this place—may Morphith cherish their souls—seem to have used it to dump all the leftover fragments of masonry. They are excessively sharp on the soles of the feet and other surfaces."

"This is an advantage. Having sated my hunger, I now propose to saw through our tether with one of these shards."

Thorian grunted approvingly. "Weaken a link and I can do the rest. The collars are too thick, though."

"I fear so." Having located a suitable fragment, I set to work filing the tether under my chin.

The bolt hole was certainly unpleasantly stuffy. It stank of wine and goose and the blood that had soaked us. It would have been cramped for two even had the second occupant been of more standard size than Thorian.

"If you detect my hands upon your person, friend Omar,

31

I hope you will not think badly of me. I purport to locate your other chain, so I may assist you.''

"Your kindness is beyond belief," I said quickly, "but I think one at a time will be adequate. After all, we have hours to kill yet before the city quietens down, and my neck can take only so much scraping and bruising."

"Of course. Forgive my stupidity."

For a while he crunched bone as loudly as I rasped on metal. Then he continued in the same diffident tone. "Your resources impress me, Trader of Tales. Will you permit a personal question?"

"Ask and I will answer."

"Then outline for me the limits of your magic. Why should so puissant a sorcerer choose to bloody his fingers rasping at a chain with a fragment of flint like a savage from the Huli Desert? Why did you suffer the humiliation and discomfort of the slave train? I am perplexed by this inconsistency."

"By my oath and honor, this is truth, friend Thorian: I am no sorcerer! I have no powers such as you postulate."

"Oh? You have demonstrated an ability to foretell the future, and you created demonic havoc upon many denizens of this great city. You contrived to skewer a tiny loop of chain upon a spike—and not just any spike. Most of them were rotted and corroded. A few had been replaced, and it was upon one of those that you secured our escape. Food and drink and a place of concealment were waiting for us, and our entry escaped notice both within and without the wall."

"Pure luck."

Thorian growled low, a sound such as might indicate frustration in a very large predator. It then occurred to me that my companion was a proven carnivore of remarkable size, and certainly capable of violence. To provoke him might be unwise under any circumstances, and all the more so when sharing very intimate confinement with him.

"I am neither seer nor mage," I insisted. "I have faith in the gods, is all."

"Yet you spurn to pray, you said."

"Pray? Prayer is whining or complaint or boasting. I do not bore the gods by telling them what they already know, nor do I presume to advise them. I accept whatever they care to send, pain or pleasure."

I continued scraping uninterrupted for a while, occasionally striking sparks like shooting stars in the darkness. Evidently the big man was considering my words carefully. I could guess at the skeptical expression on his rough-hewn face.

"You do not give thanks for their blessings?"

"If I am to thank the gods when my life is sweet, then to be consistent I should curse them when I am sick or hungry or injured or hankering for a woman. Or mourning a lost friend," I added, thinking of dark-eyed Illina mostly.

"You never seek their aid in distress? I fear they may test your resolve some day."

"They have done so, a time or two," I said. "I endure without reproach. They know they made me mortal, and breakable. One day they will kill me. No man can refuse death. I accept life, also, as it comes."

"Then you ignore the gods and deem them irrelevant?"

"Far from it! I seek always to amuse them." I chuckled. "Friend Thorian—and I am proud to address you so—you gifted me with the tale of Susian of Thereby, and I am richer for it. If you wish, I shall repay my debt with a tale of my own, the tale of my origins."

"I promise not to go away."

"Good." For a moment I gathered my thoughts. I had told stories in the dark before—for I have done almost everything before, at one time or another—but it is always a strange experience. The same story is never spoken twice the same. A tale must be molded to its listeners as a glove is cut to a hand, and in the dark I have no way to judge the reactions of my audience.

Moreover, I had not yet appraised this cryptic giant. In appearance he was brutish, although that was partly due to his unkempt condition and a natural reaction to the surroundings in which I had found him. He could be gentle in his movements, and subtle of speech. He had claimed to have battled with the Vorkans, and few survived to make that boast. The wound that disfigured his torso had come within a finger's width of gutting him. He was an interesting specimen.

"I was born," I began, "some forty years ago, in the great maritime city of Quairth, on the Peacock Coast of Leilan. It lies far to the east, across the racing seas, but you may have heard tell of its exquisite porcelain finger bowls, or even of the Quairth Grater, an amusing local device for the execution of criminals. My parents were keepers of a wayside hostelry, the Gilded Lily, not far from the docks. They were hardworking folk, and honest."

"Honest?"

"Relatively speaking. Of course they might extend to a solitary traveler of obvious means certain unadvertised services, but they were careful not to overindulge, and they always saw to it that the remains were buried with reverence. A too-strict following of the letter of the law would make it impossible for a working man to pay his taxes—so my father always said, and with good reason. Apart from that, they found a reputation for civility and fair value to be the surest stimulus to trade.

"As I mentioned, their establishment was located near the harbor, and much patronized by mariners and dealers in exotic merchandise. My earliest memories are of crawling around under the tables, searching for lost coins and licking up the beer spills."

"It must have been a happy time for you."

"Indeed it was. But I look back with even greater joy to my later childhood, when I would spend long hours spellbound by the tales the sailors told, of far lands and fabled cities. It was then, of course, harkening to their stories of peoples and gods unknown in Leilan, that I acquired my lifelong interest in anecdote as an art form."

"You epitomize that artistry, if I may say so."

"You are too kind. In time, also, I began to build a repertoire of such sailor yarns, and took to retelling them, entertaining the clientele and polishing my delivery. I confess that in my childish innocence, I fell at times into the folly of embellishing my material, but I am happy to relate that I outgrew that foible and learned never to stray from the stringent truth.

"I omitted to mention that I was an only son. My parents were blessed also with three comely daughters, older than I, and at busy times I would keep the customers amused while they waited for my sisters. It was good for business, and the family encouraged my efforts.''

"They must have been very proud of you," Thorian said. "Is that chain weak enough yet for me to heave on it a little?"

"If you can do so without dashing my brains out in this confined space, then I should be happy to profit yet again from your enviable brawn.''

Thorian grasped the collar in one giant hand and snapped the chain with a sharp yank of the other.

"I am obliged to you," I said hoarsely, rubbing my throat.

"My pleasure. Now let me relieve you of the other end, while you continue your epic tale." He fumbled for a sharp rock and began sawing at another link.

"There is little more to tell. Business had been poor and taxes were due—possibly my mother had been a trifle careless. One unusually well-dressed guest was traced by his heirs as far as the Gilded Lily and no farther. These ill-motivated persons began spreading rumors and eventually incited a riot. That night—actually it was closer to morning—I returned from visiting a friend to discover the hostel in flames and my dear parents dangling side by side from the sign bracket above the door.

"It was a shock, of course, to a tender lad of fifteen, and a lamentable end to a fine family business. I never discovered how my sisters fared, but I was told they had escaped, and am confident that they were all possessed of a fortitude and resilience that would have enabled them to prosper. Their skills were widely praised among the maritime community, although of course I never experienced them at firsthand.

"So there I was, orphaned and penniless, having no trade and no talent except a certain glibness of tongue.

Forgive me if that remark sounds boastful, but I am looking back at my early life from a great distance of years
and seeking to be impartial.''

"I am sure your judgment of your own youthful potential is justified by the fruits evidenced in your manhood,''
Thorian said politely.

I thanked him sincerely. "Of course my woolly head
was packed tight with dreams of romance and heroism,
wonders and epic valor. There was nothing I could do to
secure my parents' welfare, nor my sisters', either. I
therefore slipped away and enlisted on a merchantman, the
Perfumed Violet, trading to the Cinnabar Islands.''

I felt around in the dark to locate the wine jug. I washed
the dryness from my mouth and then continued.

"All of us, I suppose, sooner or later lose our youthful
illusions and learn to face the hard realities of adult life.
In my case, I discovered that a sailor's existence lacked
the romance and adventure I had been led to anticipate.
I found instead only monotony and hardship and heart-
breaking toil. Towered cities were almost as rare as firm-
breasted maidens breathing words of desire while they shed
silks and showered jewels. Bad food and sour water were
my daily lot.

"Oh, I admit that there was the odd sea monster and a
few skirmishes with pirates where I acquitted myself reasonably well, I think. And the ravishing maidens were not
entirely absent. But to dwell on those exceptional events
would give you an entirely false impression of the few
brief weeks I spent on shipboard.

"When the *Perfumed Violet* was wrecked on the Dauntless Rocks during a typhoon—with great loss of life, I
am afraid, although I contrived to rescue several of my
mates—I seized the opportunity to take up another pro-
fession, and eventually settled upon that of professional
storyteller.''

"A very sound decision,'' Thorian said.

"One thing I had learned, though. All those sailor stories I heard in my childhood had been entertaining enough,
and no one can doubt that the events they relate actually
happened, but I now saw that the stories were repeated

over and over, while the events themselves had only happened once. A man might have a hundred tales to tell, but ninety-nine of them would be hearsay and only one of them sifted from his own experience. This was a shattering revelation to me!

"Stories, in short, were faint shadows of reality. Having seen that, I reached my paramount conclusion, a principle which has ever after been the guiding star of my existence."

"I believe the chain is about ready to snap," Thorian said. "Well, perhaps just a little more."

"Whenever you are ready. My belief, my article of faith if you will, is this: The stories are entertainment for mortals, but the events themselves are entertainment for gods."

"Expressed like that, the truth is self-evident, but I cannot recall ever hearing it stated."

"Nor I. But I saw then that the true vocation of a trader of tales must be to witness epic events at firsthand, so that his narratives may be buttressed by the finality of truth. I decided that I would go wherever the gods sent me and see whatever the gods allowed me to see. They know me for a reliable witness. I do not pester them with pleas or imprecations or arguments. I accept hardship and luxury with equal serenity of mind, allowing neither to sway me from my duty.

"And thus," I concluded, "the gods often allow me to be present on important occasions. I observe and record. They make my presence possible, sometimes, by arranging minor incidents to advantage—as you saw happen this evening. After all, what seemed to you to be wonders were all in themselves mere trifles, of no significance. The chain you threw so expertly had to come down somewhere, so why not on a spike?"

"In total, though, such trifles add up."

"The whole world is made of grains of sand. Who but the gods can count them or decree their motion? It cost them very little to arrange my presence here."

"Just to observe?"

"And later, I hope, to recount. Oh, once in a while

they trust me to participate in great events in a small way, because they know I will cooperate without demur. How is that link?''

''Finished,'' Thorian said, and he snapped the chain without adding a bruise to my neck. ''Your narrative has moved me deeply.''

6: The Tale of Thorian

"**I** am honored by your praise," I said, reaching for the wine bottle again.

"A couple of points obtrude, though. You will not mind if I query?"

"Not at all. Ask for any clarification you desire."

"At the beginning you stated your age as near to forty. When I observed you this evening, I assessed you at little more than half that."

"You flatter me," I said cautiously. "Or I may have overestimated the ravages of recent hardship on my countenance."

"More likely. And the second thing that troubles me is that this fascinating narrative does not agree at all with what you told Corporal Fotius on the ramp."

"I had not realized you heard. Besides, to honor a thug like that with anything approaching authentic truth would seriously conflict with my professional sensibilities."

"I agree with you there," Thorian said, and there was a sound of wine being gulped. "Ah! Good stuff, er, noble vintage, I mean. Yea, I have suffered great insolence from that Corporal Fotius these past three days. Despite this wound on my belly, which still troubles me, I should dearly love to meet with him again, on even terms, man to man."

"The contest would be an interesting one!" I said, contemplating the artistic possibilities. "Action, drama, balance . . . valor rewarded or ultimate pathos? It would have to be to the death, of course."

"If the match is even close to fair I will accept the stakes gladly."

"Then be of good cheer. That is exactly the sort of

encounter the gods would find entertaining. While I do not presume to advise them on such matters, I judge it conceivable that they will arrange it.''

"Your words hearten me greatly! I shall spend some thought in planning how best I may reduce the scurvy lout to a small heap of canapés.'' The big man chuckled ominously.

"And now,'' he added, "are we ready to essay our departure from these fortuitous but cramped surroundings?''

"Not yet, I fear. We need the streets deserted if we are to parade around in bronze collars. After midnight.''

He groaned faintly and rearranged his great limbs in the tiny space. "Have we far to go?''

I admitted that I had no idea.

After a significant silence, he said, "When we first spoke, you told me of a safe refuge awaiting you within the city. I am already more grateful to you than words can express, Trader of Tales, and if your friends here will aid me also, then I—''

"I have no friends here,'' I said. "Not yet. I did not say I *knew* of a safe refuge. I said I could lead us to one. I already have—here. I should have been more humble, of course, and specified that it was the gods who would lead me and that you could follow, but I wished to discourage lengthy debate under the circumstances. Forgive me this trifling misunderstanding.''

Thorian grunted. It was the sort of grunt that might drift over the plain at twilight to stampede the shy gazelle into sharp-clawed ambush, and it made my scalp prickle. "And where do you go from here?''

I explained patiently that I would go wherever the gods led me, that they had wanted me in Zanadon and would not suffer me to be thrown out until I had recorded whatever it was that was about to happen. I even mentioned my suspicions that Krazath himself was involved.

Thorian drew breath. "Sztatch? Balor?''

"Or Phail. He is known by all those names.''

"Have you ever considered the possibility that you may be a ward of Foofang, Trader?''

"Are not the mazed held blessed of all the gods?'' I

asked patiently. I have debated this matter many times, and it never leads to profitable resolution. "If my wits are scrambled at the moment it is because of the air in here. Would you care to lift that lid just a fraction so that I may slip a pebble under the edge?"

"Excellent thinking," he agreed, and so it was done. A welcome draft of cool fresh air caressed our fevered skins. Faint light along the slit showed that lamps still burned in the windows beyond.

"We might hazard further discourse," I said, "provided we keep our voices low. It is your turn now. What is the tale of Thorian?"

There was a pause, and then a sigh that seemed to last for several minutes, the product of an unusual lung capacity. "Alas! It is nothing. The tale of Thorian will compare with yours as the mud of the paddy field below the glory of the lotus. Not only has my brief existence been totally bereft of incident, but I lack your felicity of phrase and facility of pharynx. You come from far and exotic lands, overflowing with wonders. You have viewed the deeds of heroes and the wrath of gods. Besides your peacock splendor I am the maggot in the filth of the chicken run."

"That is an inspiring opening!" I declared, impressed. "Pray proceed."

"So kind! My exact age is uncertain, but my mother has told me often that I was born a year or two after the Great Eclipse that was in Thang—sometimes she says one and sometimes the other. I am therefore twenty-three or twenty-four, as I reckoned last."

He fell silent for a space and then said, "Better make that twenty-four or twenty-five."

"Your dedication to absolute accuracy is commendable."

"It is a peccadillo of mine. I was named, of course, for the Thorian who is worshipped as god of truth down in Pulst—a minor deity, to be sure, but perhaps worthy of wider observance. On the sixteenth anniversary of my naming day I swore to be deserving of his patronage and, with excess of juvenile fervor, covenanted to strike a tooth from my mouth for every false word that I might thenceforth utter. The light is poor in here, but if you wish to run a finger—''

I assured him that I had already observed the excellence of his dentition.

''Very well. I was born in a small town not three days' journey from here.''

I refrained from commenting upon his Polrainian accent, which was quite marked.

''Sessmarsh is its name. It is a humble place, whose walls are of turf and sun-dried brick. Its protector, Urckl, is a kindly god, but so old and enfeebled that he could not put peas straight in a pod, as they say. In cold fact, Sessmarsh is a vassal state to Mighty Zanadon, and remits taxes of gold and youth to the city of Maiana and Balor.

''My father . . .'' His voice broke momentarily—an effect I normally eschew, although he did it well. ''This is not easy for me to tell, Omar.''

I urged him not to distress himself, as I had no wish to pry into matters he would rather leave covered. Naturally he did not take me at my word.

''But you were so open with your own history that I should be shamed to withhold one eyelash of mine own. Let me leave my father until later. Know that my mother was the fourth of seven sisters. My grandfather, being a man both versed in lore and educated beyond his wit, determined to name all his children after stars. My mother's name was Pulcherrima. My aunts were Aldebaran, Sirius, Polaris, Algol, Betelgeuse, and Alpha Draconis.''

''Immaterial detail always adds verisimilitude,'' I murmured respectfully.

''I noticed that earlier. Poor Aunt Alfie finished my grandmother, who died upon her very naming day. My grandfather followed in due course. Thereafter his seven daughters continued to dwell in the expansive residence he had built in the center of Sessmarsh, earning their livelihood by embroidering kerchiefs and inscribing helpful mottoes on coffee goblets, which they then sold from a window to passersby.

''Their existence was peaceful and solitary, if seven maidens may be collectively described as solitary. They employed no servants, purchased their victuals at the door from street hawkers, and found their own mutual companionship adequate.''

"It is a touching picture," I said, "and fraught with potential for romantic intrusion. They were all beautiful, of course?''

"Not especially. Polly had buck teeth and Sirius was cursed with a heavy mustache.''

"Oh? If you will pardon a minor comment from an old hand, I feel you would be wise to play down that point in future tellings. It does little to enhance suspense.''

"I am indebted to you for the advice. My father, now. My father was a mere vagabond, a rogue and wastrel. He was—and you will understand my hesitation in mentioning the matter—a vagrant storyteller.''

I beamed in the darkness and said nothing.

"One day this glib ne'er-do-well stopped by the window where the ladies sold their crafts and engaged my mother in conversation. Had any of her sisters then been present, I feel sure that the outcome would have been different. As it was, being alone, she was overcome by his blandishments, and invited him to step inside out of the heat and partake of her homemade marshmallow cookies.''

"I have never visited fair Sessmarsh," I said, "although such has long been one of my ambitions.''

"I cannot imagine why. As to the incident I was describing," Thorian continued, " I shall not speculate on the details. I do know that my parents' life together was a very happy one, although it could not have lasted for upward of twenty-five minutes. Thirty at the outside.''

"It has its romantic aspects.''

"Depending on the point of view. My aunts were understanding and did not censure my mother unduly. They did not blame me, either, when I arrived. Indeed, they were all very kind to me, and in my youth I frequently forgot which of the ladies I should address as 'mother' and which as 'aunt.' ''

"It must have been an eerie childhood, though.''

"Doubtless it seems so to you, who had the advantage

of a more cosmopolitan upbringing. Never having known any other, I accepted it as normal. I see now that my diet was overly heavy in starches. At the time I knew no better. I never went outside or played with other children, but the house was roomy, and possessed of a large flat roof, where we slept when the weather was hot. During the day I would sit up there for hours, watching the sleepy life of the little town going by in the streets. I was content.''

"How long did this last?" I inquired, awed by the tragedy so casually unfolded.

"I am coming to that. I have mentioned that Sessmarsh pays tribute to the city of Zanadon, and has done so for centuries. The rationale is that it thereby gains protection from other enemies, although one may question what greater hardship such enemies might inflict. The monetary taxes are not onerous, for Zanadon has small need of gold, but the young men of the town are required to serve a portion of their most virile years in the army of the city, and this impost is greatly resented.

"The citizens of Sessmarsh, therefore, conceal their sons from the assessors to the greatest extent possible. When small, boys are commonly dressed as girls, and treated as such. On reaching maturity they are smuggled away to outlying relatives. It is a lamentable deception."

"Heart-rending."

"My mother was therefore merely following local tradition when she dressed me in girls' clothing and taught my to regard myself as female during my formative years. My aunts concurred, of course. Together, they brought me up to believe myself a girl, and to behave in all ways as a member of the gentle sex."

He slurped a mouthful of wine, belched loudly, and continued.

"I was taught needlework and the culinary arts. When a boy should be learning skill with sword and bow, the use of plow and mattock, the ways of pony and ox, I was wielding brooms and dusters. I worked loom and spindle and became proficient upon the dulcimer. Indeed, I believed implicitly that I was female, just a younger version of my mother and her sisters."

"But surely when you reached maturity—"

"Not even then, alas," he said sadly. "My mother and aunts had no rural relatives to whom I could be sent for concealment when the impressment agents came to town. As I never met strangers, the deception continued undetected, least of all by me."

"But when your beard began to—"

"Did I not mention that my Aunt Sirius had a growth of facial hair? I was led to believe that my own was merely a disfigurement of the same nature, only greater. I bathed and slept alone—how could I know that there were other anomalies concealed beneath my petticoat? Even my pectoral development is not insignificant, as you may have noticed. Convinced that I was cursed with a besetting ugliness, I soon forbore even to show myself upon the roof. I stayed indoors and spent my days in delicate embroidery and gourmet cooking, knowing no company except that of my mother and my aunts."

He sighed deeply. "How long this might have continued, I hesitate to wonder. I suppose I should be grateful to the Vorkan horde. The flood of refugees sweeping through the Spice Lands ahead of those savages caused great alarm within the gates of Unvanquished Zanadon. The elders decreed an increase in the armed forces. However, instead of sending out their own recruiters as formerly, they assigned quotas of strong youths to each of their tributary towns, and by that trivial change in procedure, they unwittingly disrupted the serene flow of my existence.

"The puppet rulers of Sessmarsh, being required to provide a certain number of mobile young males, were thereby inspired to scour their constituency and root out all the hitherto concealed sons, for it was only then that they could hope to withhold their own offspring. Thus it was they lent ear to certain rumors. Thus it was that municipal officials came to call at our residence."

"It must have been a terrifying awakening for you."

"Oh, I knew nothing of it—I was in the kitchen baking cupcakes at the time. The men were brusquely dispatched by my Aunt Sirius, whose staunch demeanor I have described to you.

"Nevertheless," he continued sadly, "it was evident to my mother and my aunts that the milk was spilled, if you will pardon the colloquialism. That evening my Aunt Betelgeuse, having drawn the short straw, took me to her room and revealed to me certain anatomical distinctions that had hitherto been withheld from my attention. I was shaken then, I admit. I sobbed, for I had been brought up to believe that such was the correct reaction to distress. I sobbed even harder when my aunt explained that the bailiffs would certainly return on the morrow with intent to search the house, and that I must flee, out into a world where I had never set foot . . ."

I was overcome.

"You mock my shame with laughter, small man?"

"No, no, no!" I cried hastily. "I am chagrined by the pathos of it. The sounds you hear are suppressed tears."

"I apologize for distressing you. But my tale is done. That very night I stitched together some masculine garments, packed myself a small provision of cucumber sandwiches and cupcakes, and departed from my birthplace for the first time in my life."

So deeply moved by this narrative that I could barely keep a tremor from my voice, I inquired tentatively, "How long ago did this occur?"

"Four days since," he said sadly. "The following morning I was accosted by the villainous Corporal Fotius on a pony. Believing that he wished to pass the time of day in amicable discourse, I hailed him cheerily, and was taken completely by surprise when his oaken staff smote me behind the ear. The next thing I knew, I was chained like a beast, as you saw."

"Your outrage is understandable. But you have failed to explain that half-healed scar upon your person. It minds me of the fearful wounds inflicted sometimes by those overlong Vorkan blades—perchance upon an audacious warrior who, having been dismounted and lost his shield, but yet preferring death to surrender, dared to close with a mounted opponent."

"Oh, that?" Thorian laughed. "You must have regarded it very superficially, Friend Omar. No, I left my mother's house by sliding down a drainpipe. I had never practiced such unruly pursuits as a normal boy would have done. In my inexperience and nervous haste, I snagged a nail, and I was scratched. That is all."

"And the arrow wound on your calf?"

"I stepped on a sleeping cat. It bit me."

"Incredible!"

"You doubt my word?"

"No, truly." I reached for the wine jug, but discovered that only lees remained. I assured him that I had rarely heard such a tale, and if he and I left Zanadon alive, then I should be more than happy to take him on as an apprentice. His native talent warmed my heart.

"It was nothing," he protested. "A trivial anecdote of domestic tragedy with no redeeming moral. And while I am deeply moved by your generous offer, and have no wish to slight you or seem ungrateful, I do feel that my future lies along other avenues, where my skills may aid me in shaping a career."

"May I inquire?"

"I thought of seeking employment in domestic service. I have a knack for flower arranging."

"What about Corporal Fotius, then?"

"I mean after I rip out his gizzard, of course."

7: The Tale of Balor

✳

"**S**urely we now can be upon our way?" Thorian said after a long silence.

"Patience! Only when I am sure the city sleeps will I venture out clad in a bronze collar and hope to escape censorious glances."

He chuckled. "In my case, it will be a bronze collar and nothing but a bronze collar, as I lost my cloth somewhere. Your gods will provide, I suppose?"

"They brought me here for a reason, so I expect they will keep me alive; but I may serve their needs just as well in chains. We shall see."

There are worse experiences than being a slave, for masters feed slaves. Begging is another interesting trade, and not stressful unless the police are honest—in my experience beggars usually sleep more soundly than merchants. I have almost starved to death in a royal palace, knowing that any crumb I dared to nibble would probably be poisoned. I have lived like a king in a desert, where my wives could miraculously garner a sufficiency of mouthwatering sustenance from a tract of hot sand.

Escaped slaves, though, are another matter. They come trailing trouble as a wounded antelope brings hyenas. Every door is closed to them, from the palace to the gutter. Some of my experiences as an escaped slave . . . but I wander from my tale.

The collars were certainly a problem. I had observed no form of dress that concealed the neck. My companion must have been thinking the same thoughts, for he suddenly remarked, "Perchance we should have cut off the collars themselves, not the chains."

"It would have taken us days."

"True. Of course," he added in a satisfied tone, "only the back of mine is visible. Why do you maltreat your beard so? It looks like brown moss."

"It is part of my trade to be a stranger."

He snorted with disgust. "Whence do we go?"

I scratched myself and tried to find a more comfortable position. The confinement was irksome, even if I would not admit it, and must be much worse for Thorian. I did not know the answer to his question. By coming to Zanadon, I had fulfilled all my instructions. Perhaps the next time I slept I would be vouchsafed guidance. "I have arrived penniless in a strange city a thousand times, and never died of it yet. In this case, I think I shall go to the temple."

After a long silence, he growled, "Why the temple?"

"Well," I said in my cheeriest tones, "there can be no question of ever enslaving priests. If we volunteer to enter the priesthood, they will remove our collars for us."

"Your wits are as addled as a butter churn! Did you not observe those flabby, beardless priests at the gates? I know not Maiana herself, but the horned goddess goes by many names. Always the Passionate One demands the ultimate dedication from the men in her service. Before they relieved us of our collars, Trader, they would relieve us of other things more precious."

"I suppose you would especially regret that—having only so recently learned their function."

The carnivore growled in the forest again, and I realized I had strayed beyond the limits of a young man's humor.

"Perhaps that proposal needs more careful consideration," I agreed. "But I still am minded to head to the temple."

"Explain!"

"Not so loud. The reason is simple. You know the legend of Balor?"

"Such fables are myriad as the leaves of the forest."

"I need tell you, though. One more story, and then we can go seek some action after all this preparatory exposition."

"Make it brief."

"I shall try, of course."

I was now almost certain that this young giant was to play a role of some importance in the stirring days to come, although I could not guess what. I had sought out his company in planning my escape from the slave train mainly because I dislike solitary adventure—dialogue is more absorbing than unbroken narrative—but the gods had then arranged matters to throw us together whether I wanted a companion or not.

So I told him the story of Balor, which first I heard two years before, when I was gathering up tales in the lands of the Nathipi delta, south of the Pearls of the Sky. The Silver Shores, they are called sometimes. The cities there are old beyond imagining, and dying of it, their lore being scattered and their legends lost.

It was some pearl-fisher friends in Wraime who first told me, years and years ago, how much the sea gods dislike timber. When I scoffed, they began by showing me dock pilings speckled with barnacles, then took me down to recent shipwrecks encrusted with them, and finally—wilfully disregarding the risk of drowning me completely—they sank me to older, darker, deeper wrecks smothered in heavy coats of shell and coral. There all the wood was gone, and entire vessels had been turned to stone.

I was reminded of this transformation when I came to the Silver Shores. In places the sea has risen to drink down the villages. Waves run between deserted cabins, and fish school by the hearthstones where once the children played. The barnacles and the mussels are hard at their work of petrifaction. The coral cannot be far behind, and the villages will sink away into deeper water as their own stony monuments.

Conversely, jungle seems to abhor stone, for it has crept imperceptibly into some of the old cities, tree by tree, advancing like an army of night wraiths. Sometimes people yet remain, a cowed few creeping about their business in the shadow of the forest giants, ignoring the enemy already within the streets, as if it may wander away of its own accord if they do not encourage it. But the cause is hopeless, and in many cases the people have vanished already, long gone to unknown places. The buildings crumble under mosses and vines, and eventually the jungle eats the cities whole. But I wander.

One night in my dreams I perceived an old woman in a bluish cloak, sitting by a well near a banyan tree. Early the following morning I found the square, the tree, the well, and her, as prophesied. I knew her by her great age, her cloak, and a prominent mole. There was no doubt. Indeed she peered up at me with age-dulled eyes and shrunken face and said, "You come at last!"

I sat with her for many hours, while the shadows crept around the square, and we traded many tales. She was originally of Zanadon, and had been . . . but her own history is immaterial now. I shall enlighten you with that another day.

She told me wonders without number—why the gods of Dol Fark went mad, and where the people went when they fled from Kishmair, and who stole the Nipple of Xa-Vok—so many secrets that my head spun. And when the crows flew homeward in the dusk, I promised that I would return upon the morrow, and she sighed as if feeling blessed and said gently that she would not, because her penance was complete. But that she did not explain.

As the stars appeared I wandered back to my lodgings without remembering doing so and fell upon my pallet. All those wondrous narratives buzzed in my brain, and I did not know which one to think of first. I slept at last and in my dreams I saw a towered city on a hill, entered only by a great ramp from the plain below. I recognized Zanadon from her words and knew that I was summoned.

Among all the other marvels, the old woman had described Zanadon and had told me how it alone of all the cities of the Spice Lands had never been conquered. It was the will of Balor, she said, and she apprised me of Balor in this wise: Of the many gods that Father Sky sired upon Mother Earth, only Maiana and Balor were twins.

"Oh, come!" Thorian protested. "What of Ashfer and Bin Dos, or Sailmok and—"

"Desist!" I said sharply, and he fell silent. "Truly the

tales men tell of the gods are unnumbered, and our lives are short. To make a whole of them is beyond our mortal wit. Some may be false or incomplete, and many that seem contradictory to us may make sense to the gods themselves. Let us fix upon this one story as it is told in Zanadon, for while we are within its ancient walls, we must honor its gods.

"Cities come and cities go. Empires rise and fall, but only Zanadon bears the name of the Unvanquished. This is acknowledged fact throughout all the Spice Lands and all the world.

"It is told in Zanadon, then, that Maiana and Balor were twins. And when the gods went forth to raise up the races of humankind, then Maiana and Balor, being twins, founded Zanadon together and decreed it to be eternal. They made it great, and dwelt within it, as was the way of the gods in the Golden Days. And Zanadon prospered mightily under their rule.

"You know how the Golden Days ended, and how Sky summoned all the gods to his dwelling Beyond the Rainbow, and held Great Council, and how he there delegated certain gods and goddesses to bear thenceforth certain attributes and fulfill certain duties. All men admit the truth of this. Balor, protesting, was ordained the god of war."

Thorian made a noise as if about to complain and then fell silent.

"Of course the Fickle One has other names," I admitted. "Krazath, and Gar Grunn, and Phail. In Polrain they call him Sztatch, do they not?"

"So I have heard tell."

I wondered why he would not admit that he was from Polrain, first victim of the Vorkan invasion. There had been so few survivors that I still had not heard a good firsthand account of the disaster and was most anxious to do so. "And some who give those names to the god of war recognize Balor, also, but assign other attributes to him. As I said, we can debate theology another time.

"Thus Balor departed with lamentation to take up the duties the Father had decreed. Maiana remained behind, mourning, and ruled alone in Zanadon from that day forward.

"The legend continues. As god of war, Balor remains impartial. If he favors a people in one century, he must turn from their children in another. Thus Father Sky commanded, so that justice may be shared over the world, and truly we see that Balor plays no favorite for long. He raises up and he casts down. He inspires the weak to madness and glory, the powerful he unmans and exterminates. In Urgalon they claim that he is blind.

"The exception is always Zanadon. In Zanadon they say that in his agony at the awful burden placed upon him at the Great Council, Balor cried out until he won the pity of all the other gods, and they added their pleas to his. But Father Sky was adamant, until even Earth herself added her voice, and then the First One made a single concession—that Balor need never bring destruction upon the city he himself had founded.

"And so it has been. When an enemy comes to the gates of Zanadon, then Maiana makes special appeal to her brother. She reminds him of their twinship and the happy days they shared here, ruling jointly. She reminds him that he fathered the people and they are his children. She summons him again to be her consort and lover, as he was of yore. And because of the especial love that Balor has for Maiana, he remembers his debt to his former city and his sister. Then Balor takes on mortal form and comes to Zanadon, and leads its army forth in person. And with Balor himself at its head, that army must always triumph over its enemies."

The morning after the old woman told me all this, I went searching for her again. All day I hunted, but she was nowhere to be found, and none knew of whom I spoke. So at evening I kissed Roathina with many tears, and I walked down through the noisy bazaars to the banks of the great Nathipi, and boarded a craft heading upriver, through the gorges of the Pearls of the Sky. I came to the Spice Lands. Two years I had been journeying, and now I had arrived.

"So you came to Zanadon?" Thorian said. "And landed in a war."

"I knew I would land in a war. The gods lead me always to great events, to witness epic deeds and high romance. Love and sacrifice I have seen aplenty. Also storm and famine, earthquake and war. But I have never seen a god, Thorian! Not yet.

"Now the Vorkans are at the gate.

"Now Balor will return in wrath and save his city!"

My tale was done, but all Thorian said was "I hope you are right."

8: Maiden in Distress

Muttering gratefully, we crawled out from under the slab. Thorian stretched and rubbed his back.

I was already peering around the darkened court. No lights showed in the windows, and the city was silent. The moon was not due until just before dawn, but in the Spice Lands then the stars were brighter and more numerous than they have ever been at other times or in other places, and the sky was a golden glory. I tried not to look at it, because stars distract me.

Our needs were simple, but not few: water to remove our bloodstains, cloth to cover our nudity, tools to remove the collars, and a place to rest. The gods must know them as well as I.

First we must escape from the yard itself. The sheds at one end were likely to be storage; those at the other seemed stables and a carriage house. My brawny assistant and I could boost each other up to their roofs easily enough, but in summer they would certainly be paved with slumbering servants. The roof of the house itself was higher and out of reach. The windows were barred. All the doors and gates would be locked and bolted.

Thorian took the weight of the slab again; I removed the amphora. The rock settled back into position with a grating sound that seemed to echo across the city, but was in truth almost inaudible. Only then did I remember the chain, left inside. We would need the chain to climb over the gate— but then what? Naked, wearing metal collars . . .

I did not need to outline our predicament for my companion.

"Well?" he demanded in a menacing whisper. "Have we merely exchanged one sort of captivity for another?"

"The gods will provide."

"They had better do it soon!"

Something rattled at the street side of the court.

I dived for a corner and squeezed myself into it, trying to look like a water pipe. Only then did I search for Thorian, who had vanished with a speed incredible in a man so enormous.

We had come in over the big wagon gate, but it was the smaller postern at its side that now creaked open. Thorian was flattened against the wall behind it. A pale swath glittered in starlight as a man entered and turned to lock the gate behind him. Thorian's great hands closed around the newcomer's neck, then lowered the limp body to the ground.

I hurried over. "Don't kill him!"

Thorian was kneeling over his victim, one great paw on his throat. The look he gave me had the power to intimidate even in starlight.

"Sorry!" I whispered. He had never warned me that he was a warrior. I was supposed to guess. Warriors are tricky companions, quick to take offense and even quicker to seek retribution.

"Just fingertips on the arteries," he whispered. "From the smell of him, he's two-thirds drunk anyway. He'll have a sore head, but he won't even remember my touch."

Truly, for a self-proclaimed baker of cupcakes, my associate had some surprising talents. He nodded at the gate. "Be gone. I'll follow."

"Wait!"

Our victim was a largish young man with an enviable square black pillow of beard. His swath was an elaborate thing of pale silks, covering his legs to the ankle, and the brooch that held it was fist size, fiery with gems. Obviously he was no mere flunky, and I wondered why he would travel unescorted and enter by the trade entrance. The hour was late and the city silent.

I took up the ring of keys he had dropped. There were about a dozen of them. I selected the smallest and bent over my companion. Too small . . . the next produced a satisfying *click*. It was pure coincidence, of course, but I do not believe in coincidence.

Locksmiths tend to be as lazy as other men, and most use the same molds over and over.

I unfastened my own collar also, with much relief.

Thorian chuckled. "Now?"

"No." I hurried across to the door of the house. It took me a few moments and a ewerful of sweat to find the right key. The hinges squeaked painfully. I hurried back across the yard, pushed the gate shut, then knelt to replace the ring in the folds of the sleeping man's swath. Thorian's broad shoulders were shaking with silent laughter.

Two seconds later we were inside the mansion.

Starlight gleamed through a barred window, offering us a choice of steps down, steps up, or a door. I chose the door, and found a closet full of brooms and jars and shelves, reeking of wax and lye. There was barely room for both of us; I had one foot in a bucket. But I also had one eye to a convenient knothole.

A few moments after that, our victim staggered hard against the outer door, then a bell jangled somewhere in the cellars. The response was too slow, evidently, for the man outside began clattering keys in the lock.

As he did so, light advanced up the stair from the servants' quarters. An elderly man climbed slowly into view, carrying a lantern. He raised it when he reached the door, revealing a key hung on a nail above the lintel.

The action now became complicated. The man outside and the man inside were both trying to unlock the door, neither realizing that there was no need. The lock clicked to and fro several times. Eventually the hinges squeaked again, and the newcomer staggered forward into the light.

"Milord!" the servant exclaimed, steadying him with his free hand. "Is something wrong?"

"Just some bad wine, Hasmar," the young man muttered, his voice blurred. "Banged my head." Both he and his costly swath were smeared with dirt. "Sorry to drag you upstairs like this . . ."

"The master has been asking for you, milord."

The answer was an indistinct obscenity.

"If you wish to lean on my shoulder, milord?" The watchman was likely a slave, for he bore no weapon. His swath came barely to his knees. He was slight, stooped, and gray. He did not look capable of supporting the other's weight.

" 'Shnot neshessh . . ." The lordling straightened himself and took several deep breaths. "It—is—not—necessary. No, you keep the light. I can manage." He moved carefully up the steps, placing each foot deliberately, and disappeared. With a shrug, the slave closed and locked the door, replacing the key. Then he headed back down to his kennel in the basement.

I removed my leg from the bucket and emerged from the closet. Thorian followed. We climbed the steps the younger man had taken and soon observed him ahead of us in silhouette, weaving along a corridor toward light.

The great house was built to a plan common in those lands, an open rectangle. The central atrium was garnished with trees and flowers and an altar to the household gods. Torches burned there, scenting the air with tarry fumes. A staircase led up one side, to a gallery on the upper story. The large open space and fine furnishings bespoke impressive wealth.

We stopped in the shadows. The returning resident had crossed this central court and was poised at the bottom of the staircase. Another figure stepped out of the darkness behind him.

"Good evening, Jaxian."

I sensed the unspoken imprecation. Steadying himself carefully against the banister, the young man turned.

"G-g-good evening, Father."

"Did Hasmar not report that I wanted to see you as soon as you returned?" The older man was middle aged and stocky, but he seemed to be composed more of hard gristle than muscle or fat. His nose was prominent and hooked like a claw. In the ways of the Spice Lands, he proclaimed his exalted rank with his raiment, a rainbow cloak—scarlet, piped and embroidered and pleated in turquoise and peacock blue—but he also wore six or seven gold ribbons looped across his chest, gleaming in the torches' unsteady light. His graying hair was thin, his white-streaked beard comparatively short.

"I was g-g-going upstairs to wash first," Jaxian explained. He sounded much less drunk than before. Fathers can be very sobering people, of course, but Jaxian seemed somewhat old to be reacting that way, probably in his early thirties. He was surprisingly large, almost as big as Thorian—apparently I was destined to be surrounded by giants in this Zanadon affair—but size is a reliable indicator of wealth. The children of the poor eat sparingly.

Glaring up at him, his father made a sound of disgust or contempt. "Pah! Drunkard!"

The younger man was much larger, yet he cringed like an errant child. "Just a few friends after the militia d-d-drill. The wine was a bit off, I susp-p-pect."

"Male friends, I suppose?"

Jaxian hiccuped. "Yesh." He edged a couple of steps up the stair, and the shift in position moved his face out of shadow, for he had been under a palm. I saw that he had the same curved-blade nose as his father. In the father's case it conveyed arrogance. On the unassertive son it seemed inappropriate.

"I could forgive the whorehouse more easily than the taverns," his father snarled.

"There is nothing to forgive, Father." The big young man hung his head but failed to conceal his blushes.

"I wanted to talk to you about bread. Last night we agreed to raise the price another two mites per loaf, did we not?"

"Well, you d-d-d . . . You d-d-d . . ." The words would not come.

"Yes. I listened to your arguments, very patiently, but in the end we agreed, did we not? Two mites more. And I discovered this afternoon that you never issued the order!"

"The others hadn't! The P-p-p-pomaniuk b-b-b-bakeries—"

"Fool! They were waiting for us. They would have followed instantly!"

"But the p-p-people—"

"The people be damned!" the older man roared. "They can find the money or they can starve—that is not our concern. Have you any idea where prices will go once the siege begins? No, you haven't. Imbecile! And here you are, *giving* away our precious grain! Well, as of tomorrow, the price goes up by *four* mites. I did your work for you and sent out the orders. Do you understand?"

The reply was almost inaudible. "Yesh, Father."

"I wonder if you really do? If the others do not follow, then they can waste their supplies at whatever price they want, and we shall have all the more left for later. Got that?"

"Yes, Father."

"Go to bed, you drunken slob."

"Yes, Father."

The charming scene of domestic tranquility was ended. Sent to his room like a toddler, Jaxian trudged up the stairs. The seventh and the twelfth treads creaked. His father stood and watched his progress.

At the top, the big young man started to turn to the left. Then he glanced down and saw that he was still being observed. That seemed to change his mind, for he staggered and veered to the right, vanishing through the third door. It closed with a thump.

Shaking his head angrily, the older man stalked across the court and disappeared into the shadows. Another door shut.

"Filthy profiteer!" Thorian muttered angrily.

"Astute businessman," I replied. "Come along."

"Where to?"

"Upstairs. Find a bathroom."

"Idiot! There are probably people asleep in half those rooms!"

I was about to repeat my lecture about trusting the gods, when a bell jangled down in the bowels of the house. Someone would come to answer that summons.

Thorian and I rushed in barefoot silence to the stairs

and raced up them, avoiding the seventh and the twelfth treads. I chose a door at random, and of course it was the bathroom. I waited before closing the door. I saw old Hasmar hobble across the court with his lantern, and in a few moments I heard voices . . . More arrivals? At this time of night? Interesting!

The fittings were impressive—marble and fine porcelain, and downy soft towels, which I recognized as produce of the Silver Shores cotton fields. A golden spigot dispensed water from some hidden cistern that was doubtless filled from the roof by winter rains. There was even a drain to carry the discarded water down to lower levels for other uses.

To risk a light would have been foolhardy—trusting the gods is not the same as tempting them. We completed our toilet as best we could, inspecting each other by starlight under the window. The bathtub would be left stained with blood, there were two abandoned slave collars down in the broom closet, food and wine had disappeared. Hasmar would have some explaining to do in the morning, but probably other watchmen would relieve him during the night. If the owner of the residence flogged several men for the sins of one, his injustice would make all his servants resentful and uncooperative.

"Your magic continues to serve you well," Thorian remarked softly. He was anointing his long limbs with copious quantities of fragrant oil. "How about clothing?"

"Wait here!" I slipped out the door to the gallery. Standing well back from the railing, I scanned the court below until I was sure it was deserted.

Staying close to the wall lest the floor squeak, I worked my way along to the next door. I listened, then opened it gently. Still hearing no breathing, I peered in and then entered.

Starlight flooded through large windows, revealing high writing desks and many shelves laden with rolls of vellum. Obviously this was the master's counting room, and not the sort of place I would normally look for clothes. One wall, though, was draped with weavings, depicting flowers and birds. The colors were much paler than I would have chosen for nighttime skulking, but they would suffice— perhaps they would even avert suspicion. I yanked down two of them and looked around for something to represent the obligatory belly pins. I found some ribbons bearing wax seals and took those, also. Then I returned to the bathroom.

Thorian was standing on a tall ewer, attempting to peer out the high window. He stepped nimbly down, and we began to fashion swaths for ourselves. He was no more practiced than I was, and mine kept falling off completely. He grew angry; I had to fight a powerful desire to laugh. Eventually we decided that we would pass muster—at a fair distance, in pitch darkness. We had settled on midcalf as being a reasonable status indicator.

"No shoes?"

"No. Nor hats."

Now where? I had already discarded the window as a potential exit. I might just squeeze through, but never Thorian. I had heard a few troops of ponies going by in the street below, and also voices. There must be a better way out.

Doubtless I amused the gods when I opened the bathroom door again. A flood of light sent me leaping back into my accomplice so hard that the big man staggered.

Then it had passed . . . I put my eye to the chink and peered. Two women were already descending the stairway. The one in front was bearing a torch and was obviously a servant, which was why there had been no conversation to warn me.

I felt a familiar tingling of presentiment. Something unholy was happening in this minor palace in the middle of the night. The bell had indicated visitors. Now a woman had been summoned from her bedchamber. I scented intrigue. A tale was being enacted for the gods' amusement, and I had been brought there to witness.

A deep voice rumbled on the lower level. "Go to bed now. Your mistress will not require you further. Hasmar, you will stay by the street portal." A door closed as the two slaves bowed.

Finding myself being squashed, I turned my head. Thorian was leaning on me, peering over my shoulder, eyes bright in the darkness.

"Did you see that second one?" he whispered with awe.

"Of course. About time."

"What do you mean, 'About time'? She's incredible!"

I resisted a desire to ask if she was prettier than the legendary Aunt Sirius. His enthusiasm was understandable, and also a most promising development.

"I mean that every good story needs a beautiful heroine. Now we have one. Shall we investigate?"

The big man nodded and followed me. Nothing would have prevented him from following. He was bewitched.

The female servant had gone off to the servants' end of the house and the male in the opposite direction, leaving the atrium unguarded—also leaving no sharp ears at keyholes, of course . . . Yet! Finding the seventh and the twelfth treads was slightly harder when descending, but we moved in stealthy silence back to ground level and took refuge behind some ornamental shrubbery.

In the light of the sputtering torches, I took stock of my fellow burglar. Combed and washed, Thorian was an impressive sight, far from the savage brute he had seemed in the coffle. With his size and imperious glare, he might even wear an arras and get away with it, in normal times. Times were not normal, and the city guard would not let him pass unquestioned. The square-cut edge of his raven-black beard hung halfway down his chest, but it could cover only part of the great sword wound. His shoulders and arms were bright with scrapes and bruises, and his back would rouse the guards' suspicions like a Vorkan banner.

However insignificant I might feel beside the giant, I knew I was a little less conspicuous. The rough chain had grated my back and shoulders raw. For a moment we exchanged smiles, like mischievous children on a prank. It was the first time we had seen each other properly, and Thorian had apparently accepted that the gods were guiding us; or else he had reverted to his faith in my sorcery.

And now what? Well, a trader of tales could not scurry

out into the night and leave an odd little mystery like this unexplored, but whatever was happening was happening behind a closed door. Light showed below it. I felt disinclined to throw it open and announce that the gods required me to eavesdrop, carry on and pay no attention.

I tiptoed to the adjoining door, which bore no telltale slit of light underneath, sensing Thorian hot on my heels—very hot, but that second woman had been strikingly beautiful.

Heroines usually are.

The room we found was furnished with a wide table and many chairs, for dining. Leaving my accomplice to close the door, I hurried across to the far side, where arches led out into an enclosed garden. Truly that mansion was a small palace! In my time, I have known many royal houses decorated with poorer taste, too—Vlad's, for example, with its frieze of skulls.

Light streamed from the arches of the adjacent room, illuminating bushes and waterlilies in an ornamental pool.

Voices, in the night . . .

". . . waited until tomorrow?" That was the woman.

A low rumble from the man—Jaxian's father, of course.

I slid out into the garden, with Thorian still close behind me, amazingly silent for his size. Keeping shrubbery between me and the window, I began working my way around the pool in a crouch until I could see the confrontation in progress within.

As Thorian had so quickly marked, the woman was lovely. Beauty is the gift of Ashfer; it has little to do with what a sculptor may mold or an artist tint. A man or woman can be blessed with youth and classic features and shapely limbs and yet fail utterly to have beauty. This woman had it in bargeloads. As anyone seeing Thorian for the first time would automatically think *big*, so she bore *beauty*; she had an *abundance* of beauty. It made a man's head swim.

She was tall and slender, a girl poised on the brink of womanhood, a butterfly stretching its wings for the first time on the lip of its cocoon. She wore a cloak of royal blue, bound by a golden girdle just below her breasts and falling from there in many pleats to her golden sandals. Clipped by a simple gold band and shining like black water, her hair tumbled loose to her shoulders. She had probably been summoned from bed and had had no time to dress it. Her lips were pigeon-blood rubies set in ivory.

Her pallor raised my masculine fires. I wanted to rush to her rescue and carry her off. I wanted to frame epic tales about her. Even more I wanted to see invitation in her eyes, daring me to unfasten that cord and lift back the silk and possess the flawless body within. My heart thundered. I heard Thorian panting in the night.

The man was the one we had seen earlier, of course, Jaxian's father. He waved his hands as he spoke, flashing the jewels on his fingers. He would do very well for the villain of the story—old and sumptuous and obscene beside the girl's youthful grace. His nose was a vulture's beak.

"I accept that he is young and wealthy, Father," the woman was saying. "I agree that he is entertaining and witty. But his morals are notorious. You can *smell* the corruption on him. His body is warty as a toad's with oozing pustules. If you—"

"Absurd!" the man boomed, clearly audible for the first time. "Where do you gather such slanders? Filthy women's gossip!"

"Jaxian told me, since you ask. He saw him at the baths, a week ago, after the sword drill. Half the militia changed their minds and went home to bathe, he said. He said they would rather share a pool with the entire Vorkan horde than with Dithian Lius." Her voice was tuneful as a chorus of nightingales. She was being properly respectful to her noble parent, yet her manner was firm; she was displaying astonishing poise for her age. As she met his furious gaze, I noticed that she shared the family nose, although in her it was a subtler curve, a sign of dignity that added hauteur without reducing her beauty at all.

A sudden tap on my rump stopped my stealthy progress around the shrubbery. I glanced back and then looked where Thorian was pointing. We were not the only eavesdroppers. Blurred in the dark, three robed figures stood close by the arches, on the far side. Intent on the conversation, they seemed unaware that the garden had just acquired additional population.

That explained who had arrived when the doorbell rang. And if the owner of the house had not set the visitors there to spy on his interview with the girl, then who had?

This was turning out to be a very interesting night.

"I cannot believe you want your daughter infected with his foul diseases!" the girl said. "Forget Lius, Father, I beg you!"

"You are being perversely obstinate!" The man shook his jeweled fist in her face.

Thorian and I continued to creep around the bushes, and finally wriggled under the foliage at the far end of the pool and lay prone. The water would carry the sound, and we now had a much better observation post than those three earlier arrivals had chosen. Probably their dignity would have balked at the wriggling.

The father's next remark had been inaudible. He was pacing to and fro in his anger. To my skilled eye, that anger seemed false, but the girl would probably not detect that.

"Now you confuse me," she protested. "At first you said a merchant family. You said it must be a mercantile compact. The Quairts are a military clan."

"I am pandering to your ridiculous quibbles."

She straightened her shoulders, withstanding her father's anger superbly—holding her ground, keeping her voice level and her hands at her side. She was nervous, yes. Of course she would be, but the man might be meeting firmer resistance than he had expected. Where was her mother during all this?

"Very well. I do know Soshiak Quairt. He is a captain now, is he not? His last wife died of a fractured skull. The one before bled to death; the story was that she was pregnant and he kicked her. There was another before her, wasn't there? We must all feel regret at the poor man's misfortunes, of course. Would it be fair to expose him to the opportunity for further suffering? I would hate to think of him having to bury yet another wife."

Thorian shivered with fury. He wanted to rush to her defense. If a man has any mettle at all, then innocence in peril will make his sword arm twitch, and beauty does not reduce the effect. I could feel my own ire rising, although I always try to bridle my emotions when being a witness. All this might be a minor subplot; it might have nothing at all to do with Balor and the main drama of Zanadon. The girl might be only a floating leaf on the floods of history, but certainly my presence here had been arranged.

Her face was hauntingly familiar, too. I might have seen her in a dream, or she might be merely a reflection of my personal ideal of beauty—I did not know, but I mourned her distress. In my time I have seen more disaster than joy. I feared to hear the gods already weeping. Must I again witness tragedy and carry word of it to mortals, so that generations unborn might also weep?

"This is intolerable!" the man snapped. "I have offered you the finest bachelors in the city, and you spurn them all with absurd slurs and inventions. It confirms what I already knew and yet could not believe."

The girl put a hand to her lips. "I do not understand what you mean by those words, Father."

"You are besotted with another man!"

She took a moment to find her breath. "Father, forgive me, but how could that be possible? How could there be another man? I never go out, except with yourself or Jaxian. I see no one without you present. What other man?"

Her father paused in his pacing close to her and glared in her face. He spoke a name I could not hear.

His answer was a flood of red in her features.

Thorian issued a faint moan of dismay, and I nudged him angrily to be quiet.

The girl shook her head in silent denial, but her face was scarlet. She clasped her hands to her throat. Her resistance had collapsed, and she was vulnerable.

Her father moved closer, spoke louder. "I have seen how you look at him and how he looks at you. You have bewitched him and driven him out of his wits."

She shook her head in terror. "Me? It was he who . . . I don't know what you are talking about!"

"Shameless slut! You will destroy us all. Me. Your brother. Your aunts and cousins. All of us will be ruined by your evil wilfulness!"

She wheeled away from him and leaned on a chair back. He clasped her thin shoulder and dragged her around to face him.

"Do not deny this! The only solution is to marry you off at once—now! Before you bring down shame and ruin on the whole family. I have named you four fine men who would gladly be bound to the Tharpit clan. There is yet time to save our reputation. Choose, or I shall choose for you. Which will you take: Dithian Lius, Fathmonian Waus, Soshiak Quairt, or Osian Pomaniak?"

She closed her eyes. I wondered if she would faint, for her pallor had returned as fast as it had gone.

Her father eyed her carefully, then spoke more gently. "Shalial, my dear one! It is the only solution for us, for you. And especially for that unfortunate dupe whose wits you have addled as much as your own."

She shook her head without looking at him. "Father, oh, Father!"

"Do not presume to address me thus unless you will afford me a daughter's obedience. If you will not do what I ask out of respect for your father, or for the sake of your dear mother—may Morphith cherish her soul—then do it for *his* sake, and save *him*—now, while there is still time."

"Time? Surely I may have time? Just till morning?"

"No. It must be decided. I cannot sleep for worrying. Which?"

Her voice was so low that I could not be certain; but I thought she said, "They are all monsters!"

"Insolence! Your wilfulness is intolerable! It had best be Quairt. He will tame you."

"Father! Choose again! Select some other men!"

"No. You must be married as soon as possible. I see no other way out of this."

To my vast experience that was an obvious prompt, but she would not detect it. The whole burlesque had been very carefully planned, even to the choice of an hour when a victim's resistance is at lowest ebb. She was almost in tears now, understandably.

"There is one," she muttered. "One way out."

She was not watching, she did not see the sly satisfaction settle on her father's face.

"What?"

Her reply was another whisper.

"For why? To do penance?"

"To become a priestess."

Thorian moaned again.

"You would do this?" her father demanded.

She nodded.

"Say it! If I truly believe, then I might permit it."

"I will become a priestess."

The three cloaked watchers surged forward. Thorian tried to leap up and I grabbed his shoulder. I would have had more fortune slaying a bull with a fly whisk. Yet he sank back on his belly again—not, I confess, because of my superhuman strength, but because he had forgotten the branch right over his head. He must have half stunned himself. For a while he forgot his mad impulse to chivalry, and just lay and rubbed his damaged skull.

The girl had turned in fright and dismay as the three men entered the room. They were all priests. All were beardless and obese, and their heads were shaven. Two wore yellow cloaks, and the leader crimson.

That flash of crimson in the night cried out that this private domestic squabble did concern the matter of Balor. It was all one, somehow. The girl had raised her chin in defiance, and the pose made my niggling sense of familiarity burn hotter. If I had dreamed her, then I could recall nothing more of the tale I had dreamed.

"You heard, Holiness?" the father said.

"We heard," said Crimson Cloak. "It is customary to kneel to the high priest, child."

"That was a trap!" Thorian growled furiously.

"Of course. Be silent."

The girl sank to her knees. The high priest was short, and odiously fat. He laid a pudgy hand on her head in benediction and spoke in a eunuch's falsetto. "Shalial

Tharpit, you have stated of your own free will your desire to enter the service of Holy Maiana. The Great Mother welcomes you and will forgive your sins. Go now with our blessing.'' He sniggered.

It had been slickly done, I thought. She had even been maneuvered into making the suggestion. I wondered who the unnamed lover was.

I wondered what I was supposed to do about all this, if anything.

Shalial offered no resistance. She held her head high, not looking at her father as she went out the door with the two yellow cloaks. She knew she had been tricked, and by whom. She must also know why, which I did not.

Tharpit was left alone with the high priest. They smiled in mutual congratulation.

Very slickly done.

Even if Tharpit was one of the leaders of the city, as he must be, what grade of intrigue brought the high priest of the city from his bed in the middle of the night just to ensnare a young woman into the clergy? Now he watched impassively as his host turned and vanished out of my sight, soon returning with two brimming goblets. He handed one over.

"May this house be blessed," the priest said as a toast.

"I feel I need absolution more. I did not enjoy that, Holiness!" Tharpit tossed off his wine in one gulp.

"Of course not. Such a horrid ordeal for you! But your motives are ever so pure. You did no more than a father's duty. There is nothing to forgive, my son." The fat man sipped thoughtfully. "And there was no truth in your allegations?"

"Certainly not!"

Even at such a distance, I smelled a lie, and the priest obviously did. His forehead wrinkled all the way to his shaven scalp. "Of course it is customary," he said in a voice like thin oil, "to make an endowment upon such occasions." He sniggered again and extended a soft pink hand. "Just a little token?"

The merchant scowled. Reluctantly he lifted one of the gold chains from around his thick neck and hung it on the waiting fingers. The fingers stayed where they were, waiting for more.

"The terms were agreed upon, Nagiak!"

" 'Holiness' is the correct form of address, or 'Father.' " The fingers lingered yet.

The merchant could more easily part with a daughter than with wealth. He flushed furiously. "What need have you for gold? Why should a *gelding* need *gilding*?"

The priest's eyes shrank to nothing amid the bulges of fat. "Remember to whom you speak, my son." The high voice sounded shriller.

"And you! I lead the merchants of this city, Nagiak. We raised you up, we can cast you down!"

"No, I don't think so. Dear me, no. That is highly improbable!" The priest had a smile to panic crocodiles, but he made the chain vanish into his cloak.

Tharpit continued to glare at him—seldom had I seen a pair of conspirators less amicably disposed.

"When? How soon?"

Nagiak shrugged his shoulders like down pillows. "Do not worry so, my son! I do believe that War Lord Arksis is of the opinion that there is yet time. I think the sly fellow intends to let the Vorkans fatten on the rabble below our gates." He giggled shrilly. "That way we can take it all when Balor leads us to victory, can't we?"

The merchant turned away to pace the room, but now his agitation seemed much more genuine than the posturing he had used on his daughter. "It takes forty years to grow an olive tree! Have you seen the smoke in the eastern sky? I am not alone in this, Nagiak! Half the families in the city are being ruined while you shilly-shally!"

"Half of what families?" The priest puckered his lips. "Olive groves? Vineyards? Herds? We must also consider the lives of our brave boys of Zanadon, mustn't we?"

Tharpit turned on him furiously. "We have an agreement! When will that mad hag do her duty?"

Nagiak spread his silken arms, opening like a great crimson rose. "When Maiana wills, of course. At the new moon, or the next new moon."

"Rumor says that she has had another stroke."

"Do not believe bazaar gossip, my son! Do not distress yourself. Cultivate serenity and faith! Tomorrow the heralds will proclaim your sacrifice for all to hear. The populace will greatly marvel at your donation of an only daughter to serve the Great Mother. Such devotion! They will applaud such dedication!" He simpered. "I do believe they may even overlook the current prices in your stores—for a day or two. They will wonder also at the matching sacrifices being made by several other notable citizens."

Seemingly vague, yet the threat was potent—it made the merchant blanch. "We have an agreement!"

The high priest held out his hand again.

Purpling with fury, Tharpit lifted the remaining gold chains from his neck and passed them over.

"Your dear sweet daughter will be the jewel in the crown of Maiana," Nagiak said, and the fat lips leered. "Your honor is unquestioned. Now kneel, my dear Bedian, so I may give you my blessing."

9: A Familiar Face

✳

"**T**o the temple!" I said.

"Most certainly."

With Thorian at my heels, I sped around the pool. Bedian Tharpit was bowing the high priest out the door of the room. By the time they had crossed the atrium and were approaching the street entrance, we had emerged from the dining room and were on our way back to the kitchen quarters. I grabbed a torch from a sconce in passing.

"What's that for? You're crazy!" Thorian protested.

"You want to look like a burglar or something? Trust the gods!"

The servant had locked the back door when Jaxian Tharpit entered. I raised my sputtering light and found the key on the nail. I locked the door again from the outside, tucking the key in a fold of my swath. The gate I had left unsecured, of course. Without hesitation, I hauled it open and stepped out into the alley. Thorian hissed nervously but followed.

The priests would travel by coach, and we could not hope to arrive at the temple before the girl did. But then I had no inkling of what I expected to achieve when I got there. Perhaps the walk would clear my thinking.

"I find it ever harder to credit your denials of magic, Trader of Tales." Thorian's long legs had no trouble matching my hurried pace. "How did you know that there would be no watchers out here in the alley?"

"I wouldn't care overmuch if there were. We are clad now and bearing a light. Only the guard will question us." Of course our swaths were makeshift affairs that would not bear close inspection. We had no hats or shoes. Discreetly not mentioning such petty details, I swung round a corner and hastened along another narrow way. The air stank of camels, and the footing was unpleasantly soft in places.

"In such troubled times guards pullulate everywhere," Thorian said.

"Then we must avoid them. I think we can approach the temple without using the Great Way."

For a little while we strode along in silence, always angling uphill. The stars were a beach of jewels over our heads, lighting the back streets and alleys I was following. The summer night, warm and muggy, was patterned with curious pockets of conflicting scents—ponies, kitchen odors, flowers unknown to me.

The city was hauntingly familiar. I have seen so many cities that they blur in my memories like trees on a foggy morning. I shall never forget the diamond spires of Pael or the boat cities of Fallange, of course. There is timeless Daöl, deserted by day but thronged by night with shadows that will not meet the eye. There are the Silent Cities, where to speak is a crime. There are a few others of which I will not tell. But, by and large, step aside from the aorta and you will find the small veins in any city feel much the same.

My head jangled with a tumult of thoughts. Why had that lordly merchant tricked his daughter into the priesthood? He could have used her to make an advantageous alliance with some other prominent family. That was what daughters were for, in his gold-walled world. And why had the high priest himself connived and assisted? The two of them had admitted to having a secret agreement, but I could not imagine what it might involve.

As I said, I try to keep my emotions in check when the gods call me to witness great events, but the woman's beauty had touched my soul, and her face was a haunting ghost of a memory, or of a desire. And she was in great danger.

"Omar?" Thorian muttered.

I grunted.

"You are so sure that the god will come?"

I said I was sure.

"Miracles are rare in these prosaic times. These are not the Golden Days. How long since Balor last walked the earth?"

"Some centuries—I have no exact tally. I do not delve into chronicles or converse with the learned. The common folk are my grist."

"And what happens after? It seems to my recollection that Zanadon has several times gathered itself an empire."

"I believe so. Hardly surprising. Most cities have. The empires crumble, and oftentimes the cities, also. What ails you?" I was forcing the pace, but it was making me pant, and sweat streamed down my chest.

Thorian's deep voice was low, his breathing annoyingly untroubled. "And what happens after? When the god has come to the world and smitten the Vorkans—what then? Does he just return Beyond the Rainbow after the battle? Or does the war god himself continue to lead Mighty Zanadon? Half its rivals are dust already. Does Balor found empires for his people?"

"I don't know!" I grunted. I had not given the matter a thought.

"Does he age like a mortal and die? Does he sire sons to reign after him?"

"I don't know!" I shouted. "I don't care!"

"I do," Thorian said quietly.

He was from Polrain, where the slaughter had started. I was sure of that from his voice. He was a warrior, at the least.

After a moment, he began again. "The king of Pulst is known as Mothin. The incumbent claims to be the forty-third of that name, but he may be the fifty-ninth for all he really knows. All the kings of Pulst have been called Mothin."

"So?"

"Surely you see? Zanadon remains always unvanquished because it is impregnable upon its hill, that is all. Apparently it has water and can withstand a siege. The only miracles are those cliffs and those walls. And when a war leader arises, whether for defense or for conquest, he is hailed as Balor. As *Mothin* means *king* in Pulst, so *Balor* means *king* in Zanadon!"

"Let's cut through here . . . That is not what the people believe. The woman I spoke with on the Silver Shores was adamant. On the Reaver Road I spoke with many natives returning, scurrying home to safety, and they all expect the living god."

"I put my trust in priestly subterfuge! It will be a trick."

"I am distressed that you do not believe in the gods, Thorian, my friend."

"I believe in the gods of my homeland. They stay in their places. I distrust these strange, meddling gods of the plains."

I stopped suddenly and faced him under the pungent, sputtering flame. Two smaller flames burned in the darkness of his eyes.

"I have no call upon you," I said angrily, "nor you on me. Go in peace."

For a moment I thought he would do so. Then he said, "Answer me one question, declaring that Morphith may know of it when he culls your soul."

"What question?"

"Have you ever been in Zanadon before?"

I hesitated.

"Well?" he growled. "You have a choice of two words; neither is exactly hard to pronounce."

But it was not so simple. "In dreams, yes."

"In the flesh?"

"I don't know," I said. "I have dreamed it so often in the last two years that I just do not know. When first I dreamed it, it seemed familiar, comforting. But dreams are oft like that, are they not? Now I am here it seems familiar from my dreams." I sighed, for I knew I was not making him content with such words. "Friend, if I have walked these streets before, then it was so long ago that my memories are blurred."

He scowled, baring teeth in his beard. Indecision must be a rare experience for him.

I laughed. "I could have sworn this road led out to a

square. They must have changed it since my last dream! One city is like to another, and I have seen so many! Come, let us go this way.''

I walked away, but in a moment he was pacing at my side again, under the stars. Bats flitted overhead with their thin piping. Once a cat screamed, far off. When he next spoke there was a colder note in his voice.

''There are two Reaver Roads, you know.''

''No. Tell me of them.''

''For an army, there are but two ways into the Spice Lands. You cannot ship a mounted horde up a river—it would be neither seemly nor logistically feasible. Northward stands the Kulthiar Range, southward the Pearls of the Sky. Invaders must always come from the east or the west, by Maidens Pass or by the Edge of the Sown. Conquerors fall first upon Polrain or upon Thang, and then they head for the other. They sweep the length of the land, because they have no choice.''

''Which is why the route is called the Reaver Road,'' I said breathlessly. I was much afraid now that I was lost and would have to cut over to the Great Way to catch my bearings. The buildings were higher, cutting off my view of the stars, and I do not like to stare at the stars anyway. I paused, irresolute, and the night was cool on my sweat now.

''And in the center stands Zanadon,'' Thorian persisted.

''So?'' But I had not considered the geography so. The only landscape that ever interests me is contained within the bounds of the horizon. Thorian thought otherwise, but Thorian was a warrior, however much he had joked about cupcakes. Warriors are trained to think in ways that storytellers do not.

And the geography of this Zanadon warren was bothering me enough by itself then. I headed west.

''So two Reaver Roads, and they meet on the Jolipi, at Zanadon. Obviously, when the cities of the plain unite, it will be here that they make their stand, always, whether it is against Vorkans or against the hosts of former times—Kulpians, or Waregs, or the Ocher Men, or any of the multitudes who have flowed over the land in blood and tears. From east or west, here the final battle is joined."

I could see the expanse of the Great Way ahead now. "So you think the cities unite under Zanadon?"

"Under Zanadon possibly. *At* Zanadon certainly. And whoever is chosen leader is hailed as Balor. It would be a clever move because—"

"They show no signs of doing so now. You saw, as I did, the emissaries being turned away from the gate. Or do you think they will acclaim Corporal Fotius war lord as you suggested?"

Had that only been the previous evening? It felt like a week ago. My bones were crumbling from exhaustion, and the night barely old enough to shave yet.

"Stop!" I said, and backed into a doorway, holding the torch at my back. We were only a few paces from the Great Way. Thorian moved in beside me.

"What's wrong?"

"I need a breather." I twirled the torch against the stonework, dwindling its flame to a flicker. "You may be right, of course. That may be what happened in ancient times, and today's lesser men have fallen into folly and hubris, deceived by encrustations of exaggeration and mythification. If so, then I shall witness the first sack of Zanadon, and that will be a memorable story, also."

After a moment he chuckled. "And perhaps a more satisfying one!"

A troop of soldiers went marching past the end of the alley, heading down the Great Way. They did not see us.

Thorian uttered his lion growl. "You knew of them!"

"No. I needed a breathing spell. I told you."

A single huge hand closed on my throat, lifting me up on my toes and ending the breathing spell. "You knew they were coming!"

I choked, and the pressure was eased slightly, to let me speak. "I have told you that trusting the gods is not the same as tempting them! They are keeping us unobserved. It never hurts to make things as easy for them as possible."

The hand was removed, but slowly, and with reluctance.

"When a man lies to me I kill him," Thorian said softly.

"I suppose I shall learn that eventually. Now we can go. Those louts will not look back."

We emerged together onto the wide darkness of the Great Way, but I could sense the distrust that now walked between us. The temple lay straight ahead, and so close that we might as well head straight for it. There were lights there. Glancing behind me, I saw lights scattered all the way down the slope to the gates: fireflies, or fallen stars. I hurried along, foolishly annoyed at Thorian's easier pace. Being made to feel small is an unpleasant sensation for me, for I am as tall as most.

"Omar," he said, "this is madness! We shall be seen."

"Who is looking? I told you—only the guard will question."

The road was wide. Small groups were coming and going—groups of one or two, mostly, each with a servant bearing a torch. I assumed they were suppliants, visiting the temple or leaving it. Debts or sickness or a lack of children—when a man goes to pray for important things, he prefers to go unseen, in the quiet hours. He does not want his friends to see him praying to Machus! Besides, the gods may be less busy than by day, and more able to heed the petitions of mortals.

In these troubled times there would be more petitioners than usual: merchants like Tharpit whose estates were being pillaged, wives whose husbands journeyed in foreign lands, mothers whose sons had been inducted.

We went by them all at a distance, ignoring them, and they ignored us. They would not notice our bare feet. We were not wearing the foolish pot hats of the Spice Lands, but not everyone else was, either. Soon we reached the colonnade that ends the Great Way. We stepped through the arches and were at the temple.

The Courtyard of the Thousand Gods in Zanadon is the largest open space I know of in any walled city, except perhaps the Grand Plaza in Againro. I have seen larger in the cities of the Island Kingdoms, which rely on their navies for defense, but only there. That night it struck me speechless.

It is approximately oval, enclosed on either hand by curves of high wall, and at the rear by the great pyramid of the temple. The colonnade that ends the Great Way continues in cloisters that curve around, abutting the walls. The ziggurat rises in eighteen giant steps, each step three times the height of a man, but a flight of mortal-size stairs extends up the center of the nearest face to the summit and the House of the Goddess, whose golden roof glitters near the stars. Flanking the near corners of the pyramid and overtopping it easily stand the great Maiana and Balor.

They dominate the Courtyard. I rolled my head back to look up at them, dark against the starlight. Their heads touched the sky. They stared down at me accusingly with eyes that seemed to glow, although that was likely just my fancy embellishing again. Worried, I looked away.

Only the priesthood may walk within the cloisters or the temple itself, but layfolk may enter the Courtyard to pray. While the back of the Courtyard is defined by the temple and the great statues, the front and sides are marked out by the pillars of the cloisters and the colonnade. Before every pillar stands a god or goddess.

The plaza was empty. Oh, there may have been a hundred people or so there, but that space can hold the entire population of a city and would look deserted were it occupied by four cohorts of cavalry practicing spear drill. Perhaps two dozen lights glowed like lost stars in all the vacant blackness. In the background, a few parties of priests or priestesses paced slowly within the cloisters, as if two wheels turned in opposition; their torches blinked on and off behind pillars. Three or four small squads of soldiers moved across the central space, as did some suppliants arriving or departing.

At least half the lights were stationary, an irregular circle of specks defining the perimeter of the Courtyard like a string of beads. Each tiny flame represented a worshipper or two, pestering some god or other. The torches showed the groveling suppliants on the ground, of course, but they also lit up the god. Perhaps a dozen of the Thousand stood out in the darkness, listening to the whining at their feet. Each was flanked by a fainter neighbor on either side, like supporters come to witness. The sight made my scalp prickle.

"Well?" Thorian rumbled. "The girl will be within the temple by now. What are you planning to do, Trader of Tales? Take the temple of Maiana by storm, perchance?"

"I don't know," I said, and my mouth was dry. "And those guards are heading this way. Let us go over to one of the gods and pretend to pray, while we think."

"You lead, then."

I set off across the endless dark Courtyard as if I were a servant bearing a light before my master. I picked the widest unlit expanse I could see, headed for the middle of it, choosing a god at random.

Strictly counting, there are three hundred and forty-eight figures of gods in the Courtyard at Zanadon—the *Thousand* is a poetic exaggeration. I examined them by daylight later; I have seen similar collections in other cities. Wailman has over four hundred. Most are unnecessary repetitions, the same deity represented under many names. Some are obscure protectors of minor cities, or guardians of various lakes, streams, and so on. Some are so trivial that no one remembers who they are. A few are other than human, with animal heads, or wings, and those are usually exotic imports from distant lands.

The great majority are merely representations of handsome men and women, life size or slightly larger, standing on knee-high plinths. The men are mostly clothed, the women not, although there are exceptions in both cases. About half bear attributes, like wine jugs or sheaves or sometimes a child.

When we had arrived before one of the holy figures, I knelt down as worshippers do and touched my face to the ground. Thorian knelt at my side.

Silence. The night was warm and still, for the Zanadonians pray quietly, unlike many peoples I have known.

I felt strangely at a loss. To seek out the portal of the

temple and blunder in seemed madness. I wanted to find the beautiful Shalial, although I was not at all sure why—to warn her of her danger, perhaps. But her fate might be ordained, and by now she would have been inducted into the priesthood, and even to talk with her would be criminal sacrilege.

Were we to be arrested as vagrants by the city guard, we should be soundly flogged and then evicted from the gates, or more likely chained up as slaves again and sent to work on the walls.

But were the priestesses of Maiana to catch us trespassing within the temple, then Thorian's prediction would come true. He was right—it did not bear thinking about. We should be turned over to the city guard eventually, but bereft of our manhood. I have heard tales of dull knives, red-hot metal to staunch the blood, and even worse stories of fingernails . . . most men die of the shock, and are glad to do so.

What was I supposed to do here? Why had I been shown that strange scene in the night, a man giving away his daughter against her will? If I could not find a reason for being here, Thorian was going to laugh and call me insane. I needed to sleep, and I needed to dream.

Thorian, for variety, reared back on his heels, raising both arms in the air. "Hear my prayer, O Holy . . ." He paused and peered. "Rosh?" he muttered, reading the name on the plinth. "The name of this god is Rosh. Who is Rosh?"

He went down, and I went up, raising my arms. It keeps the blood circulating, and it would look convincing.

"Rosh is the god of history, and tides, and sometimes memory."

I went down and he went up.

"Why should tides need a god?" he demanded. "A god, just to shove water to and fro?"

"Do not mock," I said sullenly.

Suddenly Thorian jumped to his feet. He drew in his breath with a hiss. Then he grabbed the torch from my hand and thrust it in the god's face.

I rose, also, peering up where he was staring. Carven

of old weathered granite, the god Rosh was a comely youth, naked and almost beardless, smiling cryptically down at us from his plinth. In the flickering light, his lips seemed to move, as though the smile widened. I could almost believe he was about to raise his hands from his sides in greeting.

Thorian dropped back to the ground and made obeisance again. But this time he was doing it to me.

10: A Familiar Back

I knelt also. Thorian kept his head on the tiles. I rubbed my beard thoughtfully.

"It's only a coincidence," I said. "Just a chance resemblance."

He said nothing. I could hear his teeth chattering.

"I am a man. Omar, a Trader of Tales. Not Rosh the god."

Slowly he raised himself to look at me. Again the two tiny lights shone in his eyes like flames. Above his beard, his cheekbones were ashen.

"You swear this to me—that you are mortal?"

"As far as I know, I am mortal. I can't be certain, because I would have to die to prove it."

"How old are you?"

"Ah. That's tricky. I have lost count. Older than I look, yes. The gods have preserved me well because I am useful to them, I think. But I breathe and sweat and eat and piss like other men, and tell lies to girls." I smiled as genuinely as I know how, for I was truly sorry for him. "I fear and suffer and hate broccoli. It's only a vague likeness in a poor light."

"You swear this, that you are mortal?"

"May Morphith spurn my soul if I lie to you." That was not a totally convincing oath, because Morphith would have no chance at me if I were the immortal Thorian feared.

Thorian did not seem to notice the paradox; held out a hand, as if to shake. I took it. He squeezed. He could have crushed bricks with that grip. Soon sweat ran down my face and I bit my lip to suppress the cry of agony I dare not risk. At last I began to whimper. Only then did he release me.

"You misbegotten whelp of a poxed pig!" I sniffed, rubbing my hand. "If I had thought to bring a thunderbolt with me, I would toast your guts for that!" I wiped an arm over my mouth to remove the blood. I blinked away tears.

He snarled. "Did I not still believe that you have more than human powers, I would break you in pieces. What do you want of me?"

"Friendship. No more and no less."

His coal-black eyes burned in the torchlight, yet were cold as graves. "I do not give friendship lightly. It carries mortal obligations." He meant a warrior's friendship, of course. That was something that could never be extended to encompass a mere trader of tales.

"Then let us merely agree to enjoy each other's company and deal fair."

"I need no oath to make me deal fair, Trader. I suppose I find you amusing, and apparently without guile. Friends on those terms, then. Now—why tides and history? Why is the god of history shown as a boy?"

"History ebbs and flows, I suppose." I looked up at the statue and then grinned. "He's a little more than a boy, isn't he? He has whiskers on his chin, too. I would certainly keep him away from my daughters, if I had any. As History Rosh is generally depicted elderly, I think. As Memory he is young."

"Why? It seems wrong."

"Ask a priestess. Maybe because youthful memories are happiest; we all remember our youth. Furthermore, as I recall the tale . . . in his aspect as god of tides, Rosh ages like a mortal until he is old. Then he grows young again, and so on forever."

The big man scowled. "I do not find this intelligence comforting under the circumstances."

"Thorian, do not brood on it," I said. "Gods never pose for their own statues—mortals do! Some king or rich merchant, when pressed by the temple for a tithe, may be moved to give the money to his nephew the sculptor instead. Or he may wish to immortalize his mistress or lover or child. Here is Aunt Hazard as the Goddess of Pestilence . . . So there is a resemblance? I have never posed to have my likeness chiseled; I am not so proud of it. Some long-forgotten citizen here bore my features centuries ago in his youth. The gods reused them when they made me.''

"Maybe." He did not sound convinced.

I chuckled. "It may even come in handy if I need to do some monumental lying. You know, I have carried off some strange pretenses in my day. Many years ago I spent some time on Ahu Sawish. I discovered by chance that I bore a striking resemblance to the queen's junior deputy husband and—''

"Not now, please. Tell me what we are doing here?"

"I have to go into the temple and find the woman, I think.''

He stared hard at me, as if trying to measure sanity by looks. "You stretch friendship hard already! The girl is very lovely and was snared tonight by dire deceit. I think my courage will stand with any man's, but you must tell me what can we do to aid her that is worth the risk, for if the priests catch us, we shall certainly be no use to her or any other woman in future.''

I had no answer to his question, but fortunately the gods saved me from having to respond. Footsteps were approaching in the cloister behind the statues.

"Someone is coming!"

Thorian and I turned toward Rosh and touched foreheads to the paving. I felt no great anxiety, for all that would be visible of us would be two bare backs. There was some danger that I would go to sleep. The curled-over posture was very relaxing after an unusually strenuous day.

Voices murmured as the newcomers went by, heading for the temple. One was the soprano of a eunuch, and there were at least two others, a harsh baritone and a guttural bass.

That one was familiar.

I glanced sideways at my companion. I saw the white

of his eye, and I also saw bared teeth. I frowned caution at him.

"This is not the time," I whispered.

As soon as the strangers had passed, though, we scrambled forward on our knees and peered around the column. Three men were walking abreast, heading away from us. A torchbearer went before them, and they were outlined against his light.

The one on the right was a soldier, and him I did not know.

The short, broad one waddling along in the middle was a priest, but his cloak was purple, so it was not Nagiak himself. I suspected that purple meant someone important, though.

The giant on the left wore a drab-colored swath, and it left one calf bare, so his civilian status was low. His hat floated two cubits higher than the priest's shiny scalp; his back was as broad and muscular as Thorian's. I had noted earlier how well matched they were.

What was the brutish Corporal Fotius doing in this mystery, and out of uniform at that? Again I twisted my head to smirk at Thorian. "We follow?"

He nodded in grim silence.

The guards noticed nothing unusual in our move as we rose and headed toward Balor's mighty feet. Dauntless, or trying to seem so to each other, we stalked along as fast as was fitting in a holy place. To our right, our quarry followed the curve of the cloisters, their torch flickering behind pillars. They could only be going to the temple itself.

I was thinking about Ahu Sawish. In a moment Thorian said, "Shouldn't I kill the torch?"

In fact, the torch was guttering as if about to die a natural death. It had lasted very well.

"I feel safer with it lit. I promise you we look a lot less suspicious! Let's pretend we've decided to pray to some minor, forgotten god tucked away over here in the corner. Ol-Ku-a-Rann, for example, who was patron of much-lauded Pollidi. If he is present anywhere in this courtyard, it will be somewhere very insignificant. Pity the poor deity who let his city die—how the others must laugh at him! Of course he will have plenty of time to listen to us. The first rule of deception is to think like—''

"You babble!"

"Possibly," I admitted. "I do that when I'm nervous. Remember, I am not trained to courage like a warrior."

I was not alone in my fear. Whether or not he was a warrior, Thorian was sweating so hard that his skin shone bright under the flame. Courage is acceptance of danger, not unawareness of it. Brave men are just as afraid as cowards. The difference is that they do their duty.

He grabbed my shoulder and stopped me completely. "They must be going to the temple. You do not propose to follow them inside?"

"I certainly do."

"And pretend to be a priest, perhaps?"

No one was going to mistake us for priests; not with Thorian's beard and chest visible, nor even my own humbler foliage.

"No. I shall trust the gods to keep me unobserved."

"This is raving insanity!"

"You needn't come if you don't want to," I said. Of course I hoped he would come, to keep me company.

We were already fugitives. The instant we set foot beyond the pillars, we would be trespassing, and liable for the fate worse than death. In the torchlight, Thorian's face twisted in agony. "I will face steel in battle and I have spilled my blood in a righteous cause. I am not afraid to die! But *that*? Fingernails? Chained?"

I shrugged his damp hand from my shoulder. "May Krazath guard you, friend," I said. I walked off and left him standing there with the torch. I felt a little disappointed, I must admit. I have heard and told so many heroic tales that I tend to assume all heroes are heroic. I sometimes forget that heroes are human. Thorian was fallible, as we all are. I admit I even have a few faults of my own. And of course I could make allowances for him—a warrior is trained to trust naught but his eye, his arm, and his comrades. I have had many years' practice in relying on the gods to distract attention from me. His was the sensible response.

I had not gone more than a few steps, though, when the torch he was holding expired—I was still close enough to miss the light. I turned around.

"Do you believe in signs?" I asked.

He made a rumbling noise, very low in his throat. Then he came, and I had my hero back.

We paced together around Balor's great feet. I think the little nudge from the gods had merely speeded his decision. I think he would have come anyway, because warriors are always loath to let other men outdo them in courage. I have seen more warriors outwitted by a dare than by anything else.

"I'll tell you how the temple is arranged," I said. "Roughly, at least. The center of a pyramid . . . Something wrong?"

Thorian hissed like a snake. "Never been to Zanadon before, you said!"

"I haven't. At least, not that I can be sure of. Remember earlier I said I'd been to Ahu Sawish, where I looked so like the queen's youngest—"

"Be quiet," Thorian said, and the intensity of his emotion belied the softness of his diction. "I do not wish to hear any more of your maundering rubbishy fantasy. If we are apprehended, I shall gouge out your eyes with my thumbs and manually preempt the amputatory privilege of the priestesses. Now be *quiet!"*

I decided to sulk in silence.

All I had been about to explain to my brusque companion was an extrapolation from my knowledge of the palace on Ahu Sawish. That also is built to a step-pyramid design, although it has only eleven steps instead of eighteen. Nor is it made of red-brown granite, but rather a white, very smooth limestone. I suppose that point is irrelevant.

Regardless of color, a pyramid makes an imposing structure and seems to enclose a vast amount of space. In fact, it cannot. However much it may look like a square version of a dome, there is apparently no way to make the inside hollow without having the walls collapse—or roof collapse, depending on what you want to call the sides. And if you build internal walls to support them, then how can you light or ventilate the central rooms? The core of a pyramid is as useless as the core of a mango.

The palace on Ahu Sawish was originally a temple, a step pyramid of solid masonry. It was so old that no one could remember which god it was supposed to honor. The queen decided to make a palace out of it because her subjects were always revolting, and the Sawishians are devilishly good archers. Her previous three palaces had been torched by flaming arrows in the night, *zong!* through a window. She'd lost several husbands to master bowmen, too.

What she did—or had done, as queens don't do such things themselves—was to build a wall on the edge of every step, all the way around. The top of each wall was level with the next step up.

Then she roofed over the bits she wanted.

She had created, you see, a series of walled alleys, each one going all the way round in a square . . . can one go round in a square? This is hard to describe without using my hands. These alleys were wide enough to divide into rooms, usually with a corridor left alongside for traffic. Ahu Sawish is a very dry island, and all the ventilation and lighting could be done with skylights. Many rooms had almost no roof at all.

From the outside, the new palace was very impressive. It had no windows, which meant there was nothing to shoot through. The master bowmen couldn't see the skylights. Not knowing where to put their arrows, they were reduced to shooting at random. It was quite sporting, in a bizarre sort of way. Sometimes we would be lying in bed and hear an arrow go *zonk!* in the roof overhead. Once a servant dropped dead at my feet as I walked along a corridor. Palace life is often boring, but not on Ahu Sawish.

The arsonists were equally baffled. The roofs were made of timber, but the floors were stone. The worst a fiery arrow could do was burn down a room or two. That was no more serious than losing a barn or a shed, because the fire could not spread, and a few hours' work would replace the room. Cuddles enjoyed interior decorating, anyway.

Oh, I forgot one thing. The stairways had to be notched down into the old pyramid structure. I expect you worked that out already.

11: The Upper Echelon
✳

The cloister curved its way around behind Balor's gigantic heel and ended at the base of the pyramid, at the midpoint of the eastern face. Faint light spilled from the doorway. Thorian and I were perilously close to our quarry then and could hear voices raised in greeting. The priest ushered the two soldiers ahead of him, inside.

That was as expected, but they could have turned off there, through a gate in the wall. I assumed that it led to the temple grounds. Even a temple needs space for laundry and sanitation, and so on. I would have guessed at vegetable gardens, also, and I would have been right, but only a really fanatical horticulturist would come to inspect vegetables in the middle of a moonless night, and that seemed out of character for Corporal Fotius.

For a moment the voices continued, maddeningly indistinct. Then they faded, and the light faded, also. Our prey had gone on, into the bowels of the temple. If my guesses were correct, they would have had three directions to choose from. I waited a few seconds—about a thousand heartbeats under the circumstances—and then I stalked over to the door and peeked in. I was just in time to see Fotius himself disappear up a stair, directly ahead. A glimmer of light from torches up ahead of him jiggled his shadow back down on the floor. Corridors stretched off to right and left, but they were dark.

Thorian uttered a low moan and followed me, but I noted an absence of vivacity in his demeanor.

I was pleased to see that my predictions were working out so far. The stair was directly opposite the entrance, and corridors led off to right and left. I suspected there

would be other staircases in a structure so large, perhaps
one for each face.

We peered cautiously up a narrow canyon, rising steeply
to dangerous heights. Light flickered on our quarry, already past the next floor and still climbing. Their number
had been increased by the two who had met them at the
door. A second torchbearer had been added in front, and
I could see that both were young priests in white cloaks.
The man in armor was flanked by two priests, Purple Cloak
and a Green. Corporal Fotius was at the rear, where he
so richly deserved to be.

I set a foot on the first step. Thorian grabbed my shoulder with a fist like a lion's jaw.

"You are mad!" he said. "Foofang has eaten your
brains. You are utterly, completely, incurably insane!"

"It saves worry," I retorted. "They won't see us, because nobody looks behind him when he's climbing stairs.
We're in the dark, anyway." He had no reply to that, and
we set off up the stair.

Our quarry's deliberate pace suggested that they were
settling in for a long climb. I was disappointed, because
in a high building with no scenic view from the top, the
important people would live and work on the lower levels.
It would be juniors who were banished to the peak. At
least, that had been the way things were done in Ahu Sawish.

The longer the climb, the longer the strain on poor
Thorian.

My guess about the design was confirmed. On every
floor, a corridor stretched out to right and left, but none
ever led inward. The only route toward the center was the
staircase itself, and it rose steadily, never penetrating the
solid granite core. In one respect the temple differed from
Cuddles's palace—all the roofs and interior walls were of
stone. Eternal Zanadon had built its temple to last.

The torches continued to ascend ahead of us, and we
followed grimly. We did not speak, and soon had no breath
to speak anyway. Once I heard a distant chanting, and a
few times even snoring, but in the main the temple was as
quiet and deserted as the city had been.

Most of the side corridors were dark, yielding an occasional glimpse of the stars through open spaces in the roof. When the corridors were lit, though, we advanced with caution, peering nervously along the floors before emerging from the stairwells. Usually the lights burned unattended in sconces, but once we saw a small group of priestesses. I heard Thorian stifle a cry as I emerged from the stairwell and strolled across to the next flight. Of course the gods arranged that the women all had their backs to me at that moment, but I did not linger to see what they were doing. In a moment Thorian streaked after me, breathing hard.

My heart had been beating fast enough before we even started. It excelled itself before we were halfway to the top. The stone was cold under my feet, the air heavy with incense and other perfumes. My legs wobbled. My knees burned. Even my hand ached from hauling on the handrail—my other hand was still throbbing from Thorian's abuse of it. It had been a long, hard day.

Higher and higher the priests conducted their two visitors. We followed like distant shadows. I was amazed at how well the fat priest in the purple cloak was doing, but of course he must be used to this. My greatest fear was they would all stop for a rest, for then they would instinctively look behind them, to see how far they had climbed. Thorian and I might be visible against the glimmer of the lights we had passed or the faint glow through the skylights.

I lost count of the stories. I kept thinking of being discovered and trying to run *down* again with a swarm of angry priests after me. It did not bear thinking about, but I thought about it anyway. I knew vaguely when we had come close to the top and must end our ascent or learn to fly. Either Thorian had kept accurate count or perhaps he detected a change in the light up ahead, or the echo of the voices—I never thought to ask him. However he knew, he grabbed my shoulder and hauled me back into a side corridor, which was fortunately deserted. The glimmer of light on the stairs dimmed and faded out. I do not know if the soldiers and priests paused to look back at the way they had come, but it would have been a very human thing to do. Thanks to my warrior companion, they would have seen the stairway empty.

"Come!" I gasped. We put on a staggering spurt and reeled up the last two flights, to where our prey had disappeared. We were at the top of the temple. There were no more stairs.

Nor was there a corridor. The stairwell emerged in a squarish hallway, the full width of the tier. To left and right stood imposing sets of double doors. Those to our left emitted faint voices; they were not quite closed, and a streak of light led enticingly across the floor to them.

For a moment I considered sneaking over and trying to listen. I decided that even I could not be quite so foolhardy—that would fall into the category of tempting the gods. There was an excellent chance that those junior priests with the torches would be sent away before the serious intrigue began, and then they must emerge and find us.

I looked up at the ceiling. The stars shone through two wide spaces. I tottered over to the nearer of the two, leaned a shoulder against the wall, and cupped my hands. My legs were vibrating like the dancing girls of Sinishinstra.

Thorian muttered a faint version of his habitual grunt and then placed a huge cold foot in the stirrup I had made for him. My arms debated falling out of their sockets, but decided not to at the last minute. He stepped up on my shoulders, and then I was in grave danger of crumpling like a squeezed orange.

"Can't reach," he whispered.

I very nearly broke my lifelong rule by uttering a prayer. Instead I clenched my teeth and raised my hands to my shoulders, palms upward.

"You can't!" Thorian whispered.

"Get on with it!" I replied. I was certain those torch-bearers would be dismissed any minute now, and come blundering out of the chamber.

Steadying himself against the wall, Thorian put his feet on my hands. I wobbled dangerously, and when I tried to lift him straight up nothing happened—I just did not have that sort of power available. However, I knew of another way—I dropped, bending my legs and straightening my arms at the same moment, leaving Thorian more or less where he was. Then I held my arms rigid, straightened my legs again, and so pushed him up. It's a cute little routine I learned when I was touring the Valley of Gold with Pav Im'pha and his troupe of acrobats. I had watched it done often enough, although I had never tried it myself.

My accomplice found a grip on the roof and was gone. In a moment, one end of his swath came dangling down. I had to jump to reach it, but he hauled me up beside him like an angler retrieving a minnow. Even as he did so, the doors opened and light flooded out below my feet.

Apparently priests are no more inclined to look up than other men are, and especially not when carrying torches above their heads. They did not notice me, although they very nearly set my loincloth on fire. Then Thorian's great hand closed on my arm and hauled me over the lip of the opening.

I lay on my back on the roof, sweating, gasping, and was lost in the glory of the stars.

The Tears of Sky are so many and so splendid that just to look at them makes me feel like a god. In my mind I reach upward to embrace them as a miser yearns for gold. They dance in glory in the night, cold and fiery like purest jewels, uncaring of mortals crying out to them and weeping for their beauty. They dance and swirl, cold, cold! But often instead—and this is the worst, or mayhap the best, I cannot decide—often I start to feel that I am looking *down*, instead of up, and when this mood comes upon me I fall and fall. I fall free, rushing eternally downward to the stars. Then the stars themselves are no longer cold but hot and burning, and the dark places between them are secret with need and mystery and fulfillment like the dark places of a woman's body, and they draw me homeward and excite me, soft, sweet! I am told then that my breath becomes labored and my limbs thrash . . . but I will not talk more of that now.

That time it was for a moment only. Thorian leaned

over me, shutting off my view of the sky even as he shook me to see what the matter was. I heard his harsh breath above me and quiet voices below, and I roused myself, and pulled myself back from glory.

Below us, the two torchbearers were heading off down the staircase, side by side, followed by four priestesses of various colors. The priest in the green cloak had remained in the hallway, leaning back against the wall—keeping guard, I supposed. The doors had been closed. So the juniors had been dismissed and the serious conspiring could now start.

On the roof, Thorian and I had unlimited ability to spy. He had risen and tied his swath on again. He set off to investigate what was being plotted at this sinister hour of the night. I scrambled up and followed.

We were high upon a mountaintop, far above the city and the plain beyond. A gentle wind played over my sweaty skin and brought me the muddy odor of paddy fields. The world stretched out forever below us, shrouded in night and domed by the starry heavens. I could see over the towers and spires of all Zanadon to where the Jolipi River shone like beaten silver in the distance. Far to the east I saw wrinkles of flame on the hills—olive groves, perhaps, or villages I had passed in the last few days. There were the Vorkans, close enough to make me shiver; closer than I had expected.

Off to one side, and surprisingly far away, the great figure of Balor had his back to us. High as we were, he was higher. We were about level with his shoulder blades. Feeling a vague giddiness, I laid a hand on the wall beside me, the final step of the pyramid. It blocked my view of the House of the Goddess above me and Maiana herself, to the west.

I directed my attention to what lay below. The first room was almost completely open to the sky, a small court for use in hot weather. It was furnished with couches and a table, and also a contraption that puzzled me until I realized that it was a carrying chair. A lantern burned on a wall, casting shadows that seemed strangely distorted from our high vantage. At this time of year, such a court might well serve as sleeping quarters for someone important.

Had it been completely unroofed, then Thorian and I could have bypassed it only by walking along the top of the exterior wall, and then we might have been observed from the ground—or from a lower tier, for surely priests would prefer to sleep under the stars in summer like everyone else. We did not need to take that risk, for there was a covered walkway alongside the interior wall, and that stretch of roof was a catwalk for us. I followed Thorian along it to reach the chamber beyond.

These doors had been closed, also, but three large openings in the roof admitted light and air. I expect they could be shrouded with awnings against rain; on that muggy summer night they were open for ventilation. The ceiling was so high that we could easily see any part of the room we chose, just by moving to a suitable location. And we were in relative darkness. So long as we stayed close to the dark granite wall of the uppermost tier, we should not be noticed by anyone glancing up.

The room was large, extending almost to the forward corner of the tier. It was sparsely furnished, and obviously a chapel, because a small altar stood against the end wall, flanked by life-size figures of Maiana and Balor. In front of those, five people were grouped around a high-backed chair.

The chair itself was a grand affair of gilded wood, draped with fine cloths and tapestries, and fitted with wheels. I had noted all that before I realized there was a sixth person present, sitting in the chair—I had overlooked her despite the crimson cloak she wore. She was very small and very ancient. She slouched in an awkward posture, as if her back were permanently twisted, a washrag wrung out and thrown in a corner. She was asleep. Shreds of white hair protruded from under a canted, ornate headdress; the hands resting on her lap were knotted claws, and her face was a shrunken mask of extreme age. I remembered Bedian Tharpit saying something about a mad hag.

On her flat chest, and grotesquely large for her, hung a

jeweled pectoral in the shape of a crescent. When I saw that, I knew I was looking at the high priestess of Maiana, titular ruler of the temple and perhaps of the city, also.

On one side of her stood High Priest Nagiak, a smirking horror of crimson-draped obesity. I wondered if he had moved his soft mass to this great height by himself, or had been brought up in that carrying chair I had seen out in the court.

Alongside him stood the purple-cloaked priest who had escorted the guests. He was taller and slightly younger, but a little less odious. Like Nagiak, he was beardless and his head was shaven. He was still panting from his climb.

On the other side of the chair stood a sizable woman of middle years. Her purple cloak and headcloth proclaimed her a priestess, and she bore a temple pallor, yet her powerful frame belonged in the fields. She had fists like a man, and a rugged jaw. She was scowling at the lay visitors as a peasant might contemplate two pigs strayed into her vegetable patch.

These four must be the senior clergy of Zanadon, the high priest and priestess and their respective deputies. Before them knelt Gramian Fotius, and the older man in armor.

". . . your considered opinion, War Lord," Nagiak was saying, "that the situation is hopeless?" His high-pitched voice whined deliberately overloud.

"Yes, Holiness." The soldier's baritone would have crossed a parade ground and echoed back again. "Hopeless by mortal standards."

"The army will not fight without Balor?"

"Regrettably, that is so."

They all waited for the high priestess to react. She dozed on unwitting.

"I told you!" the other priestess snapped. "It is useless."

Nagiak flashed her a sneer of dislike and leaned close to the old crone in the chair.

"Holy Mother! Your Holiness! Beloved of Maiana?" He screeched right in her ear, but he would have done better to address the statues by the altar.

"Try her name," said the woman in purple. "That works sometimes."

"Squicalm!"

Older than the gods, lips and eyelids twitched . . . dry leaves in the wind. Eyes opened uncertainly, staring blankly.

"The Vorkans," Nagiak screamed. "They pillage and burn and rape through the Spice Lands."

The crone chewed in silence, the myriad wrinkles of her face twisting like worms.

Nagiak turned to roll his eyes at his purple-clad subordinate, who pulled a face. He looked to the other woman, and she just shrugged. He leaned close to the high priestess again and bellowed in her ear once more. "The city is in danger. You must summon Immortal Balor!"

The toothless mouth moved silently. She pointed a gnarled twig at the kneeling soldier and muttered something, a query.

The onlookers exchanged glances, and I realized with a shiver that Nagiak was enjoying himself.

In the temple of any goddess the high priestess rules, but the goddess of chance outwits us all. Squicalm in her infirmity had let power slip, and the high priest had snatched it up. Obviously the woman in purple was outclassed, if she had allowed that to happen.

"Gillian Thwagus? Gillian Thwagus died years ago, Holy Mother. He was succeeded by Joliak Thwagus. Then he died, also. This is Rothian Arksis. He is War Lord of the Army now."

"You needn't shout! I'm not deaf."

"No, Holy Mother. *The enemy is at the gate!*"

The crone raised her claws and pawed at the glittering crescent on its silver chain. She was confused. She slobbered.

"You must go to the House of the Goddess!" the high priest warbled in his thin soprano. "Tomorrow you must lie on the holy bed and call on Immortal Balor. The god will come to you as he came to Maiana in the tamarisk grove when they founded the city. He will touch your limbs with his hand and age shall fall from you as it fell from

Omia and Piala! He will look upon you and you will be beautiful in his sight. He will remember Maiana. You shall be Maiana for him, and he will lie with you in his strength. Great is the power of Balor!''

The old woman was asleep again.

Nagiak sighed and stepped back. "War Lord Arksis, you have done your duty. You have reported the peril to Her Holiness.''

"So what happens now?'' asked the soldier, but I thought he already knew the answer. He and the high priest were acting out a play. He was a tall, spare man, like well-seasoned leather. His face was hidden from me by his helmet; the hair on his arms was grizzled.

"Tomorrow we shall parade the old baggage around . . .'' The high priest sniggered and glanced at the other woman to see how she took his baiting. "So sorry—that was naughty of me. I mean tomorrow High Priestess Squicalm will do her duty, also. She will go to the House of the Goddess at sundown, and there wait for Immortal Balor.''

"And it is certain he will come?'' Arksis prompted.

"No. He may not find the offering acceptable.'' Nagiak giggled, with another glance at the furious priestess in purple.

"So then what happens, Holy Father?''

For devious reasons of their own, they were acting out a charade aimed at the large priestess—not at the other priest, for he was trying to hide a smirk, and certainly not to enlighten the moronic Fotius. Nor could the performance be intended for me, although the gods in their wisdom had brought me there to witness it. No, the large woman in purple was the chosen victim.

"If he does not come in glory that night, then Reverend Mother Belhjes becomes high priestess, and the following night she will await the god in her turn.'' He smiled greasily at her.

The woman's great fists were clenched, her lips pale. "As Maiana wills . . . But we must wait for the new moon.''

"That is three nights off!'' Nagiak purred. "I don't

think we dare wait so long. The danger is extreme, is that not correct, War Lord? It is very frightening!''

"The situation is most urgent, ma'am," Arksis agreed. He shifted uncomfortably on his knees.

"Tomorrow!" Nagiak insisted. "We must begin tomorrow. The Holy Mother's sickness has come at a most unfortunate time for us all, of course, but I know we can rely on you to make the correct decisions in her stead. Surely you will not imperil the city by waiting, when the war lord himself has assured us that the situation is urgent?''

Belhjes curled her lip in a snarl. She had the distrustful, petulant manner of those who have acquired authority and yet lack the natural grace to use it properly. Good deputies are often poor principals. As a leader she would vacillate between flabby acquiescence and shrill tyranny.

Still Nagiak insisted. "Well, Mother? The fate of Zanadon awaits your decision."

With an obvious effort she said, "Tomorrow, then. Begin tomorrow."

The high priest had won what he wanted. He smiled greasily. "The right decision, I am sure. But what ails you, Holiness? Are you troubled by doubts?"

"Of course not!"

She was certainly troubled by something, I decided, but then I would sooner copulate with a swampful of crocodiles than collaborate on anything at all with that priest in his bulging crimson cloak. He reminded me of the juggler in Pav Im'pha's troop, who could juggle six small hatchets and pick the onlookers' pockets at the same time.

And Nagiak might be the lesser of her worries. Until then I had never given thought to the ritual, but obviously Zanadon in peril must summon its protector somehow, and now the ceremony had been outlined for me: The high priestess would offer her body to tempt the god. A virgin of Belhjes's age could hardly find that a comforting prospect.

Now she tried to assert herself, and a tremor in her voice ruined the attempt before it was properly started.

"While the Holy M-Mother is indisposed, then I act as high priestess."

"Indeed that is so," Nagiak replied with an oily smile. "We all appreciate the great burden you bear."

"Then deliver me some explanations, High Priest. To bring laymen into the temple is forbidden!"

"There are certain exceptions."

"Yes, there are exceptions. Very few. I understand why War Lord Arksis is here. He must report to the Holy Mother when danger threatens the city, and you did right to bring him. It has been done before."

"Oh, I am so glad that you admit that it has been done before."

Belhjes shot him a glare of distilled hatred. "But why did you drag that one along?" She leveled an accusing finger at young Fotius.

Why indeed?

Thorian's heavy hand came to rest on my shoulder. He moved his lips to my ear.

"I told you," he breathed. "I warned you. Gods do not walk the world in these humble days. You came here to Zanadon to see a god, and you will witness nothing more than priestly intrigue."

12: The Plot Thins

I did not believe him.

Had she overheard his remark, the purple-cloaked priestess would not have believed him, either. I was not sure what the men were thinking, but I could tell that Deputy High Priestess Belhjes expected the god to come to the aid of the city, in person.

However, while she might be acting head of the temple in theory, she was out of her depth in dealing with the devious high priest. This meeting seemed to be going much as he had planned.

Gods are normally served only by men, but many goddesses have both male and female votaries. In those temples the priesthood and priesthood are rarely on terms of trust and endearment. Thorian had a good point—I sensed intrigues within intrigues—but the failings of mortals were irrelevant, and Balor would not be swayed by Nagiak.

"Rise, War Lord," he said, smirking. "Let us talk with your grandson."

Arksis rose stiffly and moved away from his young companion. Fotius stayed where he was, on his knees, holding his hat in his great hands and systematically crushing it to pulp. His lush hair and beard and his bare torso seemed strangely out of keeping in this company. He was a wild boar in a pigpen.

Nagiak smiled blandly. "Corporal, er . . ?"

"Gramian Fotius," War Lord Arksis said.

"A likely lad, a fine example of the young manhood of Zanadon." The high priest stepped forward, beaming at the giant—his piggy eyes were not much higher than the corporal's. "Unspoiled, innocent." He sighed. "Virile. How old are you, my son?"

The big man thought for a moment and then said, "Twenty-three."

"Did you ever kill a man?"

Fotius hesitated, glanced uneasily at his grandfather, and then rumbled, "Yes, sir."

" 'Holiness!' " Nagiak said.

"Huh?"

"You address me as 'Holiness.' "

"Yes, sir."

Nagiak licked his fat lips. "Tell me about the man you killed."

"Three men, Holiness, sir."

"Gracious! Did you slay them with your sword, or how?"

"With a club, sir Holiness. Was catching slaves and hit them too hard."

"Dear me!" The priest sighed again. "Such accidents are regrettable, but they incur no guilt. And how long since you returned from . . . where was it?"

"Fogspith, Holiness."

"How long since you returned from Fogspith?"

Fotius stared uneasily at his grandfather and moved his lips while he pondered. "Two weeks, sir. Just about."

"Two weeks!" Nagiak said, as if that was a remarkable revelation. He looked at Belhjes and spread his fat hands. "Armor bearer? When the god comes, he will require attendants. We thought an armor bearer would be a likely start. And the boy is an inspiring figure, is he not?" He smirked, trustworthy as a rabid snake.

"Armor bearer?" The priestess snorted in peasant fashion. I thought she was about to spit. "You can generally think up more credible fables than that, Holy Father."

Nagiak shrugged, as if he did not much care whether or not she believed him. "We can't offer the god dirty armor. There's a good day's work needed, and my lads lack the necessary experience. Rise, my son."

Fotius scrambled to his feet, and he towered over everyone else present. Thorian neither spoke nor moved at my side, yet I sensed a wave of hatred flow from him like heat from a stove.

"You know," Nagiak said thoughtfully. "He is almost as large as Balor, I do believe. This Balor, I mean." He turned and considered the statue beside the altar.

For the first time I noticed that these images of the god and goddess were not duplicates of the great figures that dominate the temple and the gates. They were carved of the same red-brown stone, but unadorned by either jewels or gold—plain, shiny granite. The Maiana was clothed in a cloak and headdress. She wore no horns. Her crescent symbol was represented by a pectoral matching the one hung on the sleeping Squicalm. This was the goddess as her own high priestess.

On the other side of the altar, the Balor figure was nude, exaggeratedly muscled and male—the god as a human bull.

Nagiak sniggered and waved his soft jeweled hand. "Stand beside Balor, my son, and let us see."

Fotius shambled over and positioned himself as directed. He was very nearly the same height and build, and close to the same color. Suddenly the statue seemed less improbable.

"Is that not remarkable, Holiness?" The high priest laughed shrilly and clapped his hands. "Should we remove his swath, do you think, for a complete comparison?"

Belhjes flushed furiously. "That is an obscene suggestion!"

"No. It will be interesting!"

"Sacrilege!"

"Oh, if you think so," Nagiak agreed reluctantly. He was openly playing with her. "A fine figure of a man, though, don't you agree?"

"This is blasphemy!" She did not know how to parry his baiting, or else she scorned the obvious slur.

The high priest leered. "Not at all. Tradition has always maintained that these very figures in the chapel of the high priestess were carved from life when Omia was Maiana . . . the third coming of Balor, when he smote the Waregs. You do not expect any less now, surely? Corporal, go and stand by the reverend lady so that we may see what a fine couple you will . . . she will . . . would . . . make with Balor.''

Fotius shrugged and trudged over toward the priestess. She backed away. He followed, obeying orders, and would doubtless have continued to do so had she fled from the temple and down the Great Way and out of the city. But she stopped and let the hairy giant come close to her. Tall though she was, her headdress barely reached his shoulder.

''Nearer!'' Nagiak said.

Fotius edged closer to Belhjes. She was trying not to look at him, but a sickly pallor had replaced her blushes. Even from the roof, I could see that she was trembling. Oh yes, Belhjes believed that the god would come in the flesh.

''Well?'' she demanded shrilly. ''Are you satisfied?''

''Me?'' Nagiak said. ''Oh, I am easily satisfied. What does it take to satisfy Balor, do you suppose?''

Fotius had caught up with the drift of the conversation— he leered. The priestess stalked away from him and took refuge behind old Squicalm's chair.

''I do not believe this fable of Balor's armor bearer! Invent a better tale, Holiness.''

Nagiak smiled catlike and turned to his companion priest. ''Most Reverend Thaliak, the honored war lord has performed his duty here. He must have others waiting, though, as he readies the army for the coming of the god. See him to the gate, will you, and send him on his way with fitting blessings?''

Belhjes's hard, square face seemed to swell with outrage. ''Just him? You are serious about keeping that young *ogre* here, within the temple? This is sacrilege!''

Fotius was sending pleading looks toward his grandfather, but obviously he had been informed of the arrangement beforehand, and it was not going to be changed now.

Nagiak rubbed his hands in delight. ''Monster? No, this is a young man, Holiness. One in the natural condition, you know. Unimproved. And Corporal, er, Fotius, is honorable and completely trustworthy. I have his grandsire's word on that—don't I, War Lord? Or is his the virtue you believe endangered? Can you not control your charges if they discover him, Holy Lady?''

Belhjes spluttered with fury, and at last used the obvious weapon. ''What does a eunuch know of such things?''

Nagiak's lardy face seemed to close up like a fat flower at sunset. ''As much as you, I'm sure. The man remains! I had thought the explanation would be obvious. Wait here, though, and I will spell it out for you.'' With a final sneer, he ushered the others toward the door.

Thorian vanished from my side in his usual speedy silence, and I supposed that he was intent on trailing Fotius. I stayed where I was, watching Priestess Belhjes. I could never like or admire such a woman, but I felt sorry for her. She had probably been a very effective adjutant for the aging high priestess. Now she was on her own, making the decisions, trying to deal with both the insidious Nagiak and an impending god, and probably aware that she was inadequate to handle either.

She watched in silence as the men departed, then bent to speak to old Squicalm and shake her gently. The only result was that the crone's elaborate headdress slipped further askew. There was to be no help from the high priestess.

With a quick glance at the door, Belhjes headed over to the altar. I assumed she was about to pray to Maiana, but she went to Balor instead. For a moment she stared at its shiny chest, then she bowed her head and sank to the ground to kiss the granite toes.

She rose up on her knees, raising her hands as if to speak an appeal, but the move left her looking right at the figure's exaggerated manhood. She recoiled with a shudder and went scrambling over to prostrate herself before Maiana instead.

I saw her shoulders shake.

The reverend lady believed, but she would be much happier were her faith a little stronger.

* * *

Thorian glided back, the meatiest ghost I had ever met. His eyes glinted in the starlight, but he did not speak.

In the chapel below us, Nagiak came waddling back, also, yawning and stretching his crimson arms. "These all-night vigils are very hard on us at our age, aren't they? They may get harder, you agree? For some of us?" He chuckled, with a wobble of his soft jowls.

Belhjes was on her feet again, glaring at him with pink-rimmed eyes.

He saw that his humor was not appreciated. "Oh, listen to me!" he said nastily. "Since you don't seem to have the wit to work things out on your own. Can't you see that the young lout is here as a hostage?"

She started, as if distrusting her ears. "Hostage?"

"Hostage. The Vorkans are at the gate, the city is beset. We must have faith in the gods, certainly, but that doesn't mean we can let ourselves be careless or foolhardy. The corporal remains in the temple as surety for his grandfather's good behavior—Arksis controls the military clans. The mercantile families are not so easily led, but Bedian Tharpit is their spokesman, in as much as they have one. I have his daughter here, also, and for the same reason."

The priestess studied him with a distrust I found commendable. "You fear treason?"

"Not as such. Nobody would be silly enough to open the gates to those horrid Vorkans. But we have a huge army of refugees without the walls and a restless mob within them. Dangerous times require firm rule." He simpered happily. "Fear of the gods seldom fails, but those two can aid us, if anyone can, and no one can oppose us without their help. The Tharpit girl is to become a priestess; that was agreed." He giggled. "No such solution is possible for the boy, because I had to promise he would not be altered in any way. It would be an improvement in his case, but I did promise. We'll keep him locked up, though!"

She nodded reluctantly. "I wish you had found a more appealing guest. That one frightens me."

"He should." Nagiak shook his round head sadly. For once he looked and sounded sincere. "Apparently he was all right until he was about thirteen. Then he molested a younger girl. It was frightfully gruesome. Do you want to hear the details?''

''Certainly not!''

''Oh. Well, her brothers beat him. He has not been quite right in the head since.''

''But he was all right before, you think?''

''Just precocious. The whole family has a nasty tendency to violence. They were keeping him hidden on some backwoods estate until the Vorkan scum appeared. Arksis assures me he will cause no trouble as long as we restrict his intake of red meat and keep him well supplied with women.''

Belhjes had started to relax at the more reasonable tone. Now she uttered a cry that was almost a shriek. ''You cannot be serious! In the holy temple itself? What women?''

Nagiak's cloak shook like a bag of melons. ''You will not call for volunteers?''

As she shrieked again, I felt Thorian's eyes upon me.

''Did you think a few welts on my back would so aggrieve me?'' he said softly. ''I have seen that brute satisfy his urges.''

I shuddered.

Down in the chapel, Nagiak was soothing the outraged priestess. ''. . . not worry . . . all arranged. Each day some relative will come to visit him and bring servants. But it will not be for long. When Balor comes, then the danger will be past, and we shall evict the lad promptly. He is merely a necessary precaution, Reverend Lady.''

And a very obvious one. I sat down to rest my legs, leaning my back against the cold, smooth wall and letting myself sink into my exhaustion as if it were a steaming tub.

I found Nagiak odious because he was a type I detest more than almost any other—a manipulator, one who enjoys maneuvering people to his own objectives. Now I understood his scheming. It disgusted me, but I was even more disgusted to realize that such intrigue was justifiable in the circumstances. Zanadon was under siege, or would be within a day or two. That oily politician was seeking to knot together the priesthood, the military, and the wealthy, and that was a reasonable precaution, as he had just said. Nauseating, but necessary.

I wanted to sleep. My eyelids drooped. Not only was I physically exhausted but sleep might bring me dreams of reassurance or instruction. Balor would not appear for at least another day, perhaps two. I could forget about Fotius and the Shalial girl. They were hostages for their families' good behavior, nothing more.

It was all very simple.

13: Moonshine

"**S**he will be here any minute!" Nagiak said.

Belhjes's protests seeped up to us less distinctly—something was unthinkable. I was not really listening. Indeed, I had almost drifted off to sleep. Thorian knelt beside me.

"We must go, Omar. The moon is rising."

I peered blearily southeastward and saw wisps of light above the hills, gold smeared to orange by the smoke. The fires had dwindled to disconnected specks. The air was cooler now. Dawn was only an hour or two away.

Yes, we must go, or we should be trapped within the temple.

Go where, though?

I forced my sleepy mind back to sifting the conversation in the chapel. Nagiak was adamant that Shalial Tharpit must be inducted into the full priesthood at once. Belhjes was insisting that rules were rules and she must first become a postulant.

"But honestly, I promised that her hair would not be cut off," the priest protested.

The argument snarled on like mating snakes.

"What did they do with Fotius?" I asked quietly. "Lock him up?"

"No," Thorian rumbled. "They sent the war lord away, but they put the turd behind the doors to watch."

I tried to make sense of that, and failed. "What doors?"

"The doors on the far side of the stair. He is to watch for the Tharpit girl when she goes by."

I have a foolish prejudice that says large men tend to be stupid. I know it is not true, but I can't help thinking it. Thorian was as large as any man I have ever met, but he was far from stupid. Indeed, he was probably much smarter than I was, and evidently he had seen something I had missed, for his eyes burned angry bright in the darkness.

What?

Below us, the argument was growing hotter.

"She is a sweet child!" Nagiak shouted. "And ever so devout. She knows her texts—we have checked ever so carefully. And, yes, she is a virgin. We have checked that, also."

I turned my mind away with distaste and looked up at Thorian again. His teeth shone in a grimace. He was waiting for me to work it out by myself. Why should the Fotius hostage be shown the Tharpit hostage? Why not show the Tharpit hostage the Fotius hostage likewise?

"We have no time for all-night vigils, ninny!" the high priest shrilled. "The foe is upon us. The situation is quite terrifying!"

Thorian knew the answer, or thought he did.

Belhjes said something about vigils.

"All right!" Nagiak agreed angrily. "*All right!* We can leave her here until dawn to do the vigil, if you must be so mulishly stubborn. You really are a terrible nuisance, you know? But in the morning she will be sworn!"

A mutter from the woman signed a reluctant compromise.

I rubbed my eyes and peered at Thorian again.

"He wouldn't *dare*!" I said.

"Are you so sure of that, Trader of Tales?"

No, I wasn't. "Can he? Is it possible?"

It was time to explore.

I heaved my leaden body to its feet and headed toward the city, staying close to the wall. Thorian rose and followed. When I reached the end, I was beyond the lighted skylights of the chapel. A single aperture in the roof showed that another small room must lie beyond it, but no light showed. I wondered briefly about that room—how was it entered? It lay behind the altar, and there had been no door there. Was it approached from some other staircase?

I peered around the corner and inspected the front face of the pyramid. The great ceremonial steps rose like a ramp up the center. Beyond that, Maiana had her shoulder to me, but I could just make out the jutting curve of her breast. Her horns were dark against the stars—I looked away quickly, not trusting myself among stars in my present bemused state.

The pavement before me was an unbroken surface of smooth granite, gleaming like water in the night. There were no skylights. All the lower tiers, of course, were invisible beyond its edge.

I started to creep forward, crouching so I could not be seen from the ground. My calf-length swath was a nuisance, and like to become more of one. After a moment I unfastened it and let it fall. The key to the Tharpit mansion struck the stone with a tiny metal chinking sound that I expected to waken the whole city. Free of my garment, I scrambled forward until I neared the edge, then dropped to crawl the rest of the way. In a moment Thorian lay beside me.

No one has ever explained to me why heights always seem so much greater looking *down from* than looking *up at*. Old Thumbal of Thank used to insist that the gods arranged it that way to help them feel godlike, but I don't think I believe him. Be that as it may, Thorian and I were very high and godlike that night. I remember feeling astonished that the pyramid was so high.

Far below us, scattered fireflies in the Courtyard of a Thousand Gods showed where the devout knelt at prayer. Beyond that the Great Way sloped away toward the gates, and flickers moved on it as the guard patrolled. A few lighted windows in houses located the sick and the guilty. But the city was not what we had come to see.

The temple was. The next tier down was another unbroken plain of dark granite.

I glanced at my companion. He nodded and said nothing.

We worked our way back a short distance, and then I rose to a crouch again and hurried to the eastern edge.

Balor was a great darkness against the moonrise, his golden sword aglint.

Again I prostrated myself to peer over and view the tier below. The difference was obvious—many darker openings and a few brighter ones marked the rooms and corridors within it. I wished I could see all the lower tiers, but I could guess that they would repeat the same pattern.

A sound of women chanting soared from the three bright skylights of the chapel and sweetened the night.

I looked up at Thorian, who had joined me again.

"We must go up to the top," I said.

"Holy Foofang looks after his own."

I smiled, reflecting proudly that my companion had begun to put more faith in the gods than in his own cunning and strong arm.

There was little point in concealment. If anyone looked up from the Courtyard, we were going to be seen. The witnesses might not believe their own eyes, of course. The stonework was about the same shade as human skin, and we were both nude. That might help, however odd it felt. Together we stood up and ran to the great staircase.

Side by side, we sprinted up the wide steps to the uppermost level. The tall House of the Goddess stood in the center, starkly beautiful—a smooth cylinder of granite roofed with a golden dome. Somehow its curves were enhanced by the square angularity of everything else. The only break in the walls was the archway in front. We did not break stride until we reached it.

I entered, saw Maiana before me, and fell on my knees.

Thorian went farther, throwing himself prostrate. "Forgive us!" he moaned. "Holy Lady, we seek only your glory."

That was prayer, and I remembered with some difficulty that I disapproved of prayer. The goddess would know we were there and why we came. I sat back on my heels to adore her.

From the ground, of course, the House seems tiny. Even within it, I had trouble appreciating its expanse because it is so high, yet I have known many kings' halls that were smaller. The empty floor was an unbroken expanse of shiny granite paving. Against the darkness of the far wall stood the Passionate One, wrought in silver, thrice my height.

Of all the goddess images I have ever seen, this is the most gorgeous. That night she was clothed in traces of moonlight, which is her mystery. Dim as it was, it shone on her horns, sparkled on the diamonds of her hair, lit ruby flames on her lips and nipples, and burned with a dark seductive blue fire at her groin. Her eyes watched me closely, striking fear in my heart. Eternal mother, eternal consort! Fear, yes—but I also felt a rush of desire that stopped my breath. My limbs trembled before her challenge. Truly, in all my many days, never before had I been so presumptuous as to come naked and uninvited into the very house of a deity.

Well, perhaps I had been invited? And there are some gods and goddesses who insist on nudity in their presence, regarding clothes as pretense and vanity. Or impediment, in other cases.

I rose unsteadily to my feet and began to explore. When I had inspected the interior, I wandered out again and strolled around to the north edge of the platform, the back of the temple, dropping to my knees and crawling the last part of the way. I looked down at the level we had recently left. Again I saw skylights into rooms within it. Again the lower levels were hidden from me, but I felt certain that they would all show much the same—plus some glimmers of torchlight, likely, and perhaps courtyards upholstered with sleeping priests and priestesses.

Behind the temple, the ground fell off steeply, pocked with a few precariously clinging buildings. The city wall was close on this side.

I did not bother to inspect the west. Instead I went back to Thorian, who was still prostrate, crawling backward as the devout do when leaving sacred precincts.

"It is as we thought," I said. "On holy days, priests and prominent citizens will march up the staircase. They will see nothing but plain stone. I conclude that the front of the temple must be solid. The other three faces are hollow, and inhabited, but the interior of the temple is never revealed to the laity, not even a glimpse of the sky-lights. Dirty laundry fails to inspire awe.''

"And up here?" he growled, rising to his knees.

"Nothing. No way in. No doors. Nothing. The rock is solid beneath us.''

Thorian stood up, and even his mighty limbs seemed to move wearily. "There must be a way, and Nagiak will know of it.''

"I hope you are wrong. I am sure you are. We shall find out in a day or so.''

He uttered his lion grunt. "I think I shall kill that Fotius brute tonight, and be certain.''

A sudden stab of panic cut off my breath. "No! No! We are here as witnesses only and must not seek to alter the flow of events.''

"You may be only a witness. You are a man of words. I am a man of action.''

Needing time to think, I silently recited a vulgar poem that Illina taught me. Then I said, "Gramian Fotius is a hostage. If you kill him here, you will plunge the city into civil war.''

He grunted again—and then a third time, regretfully.

"I suppose you are right, although my thumbs itch for his throat. Now the moon is lighting the steps. How do we descend, Servant of the Gods?''

"Let us go over the far side.''

With a respectful bow to the goddess we departed.

We went around to the north side. We lay prone on the cold granite and stared down at the tier below us. It seemed a long way down. Perhaps we should risk the stair again?

"I can lower you a little way," Thorian said. "If I had my swath, I could do better.''

"Don't expect me to catch you after.''

He chuckled. "Break a leg and relieve the monotony of our humdrum existence.''

I scrambled to the edge. Thorian took my wrists and lowered me as far down as he could reach. I discovered to my surprise that my toes were dangling in emptiness and my face was against an ornate cornice. Before I could find a grip on it, he let go and I dropped. I came down harder than I expected, falling prone with an *oof!* of shock. My knees and ankles burst into flame. I hoped that there were no light sleepers under the nearby skylights.

A moment later Thorian swung over the rim above me. He, too, found that protruding frieze, and hung there for a moment, studying it. The overhang was slight, but the ornamentation ran all the way along the edge, and presumably all around the temple. I was annoyed that I had not noticed it sooner. We had not viewed the temple close-to in daylight, but I pride myself on my observation. It is the mainstay of my trade.

Thorian clambered down the carvings like a fly until he was hanging from the bottom ledge. Thus he saved himself part of the drop. He landed more nimbly than I had and immediately stalked over to the edge of the tier. He lay down and peered over. By the time he returned, I was on my feet and more or less able to walk. We set off to recover our swaths.

"None," he whispered. "Just the top one."

"Why should there be a frieze around the top step and none on the others? If offends my sense of symmetry."

"Because the carvings are there for a purpose."

"What purpose?"

Just then the skylight we were passing brightened.

Of course we looked.

The bedchamber below us was small, but not excessively so. It would be quite adequate for one person, and it was reasonably, if modestly, furnished with a cot and a table and perhaps a few more things out of our field of view. I have lived in worse many times. It became much less spacious as Gramian Fotius entered, already complaining in hectoring tones about the size of the bed.

A soprano voice told him to sleep on the floor. The light faded out and a door slammed. I heard the lock click.

I took hold of my companion's arm, although I had no illusions about being able to restrain him if he decided to seek a reckoning with the slaver.

"If he lies down, I could jump on him," Thorian whispered longingly. "That would wreck his guts for starters."

"The temptation is manifest, but I look forward to witnessing your performance. I can't admire your artistry if you operate in the dark."

"Ah. There is that."

"Come along." I led him away.

We returned to our original starting point, above the hallway at the top of the stairs. A double line of priestesses was filing by below us and down the stairs. The chanting had stopped; apparently the ceremony was over. I flopped to my belly and leaned head and shoulders through the opening, catching a brief upside-down glimpse of crimson at the head of the procession, as fat Nagiak descended in his carrying chair on the shoulders of four young priests.

The business of the night had been completed, and the temple would soon be quiet enough for us to venture departing. Indeed we must—the crescent moon had risen clear of the smoke, and at dawn everything would start up again. We did not have long.

And we were balked. In the courtyard beside the hall, the ancient high priestess was being put to bed by three young attendant priestesses. Belhjes hovered alongside, perhaps hoping for some sign of wakefulness, but the old woman was as limp as a sack of tubers. We dared not walk along the narrow strip of roof above them.

I pulled Thorian back to a safe distance and sat down. He settled beside me with a sigh of weariness. I was dizzy with fatigue myself, for it had been a long day since I awoke in the olive grove.

"Squicalm?" I said. "Tomorrow she is paraded around. At sunset she goes to the House of the Goddess in solemn procession. What happens to her if Balor does not respond, though?"

I was wondering how Belhjes' succession was arranged, and if a high priestess was deposed by execution, but Thorian's reply took me by surprise.

"What happens to her if he does?"

"You heard! By morning she is restored to youth and beauty and is consort to the god. Maiana does not incorporate, but the high priestess is her representative. Like Omia, they said, or Piala. There must have been others, in more ancient times. Doubtless not all the names are recorded.''

"But this time the living god bears a striking resemblance to Gramian Fotius and the priestess to Shalial Tharpit?''

"And I say he would not dare!" I insisted. "Even if the gods would allow such a thing, the townsfolk will not be deceived. Shalial is not Squicalm.''

Thorian grunted. "Who remembers Squicalm in her youth, or recalls what beauty she bore then?''

I squirmed, impaled by his logic. "But Tharpit is senior merchant of the city! Many people must be acquainted with his daughter.''

"Not necessarily. She has probably been sequestered most of her life, and his friends the burghers will not rouse the commonality against him. The Fotius thug has been secluded for years at some rural retreat. You heard that. He has only been back two weeks, and some of that time he has been out of town, slaving. Perfect, isn't he?''

I did not answer.

Thorian went on, "People believe what they want to believe, Omar.''

Sadly, that is often true. I have seen the sacred Well of Sailmok, where the god is said to perform cures. Thousands of people come to the well every year. They make offerings, drink the waters, bathe in them, buy trashy souvenirs, and then declare themselves cured, or many do. Yet I saw no credible miracles while I was there, and the well-documented cases all seem to be very old. The priests of Sailmok live well. I did not want to admit that.

"Remember Tharpit giving gold to Nagiak?" Thorian growled. "What for, do you suppose? It is a crafty plot. The grandson of the war lord and the daughter of the leading merchant! Arksis believes he can control Fotius-Balor, and the god's consort will look after her father's interests. Those two will rule behind the scenes. Zanadon will be their milkcow. Nagiak must have been royally paid—I wager the bidding was ferocious.''

"But the Vorkans?''

"You heard what Arksis said, that the army demands

Balor as leader. Fotius is big and savage, a good figure-head to give them courage. His grandfather will do the thinking for him."

It was unthinkable.

Thorian thumped my shoulder in sympathy. "You came to Zanadon to see a god, but all you will see is priestly fakery."

"Zanadon has never been conquered—"

"And it will prevail against the Vorkans, also! The troops will believe themselves invincible, because they are led by a god, and because they very much want to believe themselves invincible. Of course the army of Zanadon is never defeated, with that kind of inspiration! I know warriors, Omar!"

"What kind of tale is that for me to add to my collection?" I moaned. "You are saying that Balor will be a hoax! Worse, you are hinting that he has always been a hoax?"

Thorian sighed. "I suppose I am. Nagiak must know. He will have access to ancient annals, telling him how to organize the sham."

"So the old woman is removed and killed?" I muttered. "And the imposters introduced in her place? But surely the whole population will keep an all-night vigil around the temple. How can the man pull off such a deception?"

I was trying not to think about my showman friend Pav Im'pha. He would have accepted the challenge gladly—for a suitable share of the gate, or perhaps just for the chance to perform before such a house. Pav could pull a woman out of a hat on a stage. He would have produced Balor to order at the top of a pyramid very easily.

"This place," Thorian said, "must be riddled with secret passages."

"We went to the House of the Goddess. We saw no hidden door."

"We went by night. Give me an hour up there in daylight, and I will find the way. And that frieze around the top tier? There are air holes hidden in it. That is why it is there."

So the topmost step was also hollow, but not connected

to the inhabited parts of the temple. Secret, in other words. I had to admit that intrigue had now moved very close to the House of the Goddess—directly below it, in fact.

"I will not believe until I see," I said. "We must go."

I leaned on his shoulder to rise and then gave him a hand up. Weary as old men, we shuffled back to where our swaths lay, pale excrescences on the granite. The priestesses had gone and the twisted old woman snored on her couch. Otherwise, the temple had fallen silent.

As we went by the chapel, I saw a single lamp glowing, a single figure kneeling in prayer before the altar. Shalial Tharpit was keeping her vigil.

Tomorrow she might be given to the brutal Gramian Fotius. Why else had the man been allowed to spy on her, except that her beauty might motivate him? It was all depressingly logical.

"We need to find safe haven before daylight," Thorian said as we dressed.

"Trust the gods."

"If they can get us out of here safely, then I suppose they can provide soft beds . . . a substantial meal would not come amiss either. That goose has long flown."

"Never complain," I said, and headed for the stairway.

I stopped at the chapel and stared down at the small, pathetic figure of Shalial Tharpit before the altar. Whatever her sins, she did not deserve Fotius.

Suddenly I realized that the gods had already provided!

I knelt, then stretched out on my belly with my head and shoulders over the raised curb that ran around the opening.

"It beats being married to Dithian Lius," I said.

14: The Tale of Omar

She looked up with a gasp.

"Or Osian Pomaniuk," I added. "Or Soshiak Quairt, for that matter. Or even that Waus fellow."

"Fathmonian?"

"Precisely. The name was on the tip of my tongue."

"Who are you?"

"A friend. If you scream, or raise the alarm, then I will be apprehended, mutilated, and probably put to death."

"I rarely treat my friends so," she said coldly. "At least not without provocation."

"Then may I come down and talk with you?"

"Drop in by all means. I can spare you several minutes."

"I would not willingly disturb your devotions."

"I was asleep, actually. Now you have wakened me, we may as well talk."

Muttering warrior-type obscenities, Thorian removed his swath and lowered me into the chapel. I fell the last few feet and collapsed in a sitting position in front of Shalial. As there were no chairs available, I stayed there.

Her eyes were tinged with pink, yet she was still lovely— even in the dim lantern light, even with only her face visible. The rest of her was swathed in a shapeless white garment, and a headcloth concealed her hair. She seemed quite unperturbed by my unconventional intrusion, even amused. There was no softness in the line of her jaw, her nose was too much a Tharpit nose to be conventionally beautiful—and she was inexplicably, maddeningly, intoxicatingly beautiful.

No, it is not only skin deep. Ashfer starts with the soul.

I pulled my sleepy wits together. "I am Omar, a trader of tales, and you are Shalial Tharpit."

"Wrong. As of an hour ago, I am the Postulant Sanjala."

"I prefer Shalial."

"So do I." She looked up at the stars. "Who is your accomplice?"

"Just a strong-arm man. He is useful to have around but tends to speak in grunts and monosyllables. I doubt that he would interest you."

Fire flickered in her midnight eyes. "You presume to know my tastes upon very brief acquaintance! Loquacity is no virtue in a man."

"But in this case he is just a hulk of rippling muscle, of depressingly rigid moral standards and incorrigible recklessness. A serious young woman of religious bent would find nothing of value in his constant merriment and revelry."

The fires burned hotter. "It occurs to me now that I also should incur severe penalties were I to be discovered in this compromising situation. Flogging with willow twigs, I think, is traditional. I shall minimize censure by turning you in as soon as possible. State your business quickly so I may proceed."

"We come to rescue you, of course."

"From what?"

"From here."

"From here to where?"

Seldom have I been cornered so swiftly. Thorian and I knew nobody in Zanadon. We had no safe haven awaiting us, but Shalial must have lived in the city all her life, and she knew another interested party—her unnamed lover. Her father's mention of the man had caused her to blush with guilt. There was the refuge the gods had prepared for us! Surely the man would make us welcome if we arrived with his distressed beloved? If he did not—if he turned out to have a wife already, for example—then he could be blackmailed into cooperation.

However, I felt that to demand his name and address from Shalial at this stage in our friendship might seem premature or even presumptuous. First I must win her confidence. She was keeping vigil, and the old crone slept in the outer room—we would not be interrupted before dawn.

"I dare not state our objective until I know that you will collaborate."

Her expression became grim. "I recall very little of my mother, as she died when I was born. But I am certain that, were she here beside me now, she would—on balance—advise me against rushing off in the middle of the night in the company of two improperly dressed male burglars, one of whom speaks in grunts and monosyllables and the other who refuses to answer the simplest of questions."

"For a maiden in distress, you are less malleable than I had hoped."

"I think I feel a scream coming on," Shalial Tharpit said firmly.

"Were I to tell you why and how I came here to aid you, would that ameliorate the compulsion?"

"It might postpone the results," she said, and arranged herself cross-legged to listen.

I spurred my drowsy brain to a startled gallop.

"The mighty Jolipi River," I said, "flows from its source in Sourmere across the breadth of the Spice Lands, even to the Pearls of the Sky, where it laps the walls of the great metropolis of Urgalon."

"Spare me geography. I majored in it."

"Ah. My apologies. The details are germane to my tale, though, so bear with me while I provide a little local color. South of Urgalon, the mighty flood enters the dread gorges known as the Gates of Rosh. Rosh, you recall, is the god of tides, and the river is tidal there, unlike the Nathipi when it similarly passes through the mountains.

"Within those awesome canyons, the river god does battle twice daily with the mighty sea. Water surges in waves higher than houses, scouring high upon the cliffs, rinsing out the side chasms, and roaring fearsomely."

"I have heard of this," she said quietly. "My brother has told me of it."

I hate audiences who interrupt all the time. "These fateful passes are known as the Gates of Rosh."

"You already said so."

"Quite. But in the coastal lands, they have another name. There the people call them the Wrath of Nusk. The sprightly Nusk—who may be more familiar to you by the name of Nask—is the god of doorways and beginnings."

"And defloration!" Shalial grinned an imp's grin.

"You are getting ahead of me. As the river is the coast's doorway to the Spice Lands, the alternative designation is appropriate, also. All right so far?"

"I am agog."

"Thank you," I said politely. "Through this devilish trap must pass the produce of the land, and the trade goods inward bound to pay for them: lumpish bales of cotton, rosy planks of cedar wood, and dusty sacks of ore."

"You omit all mention of the dewy pearls and fire-flecked diamonds, rainbow-tinted parrot feathers, gossamer silks from mysterious lands at the rim of the world, desert gold of Shaifu, bloodred rubies like pigeons' eggs from the devil mines of Arkraz, and potent potions fashioned from ibex horn and powdered mummy?"

I began to feel more sympathy for Bedian Tharpit's handling of his domestic problems. "You are a merchant's daughter!"

She smirked pertly. "My father will not discuss business with a woman."

"But your brother does."

She took my guess for knowledge and was surprised. "He was until recently the family agent at Urgalon," she admitted.

"Did he ever mention the exquisite porcelain finger bowls of Leilan?"

"Not that I recall."

"A regrettable oversight. If I may continue? Perilous is the journey through the Gates of Rosh, and at some times of the month impossible. At ebb and flow the waters career madly through those rocky mouths, and innumerable fair craft have been dashed to fragments. Only at the full and again at low water may a vessel essay a brief voyage through the passes, darting from one known haven to another. Disaster awaits any who miss their required landfall even by minutes, and the entire passage of the range may take many days.''

"Four and a half, usually.''

"Thank you. Now among this mountainous land dwells a hardy race of rugged disposition. Their humble houses cluster around the known harbors, and they eke a skimpy but honest living by selling provisions to the sailors, repairing damage to the ships, and so on.''

She smirked again, hoping to shock me. "With lucrative sidelines in prostitution and petty theft.''

"True!" I said stiffly. "I was about to mention their dishonest livings. They also gather up the flotsam from the many wrecks, for they know the crannies where the waters will carry them, and from time to time they adjust the buoys and markers to maintain the supply of such materials.

"My own family dwelt apart, on a lonely slope above a narrow and treacherous side canyon known as Last Resort Cove. Ships would anchor there only rarely, when in dire distress and unable to reach the popular objective of Sweet Water Bay. On such occasions, my grandfather and uncles would venture forth, even in the worst of weathers, and drop rocks on them from a great height. Such was the velocity imparted to these missiles by their long descent that the victims would invariably be holed through the hull, and sink before the tide released them.''

Shalial drummed fingernails on the floor and for once remained silent, eyeing me narrowly.

Pressing my advantage, I continued. "A tricky undertow disposed of the crews, and the next nor'wester would break up the wreck and distribute its contents on a convenient beach. My family had been in business at the same location for generations and had established quite a reputation.

"My mother was an only daughter, who never knew her own mother, for she had died bearing her. She—my mother—was raised by her father and six brothers. It was a hard and lonely life she led, and so isolated was their abode that only once a year, at the annual Wreckers' Ball, did she even get to meet any of the neighbors. She is generally reported to have been a person of gentle disposition and unusual beauty."

"I think I could have guessed that."

"Her name . . . I should mention this because the romantic atmosphere is diminished if I must keep referring to her as 'my mother' . . . her name was Nugga. At the time of which I now tell, Nugga was seventeen and just come into the fullness of her wondrous beauty."

I gave Shalial an appraising stare and was rewarded with a faint blush.

"One day, then," I went on, "in springtime, Nugga and her brothers were down by the water's edge, picking over the rocks and shingle in search of trinkets and the trivial bounty of the sea. The weather was clement, but somewhat foggy. Engrossed in her task, Nugga had failed to notice the passage of time and had wandered too far from dry land.

"As a matter of strict fact, she had been tempted out by the opportunity to loot a couple of dead sailors, but I usually omit that particular detail."

"Understandably so."

"Tragedy struck—or so it seemed. For now my tale diverges. What my grandfather and his sons saw was this. The great bore of the incoming tide normally announces its arrival by a blood-freezing roar, like to the bellowing of a thousand sea lions. That day the breeze was off the land, and they failed to hear the warning until it was almost too late. Shouting to one another, they all fled, and only when they were almost to the safety of the cliffs did they realize that Nugga was no longer with them. They turned in dismay and saw her running seaward, seemingly heading for the shelter of a jagged rock of some height, although she must have known that it would afford her no protection in that season of spring tides. Then the wall of water came sweeping up out of the mist and engulfed her, and she was gone."

"Seventeen, you said?" Shalial bit her lip.

"Seventeen years and four days."

"You were not born yet?"

"Of course not. What my—what Nugga saw was completely different. She heard a note as of great music, sweet and tuneful and totally dissimilar to the gargling of numerous sea lions, and she observed, to her great surprise, a young man come running out of the mist, his arms open to her. He was smiling, and he was exceedingly fair to look upon, especially to a maiden who so seldom met men other than her immediate kin."

Shalial raised her eyebrows—very lovely eyebrows they were, too. "May I inquire how he was dressed?"

"I doubt that it is necessary. On the face of it, of course, he must have been Rosh, god of the tides, for that is his realm. Those are his Gates. But Rosh has not often been credited with exploits of the type that now transpired, but which I need not describe in detail. You see why I mentioned that the region is also known as the Wrath of Nusk, for Nusk is notorious . . . well, let us say that he is the god of openings and defloration, and a god does not get that sort of reputation for nothing.

"Perhaps Rosh may take on certain attributes of Nusk in that region. Similar convergence has been reported elsewhere. Be that as it may, Nugga knew at once that he was a god, and she made her decision without hesitation. Ignoring the obvious danger, she hastened to his embrace."

I fell silent for a space, and finally my listener inquired shyly, "What happened then?"

"In detail I cannot say. I suppose the usual, only more so. One does not discuss such matters with one's mother. She spoke to me sometimes in a general way of being swept up in a glory of mist, and suchlike. The particulars were always vague, often containing clumsy symbolism of spray and surging tides, and so on.

"Eventually, of course, came the ebb. My uncles went sadly down to the sea again, fervently praying that they might find Nugga's body, to give it decent burial. They found her alive and well, sleeping peacefully on a small stretch of white sand. Her clothes were missing, but she was unharmed."

"Rosh, of course, would have returned her?"

"One assumes it would be in his nature to do so."

"And nine months later . . ."

"Eight. I was a premature baby, which may explain a slight tendency to impetuosity in my character."

Shalial said, "Mmm," thoughtfully. "What exactly does all this have to do with me?"

"Ah. I am getting to that. The one incident that Nugga clearly recalled and was willing to relate—indeed she never tired of telling it—was this. Right at the end, she lay in the god's arms on the sand as the last waves were sweeping around them.

" 'I must go,' he said sadly, 'for it is my invariant resolve to wait for no man, or woman, either. And you now must choose. You may come with me and I will see you safely to Morphith's realm, or you may return to the world of mortals. If that is your choice, know that you will never meet me again. Nor will you ever love a mortal man, for none who has known the love of gods can ever be satisfied by less.'

" 'And of course I will bear your child?' she said.

" 'It is obligatory,' the god remarked, somewhat smugly."

Shalial sighed. "A touching tale! Not overly original, but embellished with some notable digressions."

"It is not done," I said. "For now Nugga inquired of her lover, 'But is it not customary for a god who has sired a child upon a mortal to honor his offspring with some divine gift?' "

"Aha! Resourceful of her! We come to the bones of the matter?"

"Verily.

" 'It is so,' the god said, smiling the radiant smile of his divinity. 'Choose, then, what blessing I may bestow upon him.' "

Shalial sighed again, and even in her shapeless novice's cloak, her sigh was an endearing motion. "And what did your mother—Nugga, I mean—what did she say then?"

"She said, 'I would rather have a girl.' "

Shalial opened her dark eyes very wide and pursed her scarlet lips. "Oh! A little tactless, maybe?"

"The god was perturbed, yes. He frowned divine anger and told her she should have said so sooner. So Nugga made the best of it, and demanded that the son she was to bear might be granted the gift of foretelling the future."

Shalial whistled silently.

" 'You ask much,' the god said. 'The gift of prophecy is rarely bestowed, and invariably brings such unhappiness to mortals that I shall not wish it upon any child of mine.' "

"Nugga insisted?"

"She had a stubborn streak, I fear. And she knew her rights."

" 'Very well,' the god said, rising to his feet. 'He shall see the future in dream, but in my divine mercy, I shall so limit his gift that he may foresee only the future of others, and even then only when he may use it to avert great sorrow.'

"And so he ran off the way he had come, and vanished in mist."

The chapel fell silent with the wistful stillness that follows the conclusion of a fine tale well told, a bittersweet nostalgia as the fable dissolves away into memory.

I could see that Shalial was impressed. She was very young, of course, and my heart was warmed by her innocent loveliness, as revealed in the gentle light of the lamp upon the altar. That lamp had begun to flicker and jump in a way I had not previously registered . . .

"You can foretell the future?" she asked.

"I dream of things yet to be. The gods speak to me in dream as they speak to us all, but to me they seem to speak more clearly."

"You have dreamed of me?" she asked, and again a faint pinkness suffused her cheeks.

"Indeed I have, many times. The dreams began almost a year ago, when I sojourned at a distant city named, er, Fogspith."

"I have heard of Fogspith," she said, frowning.

"This is another Fogspith, much farther way. Summoned by the terrible sorrow I sensed in my dreams, and knowing that by the god's gift to me, I—and only I—could avert that tragedy, I set out at once in search of you. I have journeyed far and long, and ever as I drew nearer, the dreams grew clearer.''

She twisted her hands together, staring down at them. "What did your dreams tell you?" she whispered.

"They told me of great beauty, of course, and of youth and innocence and virtue. They told me of love denied.''

"Oh?'' The hand-wringing grew more urgent.

"They told me of the awful choices thrust upon you— Fathmonian and that gang. They showed me how you spurned them, how you were cruelly cast out in the middle of the night, and brought here, to the temple, to face a lifetime of deprivation and hard service. They told me of a faithful lover weeping, never knowing what had become of the woman who owned his heart.''

"Oh!'' Shalial kept her eyes averted from me, but her hands fell still. Somewhat perturbed by that, I continued.

"And they showed me that I must risk my own well-being and even perhaps my life to break into this fastness, spurning the awful risks involved, to bring you these tidings. And lastly, they showed me how I would spirit you away *now*, in the dead of night, and guide you to the eager arms of the man who loves you.''

In the ensuing silence, I dared to wipe my forehead. I thought I had done rather well, considered how weary I was. Yet I had to wait a long time for her response, and when it came it was almost too quiet to hear.

"It is a fanciful yarn.''

"But the gods work in fanciful ways, oftentimes. And I have given you proof of my tale by naming for you the four men who were offered to you—the four foul demons who sought to usurp the place of true love in your heart. How else could I have known them?''

Shalial raised her eyes and studied me. "If the ichor runs so nearly pure in your veins, then you must have lived for hundreds of years, like those first mortals of the Golden Days?''

"No, I am the age I seem, but of course I hope to have many centuries of life left to me.''

"The way you are going, you should perhaps not count on them."

"You comprehend what I am risking for your sake."

"You expect me to go with you now? You and your taciturn henchman?"

"You must, or you will be buried in this mausoleum for the rest of your life. This night is the turning point. Now you must decide."

"Go where?"

"To the arms of the man you truly love, and who truly loves you."

She said, "Mmm?" thoughtfully. And then, "Indeed?" And finally, "I think I have one other question."

"Ask."

"Why are you clad in one of the wall hangings from my father's scriptorium?"

"You are deceived by a chance resemblance."

"I wove that myself."

"I wish you had mentioned the fact sooner," I said sadly.

"It might have altered things?"

"It might."

"Your parentage, even?" Shalial Tharpit impaled me with a glare that her father could not have bettered, cold as a midwinter midnight, dangerous as snakes.

I sighed. "Perhaps even that."

"I think I feel that scream coming on again."

"Then perhaps the time has come for me to leave. How long have I got?"

"About five seconds."

"I fear that may not be long enough."

Fortunately, at that moment Thorian stepped around from behind the statue of Balor.

15: The Tale of Thorian

Shalial said, "Oh!" yet again, and put her hands to her mouth. She gazed at the newcomer with wide eyes.

As I may have mentioned, Thorian was a striking figure of a man, notable for his square beard of ebony ringlets, the gory scar across his chest and abdomen, and also sheer quantity. He kept his eyes fixed on the woman as he stalked over to us. He sat down, contriving to ripple ostentatiously all over as he did so.

They continued to stare at each other in silence.

I decided that the scream had been postponed indefinitely.

"This is the man I told you of," I said. "He goes by the name of Thorian, but that is merely a *nom de guerre*, of course."

The silence continued. I glanced upward, and it seemed to me that the sky was brightening above the windows.

"His is a curious tale," I remarked. "I wish I had time to relate it."

More silence.

"Oh well," I added. "Let us make a start, anyway.

"The Kingdom of Polrain—as any accomplished geographer will know—is located far to the east of here, in the hill country where the Pearls of the Sky meet the Kulthiar Range. It is a rugged frontier terrain, whose people have for immemorial ages been guardians of Maidens Pass, and thus the Spice Lands' first line of defense against invasion. Their women are deep breasted, loving, and virtuous. Their menfolk are known for their rugged integrity, their toughness, and an overt masculinity often verging on deformity."

I dislike audiences who interrupt all the time, but it is

nice to win some response. In this case, I might as well have been talking to Maiana and Balor. Indeed, they were watching me with a stony stare fraught with suspicion, whereas the other two had eyes only for each other. I had begun to feel that I should cough politely and leave.

I didn't. "For many years, the king of Polrain was a man by the name of Nestran, a ruler of wisdom and strength, beloved of his people. Renowned for his justice, he yet tolerated no dissent, and he kept the peace with a firm hand. In the days of his strength, he sired two sons.

"The elder was named Thorax, and the younger Bindlis, and they were as alike as wine and mud.

"Thorax from his earliest days was a husky and lovable youth, gifted with innumerable virtues. He was physically powerful and yet exceeding gentle. He was fearsome in his duty, but mirthful in company and faithful to the gods. The family and the palace staff adored him, and as he grew in years and became more widely known throughout the land, the people's love for him spread until it knew no limits. He achieved a remarkable manhood, gifted with an awesome physical presence and unsurpassed skill in the use of arms. He was upright, just, and devout. His mind was as sharp as his sword, and all were agreed that he would equal or perhaps even surpass his father Nestran when the time came for him to rule over his people."

Still the only reaction was a flickering from the lamp.

"The younger son was a weakling and a coward. He was ugly to look upon, despicable in his behavior, and corrupt in his morals. When his brother was mastering sword and bow and pony—even as a stripling surpassing men of mature years—Bindlis would skulk among the palace kitchens, harassing the juvenile servants and dabbling in surreptitious baking of cupcakes. Upon reaching adolescence, he swiftly embarked upon a career of lechery and unnatural vice.

"Thus the whole kingdom rejoiced that the elder prince was so wholesome and a fitting successor for mighty Nestran, and that the younger son had little chance to ascend the throne.

"And in time it came to pass that the old king sank into

a grievous sickness, and the people mourned his imminent passing, while yet rejoicing that he would be so well followed.

"But, alas!"

Thorian shot me a surprised glance. It was brief, but it was an improvement.

"One day, when the king's final breath seemed but hours delayed, Thorax received an urgent appeal to visit one of the humble cottages situated on the hills overlooking the palace. Normally nothing would have dragged him from the vigil he kept at his father's sickbed—and I should mention that Bindlis was elsewhere, having chosen this inauspicious time to indulge in an orgy of simony and sophism—but in this case the stringency of his affections caused the elder prince to rush to the stables, spring on the back of a mighty pony that none but he could ride, and speed like a hungry swallow to answer the summons.

"For in that lowly hovel was expiring a woman by the name of Dumpith, an insignificant peasant of no visible merit. Her one claim to note was that in her youth she had been employed in the palace as nurse to Prince Thorax."

Now both of them were giving me their attention, or at least some of it.

"The prince, being of an affectionate and loyal disposition, had always loved the simple woman who had cared for him in his childhood. He had seen that her later years were eased by a generous allotment, he had never forgotten her birthday, and he hastened now from the sickbed of his father to the deathbed of his nurse.

"It was a noble gesture, and a tragic error."

The sky was definitely growing brighter. I could see the skylight at the far end of the long chapel.

"In that hour of disaster, the woman Dumpith repaid the prince's devotion with a gruesome disclosure. Gasping her final breaths, she revealed the true story of his origins. She narrated how a band of vagrant warriors had come wandering through the hill country in the days of her youth, and how one of them had chosen to dally with her as she tended her father's goats. Surely I need not detail how the simple rural maiden succumbed to the hardened voluptuary's blandishments? The tale is all too familiar, and in due course the usual events produced the customary result.

"Abandoned by her paramour, shunned by her relatives, and terrified of her transgression, the girl crept away to a remote place of concealment and produced her child. The timing was such that the birth occurred on the very day that the queen in the palace was delivered of her firstborn.

"The royal labor was hard, harder perhaps than that of the sturdy peasant wench. To save further stress upon the queen and to ensure the health of the royal heir, word was passed for a wet nurse."

Now I had their attention, all of it.

"Dumpith draped her best shawl over her head and went down to the palace and volunteered to suckle the royal babe. And she falsely proclaimed that her own child had been stillborn."

Shalial said, "Oh no!"

"Alas, yes. And at the first opportunity, she substituted one for the other."

"It could not be!" she cried.

"I assure you that it is quite a common plot."

"What did she do with the prince?"

I shook my head sadly. "It does not bear repeating. This terrible crime she had concealed all her life, but at last confessed upon her deathbed, to her own grown son. And having done so, she fittingly expired.

"As Thorax rode slowly back to the palace, he heard drums beating for the king whom he had always believed to be his true father."

"But surely?" Shalial said, her eyes wide with horror. "He was the perfect successor, you said? He was the one the people wanted, you said."

"But I also said that he was a man of honor."

"Oh, gods!"

"Yea. Thorax never hesitated. He at once sought out his despicable brother and told him—as soon as he had sobered him up enough to understand—that he was the only rightful heir. And having thus performed his duty, Thorax saddled a pony and rode away into the hills."

Shalial turned to stare at Thorian. "That is awful!"

Thorian raised a bushy black brow at me and then spoke for the first time.

"It would be his duty to the gods, milady. A warrior must be true to his honor, or his life will be without all meaning."

Her gaze dropped to the jagged red line upon his chest. "That scar?"

"That scar," I said, "demonstrates the true horror of the crime. Hardly had the despicable Bindlis mounted the throne when the Vorkan fury swept over the passes and fell upon Polrain. A strong and crafty leader like Thorax might have rallied the fyrd in time, inspired it with courage, led it with flair, and doubtless crushed the evil horde upon the hills. He would have spared the Spice Lands their present travail. The craven Bindlis fled in terror, leaving the land leaderless. Polrain was overrun and destroyed."

Shalial buried her face in her hands.

"When Thorax heard of the invasion, he hastened back to serve his homeland, accompanied by a single retainer, a faithful groom who had been his friend since childhood. He was surprised upon the road by six of the Vorkan raiders. He dispatched all of them single-handed, but in the process suffered a grievous wound. The groom bore him away, and somehow kept him alive during the terrible journey that ensued, as they fled amid the sea of refugees outrunning the infestation."

She looked up with tears sparkling on her lashes. "And then?"

"And then, when his magnificent physique had recovered sufficiently that he might hope to wield a sword again, Thorax resolved to come to Unvanquished Zanadon and offer his expertise in the service of Balor, that he might thereby be revenged upon the reavers who had destroyed his people."

"But those scratches upon your necks?"

"Alas, yes. The officers of Zanadon spurn warriors from other cities. Prince Thorax was seized and fettered as a slave."

She moaned. "And you, also, the faithful childhood friend!"

I had not seen myself in the lowly role of the groom,

but it seemed wisest just to mutter humbly "One does what one can."

"That is terrible!" Shalial said. "I am glad that you managed to escape from the chain gang. But I do think that you should not linger longer around these holy precincts. You are sure to be discovered, and that could only bring trouble."

The chapel was all visible now, and dawn was imminent. I wished our young priestess were a little easier to convince.

"Milady," Thorian rumbled, "our fates are insignificant compared to the terrible intrigue that we have stumbled upon tonight, here in the temple. Tomorrow evening the venerable High Priestess Squicalm will be transported to the House of the Goddess to summon Immortal Balor."

"About time, too!"

"Perhaps. But we have certain knowledge that High Priest Nagiak does not expect the god to respond and has thus laid plans to effect a deception. The old woman will be secretly removed before dawn. You are to be substituted in her place and represented to the people as Squicalm rejuvenated. Your father is privy to this plot, and a willing accessory. Worse yet, the role of Balor will be assigned to one Gramian Fotius, grandson of War Lord Arksis. The man is a monster and a halfwit. You will be required to be consort to that brute, and I assure you that he will be worse than any of the four potential husbands your father named, or even all four of them together. This is the fate from which we seek to save you now."

Shalial clapped her hands, smiling happily. "That is the most expressive monosyllable I have heard in weeks!"

Thorian spun around on his knees to face the altar. "Mighty Sztatch, God of War, witness my oath. If I lie or have lied to this woman, may my sword fall from my hand when next I draw it in anger, may my bowels run in terror, and may I die like a cur disgraced. So be it."

He touched his face to the floor, then swung back to the girl. "I do not attest to one word of the various rigmaroles that my companion has babbled to you, but I swear on my honor as a warrior that I have spoken true."

The color had drained from her face. "You talk of sacrilege! The high priest?"

"Nagiak is the chief conspirator." Thorian was doing so well that I decided to stay out of the conversation. He was an apt pupil.

Shalial glanced nervously at the goddess by the altar. "My father? But my father is a pious man! Oh, he is a hard trader in business dealings, I grant you, but that is business. He honors the gods. He brought us up—my brother and me—to honor them, also." She turned back to Thorian, but the rising appeal in her voice sounded more as if she sought to convince herself than him. "He gives generously to the temple!"

"I am sure he does, milady."

"My brother is very devout! And I . . . I would not be here if I did not wish to serve the Great Mother. My decision tonight was not arrived at on the spur of the moment! I have thought about taking the veil ever since . . . well, for some time. The conversation with my father may have hastened matters along, but he did not force me!"

"I am sure that the high priest believes in the gods, also," Thorian said, and his deep voice held a strangely gentle note, as a statue of Fairest Ashfer may be carved from adamantine rock. "I did not say he did not, nor that your father does not. But belief in the gods is not quite the same as believing that a certain miracle will happen to order."

The child was shattered. She stared at Thorian aghast. "You, too? You think Balor will not come?"

He shook his head.

"But the Vorkans?"

"They are men and can be killed by men. Not only do I not expect Balor to come in the flesh, but I doubt if Balor has ever come in the flesh, even in ancient times. Belief in Balor may be sufficient in itself."

She licked her lips. "What can we do?" she asked hoarsely.

"Omar and I must leave at once, or we shall die and achieve nothing. You should come with us. Your absence may not stop them for long, but at least you will not be damned in their vile machinations."

"Go where? Where could I hide?"

"Where indeed, milady? We are strangers here, and know no one. You must have friends."

Dumb with horror, she shook her head.

"Your father thinks you have a, er, romantic association."

She flushed—angry and heartbreakingly vulnerable. "A lover, you mean? He is mistaken. I have no lover. And I know of no one who could or would hide me . . . neither from my father nor from the temple. I doubt if anyone in the city would do so."

The final part of that was probably true, but she was still lying about the lover. Whoever he was, I decided, he must be very prominent, and very married.

Thorian raked both hands through his hair. "Surely not everyone is so bespelled by the priesthood that they would refuse to listen to our story?"

She hugged her arms around herself and seemed to shrink. "My brother . . ." She stared at the big man for a long moment, completely ignoring me. "But Jaxian will never oppose my father! And if what you say is true, then this masquerade is necessary to give the city hope in the coming war?"

She had seen to the heart of the matter very quickly.

"I fear that is so. If you think that way, then your duty may be to cooperate with them—but you had best consult your soul and your goddess."

Shalial wrung her hands. "And you had best go."

Thorian rose to his great height and looked down sorrowfully at her. "I deplore this evil. May the gods have pity on you."

She stared at his ankles. "And on you."

"Come, Omar," he said sternly. The sky was starting to turn blue.

For once, I could think of nothing to say.

I rose and followed Thorian around the statue of Balor and out through the secret door.

16: The Coming of Rosh

✳

Thorian swung the ornamental panel closed. It shut with a *click*, leaving us in darkness.

I heard fumbling sounds; flint sparked, tinder flared into life. He lit the candle in a small horn lantern. I peered around the hidden chamber, seeing a couch and chairs and several mysterious chests. Moldy scrolls were piled in one corner, mildewed rags in another. The air had a rancid, unused smell to it.

"This place stinks," I said. "I scent some ancient evil awakening, an ancestral conspiracy shuffling its coils as it rouses from centuries of slumber."

"Just dust. I raised some dust when I came down." Thorian moved the lamp and pointed to a patch of mossy humus on the floor under the skylight. The marks of his landing were clear.

"You took quite a risk," I said, "dropping into an unknown room in the dark."

"It was better than listening to your maundering about the Gates of Rosh."

"There was much truth in that tale—more than you perhaps believe."

"There could not be less. I decided that this room must have access to the chapel, and the opening would be easier to find from this side. Now come here." He bore the lamp to the innermost corner. "See? A stair going up and a stair going down."

"Down," I said, and down we went.

The walls were rough and damp in places, the treads often treacherous. The stonework was narrow and uneven, in marked contrast to the fine finish of the rest of the

142

temple. Thorian went first, carrying the lantern, and I had to stumble along as best I could in his shadow. The passage seemed to go on forever, down and down into the heart of the pyramid. One thing I was sure of was that we were not going to meet fat Nagiak running up to meet us.

In fact, the draperies of cobweb said that no one had traveled those stairs in centuries. They might well lead to a dead end, and in that case we should be trapped within the temple until nightfall, without food or drink. Worse— with the high priestess keeping vigil in the House of the Goddess, worshippers might soon become so rife throughout the whole edifice that we should be unable to escape for days. The gods had brought me to Zanadon to be a witness; they had never promised I would grow fat on the job.

Nor had they ever promised that I would see Balor appear in glory. Thorian's deadly logic was becoming more and more convincing, because my divine masters were backing him up—obviously I had been led to the chapel of the high priestess to overhear the conspiracy. I had been prevented from rescuing the lovely Shalial because she was a necessary part of the plan. Whatever she might be going to suffer from the odious Gramian Fotius, and however much I might deplore her suffering, that also was decreed. The tale I would carry from Zanadon was not the tale I had expected.

Thorian stopped dead and I walked into him. It was a similar sensation to ramming a moderately sized cedar. He hardly seemed to notice.

The stairs had ended and we were underground. The lackluster yellow glow of the lantern revealed a dismal catacomb stretched off on either hand. Arches divided it at intervals, helping to support the corbeled roof. The air was fetid with decay and a stink of rats, making my head swim.

Thorian grunted and headed to the right, holding the lamp high. Dust rose around our feet. The first two sections were empty. The next was not. We walked over together and looked down at the debris against the far wall.

My belly knotted, and the lurching throb in my head grew worse.

At first I saw only a spread of dry sticks, all coated with monochrome dust to match the floor, indistinct in the shadowy light, and yet I knew I was seeing more than that and my mind would not accept what my eyes were telling it. Among this litter, round things like ostrich eggs stared with empty sockets and grinned with teeth.

"Six of them," Thorian muttered. "I think six."

"At least five," I agreed. It was hard to speak without gagging. There might even have been more than six, for the oldest bones had crumbled, and shards of pottery mimicked skulls. At least one of the skulls had been cleft by a blade, but I could make out chains and fetters. Shreds of skin and dried flesh and cloth clung to others . . . hair, too, in the dust.

Thorian bent and lifted a long bone. He measured it against his own thigh. "A big man."

He threw down the relic and turned away. I tottered along the crypt behind him without another word, my legs wavering like cornstalks. We must escape quickly, or the foul air would add our bones to that gruesome ossuary.

I still have nightmares about that place. The pottery bothers me more than anything. I can believe that the chains were no more than an oversight, left there because leaving them was easier than stripping them off corpses, but pots suggest food, and water jugs. I want to believe that the victims were already dead or as good as dead when they arrived. For all I truly know, they may have been criminals or renegade priests or anyone, but I knew then what Thorian was thinking, and I believed it myself. I still do.

A chirurgeon or apothecary could learn much from those bones. He could tell us whether any of the victims had been women. He might reassure us that some of the men had been old when they died. I would like to believe that Balor, once he has saved his people, is allowed to reign over Zanadon for a human span, if he wishes. After all, a living god must eventually return whence he came, vanishing as mysteriously as he arrived. Even if he eventually expires peacefully in bed, he must not leave a rotting corpse behind him. The temple does need a secret tomb to hold his remains. I want to believe that Thorian and I that night stumbled into nothing more than that, a communal tomb.

But earlier in the evening Thorian had asked what happened when Balor had completed his task of saving Zanadon. If the gods had not now answered the question, at least they had dropped a weighty hint. Little as I cared for Gramian Fotius, I could never wish such a fate upon him— chained and helpless in that tomb, waiting to die. Worse yet was the possibility that Balor's consort might sometimes suffer the same grisly fate. I dearly wished that I could drag Bedian Tharpit and War Lord Arksis down there to show them the evidence.

We passed the stairway by which we had entered. The next few sections of the tunnel were empty. The two after that were cluttered with collapsed remains of shelving, rotted chests, piles of decaying leather. A few scrolls had rolled away from the others and were recognizable as having once been documents. These were the temple archives, and some of them must be centuries old. The rats had enjoyed them.

Now we had traversed the catacomb from one end to the other, and were faced with a flight of steps and a trapdoor. Perpetual night reigned in the crypt, but outside the day was beginning, and the temple dwellers would be stirring.

"Well, Trader of Tales?" Thorian said, studying my face in the spectral light of the lantern. "Will your gods guide us safely out?"

"Of course." I mounted the steps. In truth, I was so ill from the foul air that I hardly cared what was waiting for me—but I thought it better not to say so. I placed my hands against the stone and heaved.

It rose silently, and apparently into darkness. Reassured, I lifted it farther. Light poured in so suddenly that I almost dropped the trap—the crash would have roused half the temple. At the same time dust swirled into my eyes. I was under a rug, and I had not realized that. I listened and heard the unmistakable sound of snoring. As

I wriggled through the gap, Thorian took the weight, and I thrust my head out from under the cover to survey the room. It was large and luxuriously furnished, with colorful hangings and shiny woodwork. Dawn shone in through a high window. The brutish snortings came from High Priest Nagiak, bloated in crimson silk pajamas, sprawled on a downy bed.

Had he awakened in the next few minutes, he would have observed his carpet doing some very strange things—bulging, excreting a skinny man with a close-cropped beard, then rising even farther as a second, larger man emerged, also. He might have heard whispered curses when the two intruders broke fingernails in lowering the flagstone gently back into place. But the gods and a very late night kept him snoring.

We straightened the rug, padded silently across to the door, and departed. The corridor was, of course, deserted.

I have a very good sense of direction, and I had no doubts that we were now on the west side of the temple, and at ground level. We marched quickly ahead, heading for the patch of brightness that spelled exit, and safety—relative safety, that is. We must still avoid the city guard, but once away from the sacred precincts, we need fear nothing worse than a quick death. Flogging and slavery seemed minor perils now.

Perhaps it was the aftereffects of the foul air in the cellars; perhaps I was merely shocked into insensibility by the bludgeoning of a long, hard night, but I was too numb to be worried. I think Thorian was in much the same mood.

"Where do we go now, Trader?" he growled, without bothering to lower his voice.

"To find the lover, of course."

"The girl's lover? Shalial's? You know who he is?"

"I know who can identify him for us."

Just before we reached the exit, a side door opened and a young priestess emerged. We stopped dead to avoid running into her. She clasped her hands to her mouth in rank disbelief. Then she slumped silently to the ground.

We stepped over her and kept on going.

"You always have that effect on women?" I asked.

Thorian grunted. "No. They usually fall backward."

We swung out boldly through the main portal. The sun was not yet up, but there was plenty of light. To our right, the gate to the temple garden was just closing behind someone. Ahead, in the cloisters, five or six priests were immersed in conversation. They did not notice us as we turned left, went out between the pillars, and continued our journey across the Courtyard. Now we were off forbidden ground and could breathe a little easier.

A few diehard worshippers still knelt before their chosen gods, but the guards had gone. Tiny as bugs, we passed Maiana's lofty ankles and headed across the Courtyard of a Thousand Gods.

Thorian had been thinking. As we passed through the arcade of pillars onto the Great Way, he demanded, "You are going to talk with her brother?"

"Of course."

"It is unthinkable!"

"I don't think he is part of the plot. He has a conscience—you heard how he felt about the price of bread."

Thorian snorted furiously. "That was a minor detail compared to this!"

"Exactly."

We passed a few arriving worshippers. They glanced curiously at our irregular attire, but seemed to conclude that it was none of their business—which it wasn't, of course.

I risked an upward glance. Maiana glared down at me out of the corner of her eye as if warning me never to reveal the terrible secret I had learned. Hastily I checked Balor. He seemed no more threatening than he had the previous day—indeed, perhaps less so, almost amused. Balor or Krazath or whatever other name he is known by, he is always the Fickle One.

I had come to Zanadon believing I had been summoned by Balor himself, but now I wondered if some other god might have been meddling. Any mortal who becomes involved in divine politics can anticipate serious trouble. Here in Maiana's city, I was totally in the power of the

Passionate; few of the gods can withstand her at the best of times. If she chose to stamp on a humble trader of tales prying around in Zanadon itself, then what god would dare incur her wrath by coming to my defense?

Thorian was still scowling ferociously. "You think the brother will help us?"

"If he doesn't, then I don't know who will."

"The girl said he would never oppose their father."

"She also said he is devout."

"You will tell him about the trickery?"

"I expect so," I said, yawning. "Let's try this alley here."

We turned aside from the Great Way, which was becoming dangerously well populated.

"You are crazy!"

"So you keep saying."

Roosters crowed hoarsely in the yards and dogs barked. Once or twice we saw people moving in the distance; we heard voices and caught tantalizing whiffs of bread baking. Shutters were being thrown open. Soon the sun's first rays would rouse the eagles that nest on Balor's helmet, and already there was a sense of the heat of the day to come. I forced my aching legs along the shadowed canyons, seeking always to move downhill. I was pondering all the things that had happened to me since the previous dawn, and my mind was as clogged as the weedy bayous of the Nathipi delta. I could feel twinges from every weary muscle in my carcass.

"Omar," Thorian growled, "this is folly! You have amply shown me that the gods will aid you, but you told me yourself that there is a difference between trusting them and tempting them. We have no reason at all to expect succor from Jaxian Tharpit! He is more like to have our heads chopped off, for we possess information inimical to the fortunes of his house."

Alas, in my fatigued condition I had no patience for my companion's misgivings.

"You are wrong," I said. "The gods have given me a way to win his support."

"How?"

"You saw it yourself. Remember that Jaxian Tharpit is a devout man and was for some time his father's agent in Urgalon. The girl told us so."

"My life is at stake. I will not play your silly guessing games!"

"Then trust me!" I snapped. The alley we had been following now divided, and I was trying to choose between two equally insalubrious alternatives. Both sloped steeply, both were rank with garbage, and both so narrow that we could not walk abreast.

"I am not inclined to do so. Be reasonable! Surely we can find some safe refuge in this warren—an attic, or a granary? We are nimble and resourceful. I will guarantee to rip open any shutter you care to select, and we shall spy out some place to lie low until dark, even if we must endure hunger and thirst. I would rather bake on a roof all day than fall into the hands of the city guard. To return to the Tharpit establishment is madness. Abandon such folly!"

Regrettably, I allowed my weariness to overrule my customary good manners. I did not even bother to reply.

"Fare you well, friend," Thorian snarled behind me.

"You, also."

I stumbled along the cobbles in silence. When next I looked around, sunlight blazed on Balor's golden helmet, and I was alone.

The gods guided my feet back to the gate I had left unlocked. For a few minutes I leaned against the wall, mourning my discourtesy and the absence of my doughty companion. I was so weary that I could have stretched out on the dirt of the alley and tumbled at once into sleep. I was too weary to be nervous. I pushed open the gate and slipped into the yard—familiar, yet seeming larger in daylight. I fumbled in the folds of my swath to find the key I had stolen, and that episode felt like years ago, instead of merely a few hours. Once inside the mansion, I relocked the door and replaced the key on its nail.

The house was silent still. I advanced from vantage point to vantage point, neither seeing nor hearing a soul. Eventually I forced my wobbling legs into a run and scampered up the stairs. I headed for the door of Jaxian's bedchamber.

It was time for me to become a god.

In my bemused state, I rehearsed for myself the arguments I wished I had bothered to speak aloud for Thorian: "Jaxian Tharpit was posted in Urgalon. A merchant in that city must of necessity be greatly concerned with the passage of vessels through the Gates of Rosh, and his sister said he is a devout man. He will have prayed often to the god of tides. Since he returned to Zanadon, will he not have continued the practice?"

I opened the door with all the slow deliberation of a flower opening petals. I slid through it and closed it again with equal diligence.

In a room both spacious and bright, the wide bed lay empty, a smooth plain of silken weaving. Everywhere I saw riches: wall hangings of flowers and seashells, garment chests inlaid with precious stones, floors softened by rich wool, low tables of onyx and jasper bearing golden combs and pins, alabaster jars, and a polished silver mirror as large as dinner plate.

At the far side, wide doors led out to a trellised balcony. The couch there was occupied. In summer the people of the Spice Lands sleep below the stars.

"You see, Thorian," I said in my mind, "even in the uncertain light of a torch, you noticed the resemblance. Such a coincidence can only be sent by the gods as a sign."

I unfastened my swath and let it fall.

"The enemy is at the gate," I explained. "The inhabitants of Zanadon expect a god to appear to them within the next few days."

Mother-naked as the statue, I paced across the floor.

"If one god can appear, then surely another can?" I asked the absent Thorian. "And Jaxian is a devout man. He will recognize the likeness." I was on the patio, standing by the bed. My heart was pounding in a most ungodlike fashion.

"It is a blasphemy to impersonate a god, I admit, but I have been directed to do this."

I put my hands against my thighs and donned the cryptic smile of Rosh.

"Mortal!" I proclaimed. *"Awake! I have business with you!"*

The figure in the bed rolled over.

She sat up, honoring me with a view of lush but shapely breasts. She stared at my nudity in horror. Equally dumbfounded, I stared back at hers. We awoke from our trances simultaneously. She pulled the cover up to her sagging chin. I spun around and headed for the door. She . . . I have heard some screams in my time, and perhaps even some louder screams, but for sheer persistence, never any to better hers.

17: Another Hard Day

❋

I was halfway down the stairs before I noticed the four armored men waiting below with drawn swords. Deciding that the upper floor might yet be more hospitable, I reversed direction. Three more soldiers were closing in at the top. I stopped, trapped in the middle. The screams continued unabated, like a fire alarm. More people were emerging from doorways all around the gallery and innumerable servants came flooding into the atrium.

I had no clothes on.

The usual penalty for rape is torture followed by slow impalement. In cases of attempted rape, the torture may be omitted—but not necessarily. It depends. I had no evidence that penal laws in Zanadon would be more enlightened than those elsewhere.

The situation called for clear thinking and a cool head. Unfortunately, while the shivers traversing my spine were cold enough, my brain seemed to be packed with boiling mud. I had certainly blundered badly. I can only blame my fatigue. Obviously those bronze-scaled thugs had been waiting for me, and they should not be able to breathe without making leather creak and metal clink. I ought to have heard them, or sensed them. I had not.

The gallery military force continued to advance, prompting me to resume my descent. When I stood on the bottom tread and the captain's sword point hovered in front of my navel, I stopped and smiled winsomely. Upstairs, someone cut off the screaming with a hard slap.

Bedian Tharpit himself came jostling through the crowd to stand at the captain's side. He wore a simple bathrobe of blue cotton. His gray beard and hair were tousled, his eyes blurred with sleep, but his hard, coarse face bore a scowl of pleasure.

"You were quite correct, Captain! They did plan to return."

Probably Tharpit had discovered evidence of intruders soon after escorting the high priest to his carriage. Perhaps he had decided to take a bath or check some record in his accounts room. Naturally the civic guard would jump when a mogul like Tharpit jerked its string. The missing key and the unlocked gate . . . I am not usually so careless, but this seemed a poor time to say so.

The captain was a rough-faced character with an unfashionably forked beard. He did not look friendly. "Only one of them, milord."

"Make him talk, then."

"Why, you must be Jaxian's father!" I exclaimed. "I am honored, milord." I attempted a bow, but the sword flicked at my face. I straightened up hastily.

"Where are your accomplices, rogue?" demanded the captain.

I allowed my face to indicate shock. "Accomplices?" I looked an appeal to Tharpit. "Milord, is there some misunderstanding here?"

An amused expression merely increased the menace in his face. "I don't think so. The facts seem plain enough. Or are you merely one of my son's drinking companions come looking for a final nightcap?"

I was aware of Jaxian standing in the background, peering over heads. I pretended not to be.

"I am a business associate of his," I said confidently. "He must have mentioned me—Omar of Arkraz, a dealer in gems?"

A faint trace of doubt glinted in Tharpit's eyes, or it may have been cupidity. The soldiers were grinning in anticipation of the coming interrogation. A sidelong glance encouraged me to believe that Jaxian's hangover despair was now tempered with confusion.

"Your business attire is unorthodox, Merchant," Tharpit said.

"Urniamist."

"What?"

"I am a devotee of Urniam," I explained, "goddess of babes and innocence. To avoid the temptations of vain display, the Ingenuous forbids us to wear clothes except in public places or within assemblies of unbelievers. Had I realized that this gathering would be so large, I would have stretched the point and remained clad. If it distresses you, I will waive my scruples and accept a suitable garment."

"Incredible impudence," Tharpit muttered. He turned his head and bellowed. "Jaxian?"

The tall man pushed through the crowd. His eyes were storm-weather sunsets. I could hear his headache.

His voice was a thin croak. "Father?"

"Do you know this man?"

Jaxian blinked blearily at me. I was wearing Rosh's cryptic smile, although it required considerable concentration under the circumstances.

"P-p-perhaps his face d-d-does seem familiar," Jaxian said uneasily.

"Balor preserve me!" his father growled. "One of your tavern cronies, I suppose?"

"Sir!" I barked, making Jaxian wince. "I have told you that I am a follower of Urniam! Red meat and spirituous fluids are strictly forbidden to the Elect. No, your son and I were introduced in Urgalon by a mutual friend, a shipping broker. We opened negotiations on a sizable shipment of the arterial rubies for which Arkraz is infamous, but Jaxian's departure ended discussions for the time being. I promised to look him up when I arrived in Zanadon. Then last night we met by chance in the street—"

"No," Jaxian said with an effort. "No, I do not know him."

"You're sure?" his father asked, as if that situation would be unusual.

Jaxian closed his eyes and mumbled. "C-c-completely. I never forget voices."

I had been hoping that the large young man's memories of the previous evening would be less distinct. That plan had just collapsed, evidently. I needed another right away.

I shot him a glance of incredulity and then chuckled with sudden understanding.

"What he means is," I whispered, "that the matter is highly confidential and we should repair to some more private place to discuss the details."

"What he means is that you haven't spoken a true word yet!"

I am always disconcerted when the chosen villain turns out to have a sense of humor—the only truly satisfactory villains are the utterly despicable. On the other hand, it can be an advantage in the confrontation scenes. Bedian Tharpit was enjoying my performance. His pleasure was nastily reminiscent of small boys vivisecting a kitten and not the sort of artistic esteem I normally pursue, but at least I had not started to bleed yet.

Starting to run short of good ideas, I decided to gamble that Jaxian's tortured expression indicated some remaining shreds of doubt and was more than the effects of his thunderous hangover.

"Naturally," I said, "in a matter so confidential, I have spoken more elliptically than is my wont. Once we are rid of the spectators, I shall disclose the meat of the matter."

"You have nothing left to disclose that is not already visible," said Tharpit Senior. "Captain—"

Jaxian groaned. "I'm not sure!" he wailed. "P-p-p-p-perhaps I have seen his face b-b-b-before!"

His father, the captain, and I all looked up at him in disgust. Jaxian Tharpit had no more substance to him than a bad smell.

"Did you invite him to this house?" his father snapped.

"Oh no! Never."

A grunt of satisfaction. "Then we can proceed with confidence."

"Insanity?" I said. "Not Urniam but Foofang? Obviously I must be insane to return here. If this approach interests you, I can do very good convulsions. You'll have to stand back and give me more room, though."

Tharpit ignored my offer. "Well, let's see what the charge is." He looked up at the spectators in the gallery. "Mandial? Was the woman harmed?"

An elderly, hard-faced matron answered the question. "No. Just fright. He didn't touch her."

"He would have had to be a very fast worker," the captain remarked, eyeing me with distaste.

"But he left this by the door." The Mandial woman unfurled the wall hanging, dangling it over the rail for all to see. My night's activities had not improved its condition. Filth from the temples catacomb fell off like smoke.

"So where are your accomplices?" The captain prodded the top of my right thigh with the point of his sword, drawing blood.

"I have no accomplices. I never had accomplices."

"You wore *two* slave collars?" Left thigh, closer.

"I don't know where he is. We parted when we left here." I am chagrined to admit that I could think of nothing *constructive* to say. That is a very rare experience for me, and always unpleasant. In this case the truth was going to be of very limited use. If I mentioned priests or temples, or even Balor, Tharpit would have my tongue out in an instant.

I set to work on Jaxian again, applying my best You-are-making-a-terrible-mistake look.

Up in the gallery, the Mandial woman howled. "Bedian! Where is Shalial?"

Four or five other women screamed in chorus as they recognized the absence. A group of them rushed to inspect one of the bedrooms.

I caught Jaxian's eye meaningfully.

His father flushed with fury. He would have preferred a more discreet family gathering to make his announcement.

"Shalial is well!" he bellowed. "Her absence has nothing to do with this man."

I raised my eyebrows at Jaxian and shook my head. He blanched, or perhaps the greenish tinge above his beard turned bluer, but he definitely changed color. Progress!

Bedian noticed. He regarded me with startled suspicion. I felt a cold trickle of sweat emerge from my left armpit. I needed to pass a message to the son without informing the father—who was smarter, better informed, and infinitely more clear-headed at the moment. To inform the father of my knowledge would be worse than failing to inform the son. . . .

Everyone was waiting on Bedian to explain. He did so without taking his eyes off me. "The lady Shalial has chosen to enter the service of the Holy Mother. We discussed the matter last night, and I gave her my blessing. I delivered her safely into the hands of the temple."

Evidently young Jaxian had not been informed earlier. His jaw hung slack and his eyes bulged. I could forget about help from him.

"May we move the prisoner outside for questioning, milord?" inquired the captain. "I don't want to get blood and stuff all over your floors."

Tharpit frowned. He was working out the timing. He must see that I could have overheard his talk with Nagiak. He wasn't sure what I might start spilling in addition to my bodily fluids.

"I think we can assume he is just a common thief, Captain."

The soldiers looked disappointed, especially the captain.

"Whatever you want, milord. We can turn him in for rape and burglary, or just kill him here, if you wish to be merciful."

"That would be very messy," I complained, "and contrary to due process. I have a good line in curses, too."

The twin prongs of the soldier's beard twitched. "Take what you can get, lad. Rape executions are the most popular of all."

"Slain while resisting arrest?" Tharpit was obviously attracted by the thought.

I had no wish to be the main event at a public execution, but I have always believed that death should be faced with the firmest possible procrastination. "You have far too many witnesses who know I made no resistance!" I said.

The witnesses had lost interest in me, though. Servants and family alike were whispering excitedly about Shalial. They would neither care nor notice if I was embalmed alive where I stood.

"He could try to escape when you get him out in the yard?" Tharpit suggested.

"Oh, certainly," said the captain. "We can set up something convincing with that spiked gate."

"I protest!" I said bitterly. "I have religious scruples against shedding blood." I was ignored.

"Oh, Bedian!" said the Mandial woman. "You won't leave him hanging there screaming for hours like the last one?"

"What about the Escaped Slave reward?" I said, having nothing better left up my sleeve—and no sleeve.

Soldier and merchant suddenly became thoughtful. Tharpit's eyes glinted as they had when I had mentioned rubies. "That would cover your fee?" Tharpit said.

"Most of it." That warrior must have merchant blood in him!

"More than cover it, Captain, if I recall the amounts correctly." Who could doubt that Bedian Tharpit would recall the amounts correctly?

He eyed me appraisingly again, weighing my monetary value against the risk of letting me live. Inevitably, cash won. Even if I knew something—even if I told it to every slave on the walls—what harm could I ever do to Bedian Tharpit? I would be dead in a few days anyway.

"That's best. You can have him, Captain. Turn him in and keep the reward in lieu of a fee. See your men get a fair share."

I jumped as the warrior swung his sword up in salute. I looked for Jaxian, but he had gone. He had worse things to worry about than a mad burglar. And I had worse things to worry about than him.

At this point I could attempt to narrate how it feels to be marched in fetters across a city, being driven at sword point by a squad of sadists who have just been deprived of an enjoyable interrogation. I could outline the sensation of arriving starving at a slave camp after the daily meal has been served, too late to partake of it. I could perhaps even sketch my feelings during a day of enforced hard labor on an empty stomach after a whole night without sleep—all under the merciless sun of the Spice Lands.

I won't, though.

It might sound like complaint.

18: The Tale of Omar

❊

The ancient walls of Zanadon stand at the top of the precipice that encircles the hill, but no cliff is ever unbroken. Here and there, even that impregnable escarpment is notched by gullies which the battlements must span. At one of these, on the western face, water had undermined the foundations, and the wall had collapsed. From the look of the trees growing amid the debris on the slope, the failure had happened generations ago. Lazy and secure, the citizens had never bothered to mend the gap—until now, with the Vorkans almost upon them.

I was assigned with five others to a capstan, and that was a comparatively easy posting. The job description was well within my comprehension. All I had to do was push on a beam and walk around and around and around and around . . .

Every hour or so, a halfwit boy brought us a smelly waterskin. Gears and ropes creaked, and blocks of stone rose from the depths. The overseer preferred to sit in the shade and watch. When he felt required to motivate, though, he tended to express his irritation with excessive zeal.

There was a fair breeze on top of the walls there, and a splendid view, and those helped lighten the day. The sky of the Spice Lands is enormous and deep blue. Westward the paddy fields and orchards of the plain stretch off to eternity, for they meet the Huli Desert somewhere beyond the curve of the world.

The work site was a busy, bustling place. Slaves and slavedrivers toiled together under the watchful eyes of clanking soldiers. Far below us, gangs of men and ponies gathered up the fallen blocks, uprooting forest to get at them. Along the rising wall, masons and more slaves levered and hammered and slapped mortar, rebuilding the noble buttresses. On a better day, I could have felt proud to be helping raise such a monument, knowing it would endure for centuries to come.

My neighbor to the fore was a farmer from the Farbloo Hills. He was cheerful enough, considering that he had lost his wife and four children and had no idea what had happened to them, while having a very good idea of what was going to happen to him. The younger man at my back was a deserter from the Forbin militia, who regarded his present torment as divine punishment for cowardice. I was disinclined to argue the point. His guilt and melancholy made him very poor company.

The blocks we raised were deposited on sleds and then dragged to the construction site by teams of four men. Thorian appeared an hour or so after I did and was assigned to dragging one of the sleds. He had obviously resisted arrest, for his face had been pulped and his back was a shambles of bleeding welts. I waved a cheerful greeting, to which he responded with a gesture I did not recognize. I am still not sure what sentiment it conveyed, but it amused his companions.

Yes, that day was irksome. I passed most of it with my eyes closed and in a taciturnity foreign to my nature.

But I had come to Zanadon and I was still alive. I had been shown the truth behind the Balor legend, and now the gods had put me away in a safe nook to await the events I must witness. They could have chosen a more comfortable nook, of course, but this one was at least secure.

I assumed that I was being instructed to meddle no further in the affairs of Shalial Tharpit and Gramian Fotius. I had no means to do so anyway—a slave's life is mercifully free from worrisome decisions.

My only danger was that of dying from heart strain and exhaustion, and those are relatively unlikely perils. Another major benefit of being a slave is that there is nothing much left to fear.

* * *

The sun was drooping near the horizon when a sudden shout halted our work. Chocks were thrown in to immobilize the mechanism while the block we were raising still spun in midair. Our minds were all so blurred by exhaustion that we did not question this change in routine; we just collapsed over our beams with gasps of joy.

Suddenly I was hauled upright and the overseer unlocked my chains. I slumped to the ground. He kicked me a few times, but I was beyond responding to kicks. Eventually two soldiers arrived to drag me to my feet and march me forcibly over to the shade of the supervisors' awning. I heard cracks and groans as the remaining five men were set to work once more. I felt badly that . . . No, to be honest, I didn't.

I peered blearily at the group waiting for me. Half a dozen or so were unusually shiny soldiers, two or three were civilians, who looked notably clean and colorfully garbed. One of those was obviously the leader. He was tall and broad. He had a proud beak of nose above a magnificent jet beard. He was clad in a swath of rainbow hues, clasped by a richly jeweled pin. His flower-pot hat almost touched the canvas overhead, and he stood with thick arms folded across an admirable chest. I was swaying on my feet in front of him before I realized that he was Jaxian Tharpit.

"I think that's the one," he said. "Is he conscious?"

Someone punched me in the kidneys to see. Then they picked me up again. I tried to make my eyes focus, struggling to reconcile this splendid noble with the drunken, stuttering ninny I had seen earlier.

"What is your name?" he demanded.

"I told you," I said, drifting out of focus again.

I was punched again and lifted to my feet again. That time someone had kicked dirt in my face, and I had to blink away tears.

"Omar of Arkraz?"

"Correct."

He frowned threateningly. I could guess that he was wary because of all the listeners, but I had no sympathy for him. I assumed that he had spent all day in an agony of irresolution, trying to find out exactly what had happened to Shalial, trying to remember where he had seen my face before, trying to screw up his courage to come to the work site and screw down his dignity to interview a slave, trying to imagine what his daddy would say if he found out, and meanwhile I had been going around and around and around and around . . .

"Why did you come back to the house?"

"To talk with you, of course."

He barked, "Leave him be!" just in time to save me another blow. I was running out of kidneys, and knees.

"I'm a very busy man. I didn't come here to play guessing games. What did you want to talk with me about?"

I pulled my wits in another notch. "About a very confidential matter."

He shrugged and glanced at the sun impatiently. "You will have to do better than that!"

"It is not something I can discuss in this company," I retorted, indicating the military with a shaky wave. A few hands went to sword hilts, fists clenched, and the overseer raised his whip.

Jaxian cleared his throat and they all froze. "Put him on that chair. And the rest of you may withdraw. This will only take a moment."

I turned around and departed. I must have surprised everyone, because I had staggered halfway to the capstan before I was grabbed and hauled back to the presence. I was dropped onto the chair, and all my joints cracked at the sudden change of position.

Jaxian eyed me with a little more interest. "What was that for?"

"Just give me a few minutes, milord," the overseer begged, "and he'll cause no more trouble. A dozen lashes? Six at least!"

"Silence! Explain, Omar."

"If you want to hear what I have to say," I retorted, "then you will have to make me a better offer than a few minutes in a chair. If I talk now, you will go away, and Musclehead there will beat me to shreds. I haven't slept in two nights or eaten in days, and all because I tried to do you a good turn."

Several men tried to speak at once, but Jaxian silenced them with a glance. He seemed amused at my insolence. "Give me one clue that you have something of value to say."

It was fair enough. A man of any real gumption would have told the overseer to start in on my hide, just to see what would happen.

"Postulant Sanjala," I said.

He recoiled. He paled above his beard. "P-p-postu . . . ?" He chewed his mustache and then switched to fingernails. Now I recognized the Jaxian I had seen before. Everyone else watched him in puzzled silence.

"Very well, Omar," he said at last. "I'll see you g-g-get a square meal and a night's sleep in comfort, whatever you have to say. If it's worth more than that, then I shall p-p-pay well. Even your freedom, maybe." A weak smile flickered under his facial shrubbery. "Isn't that a fair offer?"

"Not bad. But my friend is here, also. Include him."

Soldiers growled. The overseer rolled his eyes; his knuckles were white on the butt of his whip.

Jaxian sniggered. "I think I'll hire him as a t-t-trader!" He smiled expectantly at his companions. They just looked bewildered. "Well, you see I've never been haggled so well by someone with so little to haggle with," he explained lamely.

"Milord!" said the overseer. "There's no need to waste food on this scum. I can make him talk for you! I can make him do anything you want."

"Well . . . er . . . Um? No, I just gave my word. P-p-p-point out your friend, Omar."

I pointed out Thorian. Two soldiers marched over and unharnessed him. He was more mobile than I was and looked infinitely more dangerous. They escorted him back with drawn swords.

I had not realized how bad a mess he was in. His entire face was purple and bulbous like an eggplant, his hair and beard were matted with gore, and he had lost a couple of teeth. He managed to grin bloodily at me when he arrived, but the move must have hurt.

Jaxian looked so alarmed by this monstrosity looming over us that I could feel my deliverance fading away.

"Milord," I said, "may I have the inestimable honor of presenting His Royal Highness, Crown Prince Thorian, heir presumptive to the throne of Polrain, Grand Duke of the Thistrain Valley, Vizier of the Order of the Bronze Glove, Lord of the Eastern Marches, et cetera?"

"Really?" said Jaxian.

"Absolutely," said I, and probably none of us knew how close I might be to the truth. I could not be far off, for my large friend was certainly a member of the warrior caste and certainly from Polrain. There had been so few survivors, especially among the military families, that he could probably claim half the titles in the kingdom. It was no time to quibble about details, anyway.

What Thorian thought of his promotion was not readily apparent on his mangled features. He did not argue. He bowed. "I am honored to meet so outstanding a civic leader as Jaxian Tharpit. I congratulate you on your magnificent city of Zanadon."

The overseer had started to weep with frustration.

"Er, quite," Jaxian said. He and Thorian had both straightened up, eye to eye. Jaxian had a slight edge in height, probably only because he was wearing sandals. "I have some warrior friends who would like to meet you, er, your . . ." He could not bring himself to address a slave as royalty.

Perhaps he had also realized that his soldier companions were all scowling murderously. Whereas any merchant will always assume that any other is a liar and a cheat—justifiably—the warriors of one city regard their equivalents from neighbor cities as spies and dangerous enemies—also justifiably. I had probably marked Thorian to die as soon as Jaxian removed his protection. But that was a problem for another time.

He turned around and ordered us taken to his carriage. In a few minutes he appeared there also and climbed in beside us. Off we went. Thorian bled on the cushions.

* * *

The carriage was a sort of boat on wheels with a canopy. Four white ponies pulled it, and mounted guards rode ahead. It would have held four normal-size people comfortably, but I was crushed in a corner by Thorian's bulk and Jaxian took up the opposing seats easily. The well between was crowded with oversize legs and feet.

The roads of Zanadon are paved with granite cobbles; the carriage had no springs. In my already sensitive condition, I found the jostling painful, but at least it kept me awake.

Had I been in better shape, I should certainly have enjoyed that ride. The streets we followed were not the Great Way, but they were fine avenues, and wide by the standards of walled cities. Ornamented facades of high buildings flowed by on either hand. The crowds were colorful and pleasing to the eye. After weeks of footslogging among the ragged refugees, I could have appreciated the prosperity and the cheerful faces—had I been able to keep my eyes in focus and my mind alert. This was the Zanadon of my dreams.

Wheeled traffic and swarming pedestrians slowed our progress, but the racket of the wheels made conversation difficult. Jaxian needed reassurance, though. He was looking more worried than ever, probably afraid that he had let me make a fool of him. I could just imagine him trying to explain to his fearsome daddy how the family landau had become so bloodstained. I suppose he was imagining the same scene, and with more vivid detail.

"Start talking!" he shouted. "I don't have time for the whole story now, b-b-because I have to attend a very important ceremony. I may be late already. My d-driver will take you to a hostelry to eat, and I'll come there as soon as I can. You have my word—all you can eat and a comfortable night's sleep. Now talk!"

Thorian kicked my ankle.

Muddled though I was, I did not need his warning. Jaxian Tharpit was a feeble ally. If I blurted out what we had discovered about his father's sacrilegious activities, he would fly into a panic. He might throw us out of the city or he might send us back to the slave gangs, and then the overseers would flog us to death out of spite. The gods themselves would not lay bets on what Jaxian Tharpit might do.

A digression was called for.

"We did meet in Urgalon," I said. "Do you recall?"

He shook his head, looking worried again. "I know I have seen you somewhere . . . more recently, I should have said."

"No matter. It was briefly, and some time ago. My name is Omar. You will have heard of my family, the Angilths."

"What sept?" he demanded suspiciously. I felt Thorian twitch. The Angilths own some of the most productive pits in the notorious devil mines of Arkraz; the clan is rich and widespread. There would be an Angilth representative in Urgalon, and perhaps even in Zanadon itself. Jaxian must know some of them.

"Jailpor," I said confidently. "My grandfather is the Jailpor of Thraiman. Pray do not judge me by my looks, milord. My father always refers to me as the brown sheep of the family. He accuses my mother of having been overly friendly with the local miller."

"That is a terrible accusation!" Jaxian shouted. "Scandalous! Has she no b-b-brothers to defend her honor?" He seemed genuinely outraged.

"I speak in jest, milord! I imply only that my brown hair and gray eyes are a cause of ribaldry within the family, which is known for the darkness of its pigmentation."

Jaxian was reassured. Thorian relaxed. To raise suspicion and then allay it is a very useful technique, and one advantage of my trade is that I have been to so many places and heard so much.

In any case, I think I was married to an Angilth girl once, briefly.

"The family was naturally very concerned to hear about the war in the Spice Lands. The elders are especially worried by the possibility of danger to Zanadon, of course."

He frowned. "How so?"

A sudden burst of speed began bouncing us brutally,

raising the clatter to an ear-splitting roar. I waited until we slowed down again. Then I forced myself out of my stupor again.

"Because of the possibility that the Vorkans might sack the city. Even if they did no more than loot the holy figures on the outer walls, they could strip several cartloads of rubies from Maiana. The price would fall disastrously."

He nodded again, impressed by such mercantile sentiment.

"So I was dispatched to investigate. Indeed, I was sent on a mission of mercy, although of course it has its commercial aspects."

"Of course," he shouted agreeably.

"I assembled a small flotilla, and loaded it with weapons and armor. We sailed up the Jolipi, and my ships wait even now at Pulst. I came on ahead to make arrangements, but had the misfortune to be waylaid by one of the ragged gangs of cutthroats now preying upon the refugees. They attacked our camp during darkness. I managed to escape, fleeing naked into the night with nothing but my moneybags, only to be cornered in a caraway plantation. My companions, I believe, were all slaughtered. I should have shared their fate, had not Prince Thorian arrived upon the scene . . ."

I had a very stirring rescue coming up next, but I saw that my audience was losing interest. Talk love to a woman, war to a warrior, and money to a merchant—I learned that strategy ages ago. With priests, stick to the weather. I steered the conversation back to the flotilla. Two dhows, three coastal barks, and a couple of luggers, I explained. All of them would be able to navigate the shallow summer waters except possibly the dhows.

Jaxian demanded details of the cargo. He had totally forgotten about his sister.

"I do not recall the final detail on the bills," I explained. My throat was sore from shouting. "Four thousand swords, at least. Nearer five. All good Againroian workmanship. Shields and spurs and corselets. A full cargo of horse tackle. Had I not lost my records when the brigands attacked, I could be more specific."

He nodded understandingly, and tried to yell something over the roar of the cheering, but I could not hear. The carriage bounced to a shuddering halt. Thorian and I stared, Jaxian turned around to look.

Nowhere have I ever seen briefer twilights than in the Spice Lands—the sun moves faster than a pickpocket's pinkie. Dusk had fallen. Directly ahead of us was the Great Way, but our progress was blocked by an unbroken carpet of people. A glittering procession was proceeding up the hill to the temple: priests and priestesses, soldiers, dignitaries, torchbearers, musicians. Whatever those cornets and dulcimers were playing was completely lost in the din. The entire population of the city lined the way, overflowing into side streets, and thousands of throats clamored in unison: *"Maiana! Maiana! Maiana!"*

Even as we watched, the culmination of the parade went by the end of the street where we sat. A litter borne by sixteen priests supported the diminutive figure of High Priestess Squicalm in divine panoply on a silver throne. She was clearly visible over the sea of heads and hats. A hundred torches flamed around her, while the onlookers roared in hysterical jubilation.

The old crone was either asleep or unconscious, but that did not matter to the citizens. She would be transported in solemn triumph to the House of the Goddess. Tonight Balor would come to his beloved.

Jaxian squealed in alarm. "I'm late! I must g-get to the t-t-temple!"

His guards had already perceived the problem. One of the soldiers forced his steed through the crowd until it was alongside the carriage. Then he dismounted, and Jaxian scrambled across into the saddle without as much as a glance back at Thorian and me. Another mounted soldier forced a path for him, and our host disappeared into the mob.

"Beautifully done, Omar," Thorian yawned.

"You are too kind," I said graciously, and went to sleep.

19: One Down

✳

However ineffectual Jaxian might seem in person, he wielded the wealth of his family, and his word was good. He had left instructions with the coachman. When Thorian shook me awake, we had arrived at the promised hostelry.

The Bronze Beaker was not prepossessing on the outside. The stable yard was cramped and smelly, enclosed like a chimney by high buildings. The entrance steps were old and sagging. Inside, though, we were greeted with lights and tantalizing aromas of food and wine. Laughter and music drifted out from behind a rough plank door as the populace celebrated the imminent coming of Balor.

In front of that door stood the innkeeper—a short, broad man, scowling threateningly at us with his arms folded. We were a filthy, bloody, near-naked pair of indigents, and his dislike was understandable. But the coachman spoke the magic words, and thereafter our host could not do too much for us. Probably the Tharpits owned the place.

Following Thorian's welted back, I staggered up a narrow, creaking flight of stairs and into a stuffy bedroom. It contained two wide, soft-looking beds, and I started to yawn at the sight of them. The innkeeper was apologizing . . .

"It will suffice," Thorian said generously.

"The city is so crowded, you understand, milords? To allot you separate rooms, I shall have to evict—"

"This will do admirably," Thorian assured him.

Sleep!

But before I could fall from the vertical—the almost vertical, I mean—I discovered we had company. Jaxian had specified complete service, and complete service was what we received. If our host went beyond his instructions, then I make no complaint. I decided that my nap in the carriage had revived me.

They told us their names, but I was so sleepy I forgot them right away. It did not matter. They were both very lovely. Thorian's was tall and buxom. Mine was slim and slight. She bathed me in a copper tub and tended my wounds. She massaged me with scented unguents. And then, because the room was cramped, my handmaid spread my meal out on my bed. I lay on one side of it and she lay on the other, and she fed me like a child, popping little morsels of roast duck in my mouth and letting me lick her fingers. Also melon and sweet berries and delicious pastries. I did the same for her, and we pulled faces and sniggered a lot. We drank from the same cup. Finally she cleared away the dishes and kept me awake a little while longer so that I might sleep more soundly later. That was the excuse she gave, anyhow. She was lithe in my arms. She was totally delicious.

I am not a praying man, as you know, but sometimes I stretch a point and mutter a word of thanks. That is mere politeness.

Splatters of blood glistened brightly red on the laurel bushes. Wind sighed.

I stood on a battlefield below a darkening sky, while the first stars opened their eyes in horror. Bodies lay all around me, men and horses. The slaughter had not long ceased, for the cries of the wounded told me Morphith was still at his gathering. I heard wailings far away as women advanced onto the field, searching out their dead. I could see blood drying on the torn turf and could smell the bitter smoke of the first pyres.

Death and desolation . . .

Strangely, in the way of dreams, I could not identify the style of the fallen or the emblems on their tumbled banners. So I could not tell who had fought, let alone who had won and who had lost.

And as I stood amid the carnage, weeping for the folly of it, I heard cheering approaching. A man on a black horse was riding toward me—a big man, in silver armor, bearing a sword. After him came his warriors, the victors who had held the field. Many were limping, many bandaged, but all were acclaiming the leader who had brought them victory. As he passed them, the wounded struggled to rise and follow, if they could, or to wave if they could not, and they also joined in the shouting.

In the way of dreams, he came to me. He reined his horse and looked down at me from his great height, and his multitude of followers fell silent, all staring at me reproachfully.

I saluted the leader. He sheathed his sword. His beard was matted with sweat and gray with dust.

"It was prophesied!" he told me angrily.

"It was prophesied," I agreed. "You did as required, and the gods applaud."

He nodded, as if relieved. Then he removed his helmet to show his face. He was Thorian, of course, and he wore the golden diadem of kingship.

The day was bright when I awoke. Little light managed to reach our window, but it sufficed to tell me that dawn had long passed. I lay with my eyes closed, trying to remember where I was and why I felt as if I had been beaten all over with rods. I smelled old wine and candles and soap. Dreams . . .

"Omar!" said a deep voice again.

I opened my eyelids, and even they seemed to ache.

Thorian was standing over me. "The door is barred!"

"Doesn't . . . argh . . . surprise me," I said around a yawn. The girls had gone. They would have had other clients waiting, of course.

"We must leave!"

I moved one toe, and it ached. That left a few thousand other joints and muscles to try. "Why? I'm rather happy here."

He uttered his lion grunt, and I found it an oddly comforting sound. "Because Jaxian Tharpit will be coming to hear the message you are supposed to have for him. He will turn us over to the slavers again."

I thought about that. I thought about the message. Sleep receded swiftly. I bent a protesting arm and scratched. "It's morning!" I said—not too intelligently, I admit.

"Yes it is."

I scratched more of me. "Then his sister is now Maiana and Gramian Fotius is . . . Urckl preserve us!"

"Who?"

"Never mind. I don't suppose there was anything we could have done anyway."

Thorian sighed and sat down on the edge of my bed. It creaked and canted. He seemed to be as stiff as I was, and his back was a tartan of purple and red stripes where he had been flogged. His face looked better than it had the night before, but he was still the obvious loser of a major battle.

"I don't suppose there was," he said sadly. "And I can't believe that the Holy Gramian Fotius is in any danger from me now."

"Well, you never can tell. We don't have any clothes, do we?"

"No."

"And we can't climb out that window. What's wrong?"

"Listen!" Thorian said.

I listened. "I can't hear anything."

"Neither can I."

Morning in a crowded inn, in a busy city—a city with cobbled streets and many soldiers? Not a sound. Nothing.

There is an old legend about a traveler who arrives by night in a strange city to find a carnival in progress. He joins in the dancing and merrymaking, and wakens in the morning to . . . but I expect you know the tale.

I remembered it then, and every hair in my beard stood on end.

Thorian turned his head to look at the bell pull on the wall and then looked at me. His unease showed through the swellings and bruises.

"I feel strangely reluctant," he muttered. "Who might answer? What if no one does?"

"Why don't we just go back to sleep?" I suggested. "Perhaps when we wake up, we'll find that we aren't awake now.'' I could think of no earthly explanation at all for that eerie silence. Tired though we had been, if the Vorkans had crept in by night, we must surely have heard the massacre—and why would they have spared us?

"Mayhap Balor has marched out to give battle and the whole population went with him?'' Thorian suggested, running his hands through his beard.

"Try again.''

"You try.''

"Fast-acting plague?''

He snorted. "Is this what your gods brought you here to witness?''

"I had best get to work if it is, because it may be already over.''

Then a stair creaked, and I knew I had heard that sound many times in the night without really noticing. Another tread responded. Thorian moved to the washstand that was the only item of furniture other than the two beds. It bore a basin, a ewer, and fresh towels. He threw a towel to me, wrapped another around himself, and laid a hand on the ewer. It was, as I now realized, the only possible weapon in the room. There were several feet trooping up the stairs.

A bar clattered and the door was pushed open. Our host entered, bearing a tray. His beard was streaked with white dust. He did not speak. Keeping his eyes downcast, he tiptoed across to the table and laid his burden on it, taking care to make no unnecessary sound.

Jaxian Tharpit followed him in, ducking his hat under the lintel. His beard was filthy as an old broom. Even more astonishing, he had folded his swath in such a way that it reached down to his ankle on one side and yet left the whole of his other leg bare. As the innkeeper vanished out into the corridor, I saw that his cloth was arranged in the same lopsided fashion. I also noticed that there were at least two armed men outside.

Jaxian closed the door softly, then leaned his back against it, folding his arms under his white-and-gray beard.

"Please eat,'' he whispered. "And talk at the same time if you can.''

Thorian frowned at me in perplexity and reached for

the steaming jug on the tray. The absurdity of the one bare leg must be a local Zanadonian custom—it was certainly new to me. Most places favor lamentation, the louder the better, but I had heard of silence as an alternative. Ashes in the beard are recognized almost everywhere in the Spice Lands, and in many other lands, also.

"Milord?" I said softly. "You are in mourning?"

He nodded.

"May we ask why?"

"All Zanadon mourns. You have not heard?"

"We just awakened, milord." I felt very foolish, conversing in whispers.

"Balor did not come."

Thorian and I exchanged startled glances. Had High Priest Nagiak changed his mind, or had we misunderstood the plot? I had become so convinced of our prediction that Jaxian's news blew all rational thought out of my head. Vague fragments of ideas swirled around in there in terrible confusion. So Shalial was still a priestess. Gramian Fotius was still cleaning armor, not being acclaimed as the avatar of Balor. Fat, slimy Nagiak, and Deputy High Priestess Belhjes . . . Sudden dismay caught my breath as I remembered the old woman being borne in triumph to the House of the Goddess. "And High Priestess Squicalm?"

Jaxian nodded sadly.

"Dead?"

A frown. "Of course."

Thorian said, "How?" but I had already guessed the answer.

How much of the mourning was for Balor, and how much for the old woman? Now I understood why Deputy High Priestess Belhjes had been so frightened.

Jaxian claimed that the temple was fifty-two spans high. I would have estimated more than that, but he may have been judging by his own reach. He had been present in the House of the Goddess when the high priestess was taken there. He had returned with the other dignitaries at dawn to greet the god, but they had found no miracle, no god. Squicalm had been discovered in much the position in which she had been left, as if she had not moved a finger in the night. Rejected by Balor, she had been ejected by the priests. She had screamed once and then rolled all the way to the bottom.

As we listened to the macabre story, Thorian passed me a steaming mug of broth and a couple of fat peaches. I was still sitting on the bed. He moved over to join me.

Jaxian remained leaning against the door. I thought he looked ridiculous with one long furry leg showing, but mourning customs are often ridiculous. In many places women are expected to cut off their hair. I hoped that Zanadon was not one of them.

"You came back to the house last night," he whispered. "I want to know what happened earlier—the first time."

I bit into a peach while I gathered my thoughts, and juice soaked into my beard.

"May I speak, milord?" Thorian said softly. "My companion is a ward of Foofang, and he does not always understand the distinction between fiction and truth."

Jaxian nodded. I stared resentfully at Thorian, but he ignored me.

"We had escaped from a chain gang, as you know, milord. We climbed over your wall and hid in your yard, under some steps. We emerged in the middle of the night, just as you came home."

"Ah!"

"I knocked you down. I admit it. Then we used your key to enter the house. If you will accept a defense, recall that Zanadon had committed unprovoked assault upon us. Morally we had a right to treat you as our enemy."

Jaxian had a wry smile. "I admire your nerve! I could have you impaled for that admission, of course." He tapped his belly pin thoughtfully—there was a fortune in gems there. "But you could have robbed me or killed me. We appear to be even now. Continue."

I raised my eyebrows, and also my estimation of the man. I noticed that his stutter was missing. He was more sure of himself, as he had been when he came to the slave camp to rescue me.

"We made free of your house, milord," Thorian continued. "And then . . . Then your father summoned your sister from her sleep."

"You saw this?"

"We saw her. In all my life, I have never set eyes on a more beautiful woman."

Jaxian flushed darkly.

"Forgive me!" Thorian said. "I was not always a slave, milord, and she is so very lovely!"

"Carry on!" The merchant had lost his smile, and Thorian was walking a sharper edge than he knew.

"We watched your father deceive her, milord. He tricked her."

Jaxian glared in silent disbelief, chewing his mustache.

"Nagiak was eavesdropping, also, and—"

"The high p-p-priest? In our house?"

"Yes, milord." Thorian described the scene in the garden, and the merchant began to look less skeptical. He became no more friendly, though, as he learned how we had spied on his father and Nagiak.

"Later we went to the temple—"

Jaxian stiffened. "You t-tried to speak with her?"

If Thorian continued to report in his detailed military fashion, he was going to blunder into disaster. It was time for me to intervene. "We overheard a conversation between High Priest Nagiak and War Lord Arksis," I said.

"That is totally impossible!"

"Sanjala!" I said softly. "How else could I have known that name?"

He stared at me menacingly. "I t-t-tried to see her yesterday and was refused, but I learned her new name easily enough. That p-proves nothing."

"We heard other things," Thorian murmured. "Have you ever met a young man named Gramian Fotius, milord?"

Jaxian absently scratched his beard, and a cloud of ash fell from it. "No, I . . . O Holy Mother! I have heard of him, I think. A g-g-grandson of the war lord?"

"Yes. An animal! He also is in the temple."

"What has he to d-d-do with my sister?" Jaxian cried shrilly.

"A great deal, I fear. Do you truly expect the god Balor to come to the aid of the city, milord?"

Pale to the lips now, Jaxian nodded again.

"Your faith does you credit," Thorian said cautiously. "But we heard enough that night to know that High Priest Nagiak does not share it. He has other plans. So the god has refused the first appeal. What happens next?"

"There is a new high p-priestess. This evening she . . . *What are you implying?*"

Thorian drained his beaker and laid it on the bed. "Your father is privy to this. A foul deception. Maiana and Balor—daughter of the senior merchant, grandson of the war lord."

Jaxian Tharpit was a weak man, but he was not a fool. He could follow Thorian's laconic military style of speaking. He caught all the implications at once. He covered his face with his hands.

I waited with some interest to hear his reaction. Would he believe, or would he accuse us of blasphemy and send us off to whatever horrible end that provoked? When he looked at us again, his eyes were wide with agony.

"Gramian Fotius? The one who . . . ?"

"The rapist," Thorian said. "The killer."

"His grandfather believes he can control him," I explained.

"I d-doubt it. And the Vorkans?"

I laid a hand on Thorian's meaty shoulder. "This, milord, is a warrior. Tell such a man that he is being led into battle by a god! Tell him his cause is just and holy and cannot lose! Tell him that if he dies his soul is safe. If he believes half of that, milord, he will fight until there is no blood left in his veins and his limbs have been cleft from his body."

Thorian grunted. "He's right."

Jaxian nodded in horrified silence.

I shall always remember that conversation for the eerie contrast between the soft whispers in which we spoke and the stark evil of the topic. Once in a while I would hear a horse whinny in the distance, but that was all. Hooves could be muffled, of course, but wheeled traffic must have been banned altogether.

"You can believe this of your father?" Thorian asked.

"I might," Jaxian admitted.

"Tonight Priestess Belhjes? Tomorrow?"

Silence.

"Tomorrow is the night of the new moon," I murmured. "Holy to the Horned One."

Jaxian licked his lips. "There are hundreds of priestesses senior to her."

"Who decides?"

"The gods know! Nagiak, I expect. That may not be what the rules say, but that will be what happens. But how can this deception be worked? The high p-p-priestess keeps vigil alone."

"There will be a secret passage."

"Yes, I suppose so. I would put few things past that slimy eunuch." Jaxian shuddered and then stared hard at me.

"This was why you came b-back to the house?"

"It was. I wanted to speak with you, and warn you."

A gruesome smile twisted his beard. "Yes, I realized afterward why you had gone to that door. You had watched me earlier!"

I nodded.

For a moment, he seemed genuinely amused. "Serves you right, spy!" But only for a moment. He began scratching at his beard again. He would have it clean soon, I thought. "And why did you think I would oppose my father in this?"

"Because he had not invited you to be present when he summoned your sister." I can lie convincingly when I have to, and he believed me. The danger passed.

"I must d-d-discuss this . . ." he muttered. "This sacrilege! Talk with several p-p-people. G-G-Gramian Fotius! And yet, with the city in p-peril . . ."

I could see that Jaxian Tharpit had enough grist to keep his worry mill revolving for days. Whom could he possibly talk with? Certainly not his fearsome daddy, and to speak to anyone else would be betrayal. He would fret and worry and try to visit his sister and be refused and finally achieve nothing. What would he do with us in the meantime? I rose and went over to the breakfast tray. If I was going to be sent back to the chain gang, then I would rather it be on a full stomach.

"Who are you?" he demanded sharply. I turned around, but he was addressing Thorian.

"Just a warrior, milord. From Polrain, yes. The rest was moonbeams."

"Not a prince?"

Thorian shrugged. "Just a warrior."

"And him?"

"A wandering storyteller. He came to Zanadon because the gods ordered him to do so, in dreams."

Jaxian raised an eyebrow, Thorian nodded sadly. Had they tapped their temples and rolled their eyes they could not have expressed the thought more clearly. I am used to it and don't mind. It can even come in useful at times.

"I have seen your face b-before, though," Jaxian told me thoughtfully.

"People often think that, milord. It is a common enough sort of face."

He turned as if to leave. He even had his hand on the latch, and then he suffered another attack of indecision. Finally he turned to Thorian again. "I may need you both as witnesses. Will you continue to cooperate?"

"Aye, milord."

"Give me your warrior's p-parole, then. You will stay away from the t-t-temple and my father's house. You will d-discuss with no one what you have told me. And you will meet me b-back here tonight an hour after sunset." He did not state an alternative. He did not need to.

"I so swear," Thorian said.

"Can you c-control your friend?"

"No, he can't," I snapped, "but I also give my word. Do you think a trader of tales would run away from this one?"

The other two exchanged shrugs.

"We shall both be here this evening," Thorian said softly.

"Good. I'll send up some clothes for you." Jaxian reached into the folds of his swath. He pulled out a handful of gold and tossed it on the bed. "I said I would p-p-pay well."

The door eased shut behind him.

For a man without a backbone, he was surprisingly likable. I felt guilty at having told him so many lies.

"He really ought to keep us locked up," I whispered.

"He really ought to cut our heads off," Thorian said.

20: The Tale of Jaxian

※

Once again, Jaxian was as good as his word. Soon Thorian and I emerged from the Bronze Beaker to a hot, sunny morning. For the first time we were at liberty to move around the city without fear, for we were respectably clad, from comfortable sandals all the way to pot-shaped hats. Now we were designated as employees of the powerful Tharpit family, and none could dispute our right to walk the streets. With the aid of the innkeeper, we had wrapped ourselves in the current style of mourning, right legs bare. We had smeared ashes in our beards, although they showed better in Thorian's black forest than on my brown turf.

The streets were relatively empty. There was a tense, worried feel in the air, and the silence was uncanny. Even the armored soldiers seemed to tiptoe. A few horsemen went slowly by on muffled hooves, but wheeled traffic was almost nonexistent. I was relieved to see that the women still had their hair. They wore it unbound, hanging loose, and some of them looked very good that way. Most wore brightly hued sarongs. Every man we saw had ashes in his beard and one leg uncovered.

A couple of times guards noticed Thorian's tattered back and challenged us in whispers, but once they had inspected our swaths, the way they were folded, and the pins that held them, we were permitted to go on our way.

With no discussion, we began by walking down the Great Way until we reached the gates. One huge flap was closed and the other ajar. Few people were being allowed in, and no one was departing.

Then we ascended to the top of the walls and met a real

crowd for the first time. Worried citizens were coming in droves to stare out across the plain. News and rumors were being passed around in anxious whispers.

As yet there was no sign of the Vorkans, although the word was that they had reached the river. Someone had managed to impose some organization on the great chaos of refugees. I could see a military order to the sprawl of camps that stretched off into a purple haze where land met sky.

So the Vorkans' victims had turned at bay, prepared to give battle again—fight to the death or starve. The Vorkans themselves might not be eating well now. Who was gathering harvest in the Spice Lands this year?

Thorian burned in silent anger. He felt that the Zanadonian army ought to be down there also, prepared to give battle, but we both knew what Nagiak had told Tharpit: War Lord Arksis would let those ragged, battered refugees bleed the Vorkans a little more for him before he committed his own forces. It was morally despicable, but perhaps it made military sense. I did not feel competent to judge.

Having given his word to Jaxian, Thorian intended to keep a close eye on me, but I needed to gather information. In that mob, I had little trouble losing him. I took off on my own to explore Zanadon. I could not stop Balor and Maiana watching me, of course, but again I thought Balor seemed slightly more approving than hitherto. Maiana was still distrustful.

The conventions of mourning decreed that no one should indulge in any unnecessary conversation. Such unwelcome behavior is impossible to impose on a whole population, especially when the people are afraid. Balor had not answered the summons, and the people were very much afraid. I do have certain skills in encouraging people to talk. I spent the day doing so.

The official mourning ended at noon. As the sun reached the zenith, sounds of life began to return to the city. Carts and wagons reappeared. Woman bound up their hair. Men vanished indoors to comb out their beards and rearrange their swaths in symmetrical fashion. To get mine right, I had to enlist the aid of a sarcastic young whore in an alley. Then I bought her lunch with some of Jaxian's gold. She knew a lot about Bedian Tharpit and confirmed most of what I already learned. By an astonishing coincidence, I had met her sister once, briefly.

That afternoon, Zanadon was a more cheerful place, and I traded tales to my heart's content.

As the sun dipped near the horizon, the whole population began drifting toward the temple. Latecomers lined the Great Way, but I had foreseen the problem, and I had no duties to detain me. I was in the Courtyard of a Thousand Gods when the procession came through.

There were many thousands of people there, but as the sounds of music and cheering drew closer, I was not at all surprised to see Thorian's head nearby, towering over the mob—I have told you that I do not believe in coincidence. I shoved and jostled my way to his elbow.

"Good evening, your Majesty," I murmured.

He started angrily. Then he smiled, and it was a comforting sight. He stroked his beard. "The face is familiar. You remind me of a god I knew once."

"Then you had best stay very humble."

"That is never easy! Omar, I am worried about the girl."

"It is not our affair."

"But she is so lovely! Her father is a snake, her brother has the heart of a fieldmouse, and Gramian Fotius is a killer."

"I don't think the priests can hope to substitute her for Belhjes, as we thought they would substitute her for Squicalm. That is not the plan."

"Probably not. So she is safe for at least one more day?"

"I think so."

He nodded in agreement.

Torches blazed in the gathering dusk as the procession entered the great court. Further talk became impossible, and we joined in the universal roar: *Maiana! Maiana! Maiana!* Thorian probably went no deeper than that, but

I enjoy crowds. I joined the crowd. I was no longer Omar,
I was Zanadon. *Maiana!* I was crushed breathless in the
surging, sweaty mob, choked by the suffocating odors—
garlic is much cheaper in the Spice Lands than soap—but
I did not care. Soldiers wrestled to clear us from the path
and I fought back frantically, striving with all my strength
to draw near to the goddess. I shoved and yelled with the
best of them. *Maiana! Maiana!*

The litter passed close by me. I had a clear view of the
high priestess on her silver throne. *Maiana!* She stared
straight ahead, ignoring the accolades; she was majestic,
regal, divine. Surely Immortal Balor would not refuse us
again?

I did not see a big peasant woman in an ornate costume,
sick with terror under her paint and jewels. I saw Maiana,
and she was beautiful and I loved her, and I was wild with
excitement that the goddess had passed so near to me. As
I said, I love crowds.

Maiana!

The light was too dim and the court too wide to distin-
guish the dignitaries in the smaller procession that continued on, up the hundreds of steps of the pyramid. I knew
that Jaxian and his father would both be there, and the war
lord, also. It was a long climb. It must have been hard for
fat Nagiak.

By the time the noble company had reached the House of
the Goddess, the sky was dark. We had grown hoarse with
cheering, and now we joined in the singing. We all knew the
words after the third or fourth repeat, and we sang them over
and over, hailing our goddess, calling on her to bring the
god. Torches shone out through the doorway as the final
ceremonies were performed. Stars shone overhead. Then
lights began moving down again, while the archway shone
like a beacon above. It was so beautiful that we wept.

When they had all gone, only poor Belhjes remained,
waiting alone for Balor. But I did not think of her then as
poor Belhjes. I thought of her as Maiana.

The court emptied surprisingly quickly, people pouring
off down the Great Way like the Jolipi in spate, and in a

determinedly jovial mood. Thorian was still with me, holding a ferocious grip on my arm.

"You think the merriment sounds a little forced?" I asked.

He peered down at me. "You're better now?"

I laughed. "Did I scare you?" I was hoarse and exhausted and sore all over. And wonderfully content. "Oh, Thorian, I feel as if I made love to all of them, everyone there, and they all made love to me! But now I don't think we—they—are quite as cheerful as they're trying to seem."

"Yesterday they were certain. Today they know he is not called the Fickle One for nothing."

We walked on. My passions cooled further.

"Poor Belhjes!" I said. "How frightened she must be up there on her throne!"

"Afraid Balor will not come?"

"Or that he will."

Thorian took hold of my arm again. "You are still confused. Why should she be afraid of that?"

"A great bull like the statue in the chapel? She . . . Well, never mind."

When I showed no further signs of raving, he released my arm. "You are coming back to the inn?"

"Of course. Why not?"

"What do you expect to find there, then?"

"That depends," I said. "If Jaxian has talked with his poppa, then we shall be put to death as soon as we enter. Strangled, probably. It's tidiest."

The lion grunted.

"On the other hand," I continued cheerfully, "if he did not talk with his father, then he can have talked to no one. He will have concluded that there is absolutely nothing he can do."

"And in that case?"

"In that case, he will be there in person. He will apologize to us sincerely and *then* have us put to death. It is his duty to his family and his city."

Thorian walked a few paces before he began to laugh. "So why are you going back there?"

"Why are you?"

"Because I gave my word, of course."

"So did I."

"But I am a warrior!"

"That means you're crazy?"

"Sometimes. And you are . . ." He sighed. "You are whatever you are."

"Quite," I said.

We went in by the stable yard and the back door, as we did not know the front entrance. The little hallway seemed to be empty, but the door slammed at our backs. A man had been standing behind it with drawn sword. At that signal, other doors opened, other swordsmen emerged. They were civilians, not soldiers, and Jaxian followed them out, not his father. Tharpit Senior would have brought the city guard, while Jaxian had hired bruisers. It did not matter. They were all muscles and hair and sharp edges. Half as many and half as big could handle any heroism that might occur to us.

I removed my hat and bowed respectfully. Thorian copied me, a moment later. The merchant's face was haggard—I suppose he had been hoping we would not come. He licked his lips . . .

"Before you commit yourself to any particular course of action, milord," I said, "will you grant me a few words in private? There is something I should have told you earlier. I did not, because I was not certain of all the details."

He hesitated, as he always did. He looked to Thorian, who was probably calculating his chances of taking a man or two with him and who just shrugged in response.

"A minute, then. In here." Jaxian reached out to the closest henchman and took his sword. Then he retreated into the room from which he had emerged. Thorian and I followed him, and the door was pulled shut behind us.

We were in the innkeeper's private parlor, I assumed—a small chamber, stuffy with the heat of the day. It was cluttered with several stools. Three candles shed a flickering, deceptive light, muffling the wine stench with an odor of cheap tallow. Sounds of tipsy laughter drifted in through chinks in the plank walls. A small table littered with slates and fragments of chalk stood under the single window, which was small and barred; there was no other exit.

Jaxian leaned against the table and rested the point of his sword on the floor.

"B-b-be quick," he said hoarsely.

I did not presume to sit. "Some families seem to be cursed," I began. "I need tell you of one such. There was a man who had three sons. He was a merchant; his name does not matter. His first two sons did not survive infancy. He himself had several sisters, but no brothers, and he wished to continue the family name. Thus, although he loved his wife dearly, and although her first two labors had been hard, he chose to father a third child upon her. When that third son was born, the mother contracted puerperal fever and died."

Jaxian's face was already thunderous with anger. I knew I did not have much time left.

"The third son thrived. He was a strong child, unusually large for his years. But his father could never forgive him for the death of his mother and would have little to do with him. Much later, the merchant married again, and again he met with tragedy. His second wife died in giving him a daughter.

"Again, he was resentful of his wife's death, and the second death did nothing to reconcile him with his son. If anything, his anger seemed to increase, and he missed no opportunity to remind the boy what his existence had cost. When the son reached early manhood, his father packed him off to a distant city, where the family had offices. There he was supposed to learn the trade."

"You p-p-prying, snooping, meddlesome b-b-b—"

"The son had known the daughter only as a baby. She did not know her brother at all. When the son reached the age of twenty or so, his father sent orders that he must marry, to raise heirs. The young man made an unfortunate choice. The marriage was unhappy, and childless. The woman died."

I paused for breath, but this time Jaxian did not speak. My skin was running wet in the heat of the room.

"When war came to the Spice Lands, the son was summoned home to the safety of Unvanquished Zanadon. It was a city he barely remembered, and he had no friends here. He was thirty-two. His sister was seventeen. They met, in truth, for the first time. And then the family curse reached its fulfillment, for there can be no greater sorrow than true love impossibly barred, and theirs is a love forbidden by both men and gods."

I stooped and waited to see if I had just sealed my death warrant.

Jaxian Tharpit took several minutes to decide. Then he moved to a stool and sat down, laying his sword on the floor.

"Sit," he said.

I sat. So did Thorian. I dared not look at him. I knew what warrior honor would say to such a tale.

"Shalial told you this?" Jaxian demanded. He was pale now and keeping his hands out of sight. His face shone wetly in the candlelight.

"No, milord. We overheard your father tax her with having a lover. She denied it. We spoke with her in the temple, later that night—"

"Impossible!"

"No, milord. Unlikely, I admit, but it happened." I dared not take the time to explain about the god wanting me to be a witness, and so on. Some people have trouble adjusting to that idea. "She did mention that she herself had woven that hanging I had stolen to use as a garment."

Jaxian nodded in acknowledgment, and I rushed on.

"But when I repeated what your father had said, she again denied it."

He hid his face with his hands. Shalial had spirit—I wondered what on earth she had seen in this human pillow. He barely had the making of a brother, let alone a lover. Forbidden fruits are sweeter, but they ought to look good, too, or who will be tempted to try them?

And of course a man as shrewd as their father would have seen the problem, and probably almost at once. The woman I had so terrified when I pretended to be a god was Jaxian's concubine, Nilgia. That was why he had gone to her room, of course. Nilgia was a very recent addition to the household. Bedian Tharpit had ordered his son to go out and hire himself a woman, in the same way he might have ordered him to get his hair cut. Apparently the effort had been wasted. Over lunch her sister had told me with much sniggering that Nilgia was finding her new employment very restful.

Jaxian lifted his head and glared at me with pink eyes. "You damnable prying busybody!" he barked, and suddenly I saw the other Jaxian—the noble, the arrogant wealthy merchant. This one did not stutter. "It is true that my sister and I were already adults when we met, in effect, for the first time. We have found the situation difficult, yes. Do you think I could be blind to beauty such as hers? And she—she meets few men of her class, and suddenly there is one living in the same house . . . Naturally we have had problems reconciling our family affections with . . . with other instincts. But if you are implying that my conduct—or hers—has been in any way contrary to the laws of the city or the dictates of the gods, then I will have your tongue!" He glared at me menacingly.

"I do not question your honor, milord."

"Wise of you! Now, if Shalial did not tell you, who did? Who is spreading such slander?"

"It was guesswork. I sensed something wrong when she gave in to your father so easily. Later I told her a story about a nurse who exchanged babies—"

His teeth showed in his beard. "And you told me some nonsense about your father thinking you were not his child!" Jaxian was a puffball, but he was shrewd.

"Yes," I admitted. "In both cases I won more reaction than I should have. Persons in what I suspected to be your predicament may well dream fantasies of that type, milord."

"Because we both had wet nurses? Because I am a cubit taller than my father? The law would require more evidence than that!" He turned his face away from me, breathing hard.

In the ensuing silence I risked a glance at Thorian. His scowl was everything I had feared.

"I was not thinking about law, milord," I said. "I am not thinking about happily-ever-aftering. Your love is doomed, I agree. What I am thinking about is an innocent young girl being brutally raped by a sadistic monster, Gramian Fotius."

Jaxian swung back to stare agony at me. "You think I haven't been thinking about that all d-d-day?"

"Do you believe the gods will countenance such a crime?" I demanded, raising my voice for the first time. "Do you think Holy Maiana will permit such sacrilege— such desecration of her temple, connived at by her own high priest? Milord Tharpit, I am only a bystander, but I say I am willing to risk my life in this cause. If you will not aid her as your sister, then by all the gods, you should aid her as the woman you love!"

"Do you know what they d-d-do to men who p-profane the t-t-t-temple?"

"Yes. Are you not willing to risk even that for Shalial? I will."

"So will I," Thorian said softly, barely audible over the clamor from the reveling customers.

"So you can carry her off and rape her yourself?"

Thorian sprang to his feet. "You will withdraw that remark!" he bellowed.

Pause. The drunken crowd behind the wall had burst into song. Jaxian's sword was on the floor, the guards were outside the door, and the unspoken threat was mortal.

I was frozen to my stool by this disaster. Jaxian had turned ashen pale.

Then he rose, making no attempt to reach for his sword. "Or?" he asked hoarsely. *"Or what?"*

I was astounded to realize that his pallor came from fury, not fear. He was face to face with the warrior, meeting his insolent challenge.

As Thorian lunged, I leaped up and tried to grab him, for I could see us both dying in the next few seconds. He hurled me aside, and I crashed down over a stool.

Jaxian landed a killer punch on the warrior's midriff—*wham!*—and then another. Thorian went down, also. He slammed into the door as the swordsmen outside tried to open it.

"Go away!" Jaxian roared. "There is no trouble here."

And there wasn't. I was flat on my back and Thorian was curled up, gasping for breath. With my clumsy interference I had spoiled his attack, of course, or else a mere merchant could never have bested a warrior of the same size, a younger one.

Or had I? Admittedly my observation had been muddled by my own fall, but I had a strange impression that Thorian had pulled his punch. Certainly that would have been the wise thing to do, for a slave does not strike a noble in his own city. It had defused a mortally dangerous situation . . . but it was emphatically not proper behavior for a warrior. I remembered how his courage had faltered briefly before the temple door, and I wondered disloyally if my elected hero was slightly flawed. Or just human, I reminded myself.

And Jaxian was obviously not quite the sheep I had believed. Apparently he could be a man when he had no time to think about it.

He sat down again, breathing hard, still glaring. I clambered unobtrusively onto my stool, rubbing the back of my head.

"We shall do no good by quarreling," I suggested weakly. "Our objective is to save Shalial."

"I withdraw my remark," Jaxian growled.

There was a pause. "I apologize," Thorian mumbled. He resumed his seat, painfully hunched over and not looking at anyone.

I began to relax slightly. "Fotius is said to kill women." Jaxian moaned.

"It is true," Thorian remarked, speaking with difficulty. "I watched him with refugees. I saw it happen. His uncle would not let the others interfere."

Jaxian slumped on his stool as if his backbone had melted.

I persisted. "And Fotius himself will be put to death

by the priests as soon as the Vorkans are defeated. Shalial may very well share his fate.''

"No!'' Jaxian protested. "No, no!''

"There is a crypt under the temple,'' said Thorian. "I know our story is improbable, but we saw it, and there are old bones there. Balor will be a considerable nuisance after the emergency is over.''

"My father would not have c-c-consented to that!''

"He can't know. But the temple hierarchy will not long endure a fake god ruling over them. What can your father do then? Or Arksis? Denounce the priests? They will condemn themselves!''

Jaxian moved as if to stand up, and seemed to lack the strength. "Even if we . . . It is not p-possible! We should be c-c-cas . . . c-c-caught.''

He was a rabbit again. I suppose in his boyhood he had always been well behaved, an obedient child anxious to please the father who paid him so little heed. Now two naughty boys were tempting him to commit mischief.

I leaned back against the wall and smiled encouragingly. "Not tonight, no. We have no idea where she is in that warren and we should need a week to search it. But I don't think she is in any danger tonight. Tomorrow, or the next night—whenever Nagiak feels he has raised the city to the proper pitch of terror and anticipation. Then he will put Shalial on that throne and parade her through the town. That night we shall know where she is!''

Jaxian shook his head like an obstinate sauce bottle. "This is madness!''

"It is better than the alternative.''

"But supposing you can reach her, what will you do with her?''

"Carry her off to some safe hiding place you will have arranged, of course. That is why we need your assistance—for that, and to convince her that she should accompany us. If you are not with us, she may reasonably fear what you yourself suggested a few moments ago. She may prefer to take her chances with Balor.''

Conversation lagged. The sounds of revelry were growing louder yet in the taproom next door.

There was no chance whatsoever that Jaxian Tharpit would commit himself to my proposal on a moment's notice. He would want a year or two to mull it over. And he would find a thousand objections.

"Nagiak?" he muttered. "The next morning?"

"That will be interesting," I agreed. "He will find no Maiana there, of course. We shall have to think about that." If Thorian was involved, Nagiak was going to discover a dead Balor, bearing a remarkable resemblance to Gramian Fotius.

Motion carried.

Vorkans were another minor problem. The Balor legend was a two-edged blade. The war god come in glory would lead his young men to inevitable victory. If he refused to come, then the Zanadonian army would collapse like straw.

I was prepared to leave that difficulty to the god himself.

21: Two Down

The guards eventually became worried, and one of them tapped on the door and looked in. Jaxian peevishly shouted at him to go away, but the interruption ended the string of objections he had been spinning.

He reeled to his feet like an old man.

"Tomorrow," he mumbled. "If B-Balor does not come . . . I shall try to find out who follows B-B-Belhjes."

Thorian and I chorused agreement.

"I shall come and see you here."

Again we agreed. Jaxian shuffled out and departed with his bodyguard. The outer door slammed. Thorian and I sank back on our stools. I wiped my face. That interview had been harder than wrestling pythons, and I speak from experience.

Thorian twisted his battered face in a smile of approval, showing the new parting in his teeth. I dearly wanted to ask him if he had let Jaxian win the tussle, but I knew better than to question a warrior's honor.

"You are serious about rescuing the girl?" he inquired innocently.

"Very serious. Obviously the gods want me to do so."

"Obviously. But earlier you said it was not our concern."

"It is now! Surely you must see that the introduction of a tragic love theme changes the story?"

He scowled. "Brother and sister? It is unthinkable! It is a crime against all that is holy!"

"Half brother and half sister. And give him his due. We have the high priest's word for it that she is still a virgin."

"I should hope so!"

"Small wonder that one took to drink and the other to religion. Equally useless solutions, of course."

"You blaspheme!" Thorian barked.

"Not at all. What does anyone hope to gain by taking a problem to the gods? The gods sent the problem in the first place! They already know of it. Why should they help the crybabies?"

"One may pray for strength."

"The gods know your strength. They may be showing you what it is good for."

"Bah! You are as devious as a priest, even if you do argue the opposite case. I may assist in the rescue?"

"You do not expect Jaxian or myself to deal with Corporal Fotius, do you? I foresee your two destinies inexorably entangled."

The warrior sighed contentedly and smiled. I suspected that other ambitions lay behind that smile, but I did not say so.

"Jaxian is an interesting character," I remarked. "He seems to act like two different people, and switch back and forth between them with no warning. Mention of his sister seems to cause the change, did you notice? I have met a few others like that in my time. Vlad the Opprobrious, for example, was one of the most doting fathers one could—"

"Omar? How would you like to eat a stool?"

While I was considering the question, the innkeeper bustled in, looking worried—he would have been given no instructions about us. Thorian reached in a fold of his swath and produced a shiny gold piece.

"Our room is still available?"

That was different! The stocky man stared hopefully at the glint in the warrior's strong fingers. "I . . . I have a better one, milords."

"Plus the best dinner and your choicest wine. Sasi and Elina?"

"They will be here very shortly, milord."

"We shall require their company for the entire night."

Our host gaped. "The entire night? But, milord! Their regular duties . . ."

Thorian produced a second gold piece. That was enough to clear the girls' calendars. We were conducted upstairs. The new room was larger, cooler, and better furnished, even to a full-size copper bathtub in one corner. The crisp white linen smelled of lavender. Our host vanished, mumbling about hot water.

"The entire night?" I murmured.

"I was not at my best last night," Thorian said, stretching his great arms and pressing his hands against the ceiling. He sighed luxuriously.

"Nor I," I admitted. "I expect they will appreciate an easy evening."

"That was not my intention," Thorian said, stooping to slap his palms on the floor.

The door flew open and I was instantly enveloped in a tight embrace by my limber friend of the previous evening, her lips sweet against mine. Greatly excited by the news that she could dedicate the whole night to me, she dug fingers in my back and squirmed her firm little breasts against my chest. I heard a guttural chuckle from my friend as he was similarly reunited.

I had forgotten to ask which one was Sasi and which Elina, so I called my companion Twin Rosebuds, and Pearl of My Desire, and Avatar of Maiana, and other foolishnesses, and she called me many sweet names, also. And we did many wonderful things together.

I stood on the walls of Zanadon, looking out across the plain. I know of no vantage anywhere from which the world seems larger. The sun had just set, and the thin crescent of the goddess hung low in the sky below a threatening black storm cloud, whose top was red as blood. The wind was rising, stirring my hair.

I turned and looked up at Maiana, shiny bright against the dark east. She had her shoulder to me, and she was half hidden by a tree with yellow blossoms.

Leaving the walls, I walked up the hill toward the temple. Leaves blew on it as the storm approached. The road

was a bare track, with grass growing in the ruts, and it
climbed steeply between rundown wooden buildings, apparently deserted. This was a dingy quarter of the city,
but soon I saw the temple wall directly ahead of me.

Someone licked my lips.

"Again!" said Sasi—or she may have been Elina.

"Of course, er, darling," I agreed. I kissed her, while
wondering what the rest of my dream would have told me.

Again I walked up the hill. The last rays of sunset lingered on Maiana's hair, staining it bloodred. In the shadows at the end of the lane, a ramshackle fence abutted the
temple wall, with a gate canted on rusty hinges. I pushed
it ajar and slipped through into a weedy junk-filled yard.

Someone tickled me.

"Again!" my companion said.

I wondered if Thorian's was as inspiringly conscientious
at providing value for money.

"Impossible," I said grumpily.

In a few minutes she whispered, "Still impossible?"

"Obviously not," I muttered. "Why did you think so?"

I never did see the end of that dream.

When dawn came, Thorian and I stood within the multitude that had assembled in the Courtyard of a Thousand
Gods. Many had held vigil there all night. Huge as that
place is, it was so packed with people that we were pressed
tight together. I have never known so large a gathering to
be so silent. I could hear and feel the breathing all around
me, and yet there was no other sound. As I slipped into
the mood of the crowd, the fear and tension began to speed
my heart, and soon I was sweating with apprehension. The
waiting was intolerable—had Balor come to save us, or
had he again rejected the priestess? The part of me that
was Omar could guess the answer, but Zanadon could not,
and I swam with Zanadon in that dewy dawn. I shivered
with anxiety as with a high fever.

The sky was pallid blue, ready for the sun. The House
of the Goddess seemed tiny against it, and the doorway
was dark, the torches dead.

The dumpy crimson form of Nagiak started up the steps, a double line of priests behind him. After them came the civil leaders, the merchants and the warriors. They moved with aching slowness.

As they neared the top, Balor's golden helmet blazed. Two eagles launched and swooped away, and the crowd sighed. All eyes were on the House of the Goddess, waiting to see who would appear within the doorway.

No one did. When the high priest reached the top, the laymen stopped, moving to the sides of the stair, a single line on either hand, so that the center was left empty. We humble folk in the courtyard moaned in unison like some great unitary beast. The priests continued to climb, trooping in through the door.

The sunlight reached the gold roof, making it flame like Balor.

Shrill and faint, screams rent the dawn. We groaned again.

Four young priests emerged, bright in their white gowns. They carried the woman prone between them, and they advanced relentlessly to the very top of the stairs. Forward, back, forward, back, outward . . .

She screamed one more time as she soared, but the sound stopped when she struck the granite steps far below. She rolled and tumbled down between the double line of onlookers, leaving a trail of blood behind her all the way to the courtyard. Our howl reached to the heavens.

Thorian pinched my ribs savagely. I jerked my mind free of the crowd's. I stifled my sobs and wiped my tears. "Thank you," I whispered, and thereafter I kept to my own thoughts as we dispersed with the others. There was no sound except the shuffling of feet and the muffled sobbing, but fear and sorrow filled the air like invisible smoke. Again Balor had rejected the appeal of his people.

The sun beat down on the Great Way. The day was going to be even hotter than usual.

Tonight was the night of the new moon.

Thorian and I had just finished breakfast in our room when Jaxian arrived. As before, he had ashes in his beard and his right leg was uncovered. From the look of his face, he had not slept all night. His cheeks had sunk into hollows, leaving his incongruous prow of a nose even more prominent. His eyes were red as cherries. He slumped down in a chair and pouted at us resentfully. Thorian said nothing, but I could sense his distaste for our spineless ally.

"What news, milord?" I asked.

Jaxian shook his head. "I c-c-could find out nothing. My father is smirking from ear to ear, if that means anything."

"Then we may have to move very quickly. The procession starts from the gates, does it not? Once we are certain that your sister is—"

"I do not believe that what you p-plan is p-p-possible! There will be g-guards everywhere! Do you think the p-priests have not considered the p-p-possibility of a rescue or a substi-ti-ti-tution?"

His stutter was worse than ever. I supposed that a man besotted with his sister might be excused a few nervous twitches. The penalty for incest was probably as barbaric as anyone could imagine—and some people have very horrible imaginations.

"To be honest, I doubt if the priests have thought about the matter," I said truthfully. "Most of them believe implicitly in Maiana and Balor, as you did before we enlightened you."

Jaxian glowered at me. "As I still do. As you still should."

This was bad. I could see great trouble ahead if he pulled out of our conspiracy, fatal trouble.

"I do believe in them, milord. I also believe in human duplicity."

"Too much so. The fraud you forecast is impossible."

"With respect, milord, you told me that you would put nothing past High Priest Nagiak."

"Magic I do! Miracles I do." Jaxian glowered at me, and then rubbed his eyes wearily. "I have been four t-t-times into the House of the Goddess. There is no secret p-passage such as you predict. The walls are solid, the floor is solid. The idol is large—too large to move, too small to contain any fanciful secret d-doors.'' He peered at me and was not convinced that I was convinced. ''The stones are a span and a half long! Maybe half that in width. It would take an entire phalanx to lift one, a dozen c-camels to haul it. That's t-t-true of the floor, too.''

''There are other ways to effect deception.'' I smiled cryptically . . . then remembered Rosh's smile and switched to a witless grin.

''Name one.''

''Have you considered the litter, milord? The priestess sits on a silver throne on a sizable litter. I knew an illusionist once who could have hidden three men inside a contraption like that. Or one Gramian and half a Fotius.''

Jaxian scowled again at my wit. ''At the House, she leaves the litter and it is removed. She is stripped of her finery, and that is removed. The notables go, leaving her naked . . . well, she has a couple of wisps of stuff on, but naked near as no matter. She is there, before the g-g-goddess, in an empty hall, *and there is no one else.*''

I avoided Thorian's eye. ''There will be a way,'' I said stubbornly. ''Is she given no marriage bed on which to tempt the god? Just cold granite?''

''The p-priests heap a p-pile of t-tamarisk fronds. It's t-t-traditional; d-divine myth.'' He paused and then muttered to himself, ''D-d-divinely uncomfortable, if you want my opinion.''

The very impossibility he was describing sounded exactly like one of Pav Im'pha's illusions seen from the audience side. Any future questions about Balor's divinity would founder on the miracle of his arrival. Apparently Jaxian's mind would not trot on that sort of track, but mine would.

''Then on the critical night perhaps the tamarisk will be already in place and Fotius will be underneath it!''

''Rubbish! T-t-total chaff.'' He was avoiding looking at me, though, as if he had not convinced himself. His next remark proved it. ''And even if I accept your c-conspiracy theory, I do not believe we can do aught about it!''

''West of the temple,'' I said, ''at about the place where

we were repairing the city wall, there is a tree with yellow blossoms. A rough road climbs the hill from there to the wall of the temple itself—it is not far, as you know. On the left there is a deserted yard. Within that yard lies enough scrap lumber to assemble a rough ladder. There may even be a ladder—I did not look carefully.''

"Why not?" he demanded suspiciously.

Artists dream, priests believe, but peasants, warriors, and merchants all have miserably practical, hardheaded approaches to life. To explain the source of my information would have whittled his confidence in the reliability of my observations.

"My inspection was interrupted," I said vaguely. "Under cover of darkness, three agile men with a ladder can easily scale the temple, step by step. If necessary, Thorian can carry your sister down on his back. I am much more concerned with where we take her then . . . milord.''

Jaxian stared at me incredulously. Thorian was keeping his face impassive, but the muscles of his arms were taut as anchor cables in a riptide. He, too, knew insanity when he heard it. Fortunately, he did not comment—he was starting to acquire some confidence in my little whims.

Jaxian had none. He laughed in shrill mockery. "And how do you get into the House of the Goddess to deal with the magical Fotius? How do you get my sister out? The torches burn in there all night. From now on half the city is going to be watching and praying in the Courtyard. Anyone going in or out of that doorway will show up against the light!''

Pav Im'pha again! I had no intention of entering by that public doorway, but neither did I intend to take Jaxian into my confidence anymore. I scrabbled among my brains, hunting for any plausible ideas that might have slipped down in there.

"The torches burn out by dawn," I said tentatively.

"By then my sister has been raped and Fotius is parading around in Balor's armor.''

"True. Unpleasant. Well, I think if a man lay flat and wriggled in through the doorway on his belly, he would not be visible from the Courtyard.''

This time Jaxian's disbelief was expressed by a spurt of obscenities that I would not have expected him to know. His nanny should have washed out his mouth more often when he was little. After that, he just stared at the floor. He wrung his hands like an old woman, although they were as huge and hairy as Thorian's. We had lost a conspirator, and were probably much safer for it. At last he looked up, but he spoke to Thorian.

"You will go along with this?"

"Something of the sort." The warrior's face was still so bruised that it was even more impassive than usual, and warriors are trained to be impassive. The training is often very cruel. "The details need to be worked out."

"Yet you know what will happen to you if you are apprehended," Jaxian mumbled. "I respect your c-c-courage enormously, both of you. But me? I have much more to lose than you do!"

"I shall be surprised if you do," Thorian said blandly.

"I didn't mean it that way! C-can't you imagine what would happen if I were with you? My sister herself would be implicated . . . my father, and my aunts. The whole family will be d-d-dragged down, our entire estate and all the faithful folk who work for us! I cannot risk so many lives, even for Shalial."

"You will abandon her to Gramian Fotius?" Thorian asked.

"I have only your word . . ." Remembering that he was speaking to a warrior, Jaxian changed direction sharply. "No, I admit I have made a few inquiries. No one seems to know where Fotius is now, so I do b-believe you. Apparently he is a huge man, well able to p-play the role of B-B-Balor."

"He is about our size," Thorian said complacently. "With the face of a gorilla and the habits of a shark."

"Really?" Jaxian was sweating. "He t-tends to be rough with women, I know. Many men are. But he cannot harm my sister while he is pretending that he is B-Balor and she is Maiana, don't you see? Balor does not blacken Maiana's eyes, or knock out her t-t-teeth! I think you are overstating her d-d-d-danger."

Even I felt nauseated. I should not have been in the least surprised had Thorian lifted Jaxian by the throat and choked him.

"I take it that the rescue is off, then?" I asked sadly.

The merchant squirmed, staring at the floor. "I will not forbid it," he whispered.

And doubtless he would be willing to negotiate a handsome reward if we asked for it. I did not dare inquire, lest Thorian ruin the hostelry's rugs with bloodstains.

"This is still a c-considerable risk for me," Jaxian told my toes sternly. "You have been seen in my c-company, and you will certainly talk under t-t-torture." He looked up nervously at Thorian. "I don't mean you, of course. But Omar is not a t-trained warrior."

"No he isn't, but he is a brave man. You may be pleasantly surprised. Don't you believe your father can defend you from wild allegations made under torture?"

Again Jaxian squirmed on his chair. He scratched ash from his beard. "I hope it won't come to that, and it's your d-decision entirely. I really must rush off now. Militia d-duty, sword drill—we're all warriors now in Zanadon!"

"Inspiring," Thorian said solemnly "Oh, one other thing, milord. Your sister may distrust our good intentions. If she chooses not to come with us, how do we persuade her?"

Jaxian fumbled in his swath and produced a folded parchment. Hesitantly he held it out to Thorian. The resulting glare was designed to remind him what true warriors thought of such unmanly affectations as book learning. He passed it hastily to me instead.

I opened it and read it aloud for Thorian's benefit. " 'You may trust the storyteller Omar and his companion. Safe refuge awaits you at the place you acquired the silver butterfly.' This is unsigned, milord."

"She knows my handwriting."

"Of course."

Apologetically Jaxian added, "I could not be more specific about the p-p-place . . . in case that falls into the wrong hands . . . Unfair to a very loyal retainer."

And he would not name the place to us because we were going to be tortured.

I had nothing more to say.

Thorian certainly did not.

Jaxian rose, but even he had trouble finding words. "I . . . You . . . My p-p-prayers go with you, milords."

We bowed in silence.

Jaxian went out with his back stiff and his face crimson.

Thorian lifted the chair the merchant had just vacated and began breaking it up with his bare hands. He continued doggedly until he had reduced it all to kindling.

22: The Name of Obelisk

We left the inn then, for neither of us was inclined to trust Jaxian in his new mood. If his father asked him what was making him look so glum, he would start vomiting the whole tale. That was why my description of our plans had been so vague. I am not a meticulous person. I rarely plan ahead—I will take any sort of head that comes along. I muddle through. I have been known to change heroes in midstory. But I am not as fanatically suicidal as I had sounded to Jaxian.

With ashen beards and one bare leg apiece, we emerged into a lost city. Not only was Zanadon silent that morning, it was almost empty. Half the people were holding vigil in the Courtyard of a Thousand Gods. The other half were on the walls, staring southward at the heat haze and the dust.

The Vorkans were on the move, apparently. In that hotbed of fear, rumor and fancy bred like maggots. Make those mushrooms if you prefer. Thorian and I formed a good military intelligence department between us. I have skills at encouraging people to talk. He could suggest questions to ask and make sense of the answers. We collected a dozen names for the leader who had organized the refugees, and Thorian eventually concluded that there must be a council or committee in charge, with one strongman dominant. The favorite candidate for the overall leader was a Polrainian prince named Obelisk, and each time he was mentioned, Thorian became more thoughtful.

There were a thousand different accounts of the Vorkans' activities; Thorian dismissed all but one of them. You could see the dust, he snorted. It was obvious—they were circling around to the west, outflanking the refugee horde south of the city.

"Does that make tactical sense?" I inquired.

"Of course. It throws the refugees' defense into chaos. It also makes strategic sense. The Vorkans can't have found much to eat in the hills, but now they're into the larder. Now Zanadon can watch the crops burn. If the western cities send help, then the Vorkans can intercept. Or the Vorkans can just keep going, crossing the river and burning as they go.

"Besides," he added meanly, "people get very uneasy when they're surrounded, and now Zanadon feels surrounded."

"You think the war lord must do something soon?"

Thorian uttered his lion grunt, but it was an amused lion. "He can't do anything until Nagiak does. They can't move without Balor now. I wonder if the priest has raised his price again?"

We left the crowd to its mourning and wandered westward, trying to follow alleyways and lanes that paralleled the walls. We both knew where we were going, so we did not bother to discuss it.

"I'm pleased at the way Balor is looking at me now," I remarked. "He definitely seems more friendly toward me than he did at first. I expect he approves of what we are doing."

Thorian bared the new gap in his teeth at me and continued to walk without saying anything.

"Maiana, though . . ." I sighed. "Well, I suppose we're planning further trespass within her temple. No woman can be expected to welcome a man blundering around like that, or trust him to be discreet. Don't you agree?"

Thorian grunted.

"Isn't Obelisk an unusual name for a prince?" I inquired.

"I know of no such prince, but that is not an uncommon name for a warrior."

"Oh, I think it is. I have known many warriors in my time, but never one called anything like Obelisk."

"If you say it is unusual, then it must be unusual, my taciturn friend."

"Do you feel manly when you mock me?"

He twitched as if I had stuck a needle in him. "It takes unspeakable self-control for me to keep my fist out of your throat. You are a permanent pest! You yap and jabber all the time, and sniff at everything like a terrier. Promise me fifteen minutes' masculine silence, and I shall explain Obelisk."

"Ten."

Thorian groaned. "Cheap at the price. Listen, then. In Polrain, when a youth of the warrior caste reaches manhood, he takes his true name and swears certain oaths to Sztatch, whom you call Balor . . ."

"I usually call him Krazath. Balor is the name he has here in— I beg pardon. Please do continue."

"Grr! His name-giving is the most solemn moment of a man's life. He recalls the feats of the great past heroes he has chosen as his exemplars, acting them out with the aid of his three best friends. This is a very potent ritual for all of them. Very often the same four pledge as name friends for one another and a group of sworn . . . But you do not need to know all that."

He fell silent, brooding as he walked—despite his height, Thorian walked with a soldier's regulation stride. I wondered if he was testing my resolve to keep silent, or just remembering his own coming of age and boyhood friends now dead. When he spoke again, his voice seemed harsher.

"The new man's name is chosen for him by his three friends, and neither he nor anyone else has any say in the matter. None whatsoever! Even the king has no say in the naming of his sons. Often the name so chosen will be that of one of the exemplars the boy has selected. Obelisk has been used that way for centuries, and thus several Obelisks have been worthy of emulation. But about fifteen years ago a certain Obelisk Pheotin led a great raid over Maidens Pass and returned with cattle uncounted, such as had not been seen in a generation. After that, many young men were hailed by their name friends as Obelisk and sobbed with pride for it. Now do you understand?"

"Not completely," I said happily.

"Hunff! Of course a man's name is often just the baby name his mother gave him continued, or his grandfather's, or a nickname, or the name of a god. But if his friends decide that Obelisk is the most fitting name for him, he will be Obelisk until the hour of his death, and honored to be so. I knew a Godlike, and a Bloodlover. I had a close friend named Hasty. That was his true name and gods pity any man who smiled at it, for he thereby gained four mortal foes. Now you see?"

"This helps explain some tales I gathered—"

"Argh!" he snarled. "You prattle like a woman and you have started me doing it. Be silent like a man."

I assumed the lecture was over, and had already turned my mind to other things when he spoke again, softly.

"If they give their friend a *very* strange name, then they pay him a very great compliment. Do you see that, Little One?"

"No." I was only little when I was near him!

"It is another pledge of loyalty, of course, but mainly it shows they believe he has the strength to bear the burden. Such names are called *antler names*."

After a few more strides he said proudly, "I had a brother named Dimples." Thereafter he walked in silence, staring straight ahead, letting the wind dry the tears on his cheeks.

We stood on the western wall and viewed half the world. Lookouts paced in the distance on either hand, but otherwise we were alone, for the crowds of Vorkan watchers had not yet worked their way this far around yet. The walls of Zanadon are wide enough for two chariots to pass. In places they stand high on both sides. In others their top is almost level with the ground on the city side, and this was one of those places. I had positioned myself with respect to Maiana's shoulder, and then found the tree with golden flowers.

"There is the road I mentioned," I said. "I have a confession, Thorian—I dreamed of this place."

"Me, too," he rumbled, leaning on the parapet and staring at the distant haze and the white clouds above the horizon. "I am very grateful to you, Omar, despite my snippy remarks."

I choked back a query and took a harder look at my surroundings. I have a storyteller's ear; Thorian had a warrior's trained vision. I had not recognized that the gully just ahead of us was where the wall had been breached and repaired. Now it was tidy. The work was done and all traces of construction had been swept away. I leaned over the battlements and stared down at the ill-used forest far below. I wondered why there were so many birds . . .

"Thorian! Down there? Do you see?"

"I saw," he said, and continued to look straight ahead.

Zanadon needed its slaves no longer. Had Jaxian not called us away, we should have been lying there also.

We climbed the weedy road between the shacks and came to the yard I had dreamed of. There was no one in sight, for everyone had gone to the temple or the walls. Much of the junk I had observed was equipment left over from the repairs—ladders, pulleys, rope, tools. In time it might be sold off and removed, but at the moment it was there for the taking.

Thorian studied the high stones of the temple wall.

"We could scale that," he agreed.

"We should be in the grounds. But we could not be far from the door we came out of."

"And you were not serious about climbing the *outside* of the temple, were you?"

"That was for Jaxian's benefit. We were shown the secret stairs inside."

He nodded thoughtfully. "Then we shall need lanterns, and weapons."

"No weapons! Try to buy a sword in Zanadon now, and within an hour you will be shorter by a head."

He chuckled reluctantly. "Which would make me about your size! All right, no weapons. A coil of rope, maybe? Useful stuff. And let us not linger here longer lest we draw attention to ourselves."

23: Two Up

✳

The rest of that day was a melancholy, nerve-wracking wait. Even after the official mourning ended at noon, the pall of grief and fear did not lift from the city. Ash-strewn beards and bare legs remained everywhere in sight. The weather grew oppressively muggy, so that the least exertion provoked breathless, prickly exhaustion and floods of sweat. Thorian and I stayed together, reluctant companions. I wanted to gather tales, and chatter made him irritable. Admittedly, few citizens were in the mood for talk.

I was encouraged to note that Balor continued to approve of my intentions; he was almost smiling under his golden helmet. Every time I caught a glimpse of Maiana over the roofs, though, she seemed grimmer than before. I did not mention the matter again to Thorian. I did not want to worry him.

Dusk found us on the edge of the crowd near the great gatehouse. We carried a leather bag stuffed with two lanterns and some other supplies we had decided upon. We had full bellies—at Thorian's insistence, for I had lost my appetite. I could see the wisdom of it, though.

The procession began emerging. The crowd stayed silent, waiting. Priests first, then the city dignitaries—and finally the torches and the litter.

The crowd roared in approval, calling echoes from the towering buildings, sending up flocks of startled birds.

It was Shalial. Even Belhjes had seemed beautiful in the guise of Maiana. Shalial was dream made real. Her native beauty shone through paint and jewels and silver and made them all seem tawdry. If she was frightened, no one could tell. She wore a faint smile, but she kept her gaze ahead,

211

not looking at the screaming mob. She did not need to—
not a man there would not have died for this goddess.

And now I knew why her face had seemed hauntingly
familiar to me since the first glimpse I had of her. I wondered if High Priest Nagiak had noted that resemblance,
and if it had influenced his plans. *Maiana!* The gentle
curve of the nose, the proud demeanor . . . The likeness
was not as startling as that between me and the Rosh
statue, but it was there if one looked for it, and I thought
that mine were not the only eyes seeing it.

I resisted the draw of the crowd and remained myself.
It was an effort, but it was required of me. And as soon
as she had passed, when everyone else flocked behind her,
heading for the temple, Thorian and I slipped away and
began running as hard as we were able in the suffocating
heat.

We paused for breath below the yellow-flowered tree
and looked out over the fertile plain. We both knew we
might not see the world like this again. I was just as conscious of danger as Thorian must be. I still had faith in
the gods, but not quite as much as usual, for I was well
aware I might be straying beyond my mandate. I was not
merely observing, I was meddling, and I rarely do that.
We were taking a fearful risk, and we both knew it. For
me to say so would have been unkind, and for him unthinkable.

The sun had just set, and I thought I could make out
the thin crescent of the goddess, low in the sky below a
monstrous black storm cloud, whose top was red as blood.
The air was thick in the throat, hot and heavy as boiled
oil.

"It will be a wild night when that arrives," I remarked.

"Sztatch and Zomapp are brothers. Let us hope it is a
good omen. Come." Thorian turned away and headed up
the slope.

In the junkyard we stripped off our bulky Tharpit garments and hid them. We donned anonymous black loincloths, skimpy enough not to impede us. Even at that

distance, the roaring of the crowd in the Courtyard prickled my skin. I knew that every man there would be looking at Shalial and thinking that if Balor could refuse such beauty then he was no true god. Zanadon could have no finer woman to offer.

We laid our ladder against the wall, and Thorian went over first. I did not argue precedence. The priests would all be occupied with the ceremony . . . wouldn't they?

We came down in deep shadow in an orchard of lemon trees. Not daring to speak, we hurried toward the temple itself. I was worried by the cropped feel of the grass under my feet, for the light was too poor to make out the droppings. Sheep I could handle, but geese are far better watchdogs than watchdogs ever are. Nothing came screeching and snapping at us. The twilight was both a blessing and a danger. If we could proceed without lights so could others, and we might not see them in time.

The crowd had started to sing, which meant that the procession was already mounting the stairs. Urgency nipped at my heels and tightened my throat. We came to the rear wall of the cloister and then to the place where it abutted the temple itself. The singing was louder now. Here began the real danger. Up to now we had been trespassing, but with the option of running back to the orchard and scrambling over the wall. From now on there would be no fast escape.

Thorian paused. I went past him and boldly threw open the gate. To my left was the temple door. To my right were the cloisters, and torchlight gleamed on Maiana's heels straight ahead in the darkness. I saw and heard the crowd, but I hurried into the temple without a pause, aware of two bare feet padding behind me. The corridor seemed completely dark, but we must show up against the glow of the doorway at our backs. My belly had knotted with the conviction that at any second someone would cry out or I would simply walk into some absentminded priest meditating in the gloom, but I trailed one hand along the wall and hurried toward Nagiak's chamber at the end. My eyes were adjusting to the darkness by the time I reached it. If the door was locked we were balked.

The door was not locked. We closed it behind us, and I knew that then I drew my first real breath in some time. I recognized the unpleasant, cloying scent of the sumptuous room, but its furnishings and artwork were just vague shadows in the faint glow of the skylights. Marvel of marvels!—the rug had been rolled to one side. That disposed of another worry, that of straightening the cover over the trapdoor when we had entered. Truly the gods seemed to be encouraging us so far. Were we amusing them? I wondered.

Had I been alone, my progress would have ended right there in Nagiak's bedroom, for a secret trapdoor is not equipped with carved ivory handles or bronze rings. Because I knew it was there, I would likely have found the right flagstone, for I am not completely stupid, but I could never have opened it—not even had I sacrificed all my fingernails and all my toenails and even my teeth. Fortunately, the ever-practical Thorian had observed on our previous visit that the flap was pivoted, not hinged. When he positioned his toes along the back edge and then rose up on tiptoe, the infernal device knew it was beaten. The front lip lifted just enough for me to gain a fingerhold. Up it came. And down we went.

You have probably heard the tale of the nervous spinster who locks her chamber door, and bolts it, and then chains it, and then bars it, and has just finished pushing the dresser against it when a voice from . . .

All right, you know it. I never said it wasn't old.

But that story was what I thought about as I sat on the hard stone steps in pitch darkness with Thorian at my side. I was panting like a dog, partly from the putrid air, but mostly from release of tension. I could hear his lungs working almost as hard. I was absurdly happy to have reached that cellar. As a charnel house it had appalled me on our previous visit, yet now it was safe haven. I felt as if the worst part of our expedition was over once we had reached the secret part of the temple in safety. After this, anyone who challenged us was probably up to no good himself, and could not summon unlimited reinforcements with a simple shout. The feeling was not very rational, but I felt much better for it. And at the same time I kept thinking of the nervous spinster, and imagining Gramian Fotius putting his lips to my ear in the dark and whispering *boo!*

I have seen people die of fright, though, and it is a very quick way to go.

Thorian fumbled with our bag of supplies in search of light. I just sat. The crypt seemed cold, partly because I was streaming sweat, and that in turn was an effect of the foul air. Already my head was banging like a tombstone shop. I knew I was in danger of fainting, and so was Thorian, for sheer physical strength would be no defense against bad air. If we passed out, then we were dead. This catacomb might be a very effective burglar trap, and I wondered if that simple fact explained some of the skeletons at the far end.

A spark flashed. And another. Either the wretched air was affecting the flint or we had purchased poor tinder. Thorian muttered Polrainian obscenities and kept striking. Sparks flew like falling stars. I felt panic stir. High Priest Nagiak might well have returned to his room by now, directly over our heads. He might decide to drop in and count bones. Even if he just stretched out and relaxed with a good book, he held us trapped down in this morgue.

Thorian had switched from scatology to prayer, and that is always a bad sign. Maybe it was a wise decision, though, because eventually a flame flowered in the tinder. We needed only one lantern, but he lit both, and I did not argue. Ancient walls and roof swam into view, and also the rotting disorder of the temple archives spread over the floor. Some small things scurried away into the darkness.

I raised one of the lanterns; shadows swelled and shrank and swayed. Thorian handed me the supply bag, which was almost empty now. He took the other lantern and a wood ax that was the deadliest weapon we had dared try to acquire. We set off along the tunnel.

I wondered if anyone had passed through there in the last three days. I was morally certain that when the fat high priest needed to enter the secret places, he would prefer to have himself carried up to the chapel and use the other entrance. On the other hand, he might have trouble explaining what he was doing for long periods in the high priestess's quarters—I assumed then, and still do, that very few of the clergy were actually involved in the plot.

We reached the stair. I turned aside and Thorian kept straight on, padding like a leopard.

"Dumb bonehead!" I shouted, starting echoes rolling. "This way!"

"Be quiet!" he muttered, and kept walking.

I hurried to his side. "Are you mad? Let's get out of this cesspit before we choke."

"Gramian Fotius will be armed with a sword," he said quietly—and yet his voice sent deep rumbles reverberating along the catacomb—"and possibly wearing armor. I will go against him with an ax if I must. But I wondered if we might have overlooked some . . ."

We stopped together, seeing that there had been an addition to the ossuary. Now a bleached solidity lay discarded among the tangle of dark and dusty bones ahead. A hundred tiny eyes glinted at us; lithe rodent bodies slithered darkly on the flesh. Thorian strode forward to inspect; I turned and fled back as far as the stairs. My feet felt heavy, my heart was pumping. I swayed as I began to climb, and I had to stop and lean against the wall several times.

Quite suddenly I felt my wits start to clear. I had not climbed far—about up to ground level, I suppose—but the change was obvious, and very welcome. I wondered if Maiana had rented out the cellars of her temple to some ill-tempered god who disliked visitors. I sat down on the steps and breathed deeply as I waited for my companion. I saw his light appear, and then he came trudging up to me, lantern in one hand, ax in the other, and his shadow gigantic on the ceiling. He stopped on the step below my feet, but he did not sit. He just stood, looking down at me and sucking in the welcome fresh air in bushel-size gulps.

"Anyone we know?" I asked hopefully, thinking of Fotius.

"No."

"Tell me. I shan't scream."

"A woman. Just a girl, really. No one special. Not a lady, nor a priestess—calluses on her hands."

"Any sign of how she died?"

"Painfully," Thorian said in a low voice. "Mostly fists. In the end she was choked. He does that when he gets carried away. Whenever you tell this story, Trader of Tales, be sure to mention that girl."

"I promise."

"She can't have been there very long."

"No."

"We must put out the lanterns now. And then you'd better let me go first, Little One."

I did not argue.

That is a long climb, up through the ziggurat of Zanadon. Comparing memories, we had agreed that the stair had been unbroken by landings or turnoffs, and if it twisted at all, the effect had been too small to notice. If we used our lights, therefore, we should be visible from the top all the time we were climbing. We had brought a glow rope with us, and it was to be my job to keep the smoldering end inside the leather bag. Thus we could have fire quickly when we needed it, but would shed no light. Like most good ideas, glow rope does not always work as it is supposed to.

How long we took to make the climb I cannot even estimate—it felt like enough time to mow a hayfield with a pocketknife. The risers were uneven, and nothing is more infuriatingly deceptive or harder to negotiate than an irregular stair, even in daylight. In the dark it is an excruciating torment. Moreover, Thorian was in a hurry. Our tactical position was inauspicious and he was a firm believer that speed is the greatest virtue in warfare. I am nimble and would have laid bets I could hold my own with him at footwork, but he outran me. At first I tripped, stumbled, stubbed my toes, walked into him, and muttered obscenities. Later he drew ahead of me, and I stopped walking into him. I continued to do all the other things, though.

Eventually, when I had given up trying to catch him and was just blundering ahead at my own pace, I heard a curious noise over the sound of my own breathing and thumping heart. It bothered me, for I could not identify it. Then I heard it again, and wondered if the temple could be settling on its foundations.

The third time it was louder, and I knew it for the voice of Zomapp. The next flash must have been closer, for I saw my accomplice momentarily, not far ahead of me. The storm was almost upon us.

I thought about that, in so far as I could spare any thought from the problems of negotiating the steps. Big storms are scary; the crowd would be impressed. If the rain was heavy enough, it would drive the onlookers from the court—but the priests might let some take shelter in the cloisters. Thunder might drown out any suspicious noises. Lightning might reveal things better not revealed . . . On the whole, though, the storm was encouraging. Balor might have sent his brother to lend us assistance. Zomapp is the gods' messenger as well as their executioner.

Then I saw Thorian again, and this time the light was steadier and he was closer. Thunder rolled again, louder.

I heard a heavy pattering noise.

He had stopped. I drew up beside him and peered around his shoulder. Straight ahead was the secret room behind the chapel, and a candle flame dancing wildly. Raindrops were coming in through the skylight. Then a lilac flash from the skylight illuminated everything, only to plunge it back into darkness.

The image had been imprinted on my eyes, and as they slowly recovered until the candle was again visible, I reviewed what I had seen. There had been changes in the past three days. The place looked tidier, and more inhabited. The table was new, its white linen cloth fluttering anxiously in the wind. Even from our low vantage I had seen that there were silver dishes on it. The couch had gone, and the chairs had been grouped around the table. I thought there were fewer chests than there had been. This might have been where Gramian Fotius had passed the last three days, but somehow I doubted it. It seemed more like a meeting room, the headquarters of the conspiracy.

Thunder crackled and then roared overhead, rumbling away into the distance.

We were in a tricky location. Enemies could come at us from three directions—up the stair from the crypt, through the secret panel from the chapel, or down that other staircase we had not explored.

"Bring a lantern," Thorian said, and plunged up the last few steps. He rounded the corner and vanished up the second stairway.

Fumbling with my bag and the glow rope and lanterns, I dashed over to the table. Awkward in my haste, I first knocked the candle out of my lantern, then burned my fingers on the glow rope—which of course I no longer needed. I was about to light my lantern at the candlestick when a swirl of wind blew it out. Then I had to scrabble on the floor for the glow rope. Eventually, though, I had a lantern lit, and the room came back around me. Clutching up everything I had brought, I hastened after Thorian. The rain tapped faster.

The stair climbed steeply, parallel to the front of the temple. Soon I saw two pine trees ahead of me, rooted on the uppermost steps, but they moved to make space for me. The rest of him was in the room above. I reached his side, held up the light—and faces appeared in the darkness around us. I made a high-pitched warbling sound and very nearly dropped the lantern.

"Ssh!" he whispered.

They were statues. We were peering into a large, high space, cluttered with statues on one hand and chests and mysterious bundles on the other. I could barely make out the roof, except to note that it had a curved, corbeled shape. The room was perhaps three spans wide and stretched out into darkness on either hand. A young man in the front rank stared mockingly at me, and I thought of Rosh down in the Courtyard, smiling with my face. This youth ended just below his waist, which was why he could look me in the eye at the moment. Behind him was a one-armed matron.

Junk. The priests used this secret attic to store junk. What can you do with a damaged god or goddess? To break it up would be sacrilege. To worship it would be blasphemy. You tuck it away out of sight, of course. This was the place where the gods went to die.

Slowly we mounted the last few steps into the heavenly company. There was a narrow path winding off on either side through the forest of clutter. Which way to go?

Thorian gripped my shoulder and whispered in my ear. "I think there was a light to the left. Cover the lamp."

I tucked the lantern into the mouth of the bag. He disappeared. Everything disappeared. I stayed where I was, teetering on the edge of the trapdoor, trying to keep my teeth from chattering—I kept imagining the statues sneaking closer while I could not see them.

Needles of light flashed overhead and were gone. On our first visit to the temple, we had seen air holes concealed in the cornice that decorated the uppermost tier of the pyramid. They would be long tubes, adequate for ventilation, but not large enough to reveal light to watchers in the city if anyone was busy up here in the dark. The thunder rumbled outside, very muffled. I heard it more from behind me, coming up the stair, than I did from the vents overhead. I could feel air moving, though.

I decided that, if a phalanx of angry priests appeared, I would hide in among the statues and smile cryptically. I might even break off one of my arms to look less lifelike.

Vaguely now I could make out a glow to the left. Where was Gramian Fotius? He might be above me, in the House of the Goddess, consummating his apotheosis upon a screaming Shalial Tharpit.

He might be off to my left where the light was, being arrayed in Balor's armor by a dozen priestly assistants. But if I had to look forward to a full day in massive armor, I would not put it on until as close to dawn as I dared. I would not want it on when I was dallying with a beautiful woman, either.

He might be down in the temple having dinner with

High Priest Nagiak and a few selected notables, being instructed for the hundredth time in what was required of him—not his duties in the coming night, of course, but in the days ahead.

Came more lightning, two flashes in quick succession, and I thought I saw Thorian near the corner. More likely I was seeing phantoms.

I set my mind to working out the geography. I must be standing almost directly below the top of the great staircase, in front of the House of the Goddess. It took no great genius to guess that the chamber was a square. The House of the Goddess must be supported by a pillar of solid masonry at the heart of the pyramid, and this tunnel would go all the way around it. The rooms on all the other tiers formed three sides of a square, because the front of the structure was solid, but this secret level had no skylights and could go all the way.

If a parade of priests came up behind me, there would be plenty of places to hide, assuming it was all as littered as the portion I could see.

The light had disappeared.

I checked to make sure my lantern was still alight inside the bag and had not set the rope on fire. I gave it some more air, then closed the bag again, but not quite shut. The flame had dazzled me, and for a while I could see nothing.

I wanted to sneeze.

I desperately wanted to sneeze.

I rubbed my nose until it hurt.

Lightning. Thunder. I had never known anyone the size of Thorian who could move so quietly. The silence was good news, though. If he ran into anyone, I would hear the argument.

My legs were already weary from the long climb, and now they had begun to go to sleep, in pins and needles. I wriggled my toes. I wanted to sneeze.

Then I saw light glowing to my right, wavering, becoming brighter. I knew it could only be Thorian, gone all the way around, but my heart thundered louder than Zomapp himself until he came clearly into view, his face lit by the candle he was shielding with his spare hand. He had his ax tucked under one arm.

He worked his way carefully through between the heaps and the gods until he was back at my side, and his teeth gleamed in a smile.

"No one," he whispered.

"You're sure?" I was shivering with relief.

"I don't think that big pig would have the wits to hide." The smile vanished. "He may be upstairs, of course."

"Is there an upstairs?"

"Yes. Some sort of trapdoor again, of course. Whoever designed this place was very fond of trapdoors. Let's have more light."

He laid his silver candlestick on a chest, and I produced the lantern.

"Is this safe?" I asked.

"It soon will be." Thorian stooped and took hold of the flap, which was made of heavy timber, bound with metal, and so laden with dust that it had obviously not been closed in years. The hinges squeaked, and he paused.

"What in the name of Balor are you doing?" I demanded.

"Waiting for thunder. Ah!" Needles of light flashed on the roof again.

"Thorian! If you shut that, then you cut off our escape!"

He started to speak, and the thunder roared, louder than ever. The squeal of the hinges sounded much louder to me, as Thorian heaved the flap over, but of course that was a closer sound. The trapdoor thumped shut. Dust swirled like fog, sparking around the candle.

He chuckled in satisfaction. "Cutting off pursuit, you mean. Now . . . Ugh! Give me a hand here." He was trying to move the nearest chest.

"No!" I said. There was no need to be quiet now, but I still whispered. "You're out of your mind!"

But I knew *how* he was out of his mind. I had known for some time that he was making his own plans. I just had not wanted to admit it to myself. Now I had to face the problem.

"What do you suppose they . . ?" Thorian lifted the lid of the chest and whistled. Gold blazed in the candlelight— and then in another flash overhead. He glanced around, and so did I. There were six of the great chests, all solid timber, metal-banded. This was the temple treasury. Small wonder they were heavy.

"Come on!" he snapped, and braced himself to push.

"And how do we get Shalial out of here?" I snapped. "She must be up there, in the House of the Goddess. We came to rescue her, remember?"

He straightened up. Then he took a long step that put us toe to toe. He looked down at me threateningly and tapped me on the chest with a cautionary finger.

"No we didn't, Trader of Tales. I think you already know that wasn't why I came with you tonight. As for you, you came to Zanadon to see a god. Well, now you're looking at one. I am Balor. You may kneel."

24: Three Up

❋

"**T**he hell you are!" I said.

But, to be honest, I wasn't absolutely certain whether he was or not. Oh, I had no doubts he was a mortal, but I had suspected from the beginning that the gods had some purpose in mind for Thorian. He had been thrown in my path, and even when we had parted in a moment of pique, we had been brought together again very quickly.

I am a witness. I had been summoned to Zanadon to observe, and I had been shown many hidden things in my first hours in the city. Without Thorian I could never have contrived to see those things. That was one possibility— that he had been assigned to me as an assistant. I liked that idea best.

I still hoped that Balor would truly appear in his glory to rescue Shalial from a despicable death on the temple steps. I still hoped to see that incorporation this night, and again my arrival had been greatly aided by my brawny companion.

But if Balor did not come in person, was it not possible that he sent a suitable mortal in his place? That might be the truth behind the legend. That might always have been the truth. That was more the way gods usually worked. Thorian himself had suggested as much on that first evening—the hour brought forth the man.

Perhaps! Thorian was a warrior, and he was unknown to the people, so that he would not be recognized. He was shrewd and capable. I found him a much more believable war lord than the loutish Fotius acting as his grandfather's puppet. He might well have been sent by the gods, and if so then it was I who was the assistant.

He put a hand around my throat.

224

"I am now Balor. I shall go up to Shalial and explain. If she has met Fotius, she will welcome the substitution. If she has not, then she will still prefer me to a horrible death. I am not unskilled with women, Friend Omar. Did you not see how she looked at me?"

Yes, I had seen.

"I shall treat her with honor," he growled. "I admire her courage beyond all words, and I shall tell her so."

"But there is a problem, Thorian," I mumbled, having some difficulty moving my Adam's apple.

"There are innumerable problems, but the gods will provide. You have been eager to tell me to trust the gods. I have done so, and here I am. Now you will help me. Won't you?"

His hand tightened. I managed an infinitesimal nod and was allowed to breathe again.

There was, after all, no way I could stop him. The trapdoor was already closed, and he would not let me open it. Perhaps I could talk him out of it later. Perhaps I was not supposed to.

I felt a strange sense of inevitability settle over me. I am an observer. This is my talent, my duty, my destiny, and now I sensed that I could do nothing else but observe, and see what happened. Events had moved far beyond my feeble abilities to control them.

History had the bit between its teeth.

I went to help Thorian. Between us, we managed to push the chest onto the trapdoor. We found one that was only half full, and somehow we lifted that on top of the first. I thought I had wrecked my back forever. Thorian bulged all over more than I had imagined was possible, causing me to wonder how Balor could serve the city if he had a severe hernia.

And finally we laid half a granite statue on the top of the pile. The priests would have to cut their way in with axes. It would take them days. We would not be disturbed from that direction.

Still rubbing my back, I took the lantern and stalked off to inspect the temple attic. There was an astonishing collection of statuary and other junk in that first gallery. I wondered how the floor supported it, and then remembered that the stone was solid below me, all the way down to bedrock.

The second gallery, on the west, was more open. I saw huge heaps of moldering vestments that seemed like dangerous firetraps. Probably such garments were just too transcendentally holy to be destroyed. Carpets, also, in rolls. Piles of tables and chairs, many broken. There were mysterious cupboards so tightly wedged in that no one could have opened them in centuries. Indescribable filth encrusted everything. I peered up at the roof and saw swallows' nests packed like pebbles on a beach. I looked for bats, and wasn't sure.

Near the end of that gallery, though, I came to an open space. Here I found signs of recent habitation—a couch with fairly clean linen, a table with remains of food on it, a couple of chairs. This, I decided, had been Gramian Fotius's lair. Seeing several more silver candlesticks, all thickly coated in spilled wax, I lit some to gain more light. All I achieved thereby was to make the darkness darker.

"Look!" Thorian said at my elbow. He pointed to the couch, and the floor beside it. "Blood, not very old. This is where she died."

I made a croaking noise. Thunder rumbled on cue.

There was a hairbrush near my feet, and also a cloth that could have been a swath, discarded by someone who preferred to store his clothes on the floor.

"And come and see this." Thorian carried his lantern farther, dissolving the darkness before him until he reached the corner. Then he lifted the light to reveal a solid timber workbench large enough to seat a phalanx of soldiers, had it been a dining table. Hot colors of gold and bronze flamed under the lantern, giving us our first solid evidence of the planned deception. Here was the armor of the god, shining back at our lights in a thousand flames and sparkles—helmet and breastplate and fauld, greaves and vambraces and gauntlets. The style was foreign to anything I had ever seen in use, but Balor was always depicted in such antique trappings.

Thorian lifted the sword and tested its balance. The hilt flickered with gems. He grunted approvingly, felt the edge with his thumb, and nodded. Then he lifted the helmet and tried it on his head. That also was inlaid with gold and silver and a constellation of fine gems. It seemed to fit him comfortably—and he did look startlingly like Balor in it. Anyone would, I told myself.

"Think he . . . you, that is . . . think a man could stand in all that?" I asked.

"I could stand in it! I could fight all day in it. It is beautifully made. Very, very old, but superb craftsmanship. I have never seen finer, not even in the palace in Polrain. It would be wasted on that unspeakable Fotius." He laid the helmet reverently back on the bench. "Much of the original leather has been replaced, of course. Even the replacements seem old, but it is all supple and well cared for. Beautiful."

The bench was littered with rags and the air smelled of oil. Fotius had been kept busy. I glanced around uneasily at the waiting dark. Somehow this was turning out to be too easy. Where was the drama? Where was the villain? The food and the signs of recent activity made it seem that he had barely gone away—that he would be back any minute.

I hoped he was not already above us, with Shalial.

Thorian moved on, and his light quarried more wonders from the gloom—a bundle of clean-looking cotton garments had obviously not been lying among the rest of the filth for more than a few days, or perhaps hours. I went over to inspect them, and realized that they were padding, to be worn under the armor.

Then a headless, silver woman turned out to be a gown on a wooden mannequin. That also was too clean to have been there long. And there was the matching headdress . . .

By now we were in the north gallery, and the junk became sparser, mostly consisting of lighter things that had been moved out of the way—furniture, largely, and boxes of scrolls. Partway along the gallery, I came to an opening with a staircase leading up into the central column. I consulted the map in my head and decided it must be almost directly under Maiana, slightly to one side. I lifted my lantern to see.

All the roofs in the temple were more than twice as high as a man is tall, and this alcove was no exception. The steps ran right up to the ceiling, which itself must be the floor of the House of the Goddess. As Thorian had said, it must also be a trapdoor, or the construction made no sense. I walked part of the way up and saw a massive handle and two huge bronze bolts. The gleam of the metal said that they had been cleaned and oiled recently.

"Well?" boomed a voice behind me, and I jumped. "Well, Trader of Tales, shall we go up and inform the lovely Shalial of the change in plans?"

I was reluctant. "What's on the east side?"

"More of the same, plus a very smelly chamber pot. One big pigpen! Move!" Thorian was very eager to meet Shalial again.

"Shouldn't you bring Balor's sword along, in case she already has company?"

"The trapdoor is locked from this side, Omar. Balor's armor is on this side. I do not anticipate finding Fotius on the other. That's called *strategic thinking.*"

Annoyed at losing the argument, I ran up the stair with Thorian close behind me. When my head touched the stone, I surveyed its wide expanse with dismay. "This is impossible!" I said. "Jaxian was right! Two men can never lift this."

"It is pivoted, you mudhead! See? There are chocks set in the walls. Now pull those bolts or let me at them."

I crouched until I was almost prone on the steps, reaching for the bolts. I heaved on the first. It slid easily. I switched hands, tried the other, and that gave me no greater trouble. So I pushed my shoulders against the cold, smooth granite above me. I suppose Thorian was lifting, also, but I pretended that I was doing it all by myself. The giant slab was so massive that I had to strain every sinew to start it moving, but then it turned by itself, lifting off my back, perfectly balanced at its center. Light poured into my eyes, momentarily blinding me, and I gagged at the rank odor of burning pitch.

When the stone had tilted roughly parallel with the angle of the stairs, the counterweight struck the chocks and it came to a shuddering halt. The whole temple seemed to tremble. Still blinking, I straightened up to survey the House of the Goddess.

Leafy fronds had been piled into a couch near the center. The heap was not high enough to sit on in comfort, but Shalial Tharpit was sitting on it anyway—leaning back gracefully on straight arms, legs outstretched, one perfect ankle crossed over another, regarding me with her dainty chin slightly tilted and a wary, quizzical expression in her gorgeous dark eyes.

"Are you sure you wouldn't rather be married to Dithian Lius?" I asked politely.

25: The Tamarisk Grove

✳

Forty or so great torches flamed and smoked in sconces all around the walls, but lightning blazed in through the door in white lilac, flashing shadows where none had been before, and we seemed to plunge back into darkness right after, in contrast.

Thunder crashed at the same instant, loud enough to scramble a man's brains. The storm was directly overhead. It was a monster. Rain roared steadily on the golden roof. Outside the arch, it sprayed up from the granite platform like silver grass. The air was cool for the first time since I arrived in the Spice Lands.

I scrambled out from under the slab and straightened up, carefully adjusting my meager attire over my extremely flat belly, while running a hand through my artfully tousled curls and donning my best award-winning smile. Shalial would have that effect on anyone with hair on his chin or any hope of ever having hair on his chin or any memory of ever having had hair on his chin. Thorian emerged on hands and knees, rose impressively, and then went through the same performance exactly. He managed to include a few ripples that I could not.

As Jaxian had predicted, she had been left nothing much but a wisp to cover herself. There was plenty of it floating around in the gusty air, but it was transparent as a thin mist. Her limbs and body glowed through it. Her hair had been dressed in ringlets, and she wore a horned coronet of silver. Nothing more. She looked understandably chilly, and beautiful as Ashfer herself.

I could not understand why the chamber was not jammed with gods.

"I do think you have come to the wrong address, milords," she said evenly. She seemed strangely unwilling to be rescued. Rather miffed, even.

Flash! I had overlooked Maiana until that moment, when the sudden play of the lightning on her silver skin made her seem to step forward. The Passionate One dominated the great chamber. She was a goddess of fire and light as her jewels and metal played with the torches—starry heavens folded into woman's form. It was very pretty and yet I did not feel the presence of the goddess there. My eyes returned to the lovely Shalial.

Crash!

Torchlight danced in sconces all around the walls as the wind whipped their flames into a mad dance. Some of them had blown out completely, trailing smoke and an eye-watering reek of pitch. A curtain of silver rain stood over the doorway. *Flash!* Lightning normally illuminates the whole world, yet I saw nothing but rain outside, and more rain beyond that.

"You may remember me. I am Omar. My friend goes by the name of Thorian. We have come to rescue you."

Shalial raised an eyebrow disbelievingly. "And what if I do not wish to be rescued?"

"He lies," Thorian grunted. He strode across and sank to his knees before her. She regarded him with an obvious distrust that he deflected with an obvious self-confidence. "I did not come to rescue you, milady. I am come to aid Zanadon in its hour of need. I am Balor."

Shalial pursed her lips. "Indeed? But your face has been well hammered, you bear sword scars, and as you came in, I thought I detected the marks of a good lashing on your back." *Flash!* "Can the god of war lose a battle? Who defeats him? Have the other gods been ganging up on you, milord?" *Crash!*

There was the problem I had tried to explain to Thorian—how could so damaged a man ever hope to pass as a god?

He shrugged. "My helmet will conceal my face. Perchance when I issue orders, the absence of a tooth or two will show, but I suspect this adds an appropriately minatory quality to my grimace—grown men shall weep at my smile. None of the wounds to my body will show through armor. You may know of them, but none else. I shall be a god in public. For you I shall be a man.''

She seemed to suppress a shiver. ''It is true that I am expecting divine company this evening, but I am not certain that you fit the description. Did you bring your credentials?''

''I call on the weather as my witness. Is not the climate auspicious for a war god's wooing?'' *Crash!* went the thunder. Huge yellow flames streamed from the torches; their fumes nipped my eyes and made me want to cough. Rain hammered mercilessly on the roof. Romantic?

Shalial had to shout over the din. ''Perhaps so, but if it foretells our future life together, then the neighbors may complain of the noise.''

She turned her head to look at me with a poise miraculous in one so young and in such peril. She must know what had happened to Squicalm and Belhjes; I could only assume that she was now privy to the conspiracy—but had she consented to Fotius? Had she ever set eyes on him?

I had withdrawn a few paces, and settled down crosslegged to witness Thorian's courtship. On my first visit I had seen this great hall as an untroubled sanctuary of peace, but now the blinding flashes and the jarring booms of thunder were unsettling. It was still virtually empty, with just the three of us and an open trapdoor and a heap of herbage marring the perfection of the huge expanse. I had a sense of floating slightly above events, of being a watcher rather than part of the picture. But Shalial wanted to include me. She was smiling at me.

''I think Omar may have better qualifications. I have it on excellent authority—his own—that he is the son of the Holy Rosh.'' A tingle of amusement brightened her eyes. *Flash!*

My heart began to race. I had never even considered such a possibility, but I would certainly be able to play the role of Balor more convincingly than Gramian Fotius ever could. True, I was no warrior. True, I lacked the bulk and muscle of either Fotius or Thorian, but I am a passable figure of a man, and I am experienced in dramatic simulation. I have been many things in my time—pot mender, clothes maker, warrior, mariner, landowner, pauper, mendicant, politician . . . the list is so long that even I have forgotten half of it.

But I had never been a god.

Shalial turned back to Thorian and caught him in a scowl. "Half a god is better than no divinity, milord. And he lacks the obvious bodily damage that mars your form. I believe he has all his teeth, for example."

Thorian shot me a very threatening glance. The rutting season was under way. He was besotted with her, and had been so since the first moment he set eyes on her, in her father's house.

"Put him in Balor's armor and he would disappear. He would fall over! The helmet would come down to his shoulders."

"Splendid! Then no one could see his face."

"You are very brave, Shalial," Thorian said. "Courage is the first requirement of a man. It is the finest adornment of a woman."

She winced slightly and then recovered her marble-cool poise. "I did not truly believe you that first night, milord. I admit it and apologize for doubting you. But today His Holiness explained to me, and my father was there and he agrees."

"What exactly did they explain to you?"

"That many centuries have passed since Immortal Balor was last summoned, and in these lesser times he may not answer our appeal. He has been given three chances. If he does not come before dawn, then it will be necessary to provide a substitute. The danger to the city is extreme, and the army needs leadership. The problem is, are you that substitute?"

"I am a great deal better man than the one they have chosen."

"Mm? You will pardon my consideration of possible bias in your assessment?" *Flash! Crash!*

Thorian smiled at her, but that may have been a poor move, because it showed his broken and missing teeth.

Kneeling before her, he began to talk, shouting over the storm.

"Lady, let me tell you of myself. Thorian is not my true name, but I am a true warrior, and of noble birth. My father was cousin to the king of Polrain. I was about fifteenth in line to the throne, although that matters little. My family owns wide estates, although that does not matter much either now. I am twenty-four years old, and unmarried. I had begun to make my name known outside my clan, but that again is now of no import.

"I was wounded at Gizath, when the flower of my homeland perished before the Vorkans. My father and brothers were among the fallen, and they feast now with the brave in the halls of Sztatch. Truly, I acquitted myself without shame to my exemplars, but I shall not boast of my exploits. I acquired this wound you see. For many days I hovered near death. As soon as I was well enough to sit a horse, I resolved to continue the struggle against the invaders. I managed to catch up with them, and pass them, and I came to Zanadon in the belief that here would be the final stand. On arriving in your country, I rode up to a party of soldiers to offer my service to your city. I was disarmed, stripped, and enslaved."

Shalial had tucked her legs in under herself and hugged her arms tight around her. Perhaps she was feeling the chill. Perhaps she felt threatened. But she was intent on Thorian. I sighed to myself and abandoned my mad dreams of being a god.

Flash! Maiana seemed to twitch. *Crash!*

Thorian continued. "Shalial Tharpit, you are without question the most beautiful woman I have ever seen. Accept my love, and I will put your happiness before my life, my body, my wealth, and all else that I hold dear. I swear this by my true name, by my honor and exemplars. Accept me as the Balor you seek, and I shall serve your city for your sake. I shall be avenged upon the Vorkans, for the souls of my brothers and those of my name friends. I know more of warfare and this enemy than anyone in Zanadon. I can lead your army to victory—of this I am certain. And when the war is won, then I shall take you back to my homeland and unite with you in marriage. You will rule our lands at my side, honored always as my lady and my one true love. For you I will forsake all others, and this above all I swear.''

It was an impressive speech, and she was moved. Color had risen in her face, and she could not meet his eye. But she was a brave woman, and she spoke with courage.

''Milord, you honor me greatly, and I doubt nothing you say. Had you made such a speech to me three nights ago, then I might well have accepted you, crazy though that may seem, considering that we were strangers. But you forget that now I am sworn to the goddess of this city. I am High Priestess of Maiana, and I can no longer consider marriage with any man, however noble his line or pure his heart.'' She blinked away a tear. ''Forgive me, milord. You come too late. What you suggest can never be.''

Thorian snarled. ''And what of this fake Balor that you have been promised?''

She looked up, surprised. ''What of him? I believe in the god, milord! It is the true Balor I await, with heartfelt faith in both him and his love for his city. If he comes, then of course a priestess must yield to a god. But if I am unworthy in his eyes, then I shall do my duty by the city. I told you how it will be. Before dawn, the Holy Nagiak and my father will bring forth a man who will play the part for the multitude. You say his name is Fotius, but I did not inquire. They tell me that he is a suitable candidate, a noble warrior, and I accept their judgment. What else can I do, for the people's sake? I shall stand by his side at the top of the steps when they acclaim him. What has this to do with marriage, milord?''

What indeed?

Flash! Crash! The echoes rolled away into the distance.

Thorian opened his mouth and then closed it. He glanced very briefly at me and then gazed down at his knees.

We had bungled! We had been deluded by the legend of the priestess and the god. We had been misled by what Thorian knew of the Fotius man and his murderous lusts.

But those were irrelevant, and that was what the wily Nagiak had seen and we had not. There would be no sacred coupling and no rape. There was no romance here, only straight politics. Shalial was high priestess. Fotius, the malleable, unknown warrior, would masquerade as Balor at the head of the army. Sex did not come into it at all.

We had misjudged Bedian Tharpit. If his milksop son knew of Gramian's reputation, then he must. If he had trusted his only daughter to this hoax, then he had certainly gained assurances that she would not be harmed. Whatever Fotius himself might have been led to expect— and gods alone knew what he might have been promised— he would be used as a puppet, deprived of red meat, and supplied with lowborn concubines. Shalial would reign as high priestess. They would stand together in public and be kept safely apart in private. It was all hard politics, and romance did not enter into it.

We had blundered horribly.

Shalial seemed puzzled by her suitor's sudden silence. "They will come before dawn, milord. If you are not the man they are to bring, then I suggest that you depart in haste. After all, I am waiting here for a god, and gods are notoriously shy. Your presence may be keeping him away. I thank you for your words. Go, with the Holy Mother's blessing."

Her spirit was inspiring. How capricious of the gods, to have given such courage to the daughter and so little to the son!

"I cannot depart!" Thorian growled. "We have blocked the passage by which we entered. The priests will surely have discovered that fact by now, so the way cannot be reopened. I am Balor at your side, milady, or I am a dead man."

I glanced thoughtfully at the torrents of rain blowing in through the archway. The storm raged undiminished, and the torch flames leaped. Several more had blown out. No one down in the Courtyard would notice two men slip out from the House of the Goddess during this downpour. The tempest might not rage much longer, but we could leave by that door while it did. With the gods' help we could descend to the next level, slip down through the skylight into the secret room behind the chapel, and scamper away down the long staircase to the crypt. When Nagiak was attending to his dawn duties, we might escape through his bedchamber. But we should have to go soon, while the weather lasted.

Shalial had paled. "You refuse to leave?"

"I cannot leave!" Thorian barked. "Moreover, the fake Balor you await cannot arrive, for the same reason. When morning comes, you will have me at your side or you will have no one. And in that case, the priests must complete the ritual, and you will follow Squicalm and Belhjes."

He was right! Our bungling might have doomed her to a worse fate than we had anticipated.

She flushed furiously. "You are a meddlesome, muscle-bound moron! I sit here expecting a god, and instead I get a two-man comedy team escaped from some rural fairground. Take your skinny, fuzz-faced friend there and crawl back down into your burrow and leave me be!"

Flash!

"Milady! First you spurn my suit—"

Shalial was bright with fury now. "I am a priestess! Your words were blasphemous!"

"But you must not deny me the chance to avenge my family, milady! Acknowledge me as Balor and I swear—"

"You swear too much! The man who should stand by me has been handpicked by the leaders of the city. If they wanted a flogged slave such as you, they could have found a thousand in the sweepings of the plain starving beyond our gates. You expect me to deliver Zanadon into the hands of a vagrant adventurer at his own behest? Begone, I say! And shut the door after you!"

Wealthy, beefy young men fifteenth in line to thrones rarely gain experience in handling rejection. Thorian was completely at a loss, helpless between fury and dismay, like a dog between two cats. "Then you will be thrown to your death, woman!"

"So be it!" Shalial was picking up a high priestess's haughty manner very quickly.

"Ahem?" I cleared my throat. She turned to look at me warily, and then Thorian did so, also.

"It would seem," I said, "that the god will not come, and the man cannot come. Is it not possible that someone else may, someone who stands between a man and a god?"

Thorian made an angry-lion noise. "If this is the beginning of another of your accursed stories—"

"Of course it is."

"Is it brief?" Shalial inquired.

"Very brief, milady."

"Then you may tell it. And then you will both leave." As if regretting her momentary loss of temper, she composed herself to listen, ignoring the furious man at her feet.

"Long, long ago," I said, "before history had learned to crawl, while gods still sometimes walked the earth, when Zanadon was only a crude village of wattle huts upon a hill—then there was no great temple, only a grove of tamarisk sacred to Maiana. In those days a band of enemies drew nigh the village. They wielded axes of stone, and they had no ponies, but they were dangerous, and the people were afraid."

"So?" Shalial said grudgingly.

"There was great dispute among the warriors of the village over who would lead the young men against the enemy. And while they disputed, the threat drew nearer, and yet nothing could be done until a leader had been chosen and accepted by all. It is the way of warriors that they are proud and do not willingly serve under one another. They choose their own leaders and will follow none but them. It had always been thus."

"So?" she muttered again, with a sidelong glance at Thorian.

"So the high priest of the village devised a scheme. He announced that he would summon a god to lead the young men, and all agreed that they would follow a god. The priest, having obtained their consent to this plan, announced that the high priestess would lie by night in the sacred grove to summon the god, who would be drawn to her beauty and would come to couple with her. When he had lain with her, then she would beseech him to take command and smite the foe, and he would agree, for who can refuse a reasonable request at such a moment of content? No man, surely, nor yet a god. Thus the high priestess, greatly flattered, went to the grove at sunset and waited for the god. The people of the village were simple folk, but they were not stupid. They saw the opportunity for deceit. To prevent cheating, the priest set guards to stand watch all night around the grove and let no mortal man enter upon pain of death.''

Thorian's eyes were shining.

''Alas,'' I continued, ''when morning came, there was no god to be seen. So the priest announced that the priestess had proved unworthy, and she was put to death at once. The village selected another high priestess, and the next night she also lay in the grove and waited for the god.''

''How long is this going to continue?'' Shalial inquired coldly.

''That was what the people began to wonder. And at last the maiden chosen was one who had a lover, a wily, nimble warrior. He was strongly opposed to seeing his beloved beheaded in the cold light of dawn—or at any other time of day, I assume. To save her, he was prepared to risk even his own life, as true lovers always will. And in the darkness, he evaded the guards and entered into the sacred grove, and there lay with his beloved.''

Crash!

''And in the dark she did not know him?'' Shalial asked pensively.

''Who knows? Who cares? In the morning he was hailed as the god, and he led forth the other young men to do battle.''

''They won?''

''Of course they won!'' Thorian bellowed. He took her hand and began to chafe it, as if it was cold. ''They were led by a man with courage and craftiness, who had proved himself worthy by risking death for his love. What else does an army need?''

She did not pull her hand away. She frowned at me. "Explain your riddle, milord. Who stands between a man and a god?''

I had no chance to reply.

"A hero," said Thorian. "A man who has proved his wit and his bravery . . . and his love. As I have proved myself tonight by coming here for you. This is why you are here, lady—to call forth a hero from Zanadon. Not a real god. Not a fake chosen by the priests. A true hero, chosen by himself, as true heroes always are.''

Shalial wiped her cheek, not looking at him. "I am moved by your friend's tale, milord. It explains much.''

"Oh, let me be your hero, Shalial!''

Flash!

"He left out the bit about fighting the dragon," said Gramian Fotius, emerging from the trapdoor.

Crash!

26: Four Up

✳

As he straightened to his full height, we saw that he carried Balor's great sword. He wore boots, and Balor's helmet, and nothing more. He was very big.

Shalial screamed. I jumped up, but Thorian was faster. I did not even see him rise to his feet. He seemed to fly over the couch of tamarisk, and a moment later he skidded into the wall beyond, grabbing for a torch.

I should perhaps describe those torches for the benefit of those who have not visited the Spice Lands, or other places where there are seeps of bitumen. When Thorian whirled to meet his opponent's charge, he was wielding a bronze club longer than a sword, and heavier. The upper end of such a torch is hollow and contains a wick of hemp, implaced with molten pitch. The wick burns with a bright light, and such lights are used extensively outdoors. One of their advantages is that winds strong enough to blow out ordinary lanterns merely cause the pitch to burn hotter. Their heavy fumes limit their indoor use, of course.

Often they have wooden grips on their lower ends, because the metal can become unpleasantly hot throughout their length. The torch that Thorian grabbed was not designed to be carried. It was cast of solid bronze, inlaid with silver and gold, and probably painfully hot in his hands.

That night the violence of the storm had been so great, even within the House of the Goddess, that half the flames had been blown out, while the rest had roared with special brilliance. Thus the upper end of Thorian's club was red hot, and whatever pitch remained within it would be close to boiling. Against a man stupid enough not to protect himself with armor when he had armor available, the torch was a considerable threat.

But it was not a sword. It had no edge, no guard to protect the fingers. The two men were of comparable age and size and strength, but the odds were with Fotius. His blade cracked into the wall where Thorian had been standing and then flashed aside to parry the first blow of the torch. They backed off a moment, taking each other's measure.

I had two options: I could attempt to obtain a torch of my own and enter the fray, or I could comfort Shalial. I chose to comfort Shalial. You may consider this cowardice. It did not seem so to me at the time, because I was risking the results of a Fotius victory. Self-interest should have impelled me into the fight. But I was present as an observer, remember, and observers must remain neutral. Furthermore, I clearly recalled Thorian yearning to settle his score with the brutal slaver, and I knew he would resent my assistance more than welcome it. I was not at all worried, for I have faith in the gods. Here was the confrontation I had sensed as preordained. Let the odds be only close to even, Thorian had said, and he would welcome the match. His prayer had been granted.

Fotius laughed and slashed down with his sword, seeking to slice his opponent's hands. Thorian deflected the blow with the torch, which he was holding vertical. The flame swirled and smoked above their heads. Fotius thrust at his belly. Thorian sidestepped and parried again.

During this opening round, I had hauled Shalial to her feet, wrapped a protective arm around her, and withdrawn to the wall to observe. She shivered and clung to me, and I was content in my observer's role.

I have possibly given a false impression of Gramian Fotius, for my thoughts of him were heavily colored by Thorian's views. The man was undoubtedly stupid, and brutal. Yet he was also possessed of a certain animal cunning, and he quickly revealed that he was no mean fighter. I am sorry—redeeming qualities in a villain are distressing, I admit.

How he had evaded us in the secret chamber I do not

know, and I never discovered. Always I narrate only strict truth, you understand, and I cannot testify to what I have not witnessed. For the benefit of dramatic completeness, though, we may speculate. You will understand that this is only speculation?

The day had been intensely hot and muggy. He had perhaps been harangued by priests, or working on the armor, and he had probably tired himself with his lovemaking, if that is a comprehensible term in the circumstances. I suspect, therefore, that he had gone to sleep on the couch. He may well have been wakened by the singing as Shalial was conducted up to the House of the Goddess. Finding the room dark, he would have lit a candle, and it is notable that only one had been lit when Thorian and I arrived.

I suspect—and again I stress that this is only guesswork—that he slipped his feet into his boots and wandered off without bothering to take the light, and in that case his most probable destination was the chamber pot that Thorian had observed. When Fotius was returning, he saw the intruder.

He had, as I said, a certain animal cunning. He could not know who this was, or how many companions he might have, and yet even Fotius could not have mistaken Thorian for a priest. There were a thousand places to hide in that midden, even for so large a man. So he must have hidden himself and watched what we did. Very likely he later made his way to the exit, meaning to report the intruders to the priests. He found the way impossibly blocked. So he took up sword and helmet, and climbed the steps after us to listen. Or so I must presume.

Flash! Crash!

The fight continued with more footwork than armwork, both men being cautious. The storm was trying to surpass itself. Wind howled around us, lashing Shalial's gauzy garment, even starting to shift branches from the tamarisk heap and skid them across the floor. Maiana watched impassively as the two would-be champions battled below her. Sheets of flame fled from the torches, and more of them blew out. Lightning blazed almost continuously outside. It was a wild night.

Still Thorian contrived to keep his burning torch upright, using it as a quarterstaff. Fotius realized that he was up against more than a club and began to work at longer range, jabbing with the point of his sword. At last Thorian saw an opening, parried the blade, and swung at his opponent's eyes.

Fotius was wearing a helmet with nosepiece and cheekpieces, and the rest of him was unprotected. He could not have been worrying much about a blow to the face, but in this case his beard went on fire, and burning pitch splashed over his chest, as well. The torch flame went out. A few moments later the fire in Fotius's beard went out also, but molten pitch is both very hot and very sticky. I do not know why he was not blinded. I do know he lost a lot of flesh. By all the rules of combat, the fight should have ended right there.

A prolonged crash of thunder drowned out the man's initial screams, or the crowd in the cloisters would have heard them clearly. They might have been audible in Polrain. Shalial and I shuddered in unison.

The fight should have been over. Had any one of Thorian's subsequent slashes connected, it would have been. But it wasn't. I hate to admit any admiration at all for a murderous pervert like Gramian Fotius, but I must pay tribute to his courage. With a feat of sheer will as impressive as anything I have ever witnessed, he kept control of his limbs in that awful torment. He parried Thorian's attack even while he was on fire. In moments he returned to the attack.

Maddened by pain, he went berserk. He screamed without pause, even over the continual crashing of thunder, and he whirled that huge, two-handed sword as if it were a rattan cane. He went after Thorian like a whirlwind.

The torch had gone out, there was no more pitch to spill, but the end was still hot. Thorian jabbed with it, branding great rings on his opponent. He smote ringing impacts on the helmet, and he repeatedly landed blows with enough force, I should have thought, to smash any normal man's bones. He might have done as well with a fly whisk, for nothing would stop the corporal. Despite his own fury and skill, Thorian was driven backward as fast as he could move by that glittering blur of bronze.

Shalial and I watched in awe. I realized that I should reconsider my scruples and start to play an active role, or I might find that I waited too long.

"Excuse me a moment," I muttered politely, disengaging my arm with reluctance. *"Look out behind!"* I screamed, seeing Thorian being driven swiftly backward. A crash of thunder drowned out my words, and the fight was over. Thorian had vanished and Fotius held the field . . . alone.

Thorian had backed into the hole in the floor—not the stairs side, but the counterweight side, which was just as large and much more dangerous. He fell on the slope of the tilted slab, shot down it, and was gone into the dark, accompanied by a roll of thunder.

A long moment later we heard his torch strike the floor below. Thorian had very likely broken both legs or even his back. He was out of the fight.

Still capering, Fotius stared at the hole for a moment, as if puzzled. Then he screamed his triumph, waving the sword overhead. His chest was charred through to the bone in places, and I did not want to see what was under the helmet.

I took Shalial's hand. "I think we should leave, dear," I said. I eyed the distance to the door. Fotius was eyeing me, and he seemed to be laughing.

He began to advance.

"Run!" I shouted, gave Shalial a shove, and lunged for the nearest torch.

An explosion of wind howled into the chamber and blew out all the flames. For an instant there was no lightning, only the bellow of the rain and the shriek of the wind. The archway should have been visible as a faint glow, but my eyes were not adjusted to the dark. I felt totally blind.

I took off along the wall, running my hand on it so I would not fall in the hole as Thorian had done, and eventually I must come round to the door. I expected to cannon into Fotius at any moment.

A couple of faint blue lights began to flicker as two torches recovered from the blast of wind.

Then Shalial screamed.

Flash! Fotius had caught her by the trailing ends of her draperies. I expected them to rip, but they didn't. *Flash!* He had transferred his grip to her arm; she was struggling helplessly.

Flash!

"Come here, Slave!" he shouted to me. "Or I cut off her breasts."

"Release that woman right away!" a new voice thundered. "Or p-p-pay the p-p-price!" it added.

Flash! Flash! Flash!

A man stood in the archway, holding a sword.

27: Five Up

✳

Yes, it was Jaxian Tharpit. Of course it was Jaxian Tharpit! Who else could it have been?

At this point in the evening, things began to move quickly, and a certain amount of confusion crept into the situation. For one thing, the two revived torches were sputtering and uncertain, sometimes close to dying again in the wind, sometimes flaring up. Maiana jumped in and out of existence at the rear of the chamber as lightning flashed in a similar jagged pattern. At times we were in pitch darkness and at other times in brilliance. The noise of thunder was so continuous and so painful that it made rational thought almost impossible. The whole temple seemed to shake with the racket.

All of which is by way of excuse for the poor quality of my observation and narration. I have very spotty memories of the events subsequent to Jaxian's entrance.

I recall running toward Shalial, and seeing her in a series of still images, contorted now this way and now that as she fought to free herself from Fotius. Her movements between these strange postures were veiled in darkness and did not register. She was a heroine in an illustrated book, and someone was flicking the pages.

Similarly, I know that Jaxian ran in from the entrance, brandishing his sword. Again, I recall a series of inky drawings, his long shadow dark before him; he seemed to jump closer in each successive picture, with no movement between.

I think I grabbed Shalial's arm in passing just as Fotius released her, as if we were a relay team and she the baton.

I do know that she was with me, that I had my arm around her, and that we were circling around to head back to the archway when a clatter of bronze announced the start of the sword fight.

I know she screamed "Jaxian!" right in my ear.

"He's coming!" I insisted, as I dragged her out of the House of the Goddess. She did not want to leave him, although what she could have done to help him I cannot guess.

I glanced back from the door and saw two embattled warriors frozen in lightning: Balor's brazen helmet blazing on a dark Fotius, and Jaxian, whose skin was soaking wet, gleaming silver like Maiana in the background. A disembodied head fighting a decapitated body.

Then Shalial and I plunged out into the storm and were almost blown away at once. What had been a wild night inside was mind-wrecking outside. The impact of the rain was a torment, a flogging with whips of ice. It was more blinding than the darkness. If you have ever tried to run across the top of a pyramid with your eyes shut in a tropical cloudburst dragging a screaming woman in a heavy surf, you will understand. If not, you can't possibly.

Shalial wanted to go back and rescue her brother. I wanted to find the ladder.

"We are all warriors in Zanadon now," Jaxian had said, meaning that all able-bodied men had been conscripted into the militia for the emergency. But I had watched Fotius outfight Thorian, and I knew that a lunch-hour swordsman like Jaxian had no hope against him whatsoever. Jaxian was as good as dead in my mind, and Balor needed a beard.

Sorry . . . have I got ahead of you?

I'll run through it, then, although at the time I had not worked it out in strict logic. Thorian had blocked the secret entrance, so the priests could not come up to the House of the Goddess at dawn to effect their production of a fake Balor. They must know that Fotius was up there, though, and the public ceremony would have to take place in the morning. They would assume that Fotius had been responsible for loading the trapdoor. They might equally assume that he had some nefarious motive for doing so, involving Shalial and a desire to remain undisturbed. They would just have to hope that she would survive the encounter and that Fotius was capable of donning the divine armor and making his appearance without further assistance from them.

But Balor is invariably depicted with a lush square beard halfway down his chest, and Fotius had lost his beard in a fire. Thorian was dead or crippled. Jaxian was about to be chopped into kebabs by Fotius. My beard did not qualify, and Shalial did not have one. So the whole deception was going to fall apart.

Obviously Jaxian, overcome with shame at his cowardice, had decided to lend assistance in rescuing his sister. I had told him an improbable tale of scaling the outside of the pyramid with a ladder. Such a feat might just have been possible with two men on a quiet night, but was manifestly impossible for a lone man in a storm such as this—except that somehow he must have achieved it, because he had arrived. So somewhere there was a ladder, and my firm intention was to find that ladder and escape with Shalial.

Does that make sense? It did at the time.

Or it did until I was outside in the storm. Half beaten to my knees by the rain, swung hither and thither by the wind, and blinded by lightning and darkness in rapid alternation, I completely lost my way in a few seconds. I made a right-hand turn, knowing that Jaxian would have brought his ladder from the west. Then I realized that he might have detoured round to the north, where he would be more likely to escape detection. Shalial squirmed out of my grip and disappeared. I decided to go back for her. On the other hand perhaps I should locate the ladder first?

And by then I could not remember which hand was which or which way I wanted to go.

Water was streaming over the paving, and I knew that there would be a slope to take it to the edge. I inched downstream. A fortunate flash showed me that I had one more step to disaster and I stopped. I realized then that the ladder might not be quite long enough to protrude above the top of the wall, and in that case I would need all night to find it. I turned around, located the House of the Goddess in the next flash, and started back.

If that sounds confused, it does not do justice to the situation. I was not nearly so well organized as I have indicated.

And suddenly everyone was outside in the cloudburst. I saw Jaxian, backing furiously, but still alive and apparently unwounded, still holding off Fotius's murderous assault. They were heading for the edge, though, and in a moment Jaxian's speedy retreat would carry him off as suddenly as Thorian's had. Shalial was heading for them. Knowing where my duty lay, I rushed over to assist. The four of us came together on the brink of the cliff as a sudden incandescent brightness . . .

Rain beat on my face and chest to rouse me. My head was full of a high-pitched singing, and I tingled strangely all over. I was also half drowned and quite blind.

I raised myself on my elbows and wondered where I was. Then I remembered and wished I hadn't. I turned my head to the left and waited, spluttering and spitting. With the storm fading, the next flash seemed to hold back deliberately. When it finally came, it revealed only water, sheeting across granite. I turned my head the other way in the darkness and waited again.

Realizing that my feet were resting on air, I pulled them back. I have seen people struck by lightning. The effects are so unpredictable that in many lands Zomapp is worshipped as a goddess. Once I saw a bolt strike half an armored phalanx on the battlements of Otranthan. Four of the men died instantly, about as many were badly burned, and the rest merely knocked down or stunned.

Thus I was not too astonished when the next flash showed me a man lying facedown at my side, but no one else in view. Dark returned but after some thought, I recalled that I had seen a swath and no helmet, so this was Jaxian. I could not tell if he was dead, nor whether Fotius or Zomapp was responsible if he was. I shook his shoulder without result. He was cold as death, of course. So was I.

As I heaved myself up to my knees, another stroke of lightning flashed on bronze near his outstretched hand. I crawled over in the dark until my fingers found the hilt of his sword.

Obviously the gods now expected me to rescue the lovely Shalial by myself, where two larger, stronger men than I had failed. Dimly, over the singing in my head, a small voice whispered that I had better get started, or I might arrive too late.

Even if I could best Fotius, what then? I did not want to think about "what then."

Reeling and tottering like a drunkard, I wound my way back to the archway and into the House of the Goddess. It seemed much larger than before, dimly lit by two dancing flames, far apart. I rubbed my eyes, drawing luxurious breaths of air that were not mostly water, and tried to ignore my resident internal choir as I strove to analyze the problem. Shalial was wrestling with Fotius at the side of the badly misshapen bed of tamarisk. He had discarded his helmet and ripped off her garment, which lay some distance away, fluttering plaintively. I concluded muzzily that he was still just toying with her, and I had arrived in time to prevent serious hurt.

I should like to record that I now bellowed "Unhand that woman, varlet!" ferociously. I did try, but all that came out was a high-pitched squeak. Perhaps it was louder than my song-filled ears could detect, though, for Fotius heard. He looked up and saw me . . . I should like to say *stalking forward purposefully*, but the truth was closer to *tottering unsteadily in his direction.*

He tossed Shalial carelessly down on the couch, proving that he could have done so earlier without trouble. He snatched up Balor's sword from the floor and came at me, fast.

I have used a sword often enough. I am not without skill in the noble art of swordsmanship, but after seeing Fotius in action against Thorian, I had no illusions about being in his class.

Nevertheless, duty is duty. I shuffled my unwilling

feet into approximately the regulation position and raised my . . .

Well, actually, I raised my hilt. The blade of Jaxian's sword, I now saw, had gone. A tiny stub remained, and the end of it showed evidence of melting. I stared stupidly at this curious phenomenon while I tried to remember my objective in challenging the heavy of the tale when armed only with a hilt.

Fotius came to a stop in front of me. He put his knuckles on his hips and regarded me favorably. There was a foul odor of burned hair and flesh about him, and I did not want to look at his face too closely. I would rather have just gone away, but that did not seem like a very probable outcome now.

He said something insulting, which was fortunately drowned out by the singing in my head. I still tingled all over, too. I dropped the sword hilt and took a step backward. Then another.

I was encouraged in this action by the point of a sword at the end of my nose. Fotius was leering down at me—at least, I think he was. What remained of his face would have been unpleasant in any expression. He was making noises that I concluded must be laughter. My back came hard against the wall of the chamber, and I could retreat no more.

Out of the corner of my eye, I observed Shalial hurrying to my rescue. She held Balor's helmet aloft with the probable intention of bringing it in abrupt juxtaposition with the back of Fotius's head. I wondered which would be the more damaged by the impact. I wondered if she would arrive soon enough to save me. I seriously doubted that she could hit hard enough to do any good. She might just make him mad.

Someone bellowed, and this time it was a real bellow. It raised echoes like the thunder. I decided it had said "Stop that!" I observed that Shalial had stopped, and that both she and Fotius were staring toward the arch. I considered the matter, and then turned my head to see what was interesting them.

28: The Tale of Lionman

Jaxian Tharpit came striding across the floor toward us. He seemed totally unharmed by his brush with the storm, except that he was soaking wet, of course, trailing dribbles from his swath. His hair and beard were plastered flat by water, and he wore a very threatening frown.

Fotius screamed in fury and forgot about me. He charged the newcomer like a bull—or a unicorn, perhaps, for he was intent on skewering Jaxian through the solar plexus.

As I said, my observation was not at its best that night. I cannot swear to exactly what happened. I think, though, that Jaxian sidestepped the sword and struck his assailant's wrist with his fist. Something like that must have happened, because I am sure that the sword skittered off across the floor, that Fotius staggered wildly sideways before he regained his balance, and that Jaxian stood his ground, merely turning to watch his opponent.

Fotius howled so loudly that even I could hear him. Then he charged again, his hands going for Jaxian's throat. That was a foolish move, or a brave one, because the two were about evenly matched in size. I don't think Jaxian moved at all, except perhaps to put one foot back for leverage, but this I am certain of—he did not even rock when the corporal slammed into him. He absorbed the impact like a granite pillar. Then he picked Fotius up and threw him.

I don't mean a wrestler's throw. I mean a javelin throw.

Fotius moved in a blur and struck the wall headfirst. The wall was at least six paces away, and he was still at shoulder height when he hit it. He crumpled to the ground like mud and lay there in one of those excruciatingly tangled positions that exceptional juvenile female contortionists may sometimes achieve, but never a living man.

Jaxian turned to Shalial and held out his arms. She rushed to him and they embraced. Wishing that the goddess provided chairs for her guests, I tottered over to the trapdoor, which still stood open, and leaned against the side of the flap. I wondered if I would wake up soon and what I would make of all this when I did.

Jaxian was still kissing his sister.

Well, it was none of my business.

I don't usually care whether it is or not.

I wished my head would stop singing and my eyes stop changing the colors of things.

The night was half gone, we were still trapped in the House of the Goddess, and we had no Balor. The rain was slackening, and the thunder seemed to have stopped completely . . . which was odd, because storms usually wander away into the distance, muttering. Perhaps Zomapp had delivered his message.

Shalial was still tongue-to-tongue with her brother.

I could relight the torches, of course, but the two that still burned were shedding a steadier light now, and it seemed adequate. I decided to go down and see what had happened to Thorian.

I ducked under the flap and found him already halfway up the stairs. He had blood in his hair and beard, and he was leaning against the wall as if he lacked strength to go farther. A sword dangled from his free hand, but I could not have been surprised at anything that turned up in that temple attic.

"How are you?" I inquired, expecting him to say "Terrible."

"Terrible," he muttered. "But I can still kill that swine."

"Jaxian beat you to it."

He peered at me incredulously and blinked. His eyes seemed to be moving independently. He was obviously very groggy, and in pain. He had taken a bad fall. "Jaxian? Tharpit? He *did*?"

"I'll help you up. Lean on me."

"I'll squash you."

I insisted. I wrapped his sword arm over my neck and more or less dragged him up the stairs—I can be stronger than I look when I want to be. We emerged from the flap.

Jaxian and Shalial had separated just far enough to look each other in the eye. They were holding hands. She was staring up at him in wonder, he was smiling down at her fondly.

I wandered across to them, with Thorian trailing somewhere behind. Jaxian turned to me and smiled. A witty remark died in my throat. There was a dark awareness in his eyes that I had not seen there before, and certainly had not expected. There was supreme satisfaction and a confident amusement that implied he knew a great deal more than I did about something. Or everything.

Vlad the Opprobrious had looked like that sometimes, usually when just about to flay someone.

"Well, One-Who-Calls-Himself-Omar?" he said—and even his voice had a resonant quality I did not recall. It jarred the ears like loud bells. "You have observed enough wonders tonight to keep you talking for years, have you not?"

I nodded uncertainly, and then mumbled, "Yes . . . milord."

Something about my answer seemed to increase his amusement. He raised a bushy eyebrow but did not comment. Then he glanced at Thorian and his expression darkened. Neither spoke.

I also looked at Thorian, and the perplexity on his face was wondrous to behold. I wish I could describe it, but words fail me. Like me, he could not place this unfamiliar Jaxian. Where was the milksop poltroon who had refused to help rescue his sister? Even the haughty noble we had glimpsed a couple of times would not compare to this. The new Jaxian looked capable of storming the temple single-handed and slaughtering every priest who stood in his way. Just the arrogance with which he held his ox-yoke shoulders made him seem larger than before. Wonderful what a little success will do for a man, I thought vaguely.

Shalial also seemed surprised, but proud, too. She caught my eye and smiled happily. Then we both realized that she had no clothes on. She blushed and I turned away in haste.

"I'll fetch your robe, milady," I said.

"That will not be necessary." The sheer finality in Jaxian's deep voice would have stopped a charging bull, and I froze in my tracks. "Take off your own swath if you want," he added. "There is no shame here."

My loincloth was sodden and unpleasant on me, of course, but I hesitated. Jaxian reached to his pin, and his own wet garment fell about his ankles. I did as he had suggested.

That left Thorian as the only one clothed. "What is going on here?" he shouted. It was a very good question. The world was becoming more unreal by the minute.

Again Jaxian gave him that dangerously unfriendly stare. "What is it to you?" he said coldly. "You have our leave to withdraw." He turned back to his sister and smiled. "Oh, Beloved!"

"Jaxian! What are you saying?"

"You are Maiana!" He bent to press his lips to hers again, and his hand moved to her breast.

Thorian uttered his most feline roar and strode over to them in two fast paces. He brought his sword up to Jaxian's throat. "That is your sister! Unhand her and cover yourself! This is abomination in the sight of men and—"

Jaxian released Shalial and turned on his accuser with a blazing anger that chilled my spine. He snatched the threatening sword and threw it away. It clattered loudly against the far wall of the chamber, behind him.

Yes, I saw that quite clearly.

He took a sword by the blade with his bare hand. However, this proves very little, because the weapon had probably been lying in the junk room for centuries, and if it had been any decent sort of sword at all, it probably would not have been there. It was probably as blunt as a spade. No, the sword incident proves nothing.

Of course he did twist the hilt out of Thorian's iron grip.

As a feat of strength, that was almost as impressive as the destruction of Fotius. Obviously Jaxian Tharpit was a phenomenally powerful man.

But then he grabbed Thorian's beard and jerked him to his knees in one fast motion. Thorian cried out and stayed there, his blood-streaked face twisted up to stare at the man above him, apparently helpless in his grip.

"Nine years ago this month you swore certain oaths to us, Lionman Thorian of Quilthan!" Echoes rumbled.

Thorian whimpered.

"Well?" Jaxian roared. Shalial had backed away, eyes wide with amazement, or fear.

"Sztatch?"

"Yes, Sztatch! And have you been true to those oaths?"

"I have!" Thorian screamed.

Jaxian gave his beard a jerk that seemed like to dislocate his neck. *"No you have not!* Oh, you did well at Gizath! We grant you Gizath. There was great rejoicing in our halls on the day of Gizath. Mighty the deeds and great the slaughter! Exemplars and name friends roared their approval and wept their pride, and none were bragging harder than Valorous Thrumin and Telobl Summinam and Rosebud Shandile. 'Look!' they cried. 'See the blood he sheds and the souls he sends to Morphith! See how Lionman honors our memories!' *Do you remember them?"*

Thorian moaned. "My exemplars! They saw?"

"Of course they saw! And when your father and your brothers entered our halls that day and were welcomed fittingly as heroes, they also praised the vulture feast mounting around their kinsman, the mighty Lionman! Their joy was unbounded."

Thorian was sobbing helplessly, the tears running from the corners of his eyes back to his ears.

"But then!" Jaxian thundered. "Ah, but then! When Morphith spared you, ah! what then? You sought revenge, yes. 'He remembers me!' Telobl cried. 'And mighty will be our vengeance!' You survived the journey—and great were the wagers being placed that you would not. But then you let the slavers catch you!"

"I had no choice!" Thorian screamed. "I was unarmed."

"You had a choice! You chose to live—live as a slave! What warrior would live one hour as a slave? One minute? *And you told them your name was Thorian!*"

The disgust in his voice made my skin crawl like maggots.

"Such is their custom! They are not of our people! They would have . . ." Thorian's voice died away in a mumble.

Jaxian's fury seemed to flame hotter. "They would have laughed at a slave called Lionman? Of course they would! That is why such names were invented! And then you could have retaliated and died, as you should. Whether they slew you with a sword or beat you to death, you could have died for your true name. It was a good name, and the three chose well at the time, but in the end you were unworthy of it. How do you suppose your name friends feel now, Slave? They do not come to the feasts. They do not speak of their noble deaths and the Vorkans they slew. They wail as shadows in the rafters. They flit like owls in mist. And your exemplars hang their heads and talk of other devotees."

Jaxian released his grip on Thorian's beard, and the warrior crumpled to the floor at his toes.

After a moment Jaxian added, *"You apologize to merchants!"* Again the maggots squirmed under my skin; I felt nauseated by such unthinkable perfidy, although at the time I had completely approved of that apology.

Thorian raised his face a fraction and whispered, "Let me go now, Lord, and I will die."

"It is too late for that. There are not enough Vorkans out there to expunge your shame. This be our judgment and our decree—that henceforth you are only Thorian and Lionman no more."

Thorian howled and slammed his face against the floor.

"My Lord?"

Jaxian turned at the whisper and his face brightened, but his brightness was deadly as the noon sun. "Beloved? Speak!"

Shalial was regarding Thorian with sorrow—he had asked to be her hero. "Is there no redemption, Lord? No way he can recover his honor?"

Jaxian frowned, and I thought of midnight terrors and

the dangers of deep waters. I wanted to flee from the frown, although it was not directed at me but at the whimpering penitent.

"There is one. There are some roads so hard that they change all who travel on them. None who begins achieves the end and none who ends began. Could this craven but discover such a road and follow it far enough, he might find his true name once more. The man who will bear it then will not be this one."

"Will you tell him of such a road, Lord?" Shalial asked cautiously.

"He knows what will be needed. He is more like to find death upon the way than honor, and shame more likely yet, because he does not always recognize honor. Go now, Escaped Slave. Take our sword and helmet and attend them. Wait below until we summon you."

Thorian backed away across the floor. He was still on his knees when he vanished through the trapdoor, dragging the smoke-stained helmet and Balor's great sword.

I said that the way Jaxian had taken Thorian's own sword away from him proved nothing, but the way he took away Thorian's name left me shaking. How could Jaxian Tharpit the merchant have known about Lionman or his exemplars? There was no fakery or threat or reward in the world that would have led Thorian to humble himself like that before mortal man.

Jaxian was looking at me now with a return of that terrifying amusement, as if he knew how confused I was. "You saw, Trader of Tales?"

I had seen, and heard, and I hoped that the warrior had not been tormented just to instruct me. Shalial had addressed her brother as Lord . . .

Nodding, I sank to my knees. I am not often at a loss for words. The singing in my head was soaring. In the dimness, the naked pair before me seemed to shift at times, taking on the texture of a faded old painting, or at times a mosaic picture like those in the ruins of Pollidi. I was no longer at all sure that this was Jaxian.

And neither was Shalial. She recoiled slightly as he put his arms around her, and she stared up in fear at his face.

"Who are you?"

"We are Balor. And we have come in person to answer your pleas as Maiana."

"You are my brother!"

And suddenly he chuckled and smiled a very mortal smile. The mosaic smoothed into reality. His voice was Jaxian's voice again. "Yes, I am. Half brother. But Balor and Maiana are twins, are they not?" He grinned with mischievous glee. "And were not they the first of the Earth-born to discover the joys of love, in among the tamarisks? A priestess may not refuse a god, my love. Can't you see—this is the answer we sought?"

Shalial was very pale. "What was permitted to the gods in the Golden Days is not permitted to mortals now."

"But it is permitted to us." The minatory overtones were flooding back.

"You will don the armor and go before the people? You will play the part of Balor?"

"We are Balor!" The full power was back in his face again.

Shalial closed her eyes for a moment. Then she turned and moved away across the floor until she stood before the towering mystery of Maiana. And where the goddess was wrought of metal, glittering torchlight from her silver skin, her priestess was still jeweled wet from the rain, and she shone also in the dimness, so that they seemed a large and smaller version of the same.

She sank to the floor and made obeisance, but I heard her utter no prayer. I do not know if she gave thanks, or made vows, or if she asked in silence for forgiveness, or guidance. Her communion was brief, for I think I held my breath all through it. When she arose she was smiling. She came slowly back to the tamarisk couch. I watched the movement of her hips and long legs with worship. She was a miracle of slenderness and lush womanhood combined. Men will gladly die for much less than the miracle of such breasts or a smile from such lips.

I thought that if I had been Jaxian Tharpit, then I also would have found a way.

She sat, she swung her long legs up, she lay down. Her brother had watched all this with approval.

I began to edge toward the trapdoor, and those terrible dark eyes flashed to me. "You will stay."

The woman had already raised her arms in invitation. She lowered them. "My Lord!"

He smiled across at her. "Do you not recognize him, Love? Remember the first day we went to the temple together? Two days after Jaxian arrived? I think it was the first day he realized that he was falling in love. It was the first day you realized you already had. We prayed to seven gods and goddesses that afternoon, giving thanks for Jaxian's safe return, and other blessings."

Shalial studied me, a crease of a frown in her brow. I was too scared to be aware of my nudity. Nudity was a trivial mortal worry, and there was something loose in the House of the Goddess now that went far beyond the world I thought of as reality. I could not even feel the stone below my knees. The large man towering over me was flickering to and fro in my eye, Balor one instant, Jaxian the next. I was aware of the singing in my head surging to new heights, new harmonies. The hall danced around me.

"Rosh?" she murmured.

"The god of memory," Balor agreed. "Our brother of history. Stay, Little Brother. For this is the coming of Balor, and there must be no doubts. Let no one say that Jaxian Tharpit was a fake god, or that Balor was deterred from his duty and his rights. Let it be recorded."

His terrible gaze had frozen me to the floor, and I could only nod.

He went to her arms then, and I remained there, and was an observer, as the gods require of me.

I witness that Balor came to the House of the Goddess and lay with the high priestess upon the bed of tamarisk. He went to her eagerly and she received him gladly. Great was their love, and they cried out together in the joy they had of each other.

29: The Coming of Balor

※

Crouched in the mystery of a single candle, Thorian was still sharpening Balor's sword at the armor table. He must have been at it for hours, and he had done a fine job, as I was shortly to discover.

I noticed he had also hacked his hair short, and squared off his beard just below his chin. His shoulders were bowed like a grandmother's. The only cure for shame is suffering, and I had no wish to be the one to suffer in this case, so I offered him no sympathy or cheer. I merely passed on the message that he was wanted upstairs. He hurried off without looking at me or saying a word. I gathered up the high priestess's finery and followed.

Beyond the archway, stars were fading above the plain. Dawn was not far off.

Shalial was radiant—still faintly flushed and tousled, but obviously as happy on her wedding day as any maiden in the history of the world. She thanked me charmingly as I delivered the costume. I wanted to offer to assist her, but Balor was approaching, bearing a torch, and I suspected that the war god might have very sharp hearing and an extremely high jealousy rating.

Thorian had already returned from the far side of the hall, bent under the weight of Fotius's corpse. It was gruesomely shapeless and yet already starting to stiffen. He dropped it callously down the chute he had fallen into himself during the battle, and then limped around to the stairs side. Balor followed him. I followed Balor, leaving Shalial to attend to her own robing.

When we reached the trapdoor to the lower level, Balor himself lifted the statue and the chests out of the way. He hardly seemed to exert himself doing so. I stooped to lift the flap, wondering what I would say if High Priest Nagiak was standing on the steps below. He wasn't.

Thorian did not ask if his escape route was clear all the way to the crypt and beyond. Perhaps he had asked earlier and I had not heard. Perhaps he did not care. Perhaps he credited Jaxian Tharpit with supernatural knowledge. Perhaps he had been trained never to question an order. The night was filled with doubts and unrealities.

Whatever the reason, Thorian and his odious burden vanished down the stairs in silence. I closed the trapdoor, and Balor replaced the blockade on it with continuing ease. How much strength need a man exhibit before you admit that he is more than human? The strongman in Pav Im'pha troupe could lift a horse with a special sling and a pulley, but I have seen a small arthritic grandmother rip a stable door off its hinges to rescue a baby from a fire. Strength by itself proves little.

"You will help me with the armor, Little Brother?" His tone was jocular, but I did not think it was a question.

"Of course, Lord."

When we reached the workbench, though, I suddenly realized that my companion was the real Jaxian Tharpit again. He scratched his hair with eight fingers as he surveyed all the equipment, and he groaned. "Gods do sweat, you know!" Then he grinned at me.

I smiled back uncertainly, and he laughed. "Don't look so frightened! Balor loves you, of course, and I am very, very grateful. I am sorry for your friend—but those who serve a hard master must expect hard discipline, mustn't they? Just look at all this antique paraphernalia! Where do you suppose we start?"

Jaxian could be an astonishingly likable man, I discovered. Shalial's love was suddenly understandable. He cracked jokes as I tied him into his cotton padding, teasing me about a voyeur now, trading in naughty tales and so on, deliberately putting me at ease. Soon I was reassured enough to venture a question.

"What about the ladder, Lord?"

He glanced around, looking puzzled. "Ladder? What

ladder? Oh, ladder! There is no ladder. We passed some ladders over there, though. Did you notice?'' He waved in the general direction of the east gallery.

''So sometimes ladders?''

''Apparently. I can't think what else ladders would be doing up here. But I had no ladder. I was feeling terrible yesterday, of course. Let's do the greaves next. I kept thinking of Gramian Fotius. I tried to believe that Father would have insisted on guarantees, and the pretense would not be carried so far as you feared. Sometime in the middle of the afternoon, I realized what your Thorian friend had in mind, and after that I felt even worse. Then I had to help escort Shalial to that chamber. As I was watching her being installed on the tamarisk, I thought how much she looked like bait in a trap, and I saw that bait was indeed exactly what she was—hero bait.''

His story was interrupted as we loaded the breastplate on him. I could barely lift it, but he shrugged it easily into place. He had no stutter now.

''Worst of all, I'd believed that the only woman I have ever truly loved was hopelessly out of reach, and now I could see that there was yet a way to claim her, if I had the courage. And I did not! I went home and didn't even want to get drunk, I was so miserable. The vambraces next, please. Is that buckle all right? Then the storm came. I took my sword and went up to the temple, suffering agonies because I was imagining you and Thorian struggling with a ladder in that wind. Tighten this strap. When I reached the Courtyard, the rain was at its heaviest and the steps were totally invisible. On impulse, I ran to them. I didn't dare stop to think—I just went up, and no one could see me in the storm. I arrived in time to witness the end of Thorian's efforts . . .'' He sighed. ''If he'd won, I think I'd have gone away again.''

Finally I handed him the helmet and he set it on his head. He seemed more enormous than ever. He looked exactly like Balor—he was Balor! The terrifying, burning eyes were full of that knowing amusement, and the intermission was over. I had been given the missing piece in the story and was being warned not to pry further. I bowed in acknowledgment.

"Come," he said, lifting the sword, and he headed for the steps.

Up in the House of the Goddess, Shalial waited in silver splendor. The horned headdress hid her tangled hair; pearls sparkled on her fingers and neck. I marveled anew at beauty that could wear anything or nothing and seem more glorious every time. She sank to her knees as the god approached. He chuckled approvingly, and raised her. She smiled up at . . . no, she *glowed* up at him, her face dazzling with adoration. Beyond the archway, the sky was brightening, reddening before the swift-approaching dawn.

"Close the trapdoor!" Balor commanded me.

Wondering why he'd bothered to bring me upstairs again, I genuflected and began crawling back to the steps.

"From this side!"

"But . . ." I had assumed that I would seal the door behind them and then wait downstairs to be rescued later that day, or the next night. "But, Lord, there will be no way to set the bolts! And if I stay here . . ."

One does not argue with gods. Scalded by his glare, I jumped hastily to my feet and leaned on the flap. It moved in its own stately time, thumping shut and remaining so, perfectly balanced. Until someone walked on it, of course.

Balor was inspecting me thoughtfully. "Come here, Little Brother."

I walked over to him nervously. He was still holding the great sword. He took hold of my chin with his free hand and tilted my head to one side.

What followed was perhaps the strangest event of the whole night. As I stared up at him, petrified, the giant shaved me with the war god's sword. Few men could have wielded that blade even with both hands. He flourished it deftly as a razor. My beard dusted to the floor. Balor left me a thin mustache and a trace of whiskers on my chin, like the statue in the Courtyard.

Then he sheathed his sword and appraised me with the teasing, knowing glance I was coming to recognize.

"History should be unadorned, of course. But perhaps,

after so long, the Omar part of you would be happier in a loincloth?''

This absolutely could not be happening! I bowed my head. ''It shall be as you command, Lord.'' Truly the god of war is not called the Fickle One for nothing.

''Naked, then. Wait here and come out when I sheath my sword.'' He turned to take Shalial's hand.

And so I became a god.

The air was cool and fresh after the rain, the world washed clean.

From the shadows we watched the procession begin its climb, bright ants far below. The Courtyard of a Thousand Gods was paved with faces like grains of sand, and I could imagine the awful tension in that crowd. Half the Great Way seemed full of people, also.

Fat Nagiak came into view, laboring hard. Somewhere in the double row behind him were Tharpit and Arksis, two men who were going to be very surprised indeed.

Shalial swept out in her whispering gown and advanced to the top of the steps. The priests halted. Seeing her horned in her silver majesty, the crowd drew breath, and I heard that, like wind in corn.

She turned to one side, adjusted her skirts, and knelt, head bowed. Balor walked forward to stand beside her.

Tumult!

The city trembled before the roar of its people. Echoes rolled from every wall. Birds flew up like dust from the rooftops. *Balor! Balor! Balor!* Zanadon acclaimed its savior.

The god drew his sword and raised it, and the sunlight caught the blade and flamed. *Balor!* He shone in the bloody first rays—helmet and armor, and mighty limbs, and a black beard halfway down his bronze chest.

Balor! Balor! Balor! Balor!

He sheathed his sword. He raised Shalial to stand beside him. He turned and held out a hand to me.

And Rosh, the god of tides, the god of memory and history, walked forward out of the archway and advanced to stand at Balor's side.

The roar of the crowd stopped as if it had been stamped on. In the leaden silence, I still heard a wild singing somewhere inside my head. The city lay before me, and the plain beyond, and they were a painting to me, laid out in odd shapes and strange pastels. But the sky was blue, and the dewy morning smelled of tamarisk.

And the wind was chilly.

Balor advanced down the center of the stair, with Maiana on one side and Rosh a pace behind on the other. Nagiak moved away and groveled—but I had seen his bulging eyes and ashen face, and I confess few sights have ever made me happier.

The tumult of the crowd had begun again: *Balor! Balor!*

At our approach, the spectators stepped to either side of the stairs and prostrated themselves. The first were priests, of course, and soon I heard a whisper being passed down the line: *Rosh!* The name outstripped our approach, for the crowd began it also: *Rosh! Rosh! Rosh!* The quick and the learned would already be discussing the significance of Balor bringing a brother god with him. He shows that he remembers his people? He had to be reminded of his people? History will be made here? The Vorkan tide is about to be turned? Theology was going to be more fun than it had been in years.

Beyond the priests were the notables, and the first two were War Lord Arksis and Bedian Tharpit. They were both white to the lips, but Tharpit was staring more at me, and not just because he happened to be on my side of the stair. Bedian Tharpit had sold me back to the slavers. If the slave had escaped again and was masquerading as a god, then he would be justified in standing up, announcing that this performance was completely unacceptable, and indulging himself in petty bluster. On the other hand, if he had sold a god, then he was in rather serious trouble for the rest of eternity. I smiled cryptically at him as his face went down to touch the steps.

Balor stopped. "War Lord!"

Arksis rose shakily to his knees, but his attempt to speak failed. Even if he knew Jaxian Tharpit personally, he almost certainly could not recognize him inside that helmet, for nothing of his face was visible except his eyes and his beard. There were a thousand such beards in Zanadon, and no other such eyes. Arksis must know that this was not his grandson.

"Harness up the wagons!" Balor commanded. "Every wheel in town. Load them with food, with weapons and armor, and enlist all the healers you can catch. Send them out to our allies. When the carts return, send them out again."

Arksis moved his mouth several times and then turned even paler. "Lord!"

Bedian Tharpit had risen to a crouch and was staring in disbelief at this unexpected Balor. Alone of all the city, he must know who stood within that armor. "Who pays?" he screamed.

"You do!" The god's fury blazed on the steps of the temple. "Tomorrow we smite the Vorkans. Go and open the doors of your granaries, Bedian Tharpit. Go and restore the price of bread to what it was last year at this time. *Now!"*

Tharpit swayed to his feet. For a moment I thought he was going to argue, for he tried to straighten his shoulders. Either he saw the god behind the face of his son, or he recognized that resistance in such circumstances would be fatal, for the priests would tear him to pieces. He bowed in submission and staggered off down the steps like a very sick man.

Balor turned back to the grizzled, blue-lipped warrior. "Give all succor to our allies, for we shall need them. Whatever they require supply, and ask nothing in return. There will be no fighting today. Summon their leaders here to us."

Arksis, also, went stumbling off down those endless stairs.

It was a very impressive show of confidence. Of course there could be no fighting today, with the plain knee-deep in mud. Even a minor god like Rosh could work that out.

And what is it like to be a god?
Well, mostly it is very boring. One smiles in appropri-

ately enigmatic fashion. Sometimes one becomes self-conscious at having no clothes on, especially when the cowering mortals include beautiful girls displaying their cleavage to advantage. One says almost nothing—which I find irksome in the extreme, always. One is horribly aware that everyone desperately *wants* something. One stands at Balor's elbow and witnesses.

History follows war, of course.

No one questioned, and he made no mistakes that I could see. If you choose to believe that Jaxian Tharpit was merely an exceptionally strong man with a remarkable acting ability, then I can offer little evidence in rebuttal.

There had been the Lionman incident, which had convinced me. He had known things then that he should not have known. And once or twice during the long day, I saw other inexplicable flashes, especially when the leaders of the refugees were brought in to worship their new commander.

The aging king of Forbin he dismissed with deadly contempt, even before he was announced.

"Remove that one!" he roared, pointing a mailed finger. "What need have we for a doddering craven whose armor is corroded by urine? Take him away and bring us that lusty, squint-eyed son of his!"

A burly youth with a cast in one eye scrambled forward to kneel before the war god.

"Behold your war leader," Balor said, and the lad grinned up at him in wild delight and adoration. So did the rest of the delegates from Forbin.

And the delegation from Polrain . . .

"*Prince* Obelisk?" Sztatch rumbled scathingly. "Since when have the Puelthines bred princes?"

Crimson-faced, the kneeling warrior gabbled something about the royal family being wiped out at Gizath.

"You are building a larder to match your quiver, milord," the god said, and all the worshippers smirked.

As the Polrainians were about to withdraw, Sztatch beckoned to that same Obelisk Puelthine. Warily the warrior drew close. He was a rugged, fearsome man, who would have been a figure of power had he not been in the presence of the god. Only I overheard what followed.

"Today a man named Thorian will enlist in your force."

"Thorian, Lord?" His craggy face brightened with joy. "Lionman? It is true that he survived?"

"Lionman is dead. This is a very minor Thorian. You will place him at the point of maximum danger."

Obelisk bowed in consent and did not question.

But the rest of the day was very dull.

I slept that night in great comfort in the temple, a visiting god. The high priestess sent some very pretty novices to attend me. By ancient law, and clearly by inclination, no priestess could refuse a god. However, there was the problem of the obligatory child to follow, and the gift that the god must bestow on his mortal offspring. Reluctantly I decided that to play favorites would be unfair. Very reluctantly!

I knew by then that I could not stand this godhood business for long.

I also discovered that gods do not dream.

What would a god dream of?

At the summit of the gatehouse, there is a small platform, surrounded by a very low parapet. There, in the cold light of dawn, High Priestess Sanjala stood with the god of history to watch Balor lead out the army of Zanadon. Hooves clattered and bronze jingled. Trumpets and drums roiled the air. Chanting their war song, the young braves marched with heads high. They were supremely confident of the coming victory, for who could defeat them when the war god himself was at their head? And perhaps they were also conscious of the eyes of history upon them.

They should have been. I was feeling most exceedingly ridiculous up there on that aerie. Once the troops were outside the walls, it was all right—they had their backs to me then—but all the time they were marching down the Great Way, I had my back to them. I wished the parapet was high enough to . . . well, just higher.

Moreover, my cheeks were aching from too much enigmatic smiling.

The top of the city walls was packed with women and
children as far as the eye could see. I bitterly regretted
that I had not insisted on the loincloth, however untradi-
tional it might be. I should have known what would happen when I let Big Brother Krazath make the decision.

But this was the only chance I would ever have for a
private talk with Sanjala, who had been Shalial Tharpit.

"Have you any doubts?" I asked.

She gave me a sidelong glance under thick lashes. "Of
what, Lord? Of victory? None!"

"I think we can count on victory," I agreed. "The
Vorkans have driven the locusts ahead of them and must
be starved themselves. Their only recourse would be to
flee on to the west, and even that would be a victory for
Zanadon. No, I did not mean that."

"What, then, Lord?"

"Please don't call me that! You know that Balor is really just your brother and that I am only a trader of tales."

"I know that you are a trader of tales, Lord, but I think
you are more than *only* a trader of tales."

I snorted angrily. "I am me, and always me. Jaxian,
now—Jaxian seems to be two people."

"He always has been two people."

Either a peacock or a pigeon, I thought, but I did not
say so. When she added no more, I prompted. "Of course
a certain nervousness can be expected in a man who has
fallen in love with his sister."

"It wasn't me!" she said sharply. "It was Father. Jax
was only a child when he left here. All his adult life, his
father has been a sort of distant god to him, sending
edicts . . . And when he returned, he was a child again.
No, Lord, it was not me! You must have noticed his
stutter? It was Father or Father's conniving that provoked
that stutter, always."

About to dispute the point, I realized that she was right.
Mention of Bedian's scheming treatment of her had brought
on the sheep every time, but in the tavern Jaxian had spoken

of Shalial herself and of their love, and then his voice had been steady.

"Now he is three men, or he is two men and a god," I said, "but which? I have seen him do strange things, and reveal strange knowledge . . . but can I be sure? I came here to see a god. I expected fire and glory. I am still not sure, Shalial. Am I witnessing only a performance by a master actor?"

My question was impertinent, if not heretical, and the only answer she would give me was a blissful smile.

The army had gone. The ramp was empty. Shalial might permissibly leave at this moment, but Rosh must wait and witness the battle. My eyesight is good by human standards, but I thought I would need to be a hawk that day.

"Yesterday I caught a glimpse or two of Jaxian himself," I said. "You must have?" I was prying despicably, but a god has responsibilities.

She granted me another tolerant, mysterious smile. "I have heard no stuttering, Lord! But yes . . . Sometimes he has been Jaxian." Then she colored, waves of scarlet crossing her lovely face like cloud shadows on a landscape. But she held my gaze defiantly, and it was I who looked away to stare out at the war again. I dared not ask what Jaxian had been doing when he returned.

So Balor came and went? Perhaps he had other wars to attend to elsewhere.

The land was still too damp for dust, but the Vorkans were visible as a dark stain slowly spreading in from the horizon. The Zanadonians were forming up in battle order.

"And after?" I demanded. "How long does Balor remain?"

"Why do you not ask him, Lord?"

"Why will you not answer a god?"

She smiled faintly, still staring out over the plain at the slow-moving columns. "Good shot! I have not asked him, but I can give you my guess."

"I will accept that."

"I think Balor will leave soon after the battle. I think Jaxian will depart a few days later."

"And I think," I said, when she did not continue, "that many men would be tempted to remain and try to rule. But Jaxian is not such a man, and I doubt that the priests would tolerate such a deception for long." There were old bones in the crypt to support my view, but I did not know if she knew of those.

"And what of Rosh, Lord? How long does he remain?"

"Just as long as it takes me to find something to wear!"

She laughed. I wanted to make her laugh again, for her laughter lifted the cares of godhood from my shoulders. It lit up the world.

"History and tides wait for no man. Other important matters call me away."

She did not ask what those were, which I had expected her to do. We stood in silence for a minute, and I saw tiny tears like day stars in her eyes.

"Jaxian will return to Urgalon?" I asked.

"He was very happy there."

"And High Priestess Sanjala?" I asked cruelly. "She must remain in Zanadon and do her duty by the city?" As much as any one person, she would rule it—her father must be very proud of his achievement. She could never leave, and Jaxian could never return.

What complex creatures mortals are! Jaxian Tharpit was only an extreme case. However villainous, his father had a sense of humor, and he may even have believed he was considering the city's welfare when he schemed to install his daughter as high priestess. Fotius, despicable killer, had been an admirable fighter, of superhuman courage. Thorian, the battlefield hero, had been human and hence flawed; twice he had declined to die for his honor. And I—I, Omar, the dedicated seeker after truth—was carrying deception to blasphemous heights.

But Shalial Tharpit was single-minded. She, at least, would be true to the oaths she had sworn to Maiana, I was certain . . .

Then I saw that Shalial Tharpit was grinning at me with a totally unexpected gleam in her eye. "But, Lord! The high priestess must set an example for all the lesser priestesses and postulants. Were I to remain here, think of the scandal!''

"What scandal?" I demanded. Her grin widened, and I remembered that some things are obligatory when gods love mortals. Certainly Shalial could not stay on as high priestess—she could not remain in Zanadon at all. "Oh! But he will be *gifted*, you mean?''

"*She!*" Shalial said firmly. "Balor says any son of his is almost impossible to rear. Terrible troublemakers, he says.''

Then we both began to laugh, and perhaps the women and children on the walls stared up in astonishment when they heard their high priestess and Holy Rosh howling with laughter together.

The worst part of being a god was that I could not put my arms around her and hug her, although I dearly wanted to do so. Had I had a loincloth on, I would have risked it.

The tale of the battle is so well known that I shall not bore you with detail. I saw most of it, but far enough off that it had none of the blood and stink and horror of war for me. Rather it seemed like a stately dance, or the majestic sweep of a flowing tide. The Vorkans blundered into Krazath's mill and were grist. Who can make war against the god of war?

Armed with their overlong swords, mounted on tough and shaggy ponies, the Vorkans had met nothing in the Spice Lands that could withstand their charge, until they tried the armored wall of the Zanadon army. They came in as a dark wave and were as spray upon a rock. Wheeling around to regroup, they found their way blocked by the storm-gorged Jolipi.

Then the refugees' forces swept in on either flank. The men of Zanadon formed a resolute hedge of bronze on one side, the river raged on the other, and the Vorkans were staked for vengeance. Krazath believes battles should be decisive.

Vorkan warriors had never shown mercy and could have expected none. Vorkan women are ugly enough that no one wanted them, even as slaves. By sunset the Jolipi ran red, the last of the children were being butchered, and the horde was a matter for history.

With a crescent moon low in the west, Balor returned through a blizzard of cheering along the Great Way. It is not easy to cheer at the top of your lungs when you have your face in the dust, but the citizens of Zanadon managed it superbly. And so did the nobles and dignitaries, and so even the clergy.

He marched straight to the high priestess's chambers, where Shalial and I waited for him.

Then he collapsed.

We stripped off the superhuman armor until Jaxian Tharpit lay on the rug surrounded by heaps of bronze and sweat-soaked cotton batting. His hair and beard hung limp and tangled, he was chafed raw in many places, his face gray with exhaustion.

Shalial knelt and wiped his face. "Lord?" she whispered in fear. "What do you need?"

"Wine," he mumbled. "And food. I haven't eaten all day. And a wash wouldn't hurt, either."

We brought all those things, for we had them waiting. He quaffed wine and looked a little better. Shalial washed him as I pushed food in his mouth—enormous quantities of food. He ate like a starving horse. He even ate lying on his stomach while she wiped his back and massaged him.

Then he waved away the rest of the food, and Shalial had finished. He still sat on the floor, a huge man worn out by a mighty battle. His eyelids drooped.

He glanced at me with puzzlement for a moment, as if bothered by something. Then he remembered. "He lives. He did very well. He made a good start."

"I thank you," I said. "A start on what?"

Jaxian shook his head wearily. "I have no idea. Who are we talking about? That's all I know."

"Can you walk to the bed, Lord?" Shalial inquired anxiously, kneeling beside him. I wondered if she and I could lift him, and decided it was just barely possible but I would rather not try.

"I suppose I could," he muttered. He laid a hand on the floor to push and then sagged again.

She glanced at me, bit her lip, and then asked, "The god has gone?"

"His work is done, love."

She nodded. He puckered his lips invitingly. She knelt and gave him a chaste kiss.

Jaxian shook his head sadly. "No, that was too sisterly." She tried again.

"Aha!" he cried, and scrambled to his feet, hauling her up after him. He enveloped her in his great arms, and they kissed with passion.

I headed for the door. As I went by them, I slapped his shoulder. "Anything else you need?" I asked. "Some tamarisk, maybe?"

"Out!" roared Balor's terrible voice.

I leaped like a rabbit. As I closed the door behind me, I heard laughter, and the bed creak.

On my way out through the tiring room, I paused to wrap a towel around myself. I felt much better for it. Indeed I sensed a rush of reality as if I were awakening for the first time in two days, or sobering. The world came into sharper focus. I saw the ancient temple stones in the walls and the dancing flames on the candles. I smelled old soap, and old soup, and leather, and the faintest hint of tamarisk. I heard distant chanting, as the temple routine continued in the ways it had for thousands of years, ever since there had been only a grove of trees upon a hill. I could imagine that grove as clearly as if I had seen it myself.

When I emerged into the waiting room beyond, I came face to face with the odious high priest. He looked stressed, and weary, and his bulging crimson robe was blotched with sweat. He sank down to his knees, but that was probably just in case anyone else blundered into the room. He was eyeing me in a way a true worshippee would find disrespectful.

He might yet fear Balor, but my smile could never be

enigmatic enough to deceive Nagiak. He knew me for a mortal imposter, and he would not tolerate me long.

"Have you troubles, Holy Father?" I inquired cheerfully.

He pursed his fat lips thoughtfully and then decided to continue the deception for at least a few more minutes. "None, Lord. Has Immortal Balor need of us? Is there anything he requires?" The man was bursting with unasked questions and dangerous resentment. And perhaps a little fear—but not much.

"We think he would prefer to remain undisturbed tonight. We ourselves have a couple of small wants, though."

His flabby face puckered in suspicion, candlelight gleaming on his shaven scalp. "Anything your Godhead desires is our foremost ambition," he squeaked, with a touching absence of sincerity.

"The city gates are closed?"

Ah! He beamed in sly satisfaction. "I expect so, Lord."

"But you have a good coil of rope and some reliable young fellow to haul it up again afterward? Perhaps a suitable swath and a pair of sandals? A handful of small change and a bag of food would be a kindness for services rendered. We are mindful to see more of the effects of the battle, you understand, so that we may record them for history."

"I think that much could be arranged." Smiling odiously, he scrambled to his feet. "You are leaving us?"

"I am. I'll even make a deal with you."

Priests take to deals as merchants take to gold or warriors to blood. He rubbed his hands. "Lord?"

"You come with me yourself and give me your solemn oath that you won't cut the rope when I'm halfway down the wall—and I'll tell you exactly how we did it."

Nagiak blinked and then began to laugh shrilly.

30: The Reaver Road

I arrived at the wide glare of a river and a ford, and they seemed familiar to me. The water was low, with many shoals of golden sand shining in the noon sun. A few dark specks here and there were probably stranded bodies, but the water was silver again, not red, if it ever had been truly red. I saw fishing boats in the far distance downstream, many-colored triangles of sail, blurred by the shimmer of heat.

Charred ruins showed where a ferryman's house had stood, but weeds sprouted within the blackened timbers, and there could have been no ferry there for many years. A legacy of a garden remained in the form of six green willows and a tulip tree flaming scarlet. I especially recognized the tulip tree.

Sprawled on the black carpets of shadow in the grove, a score or so of young men were taking rest, munching, swatting at the inevitable flies, and also keeping watch on two chomping, shaggy Vorkan ponies chomping the dry summer grass.

They were a variegated band, but most wore tattered leather breeches of Polrainian type. Some were barefoot, some wore boots. They all had their shields and swords at their sides, but whatever other armor they owned must be in the ponies' packs. Either they had very little equipment, or they had very little food. They were almost all quite young. Some were bandaged, some still had the drawn look of men suffering from wounds or the fever that follows wounds. Despite their youth and lack of polish, they were a hardened bunch, and they did not know what blinking was.

As I approached, the nearer men prepared to rise, and I waited for a challenge.

"Let him come," a familiar voice barked.

I strode through the group to the man I wanted, who was sitting by himself, his back against the tulip tree. He was a little older than most of the others. There was still a bandage around his head, and he had been adding to his collection of scars. He was a very large, hairy man, and he was scowling at me like Queen Goople's demon.

I sat down and took a long swig from his water bottle. When I finished, he was still glaring, idly scratching his unusually short beard.

"What do you want?"

"Just a chance to talk with an old friend."

"Talk, of course. What else?" He grunted like a hunting lion. "But it takes more than one to make a friendship." He glanced around to see if any of his followers were listening.

"I have a message for you. Two messages, actually."

"Then pass them and depart."

"The first one is from Sztatch. He said you made a good start."

A dark flush of fury rose in his cheeks. He did not comment, but I had heard of his exploits and I knew that they merited far higher praise than that. The presence of so many eager followers bespoke the reputation that Nameless Thorian had built in that single day of blood.

"And the second message?"

"That one is longer. We can converse while we walk."

He growled menacingly. "So you can drive me out of my mind with your ceaseless chatter and telling of tales? Dream what you like, Omar, but not that."

"Then I won't give you the message." I beamed winningly.

"You are not a god anymore?"

"Gods forbid! No, I do not enjoy being a god."

He quirked his bushy eyebrows thoughtfully. "That explains a lot, I think. Tell me true, if you wish to be my friend—where and when were you born?"

"I don't remember. I was very young at the time."

Jet eyes glinted menacingly. "If you are mortal, I can kill you. Indeed, now that I think about it, I see that I must kill you, because you witnessed my shame, and I will not have you tattling it to all the world."

"I hope you know me better than that," I said, not hiding my hurt. "I do not treat my friends so. I shall never tell of it until after, when it is part of the glory."

"After what? What glory?"

"That is the second message."

He studied me suspiciously. "Who sends this second message?"

"The gods, of course."

"Sztatch preserve me!" He sprang to his feet and stamped out of the shade, into the heat and the light. The others looked up in surprise, but in seconds they had thrust their unfinished food in their pouches, grabbed up their weapons, and were on their feet, ready to move. Two men held the ponies' bridles.

I rose and wandered out to stand by Thorian, blinking at the glare, swatting at flies.

"What news of Balor?" I asked.

"He stayed one day after you left, mostly adjudicating disputes over plunder. Then he, too, returned Beyond the Rainbow."

"And Shalial? Sanjala, I mean?"

Thorian scowled. "She vanished. It is assumed that the god took her with him."

I sighed happily. The citizens would grieve the loss of their lovely high priestess, but they would never dream of trying to find her. Urgalon is a pleasant city. Shalial Tharpit would not be known there as Jaxian's sister, and their likeness was not so marked that a stranger would suspect something so unthinkable. I sensed happily-ever-aftering! Maiana pays her debts, even if Krazath does not.

Thorian was gritting his teeth and staring down at me warily. "And you? Where do you journey, Omar?"

"I go to Polrain. I have never been there—at least I do not remember ever being there. Perhaps I went once, a very long time ago."

"Why Polrain?" he snarled.

"Because the kingdom has collapsed. Because a new king must arise and build a new kingdom. It is a job for a hero, but heroes are hard to find. I foresee a long and bloody struggle, with many great deeds to witness."

He groaned. "I knew the road would be hard, but I did not expect this hard." It was surrender.

"I was sent a dream on our first night at the Bronze Beaker. At the time I misunderstood it. It will interest you!"

"Was it a long dream?"

"No. Very short."

But the prophecy would be a long time being fulfilled—his beard had been gray.

He laughed unwillingly. "We also journey to Polrain."

"What a fortunate coincidence!"

"Not directly, though. We are minded to try a little looting, here and there."

"Excellent exercise!" I murmured happily.

"How did you find me?"

"I also was sent a message." A tulip tree.

"If you don't dog my heels too persistently, I suppose I can tolerate you around for a day or two."

"Agreed, then! And while we walk, Friend Thorian, and after I have told you what I saw prophesied, will you tell me something in return?"

His face became threatening again. "What?"

"I am most anxious to know the exploits of Valorous Thrumin and Telobl Summinam and Rosebud Shandile."

For a moment I thought he would strike me dead with his fist. Gradually the thick arm relaxed. "You really mean that, don't you?"

"Very much!" I glanced around the band of young warriors watching us. "I had never heard of that custom before. And all your companions must have exemplars of their own?"

Thorian sighed deeply and then chuckled. "They have indeed, and every one of them will be overjoyed to recite his exemplars' deeds for you, and brag of how he has already surpassed them. And some of them actually have! Let us talk on the way, then. We have a long road ahead of us."

About the Author

Dave Duncan was born in Scotland in 1933 and educated at Dundee High School and the University of St. Andrews. He moved to Canada in 1955 and has lived in Calgary ever since. He is married and has three grown children.

After a thirty-year career as a petroleum geologist, he discovered that it was much easier (and more fun) to invent his own worlds than try to make sense of the real one.